MUDRITHA

PRAISE FOR *MUDRITHA*

'*Mudritha* is an intriguing palimpsest of narratives of women and rivers, journeys and disappearances, loss and self-discovery, with echoes and resonances of myth and legend. The nuanced translation by Jayasree Kalathil successfully conveys the subtle inflections and silences of Jissa Jose's writing.'

— NAMITA GOKHALE

'*Mudritha* leaves an indelible impression on you just as the mysterious woman at the centre of the novel touches the lives of all the narrators. This is a story of many journeys, the ones that take us outside of ourselves, and within, the ones we have dreamed of and never embark on, the ones we take both in our sleeping and waking lives. What an astonishing achievement – in form, style, and language, ever flexible, ever new, ever surprising. And at the heart of it all, the secret lives of women, tethering always on the edge of the miraculous. I loved every page of Jissa Jose's startling debut.'

— JANICE PARIAT

'*Mudritha* is an extraordinary novel. Its sharp and tender eye takes in the cages we build for ourselves and others, and relays them back to us with a sly mischief that becomes liberating. Jayasree Kalathil is one of our finest translators into English. With *Mudritha* she pulls off a tightrope act in which she conveys cultural resonances deeply embedded in language while keeping the novel compulsively readable.'

— SRINATH PERUR

'A deeply moving novel about women who find – or at least dare to seek – their freedom even in the smallest nooks of life's labyrinths. Unforgettable.'

— SHARANYA MANIVANNAN

MUDRITHA

a novel

jissa jose

Translated from the Malayalam by
JAYASREE KALATHIL

HARPER**PERENNIAL**
An Imprint of HarperCollins Publishers

First published in English in India by Harper Perennial 2025
An imprint of HarperCollins *Publishers*
4th Floor, Tower A, Building No. 10, Phase II, DLF Cyber City,
Gurugram, Haryana – 122002
www.harpercollins.co.in

2 4 6 8 10 9 7 5 3 1

Originally published in Malayalam as *Mudritha* by
Mathrubhumi Books © Jissa Jose 2021
This English translation © Jayasree Kalathil 2025

P-ISBN: 978-93-6213-190-4
E-ISBN: 978-93-6213-263-5

Typeset in 11.5/15.2 Adobe Caslon Pro at
HarperCollins *Publishers* India

Printed and bound at
Manipal Technologies Limited, Manipal

Contents

I am a traveller
You are my road
I go from You to You...

ZEYNEP HATUN

VANITHA

It was in April this year that a young man named Aniruddhan came to our police station and filed a complaint about a missing woman.

He did not intend to file an official written complaint, only to report that a person had gone missing. Little did he realize, until he talked to us, that the police did not simply accept such reports and let the informant walk away. The realization made him anxious, and he tried to retract his statement. But someone, presumably, was missing, and now that we were aware of it, we had to investigate. He was connected to the incident, or to the person who had gone missing, so we could not just let him go. At the very least, we were obliged to investigate whether there really was a 'Missing Persons' case, and for that we would need his involvement.

So, obviously, he had to make a written complaint. We registered the case: Kerala Police Act 57 – Missing Person. And as with all such cases brought to our attention, we hoped that the missing woman would return soon and that the case would not expand to involve other sections of the Kerala Penal Code. As long as the incident was not complicated by other offenses or unnatural death, including by suicide, it would not be too difficult to find her.

As I was writing the report, the term 'missing woman' brought a smile to my face. Who was missing her? What if she had gone away of her own accord? It reminded me of those who disappear in order to find themselves. There never seemed to be any women among them, and this thought made me smile again. Women were always for others to find. If they were not where they were or where they were supposed to be, complaints like this came to the police.

When women do leave by themselves, often it is their phones that betray them. Now that we have a Cyber Cell, missing women are less of a headache for the police. They come right back, or are brought back, except that most of them do not return, or to be exact, are not allowed to return, to where they were before. Only women are unable to return to a home or a relationship they chose to leave. Even if they did, they would be ignored, abandoned, like an old brass pot covered in verdigris. Any hope that one could polish oneself back to an earlier shine is best discarded.

Sometimes, the courts listen to her testimony and rule that she is free to go where she pleases. The woman who had gone away of her own free will is caught and brought back to be given permission to exercise her free will! What a joke! How many of them are then able to get away free? This second going-away is not like the first time. All it required that first time was courage, like making up one's mind to jump into an abyss, eyes screwed shut.

The complaint Aniruddhan wrote down was vague. Significantly, it lacked details about the missing woman. What he gave us as proof of identity was a copy of her Aadhaar card, and that too printed out right then and there on our demand. It is usually quite difficult to figure out what a person looks like from the photograph on their Aadhaar card, but at least it gave us her name, age and address. Her age set alarm bells ringing because we knew from experience that women as old as her rarely ran away. The disappearance of a woman aged fifty or above is usually different from the disappearance of younger women. When younger women go missing, usually there is a fairly obvious reason – a love affair, or an extra-marital relationship. And all we usually need to find them is a bit of help from the Cyber Cell – the call history of their telephone numbers and the tower location of their mobile phones. All eleven cases I had personally investigated after coming to this police station were such cases.

This one, however, had all the hallmarks of being different. The missing woman was over fifty years of age, and this fact opened up other avenues – murder, property dispute, kidnapping, captivity … It was clear that we could not let the complainant walk away.

Unfortunately, Aniruddhan had very few concrete facts to give us. He told us that he had never met the woman who was supposed to have gone missing. The irony made me laugh, and I continued laughing at the young man as he sat pale-faced in front of us until Thomas sir, who was interviewing him along with me, said my name in a cautionary tone: 'Vanitha…' I tend to laugh for the merest of reasons, because of which Thomas sir, Renji and my other colleagues often say that I am not cut out to be a police officer. I agree. That I was biding my time until the rank list for assistant professorship was released was a secret I kept to myself. English departments all over the state were full of vacancies waiting to be filled…

Anyway, I was convinced that Aniruddhan was not the person who should have come to the police with this information. How come someone else, someone who was in daily contact with this woman, hadn't come forward to report her missing? Was there no such person? We began questioning Aniruddhan in detail.

According to Aniruddhan, and according to the ID proof he gave us, the missing woman's name was Mudritha. When we first asked him for her photograph and address, he said he didn't have them. Then he remembered an email he had on his phone, and with our permission, printed it out on the station printer. As the printer was awaiting a cartridge change, the copy was not all that clear.

Aniruddhan told us that he had come into contact with the woman around seven months ago as part of a business deal. Since then, for forty-five days or so, he was in regular, almost daily, contact with her, although, in all that time, they had never met in person. The phone calls between them and the two longish emails she had sent him were the only evidence he had to prove such a relationship existed. Then, suddenly, she disappeared.

'Why do you keep saying "she disappeared" when you've actually never seen her?' I couldn't help asking.

He was taken aback, and his face paled further.

'I lost contact with her. Or I couldn't get her on the phone. Would it be better if I said something like that, madam?' he asked, hesitantly.

I grinned and said yes. What else would you say to someone who had come to report the disappearance of a person he had never met before…

Their contact had started when the woman had called him requesting his services, Aniruddhan said. When we asked him what that service was, he told us, with some sense of embarrassment, that it had to do with organizing a tour. A trip to Odisha for a group of ten women. Mudritha had some strange and strict specifications for the trip, and she called him several times to discuss these. He had no contact with any of the other women in the group while arranging this trip; Mudritha was the only one he was in touch with. But, he told us, it did not feel like she herself knew any of the other women in the group personally either.

'Hang on,' I interrupted him. 'So, you run a travel company, do you?'

'No,' he said. 'I'm a managing partner in a coaching centre that prepares students for the Public Service Commission exams. I also teach there.'

'Oh, so you were a tour operator, what, seven months ago then?'

'Not really, no. I worked as a tour operator many years ago.'

I found this strange. In fact, we found a lot of what he told us strange and unbelievable. He had not run a travel company for many years, and yet only seven months ago he agreed to organize a tour for a client he had never met. He had no idea where she lived. In these technologically advanced days, it is entirely possible to do business and make and receive payments without the service provider and the client ever having to meet in person. Still, something did not feel right.

The most intriguing thing was this: Mudritha had told Aniruddhan that on 24 November, the day of the trip, she would be at the railway station at 4 p.m. She had confirmed this in an email that very morning. But when he arrived at the railway station, she was not there. She did not show up even after the other members of the group arrived. And when he tried to call her, all he got each time was a message saying that the phone was switched off.

'So, the trip was cancelled?' I asked. 'Did you try to find the address that was on her ID proof?'

'No, no, we couldn't cancel the trip,' Aniruddhan said. 'Some of the others were already on the train having boarded it from earlier stations. But that was not the only reason. You see, it was not one person's trip. It was a dream trip that involved eleven people, me included.'

'But you're only the tour operator,' I said. I suppose he didn't appreciate my comment, but I couldn't help the thought that a tour operator should see the tour he has been asked to organize for what it is – a business deal. Why romanticize it by calling it 'a dream trip' and such?

'Well, yes. But I had to finish the project. And the other nine members were not in a position to cancel the trip. So, we went ahead. We did face a few hiccups that any project without a team leader would face. And I kept trying to get in touch with Mudritha. Hoped that she might have simply missed the train and would try to get on a flight next morning or something, which would still bring her to Bhubaneswar before us.'

'And?'

'I couldn't get through to her. Not once. Her phone remained switched off. We completed the trip without any major problems. But it was not the same itinerary that we had planned – well, Mudritha and I had planned. The other women knew very little about it. So, like everyone else who visits Odisha, we too went to a few temples – Puri Jagannath, Markandeshwar, Mukteswara and so on. A whole day in Konark. Did some shopping – Sambalpuri silk, Ikat saris, sweets … And then, a journey back home as boring as all return journeys.'

Well, what else was there to see in Odisha, I thought. What else would anyone buy from there? Would anyone in their right mind choose Odisha for a leisure trip? Konark, of course, was worth a look. But other than that, why would anyone waste their time and money on Odisha? Of course, I did not say any of this aloud.

'Didn't you try to meet her or contact her after you got back?'

'Yes, I kept calling her number with no luck. I tried sending her an email, but it bounced back saying "invalid ID" – the same ID from which she had sent me those emails.'

'So, how come it took you this long to file a complaint? Even after you thought she was missing?'

Aniruddhan's response to this question was truly strange. There really was no reason for him to be worried about her. Even if she had gone missing, it was none of his concern as he had no relationship with her beyond the service she had contracted him for. With the successful completion of the tour, that contract had also ended, her absence notwithstanding. The fee and the money for other expenses had already been paid into his account, and since she was the one who didn't turn up, he was not obliged to return any of it. But when he went over his books and tallied up all the expenses, he found a surplus of over ten thousand rupees. Aniruddhan felt the right thing to do was to return that money, and that was why he continued trying to get in touch with her. It didn't occur to him that he should go to the police because all he was aware of was that her phone was switched off, not that she was missing.

'So, what changed? How did you come to think that she was missing? Besides, you could have just pocketed the ten thousand and forgotten all about it. I'm having a hard time believing that you kept trying to get in touch with her in order to return the money.'

'Look, I had already factored into my fees a not inconsiderable sum as my profit. The amount I am talking about was left even after that, and it belonged to those ten women. I didn't think, even for a minute, that I should just take it. Not even when I couldn't contact Mudritha. And I didn't think she might have gone missing until I passed by the place that was stated in her address.'

Now he had our total attention.

'I was in the area when it occurred to me that this was where Mudritha's house was, at least according to the address on her identity card. So, I began to ask people. Her name didn't ring any bells with them. Finally, someone recognized the house name and gave me directions. And I went hoping, finally, to meet her. But there was no house there – just a piece of land and a gate.'

'What? Where would a house go? Has it also gone missing, just like her?'

I picked up the printout of her ID proof and read the name of the house: Mullapparambil.

'Are you telling us that now we have to investigate the case of the missing house as well?' I realized, even as I said it, that it was an unnecessary wisecrack.

'Apparently it was an old, dilapidated house, and was demolished. That's what I managed to find out,' Aniruddhan said. 'But no one knew anything about the woman who lived there. She kept to herself, they said. I remember her telling me that she lived alone. That's when I realized she's missing, that she may have gone missing six months ago. And that's why I am here. She's no one to me – I wouldn't recognize her if I ran into her – and I don't have the right to say anything about her. To be fair, I'm not even the person who should be reporting her disappearance. I'm sure she has people who care about her…'

There was nothing more we could get from Aniruddhan at that point, so we terminated the interview and let him go.

Over the next few days, we made inquiries. Mudritha's house had been in one of the important by-lanes in the city. The land where it had stood was, as Aniruddhan had described, quite large with lots of trees, most of them laden with fruit. A few letters were missing from the name 'Mullapparambil' welded on to the rusty gate. Commercial buildings flanked the land on either side, most of them new-builds. No one we spoke to had any clear memory of even the existence of the old house. The Cyber Cell also came up with nothing useful other than a confirmation that Mudritha's mobile phone had not been in use since 10 a.m. on 24 November.

Finally, with nothing else to go on, we decided to go back to Aniruddhan. We had to complete the inquiry after all. As we were finding our way to Aniruddhan's house, Renji recalled an old case in the vicinity and made a lewd comment. It was an afternoon with reluctant, untimely summer rain.

As we arrived, Aniruddhan was getting ready to leave for the coaching centre for his afternoon classes. He volunteered to give us everything he had that might be useful for the case. This included a notebook, divided into four or five sections, which contained detailed records of the preparations for the tour. As he handed it over, he said he was uncertain why he had chosen to make such detailed notes or why it was divided into sections. He forwarded the emails from Mudritha to my account, and added, as though remembering it just then, that he had stuck printouts of those emails in the notebook.

We were leaving when I saw a woman – Aniruddhan's mother, perhaps – staring at us. I smiled at her, but she withdrew into the house without smiling back at me.

Returning with the notebook and Mudritha's emails, it was the thought of another woman that occupied my worried mind. A woman who had, at the age of fifty-nine, walked into a river near her home and killed herself. Her name was Adeline Virginia Woolf.

For women, every age is also the perfect age for suicide.

I began reading Aniruddhan's notebook that night.

ANIRUDDHAN'S NOTEBOOK – PART I

In November last year, I had the opportunity to organize a tour and accompany the travellers on the trip. A weird experience, right from the start.

The year we finished our degree, my friends and I had started a tours and travels business. Ten years have passed since – I guess I am the only one of the four of us left to remember all this. Hari, Ramit and I were friends from our schooldays. Nithin joined our gang when we began our degree. We have remained friends all through those glorious years of college and ever since.

Ramit and I were clear-sighted enough to conclude that passing exams and pursuing higher studies were impossible dreams after having spent the three years of our degree cutting classes and enjoying ourselves. So, we did not even bother sitting the final year exams. Hari tried and failed. Nithin passed, barely managing a third class. Nevertheless, all of us recognized that the time had come to make a decision about our future. We could not depend on our parents any more. Nor was there any point in trying to attempt again and again the ten or twelve papers, lab work and practical exams that we had failed or ignored. At the same time, we were keenly aware that if we went back home as complete failures, our families would eat us alive! And beyond all these considerations was the conviction that we were meant to face our futures together, that we could not – should not – go our separate ways.

And so, we arrived at the decision to start something that, at least in our estimation, would not require much financial investment: a travel company. We rented a small office, a narrow room above Raghavettan's chai shop, in a two-storey building near our college. We had a stylish signboard made – Himadri Tours and Travels – and hung it up in front of the building. For days we quibbled before arriving at the name 'Himadri'. The only thing that made us brave enough to start a new business, of which we knew nothing at all, based purely on our college friendship, was our youthful enthusiasm. I know this now, but none of us realized it then. And so we jumped right in putting our confidence in the only capital we had – the gift of the gab.

It is better not to talk about the battles we faced to make ends meet in those initial days. Every time he visited travel agencies in the city, Hari would come back bursting with stories about them – designer furniture, curtains, carpets, flower vases, glossy magazines, pretty receptionists … We didn't even have a telephone line in those days.

After twiddling our thumbs for five or six months, we finally got a break – a request to organize a tour from the Physics department in our old college. By then, the white letters spelling out 'Himadri Tours and Travels' on the blue background of our signboard had begun to fade, and cobwebs decorated the office. I was in the office, idly drawing patterns in the film of dust covering the table – we had lifted it from Nithin's house one day when his family was away – when Muralimohanan maash, the head of the Physics department, came in with the request to arrange a Bangalore-Mysore class trip. The creak of the wooden staircase as the overweight maash came up them is still fresh in my memory. Approaching travel agencies to arrange class tours was not a common practice in those days. Every college department had at least one teacher who was capable of organizing them quite efficiently, as though that was the sole purpose of their existence on this earth. The Physics department in our college also had one such person, but fortunately for us, it was Muralimohanan maash, one with no interests outside academics, who was endowed with the responsibility of being the tour-coordinator that year.

Ramit, Nithin and I had been students in that department and had constantly been pulled up for not attending classes or completing lab work. Somehow, solid state physics, statistical mechanics and such were beyond our understanding, and the compound pendulum, galvanometer and experiments made us want to run away. Luckily, our campus had many places we could escape to. By the third year, the mere thought of Physics made us retch. Muralimohanan maash might have broken all records in his entire teaching career for the amount of red ink he used while marking our papers. But he made no reference to those days. In fact, what he said as he was leaving, after giving us the responsibility of organizing a two-day trip and paying a good amount of money in advance, took me by surprise.

'This is good, what you're doing,' he said. 'It's so difficult to make a decent career out of education alone, wasting so many years in the process. Well done for setting up your own business. Opportunities await those who are willing to work hard.'

As it turned out, we were able to complete the project satisfactorily. Thinking about how we haggled, in broken Kannada with the hotel manager and in proper Kozhikode Malayalam with the owner of the tour bus, makes me laugh even today. After that, more business came our way from the college. Slowly, we began figuring out how to cut costs and make a profit, hiring the same buses and booking the same hotels, organizing tours along the same routes, and so on. They say in business you learn by doing. That was true in our case. There are lessons that can be learned only from setbacks.

Influencing college students and making them listen to our suggestions was easy. I am talking about a time before the semester system became common, so class trips were usually at the end of the academic year. Students would be in a weird state of mind at that time, what with the pain of separation and anxieties about the future … Their minds would be like balloons. All we had to do was quietly blow them up, and they would be enchanted by the beautiful colours.

There were some routes – less risky and more profitable – that we were keen on. But no matter how keen we were, we had to convince the students to choose them, and that was not always difficult. Just mention the vineyard from the romantic blockbuster *Namukku Paarkkan Munthirithoppukal* and they would pick a tour on the Theni route. Not because they liked the film or had even watched it, but merely because it was in a film. River rafting, trekking – they were ready as long as they were in the company of their friends. Drop in the words 'beach' and 'sand', and Goa it was. For them, going on a class trip was not about sightseeing, but about sitting next to their sweethearts, singing and dancing with their friends. A long bus journey, without stopping, without getting off anywhere … That would be the best trip ever as far as they were concerned. Well, it had been for us too when we were students…

The difficulty was persuading the teachers who came along as chaperones. They were, without exception, strict and cantankerous. Every route you suggested, every sight, would be met with a hundred questions and quibbles. Suggest a trip to Kodaikanal, and they would stick Pazhani onto it. Okay, a quick stopover in Pazhani then because there will not be enough time for anything else, you said, conceding. But no, they would insist on climbing the bloody hill. In the end, upsetting all our careful planning, it would be four hours in Kodaikanal and twelve in Pazhani. If the trip was to Ooty, they would redirect it via Rameswaram. 'The temple there!' they would say. 'One should visit it at least once in their lifetime, don't you think?' 'Have you got someone's ashes stashed at home, that need scattering in a holy place? Why not take that too and kill two birds with one stone?' we would mutter. In the end, we would end up absorbing the extra expenses from these last-minute reroutings because it was important we had them on our side. We needed them to recommend us to the next batch of students, vouch for our credibility. On top of all this, there would be complaints about the food, the hotel rooms, the lack of hot water … Never from the students – they were happy and willing to adjust – but always from the teachers. If it weren't for them, Himadri would have stood a chance…

The business went on, grunting and grinding, for two more years. Then Ramit joined the army, Hari got a job in the Gulf and Nithin decided to do a BEd degree in Karnataka. I couldn't keep Himadri going on my own. Continuing it would have achieved nothing. So, I, too, left. I joined a coaching institute, named 'Grandma', which prepared aspirants for the Public Service Commission competitive exams. To be fair, what attracted me to that institution was its name, something that would have better suited a company making achars and condiments. I sat the exams a couple of times myself, and although I could not pass them, within a year I became a teacher there. In this time, I had also acquired a BA in English through the distance education programme with the open university.

It is easier to try and help others achieve what we ourselves have failed to achieve. For example, my mother, who never passed her Class 10 school leaving exams, has been giving me career advice since I was a child. If you ask her why she, who obviously was so clever and good at analysing and making plans, never managed to finish her schooling and forge a career for herself … Well. The question would send her into a spiral of anger during which I would have to listen to everything she had suffered in the nine months she carried me in her womb, and the account of every paisa that was spent to keep me fed and clothed. Anyway, I decided that rather than trying to find a government job by passing competitive exams, I was better off doing the somewhat easier – well, at least for me – job of teaching others how to do it.

I also think that I may have got the job at Grandma because it required a temperament that was somewhat comfortable with a certain kind of violence. Like being able to watch from the safety of the bank when someone was drowning in a river. I pushed my wards into the bottomless water and sat quietly watching. I must admit I was a little surprised to find that the teacher in me was capable of more heartlessness than is usual. Perhaps it was the effect of the few disasters that had unfolded over the years in my personal life.

I was beginning to realize that the years between boyhood and manhood, those early twenties when we are neither boy nor man, are more complicated than one's teenage years. It is important that we have close friends, or a lover, or at the very least an inclination to explore the pleasures and wonders one's body is capable of. I discovered that the combined fragrance of creams, deodorant and sweat that emanated from female bodies gave me headaches. Even on the tours that we arranged, I avoided mingling with women and sat with the driver in his cabin, watching Nithin and Ramit and Hari use those opportunities to their advantage. As for friendships, well, it was not long before all my friends went their separate ways. That they pursued their own paths is not the issue. The issue was that they were gone far away from me. No one came to take their place. I began to feel isolated, lonely.

As for exploring the pleasures my own body was capable of … well … I did not find it pleasurable. In fact, I found it distasteful even though I tried from time to time just to convince myself that there was nothing wrong with me.

Devoid of such simple joys as friendship, love and bodily pleasure, a person can only be cantankerous and behave badly towards others. The job at the coaching centre was eminently suitable for such a person because all anyone there expected from you was to be more obnoxious and stricter than everyone else.

Daily tests, piles of homework, quizzes on current affairs, punishments, impositions … Those studying to pass competitive exams for employment are not like ordinary students. They will put up with anything, without complaint, without shirking, without cutting classes. They are machines that memorize questions and answers, and practise them even when they are in the toilet. And I, too, behaved like a machine towards them. No place for human emotions there. The more I made them work, the more my students seemed to respect me. The owner of Grandma, Krishnanandettan we call him, was also quite impressed with me. Sitting in his shop selling cattle feed and iron goods, he watched with interest as the number of students enrolling in my batch increased. It was also the time when there was more demand for jobs in the public than in the private sector.

'Helping others learn … that's an honourable thing,' Krishnanandettan said to me often, as though he was afraid I might leave. 'It's not something everyone can do. But you have a special knack for it. Don't bother attempting the tests yourself now. This is the best job for you.'

Many of my students were able to court success, and that made me proud. They – Sreenisha, Sayona, Prasanth and others – smiled sweetly at the world from the huge flex board at the bus stop advertising our institute.

Around that time, the building that housed Himadri and Raghavettan's chai shop was vacated in preparation for it to be demolished. We had stopped paying rent a long time ago and had left, abandoning our measly office furniture in the room. Despite repeated requests from our landlord, I never went back to clear it out. The wooden staircase to the top floor disintegrated slowly, but the signboard 'Himadri' remained, faded yet sturdy. Whenever I passed that way, I would look at it and be reminded of Muralimohanan maash's words. What heights of success we would have scaled by now if only things had panned out … The thought would send the name Himadri slithering across my mind like a cold whip.

ANIRUDDHAN'S NOTEBOOK – PART 2

Mudritha's call to me was like a person going to eat in a restaurant that had been closed down a long time ago, misled by the 'Meals Ready' sign left behind. I was having a cup of tea in between classes when my phone rang.

'Is this Himadri Tours and Travels?' the caller asked.

I was taken aback, and before I could say yes or no, the caller introduced herself.

'I'd like to arrange a trip for a group of ten people, all women,' she said. 'Travelling by train. Accommodation has to be pukka, and there will be no compromise on the quality of food. And of course, I would want all the expenses worked out and explained beforehand because I have no interest in haggling about them later.'

I could not guess Mudritha's age from her voice. The trip she wanted arranged was risky, especially for a company that was not in business. All-women trips were not all that strange – run-of-the-mill temple tours and trips to Kashi–Rameswaram were quite common, and the occasional adventure trips. But I had not even heard of the places Mudritha was talking about. The only thing that was vaguely familiar in what she told me was the name 'Chitrotpala', although I would have been hard pressed to say whether it was the name of a place or a temple.

She said she got the telephone number for Himadri from the old nameboard. And when she told me that an acquaintance of hers had vouched for us saying that we were youngsters who could be trusted, I could not bring myself to correct her and tell her that we were not youngsters any more.

In that moment, it dawned on me that Himadri had been a bigger dream for me than for my friends, and that I would have revived it at some stage. This phone call was a wake-up call. My life, I realized, was not to be spent shouting and screaming at the bodies packed tightly into narrow, airless classrooms, clamouring for more and more. Long, long journeys awaited me, and vast vistas. Verdant lands and sandy stretches, undulating oceans and waterways … The thought gave me goosebumps.

When she asked me whether she could make the arrangements over the phone or whether I wanted her to come to the office, I was relieved to know that she had not seen the disintegrated staircase to our erstwhile office.

'It's a bit difficult to come in person,' she told me. 'I sprained my ankle the other day and it is bandaged … How about if I call you again in the evening? You must be busy now…'

After she hung up, I was overwhelmed with the conviction that she was not going to call back. I blew away the milkweed seed of a dream that had floated on to my shoulder and begun to gather substance, and went back to my class forgetting to finish my tea.

But that night, I spent hours on Google reading about Chitrotpala. It was a river in Odisha, and the places Mudritha had mentioned were along the river's course. They were not on any usual excursion routes; it would be difficult to find tour packages with details of those places. Why would a bunch of women want to go there? Was Mudritha entertaining herself while bedridden with a sprained ankle and bored, calling around travel agencies with her dream trip? Anyway, I followed Chitrotpala until I ran out of data on my phone. All that night, I dreamt of a flowing river, and when I woke up the next morning, I was wet, my body and mind chilled, and the tension that I had not been fully aware of carrying released.

I called Grandma, told them that I was taking a half-day leave, and hung up without waiting to hear about the chaos this would unleash on the daily schedule. I wanted to call Mudritha and tried to figure out what might be a good time to do so.

Women usually are not able to attend phone calls in the early mornings in peace as the demands of the kitchen would be pulsating through them like a nasty, throbbing sore. Perhaps Mudritha was free of the kitchen currently because of her ankle? Would she be awake? Several times I brought up the number she had called me from, but hesitated. I checked to see if she was on WhatsApp on that number – I could send her a message asking why she hadn't called the previous evening as she had said – but I couldn't find her. I began, again, to speculate about her age … I made the call, finally, and she picked up on the second ring.

'Aiyo! I'm sorry, young man,' she said. 'My leg was hurting too much yesterday, so I took some pills and fell asleep early. Good you called because I was sitting here wondering what might be a good time to call you. You must be always busy with tours and arrangements, no?'

'No, no, don't worry,' I said, shamelessly. 'Go ahead.'

'Well, there's not much more to add to what I said yesterday. Tickets for ten people to Cuttack. From there to Salipur where we'll stay. Ten days including onward and return travel. Like I said, we are all women, so we'll need someone dependable with us at all times, not just to see us off and receive us at the other end.'

I took note of the fact that Mudritha's voice tended to be sterner when discussing formal details, and made appropriate acquiescing noises. Before we ended the call, we had a verbal contract. Once she transferred the advance payment into my account, I would be completely responsible for this trip. But my immediate thoughts were about taking time off from work, about the upcoming tests for the Lower Division Clerk (LDC) and village assistant posts, and the greedy students waiting to suck my blood dry. I realized instantly that these were inconsequential concerns and that I had already distanced myself from them.

Months had passed since Himadri was locked up, but I yearned to return to that office room. There is a twenty-year-old still in there, excited about the preparations for a journey. He was the only one of the four who got intoxicated by the prospect of organizing tours for others and being a silent witness to other people's journeys. For the rest, it was only a business, something to pass the time until they found their rightful perch in the world. And the moment they found it, they flew away with no sentiments weighing them down. Even now, during the occasional phone calls or messages, they did not reminisce about Himadri.

In the afternoon, instead of going to Grandma, I took the bus and got off at College Stop. The demolition work on the building that housed Himadri was under way, the staircase hung broken, but the signboard, although faded, was still there. Perhaps only for one more day … How fortunate that Mudritha saw it when she did, I thought anxiously.

There was no way to go up into our office. Still, I hung around the building. Would someone have taken away the table we had stolen from Nithin's house? I remembered hauling it down from the top floor of his house on a day when his parents were out. How we struggled to bring it down the narrow staircase! His grandmother, who was bedridden, called out from her room – 'Who's there? What's that noise?' – and even though we knew she couldn't come out to investigate, we had looked fearfully at each other with our fingers pressed to our lips. But the table and the stairs made loud noises, and Nithin's grandma began calling out his name and scolding.

'You're stealing something, I can tell! You'll sell it off and get drunk with the money, you good-for-nothing … You'll be the ruin of this family, you and your mother!'

Nithin slapped his forehead and cursed her under his breath, thanked the universe that she was finally bedridden. His muttered words still ring in my ears. He is a schoolteacher now, somewhere in Madhya Pradesh.

I hung around the place until evening. I felt the urge to go into the college but resisted it because the intervening ten years had put a lot of distance between me and the campus, severed all the veins that had connected me to it. The chai shop was closed – Raghavettan had died. In the golden days of Himadri, he would come upstairs every evening, bringing us tea and kizhangupori. We could never hear his gentle footsteps even if we listened for it, but the fragrance of kizhangupori – its deep-fried golden crust encasing melting, off-white pieces of tapioca – would announce his arrival. Suddenly, I was overcome with the desire to eat it. New buildings had come up in the area, with new shops, but none of them sold it. It was evening by the time I finally reached Grandma – just in time for the busiest class preparing for the LDC tests. Until it ended at 9 p.m., I forgot everything else.

That night, and in the nights that followed, it was not the woman who had called me that I thought about, but the river. Chitrotpala, my river. Night after night, I dreamt of her and woke up wet, ecstatic.

I never met Mudritha, and I didn't meet any of her fellow travellers until the day of our journey. Mudritha and I exchanged several phone calls, and there were times when we argued. I had agreed to organize this tour in a fit of enthusiasm, but it threw up a lot of challenges. I was not familiar with the destination. It was not part of the usual itineraries, so I had to do a lot of research and make all the arrangements from scratch. Still, when I think back, that was easy compared to facing up to Mudritha's uncompromising attitude.

I made up an itinerary after several hours of research on Google and Wikipedia. I didn't know anything about the travellers, but I could imagine that going on such a journey was not an easy proposition for any woman. It would not have been a journey conceived on a whim; it was more likely to be the realization of a dream deferred, perhaps for years. So, I was determined to make it a successful one for them, to ensure that they got to see as much as possible in those few days. I had begun to feel a kind of affection and protectiveness towards these women who were, really, strangers to me. The truth is that I began to forget ours was a business relationship.

And moved by these emotions, I asked Mudritha why she didn't consider travelling by air. That would cut down the journey time and give them more time to sightsee, I said. They could take a flight to Bhubaneswar and get to Sambalpur from there in an hour. Spend the night there and go on to Salipur. Or somewhere else – Lingaraja temple, Mahavir temple, Konark that must not be missed … But Mudritha dismissed my suggestions outright.

'Have you even been to Odisha, kutty?' she asked me in a severe tone.

I had to admit, embarrassingly, that I had not.

'I don't like unnecessary interferences,' she said. 'I don't want to travel according to your convenience. I'll pay you what you ask, and you'll take us where we want to go. That's all there is to it.'

I would be lying if I said I wasn't angry, but I swallowed it. We had several more of these altercations, but by then I was determined that I would see this through. What if this marked the rebirth of Himadri, and me? I would be doing this alone, but in some sense, it was better to be alone than with partners who would walk away halfway through.

Booking accommodation and other arrangements was easy enough, thanks to Google. Since Mudritha had not given me any specific destinations other than the five days in Salipur, I didn't have to worry about the travel arrangements once we got there. And since they were all women – and middle-aged women presumably, given that Mudritha addressed me as 'kutty' all the time, as though I was a much younger man – I imagined that their destination would be some temple along the river's course. I couldn't ask Mudritha – I wasn't sure how she would respond.

As for the worry that I didn't speak a word of Odia, I consoled myself thinking that Mudritha must surely know the language. Anyway, I too began to anticipate, perhaps more eagerly than those women themselves, the day of our journey. The truth is that I had not been this interested even in the very first tour we had organized after setting up Himadri.

ANIRUDDHAN'S NOTEBOOK – PART 3

As expected, I had a hard time getting time off from Grandma. When I submitted my letter requesting a leave of absence for ten days, Meghna, the young woman who managed our office – she was also one of the students – stared at me.

'Really, sir? At this time?'

The dates of the upcoming tests were written in huge, red letters on a chart and hung on the wall. It was not just a reminder, it was a warning to all aspirants to be scared, to try harder.

'Well, I must have those days off,' I said, pretending not to understand the look of utter disbelief in her eyes.

Whenever I saw Meghna, the entire history of the river Meghna, which originated in the mountains in the district of Kishoreganj in Bangladesh and flowed through that one country only before joining up with the Padma in Chandpur, would rush into my mind. And my thoughts would turn to Sabitri Roy's *Meghna Padma* and Abu Jafar Shamsuddin's *Padma Meghna Jamuna*. In the secrecy of my thoughts, I called her Padmameghna. Maybe this was the kind of thing that happened if one's entire reading was confined to books on general knowledge. A derisive laughter bubbled up within me whenever I thought of the meaninglessness in requiring would-be clerks – whose jobs would never amount to anything more than sitting in dusty offices, and keeping records of thandaper and land transactions – to learn the names and sizes of foreign rivers.

Even so, thinking about it later, I would find it weird that I had heard nothing at all about the river named Chitrotpala until Mudritha mentioned it. I knew of other rivers in Odisha – Mahanadi, Baitarani, Brahmani … But Chitrotpala … she had been flowing all this while beyond the realms of my knowledge. It is possible that I may have said her name as I mechanically recited the names of rivers that I had learned by rote. But when Mudritha talked about her, it did not sound like repeating something she had committed to memory. She brought her alive, and that river had started flowing inside me.

Padmameghna looked at the wall. The date for the LDC test had not been announced but a tentative date was marked there. It was the most popular test; almost ninety per cent of Grandma's students attempted it. And because it was so competitive, our responsibility as coaches was immense. Among the aspirants were those who prepared seriously for years and those who were attempting it for a laugh, those who were almost at the age limit and those who had just turned eighteen. It was not easy handling a class like that. The date for the test for the village assistants' posts had already been declared, and there was a considerable number of students attempting that too. Padmameghna herself was getting ready to try both tests. Krishnanandettan gave her a reduction in fees in exchange for managing the office. It was her job to collect the fees from students and issue receipts, and maintain the attendance register.

'Sir, there is no need for a leave letter,' she said. 'Can't you just talk to Krishnanandettan?'

'Put it in the file. That's the official procedure, isn't it? I will talk to Krishnanandettan.'

'But sir … At this time? Do you think he will allow it?' Padmameghna persisted, frowning. 'As it is, we don't have enough teachers at the moment. Vikas got another job and Sayant is never regular…'

I was beginning to get irritated. Explain myself to this slip of a girl … Besides, just that morning I had been in yet another argument with Mudritha and was again made to swallow my opinion and defer to hers, the distaste of which lingered on my tongue.

'So what?' I said, raising my voice at the thin, frail young woman. 'I need the time off, so I am taking it. I haven't signed any contract saying I'll be here permanently. If I feel like leaving, I will. That's it.'

My voice attracted attention, and as people glanced over, Padmameghna's eyes began to fill. Trying to hide them from me, she picked up the leave application and stuck it in a file, muttering, 'Okay, sir,' with her head bowed. There was no reason to shout at her, I knew that, but I did not feel like apologizing and went on to my classroom. Padmameghna did not attend the class that day. Well, never mind, I thought. There was only a split-bamboo screen between the classroom and the office, and sitting on the other side, she could hear everything that was discussed in class. She did that often anyway.

When I finished my last class of the day, the 9 p.m. batch, and walked downstairs, Krishnanandettan's shop was still open. It often remained open until late on days when the merchandise arrived. He might have been expecting a delivery of cattle feed – orange sacks with the name 'Shubhlabh' printed on them – all the way from Jaipur. Krishnanandettan invited me inside. Goods that were neatly arranged at the shopfront during the day were strewn haphazardly everywhere: hoes, sickles, pathalakkarandi – those lethal-looking cluster-hooks used to retrieve stuff from wells –

and sacks upon sacks of cattle feed. Everyone else had left. It was difficult to breathe in there. I yearned to stand in the fresh air of the night and wished he would step outside. I had already been indoors for over three hours, sweating.

Krishnanandettan did not come outside. 'Come in,' he said, again. 'Come, sit. The truck hasn't arrived yet. Who knows when it will be here.'

There was nothing to sit on, so I stood around uncertainly. As though only just realizing that he was sitting on the only chair available, Krishnanandettan stood up and said, 'Come, then, let's go get a kattan.'

I really didn't want a black coffee at that time of night but grabbed the opportunity to get out of the stuffy room. As we stood waiting for our coffee at the food cart, he kept offering to buy me bread-omelette or kothuporotta, and I kept refusing, saying that my mother would have dinner waiting for me.

'Don't you have any friends?' he asked, launching into a completely different subject suddenly. 'You're always alone…'

I might have said something about us meeting only at the institute and how one might not bring their friends along while teaching a class.

'Ottappooradam. That's what I always thought you were – a loner,' he said, nodding as though he understood. 'Aloof, always. And I've never seen you talk to women. Good to know you have friends.'

Our coffee was ready. The memory of that night, complete with the smell of the coffee and the food cart frozen in the cold, is still fresh in my mind. We must have been the last customers of the night. Ours was a village that was trying to be a city, and it displayed all the desperation that went with it. It seemed aware of the limits of its ambition given that there was a college only two or three bus stops away and an actual city a further four kilometres from there.

'She said you asked for a few days off … Planning to go somewhere? With friends?'

I nodded, realizing in that moment why he had broached the subject of friends.

'Yes, a ten-day trip, with friends,' I said, suppressing a smile. Friends! Ten women I have never met!

'Good,' he said. 'A change from routine is good every now and then.'

He then went on to tell me that, if it weren't for Grandma and the cattle feed shop, he too would have considered travelling. He could have Meghna look after Grandma, capable as she was, but he could not shut the shop. Too many people depended on it, he said. They would have to go all the way to the city in search of cattle feed, which they would struggle to find. For whatever reason, cattle-feed shops were rare in the city. And they could scarcely let their cattle starve … Finding someone else to mind the shop was impossible. He went on like this for a while before coming to the point.

'You go. You should go because you've never gone anywhere in all this time. But, listen, it's my humble request. Don't go just now. A month or two from now … you can take as much leave as you want. If you go now, it will be difficult for all of us.'

Our journey was scheduled to begin in exactly a week. So, I shook my head even as he continued with his entreaties, even as, for a moment, I considered cancelling the whole thing. Even the strongest wall would have crumbled in the current of his pleading. Thankfully, I remembered that the tour was not something I could cancel based on my personal circumstances, that it involved other people. It was getting really hard to keep saying no. I had to get away from him, but the last bus home was already gone. I wasn't sure why he was pleading with me so hard. It was not that difficult to find someone to replace me – there was no shortage of educated, unemployed people who would grab the chance of earning ten thousand rupees a month with both hands. Still, he went on and on, until I jumped into a passing autorickshaw. He kept at me over the next few days.

Finally, I told him that the planned journey was one I could not cancel even if it meant losing my job. That changed things. On the day before I was set to leave, he approved my leave, adding that I should come back to work as soon as I returned. He came to the office that day and, handing me a bundle of money, asked Padmameghna to write out a receipt. I knew it was a trap, but I took it because I needed the money. Even if I decided to leave the job later, I could work for an additional month and pay it back, I told myself. It would take a while to reopen Himadri even if I decided to do so, and I could continue teaching while I made the preparations.

As she wrote out the receipt, Padmameghna avoided eye contact with me. When she pushed the book towards me for my signature, her bangles tinkled. In that moment, I promised myself that I would bring her some bangles when I returned. Every temple had stores that sold fancy items to attract the pilgrims. Odisha would be no different. I didn't say any of this out loud though – she would never know I was thinking such thoughts. Words that go unuttered, that would not cause any harm if uttered … How stubbornly we keep them to ourselves, stop them from providing even a semblance of solace … I signed the receipt book and went to my class without smiling, without saying sorry or thank you.

ANIRUDDHAN'S NOTEBOOK – PART 4

If what happened at my workplace was emotional blackmail, what happened at home in the wake of announcing my travel plans was full-on drama. I had assumed that they wouldn't care if I went to hell, let alone to Odisha. Although I didn't quite meet their expectations of who I could have been by this stage in my life, I did bring home a regular income, lived a more or less orderly life. In their own estimation, I had no bad habits or unsavoury associations. Above all, I was a thirty-year-old man. So, I did not expect them to interfere in my affairs, try to curtail my freedom. But they did – my mother and my older sister.

My acchan had passed away six years ago. His death was quite a shock to all of us, and we had struggled to come out of it. After his death, Amma began talking really loudly and dressing up in gaudily coloured saris. She became a regular customer at the beauty parlour that Preetha chechi, our neighbour, ran from her home, to have her hair dyed black and for facials and other beauty treatments. She also began going to the cinema on her own. And her trips to the treasury to collect Acchan's pension turned into celebrations. She came back from them sowing, or at least pretending to sow, seeds of joy around the house, talking about the biriyani from Paris and the ice cream from Saiboo's.

As for my sister, I did not realize until much later how she was dealing with our father's death. Ever so slowly, Chechi began to remove colour and joy from her life. She went to work and came back home, each day a series of mechanical routines. Booklets and CDs addressed to her from Vipasana and Rajayoga retreat centres began to arrive. Sometimes, she observed silence for days on end, and if Amma or I said anything about it, she shut herself in her room. Even in the intervals between these periods of silence, it was pointless trying to talk to her. She would just smile back. Why speak, she would ask, if one finds oneself in a situation where it is possible to live without speaking? The tongue is an organ to experience taste, but we use it to utter so many distasteful things. Everyone seems to rejoice in using words to kill taste. It is better to keep quiet, she said, since she didn't have anything good to say. Then she would ask me: 'Do you speak to anyone properly these days except when you are in your classroom?'

She was right. I spoke non-stop in class, but after that? I spent days not saying a single word to anyone. On the way back from work, I hand over eight rupees to the bus conductor and he gives me a ticket. That late in the night, as I walk home from the bus stop, the lane is usually deserted. Once home, I push open the front doors left unlatched, eat the dinner left for me on the dining table, wash the plates, switch off the lights and go upstairs to my room. Amma eats early as she has to take her medication and goes to bed after watching TV for a while. I don't think Chechi eats in the night or spends time in front of the TV. The door to her room is always shut. I don't think they know when I come home – I wonder if they will notice if I didn't come home.

'Well, like I said, it is better not to speak. It's not that difficult. The only reason we speak is because we have needs and wants. If we don't, then we'll be able to keep quiet, at least speak less,' Chechi would advise me.

I am scared that one day very soon she will give up speech altogether.

Chechi was the one most affected by our acchan's untimely death. She changed, in front of our eyes, like a polished metal lamp blackening over time. She was only twenty-six at the time, still unmarried because she was adamant that she would marry only after she got a job. That was the year she got a job, and pretty soon, an alliance was almost fixed. Acchan set out to visit the prospective groom's home in Pazhayannur with my ammavan and elayachan. He never came back. When we called Ammavan, he said that, after the visit, Acchan had left them saying there was some emergency he needed to take care of. Amma and Chechi waited, wanting to know all about the groom and his family. Our phone calls went unanswered.

All I can remember clearly of that night now is the rain. Water gushed through the front yard submerging the stepping stones. Power was out since dusk. On days when he worked late, Acchan used to spend the night in a little, narrow room below our shop in the city. We had always assumed that it was because he didn't want to come home in the dark or disrupt our sleep. We never asked for reasons or explanations – that was a peculiarity of our family.

Our shop in the city was rented out to a tailor. The room below it on the ground floor was on a lower elevation than the road. Once the door was closed, even light and wind hesitated to make their way in. Acchan had equipped it with a cot – just a metal frame woven with plastic strips – and a mat. He had spent the night there, and he had not woken up from his sleep.

But that was not what shocked us. In the room with him was a woman, a stranger. Both dead, both naked. Acchan was fifty-seven years old.

I worried about the shame Amma was sure to feel, a feeling different from what Chechi and I experienced. But as I watched her wailing over his dead body, I felt I was watching a performance, that she was acting as though to win some award in the Best Actress category.

It was the boy from the tailor shop, who was disposing off the fabric remnants and debris, who saw smoke rising from the room and raised the alarm. When they kicked the door in, the two of them were lying dead, turned away from each other. Perhaps, in the panic of imminent death, they had pushed each other away, they who had been holding one another closely until then, with not even the barrier of clothes. The fear of their secret liaison being found out must have exceeded the intense despair of death. I marvelled at the thinness of the line between love and hatred.

Later, we heard detailed descriptions of how it all had happened.

A cigarette that had not been extinguished before falling asleep had set fire to the plastic bed. They must have woken up when the room filled with smoke. Or was it when they felt their skin burning? It wasn't clear. What was clear was that they had woken up because otherwise they would have died in each other's arms. It was because they woke up that they were found away from each other. Their mutual revulsion, the urgency they felt to push the other one away, was evident in the way they lay. If only they were found in an embrace … If only they had tried to give the other one last breath of air through a kiss … I couldn't help wishing. What I felt acutely was not the shock of finding out about my father's secret affair, or our neighbours' scorn, but sympathy for the love between them that had been betrayed in the end. I guess, in that moment, I might have sworn never to love anyone.

It didn't surprise me when my sister, too, came to the same conclusion, but it was inconvenient. After the confusion of a couple of years, she began receiving marriage proposals again, but she refused every single one of them. When Amma saw me trying to persuade her, she would say, in an off-hand fashion, 'Why force her if she doesn't want to?' and continue whatever she was doing – sitting in front of the sewing machine attaching a fall to yet another new sari or interlocking its hem. The sewing machine had arrived after Acchan's death, like a gift from the tailor who had bought the shop and the room downstairs from us, and Amma had, by then, learned to sew from Preetha chechi.

I have often felt I am living with two mentally unstable women, and that is why I had assumed they would not be bothered by my impending journey. Amma's reaction was to forbid me in no uncertain terms. She then set out to impress upon me the risk in even considering restarting the travel company.

'Oh, how we hoped you'd make something of yourself … You have no idea how much your father and I worried when that didn't happen. Then you spent years gallivanting about in the name of that business. By God's grace, you now have a proper job. And now you come up with this new idea, only to go back to time-wasting … I'll never allow it, I swear!'

Entreaties and arguments that went on and on for days. Perhaps because she was between observances of silence, Chechi spoke up in support of Amma. This is what I want to do with my life, I told them, this is my passion. I told them about the trip, that I had been asked to take a group of ten women on a pilgrimage. I knew I would go ahead without their permission, but I didn't want to hurt them if I could help it, so I tried my best.

'You could come with us, Amma, I should have thought of it sooner,' I said. 'You haven't been anywhere outside Kerala. Odisha is famous for its temples. I have heard there are over two hundred temples in Bhubaneswar alone…'

I was being honest when I said this. If it had occurred to me earlier, I would have talked to Mudritha about bringing my mother along. But Amma scoffed at the idea.

'Temples! Ha! Like I am at the age or in the mood to go on pilgrimages … You just want an excuse to wander around with a bunch of women!'

She kept up her objections until the day before our trip. It was hard to fend off many of her arguments. I was only beginning to learn, through my dealings with Mudritha, about the unshakeable certainty with which women held on to their convictions and preconceptions, and now my own mother seemed to be even more hard-hearted. I also thought, unnecessarily, of Padmameghna, who stubbornly continued to avoid me. All in all, I was so frustrated that I did not even feel the excitement of getting ready for a ten-day journey. Finally, the night before our departure, when I got home after shopping for a couple of things necessary for the journey, Amma was still awake, waiting for me.

I will never ever forget the things she said to me that night.

'Can you even imagine the feeling of complete and utter shame in your husband being found dead with another woman only a few minutes away from your own home?' she asked. 'For six years I have been burning in that shame. The memory of it will make me sit up even in my grave. If he was alive, I could have asked him who she was, made him tell me what he had to do with her. I could have spat in his face, chucked him out of the house. Could I do any of it? He was dead! With her! Like a slap on my face!'

It was the first time Amma talked about Acchan's death. Watching her life since – enjoying herself as though she was trying to gather together all the colours that had leached out of her life – I had assumed that she was rejoicing in his death, had often felt irritated that she was overdoing it.

'When you found out he was a smoker, you were all surprised, weren't you? Well, he smoked, you just never saw him. Some nights, after, you know, doing *it*, he liked to smoke, and he always did it lying down. So many times I've tried to stop him … Sometimes, he would fall asleep before finishing his cigarette. But I would be waiting to take it off his fingers before it fell on the bed. For so long after it happened, I used to think – if it was me with him that night, I wouldn't have fallen asleep, I would have put the cigarette out before it fell off his fingers…'

I could understand what Amma was trying to tell me, feel the helplessness she would surely have felt in talking to her thirty-year-old son about it. None of us had bothered to find out who that woman was. All we heard later was that no one had claimed her body from the mortuary. The municipality must have buried her in the public grave. The ultimate loneliness of a woman who had come looking for love … But Amma, obviously, thought about her still, about her carelessness in falling asleep after making love. If she had stayed awake until Acchan had finished smoking his cigarette, he would be here now, with us. Faithful husband, responsible father … What happened was for the best, I thought, a shiver running through my body. What I had believed as the truth was a shameful, black-faced lie!

'And you want to go away too…' Amma said. 'I don't think I could bear it if you too ended up in a similar situation.'

I found that funny, but at the same time, I was filled with rage. Did she think I was going away to have a clandestine relationship with some woman? How dare she think of me that way, my own mother, this woman dressed in a red nightie with a large floral print?

'I'm not like that,' I said, feebly. I always found it difficult to speak when consumed with anger.

'Well, I didn't think he was like that either. Not once had he slept apart from me when he was home. I don't have a single memory of him fighting with me. When he died, I tried to recall everything that had happened between us, right from the time we met, wanting to find something – anything – that would make me hate him. I could barely come up with even small instances of us falling out with one another. Neighbours, relatives, everyone used to say, "Look, oh, made for each other they are!" Then he goes away to fix his daughter's marriage. And? It wasn't the first time either. Apparently, the relationship had been going for a long time! I just had no clue!'

'Amma, I am going on a business trip. As part of the work I love doing. I am not off to do stuff like you're conjuring up…'

'I don't trust men, not any more! You're his seed, after all, aren't you? Did you know, when my daughter decided not to get married, what I felt was relief. Even if she decides to become a monk, I will only be happy. That life will be so much better than being floored by betrayal. If you were to marry and bring a woman home, I will only feel sorry for her, for what she would have to endure.'

On and on she spoke, her voice dry, merciless. I was fed up, and hungry – I had not had my evening meal. Amma had forgotten all about it. I had to pack, be ready to get to the railway station by at least 4 p.m., have enough time to get to know my fellow travellers before the six o'clock train arrived.

'Enough, Amma,' Chechi said, finally interrupting her. 'He won't change his mind. You've said all you could. Whatever happens now – good or bad – just accept that you were not able to change his mind.'

I picked up my things and quietly climbed the stairs as she began talking Amma down calmly. All thoughts of food had left me. It was easier to starve than spend any more time with these women. I shut the door to my room and lay, exhausted, in the little space left on the bed strewn with my stuff, pulled out my phone and connected to the Wi-Fi. Notifications began pouring in. There were at least five or six WhatsApp groups connected with Grandma. No matter how many times I swiped left, they added me back in. Three hundred and ten messages in the Grandma LDC group alone! I pressed 'Clear chat' in an effort to purge my phone. Even personal chats were full of questions and doubts, almost all of them from my students.

In that moment, I yearned for a tender, personalized message, realizing, almost immediately, that I had no one who would send me such a message. Hari, Ramit and Nithin … it was unlikely that any of them would even think about me. I would have loved telling them all about the journey I was about to embark on. But the truth was that my messages to them often languished in our chat history. I stared at their dark-grey double ticks and told myself that they did not have the time to spare to open and read them. If they did, they would have responded.

I was about to fall into an exhausted sleep when my phone pinged. A message from an unknown number. Curious, I opened it. It was a fragment of a poem:

> I am an eye
> You are my sight
> I am a spring
> You are my water
> I am a rambler
> You are my trail

I had no idea whose poem it was. Who was the sender? Was this their own creation perhaps? I might have been able to find the identity of the sender using the Truecaller app, but I didn't try. Instead, enveloped in the soothing pleasure of the poem, I fell asleep.

That night, too, Chitrotpala came into my dreams. She looked like Padmameghna and Mudritha who I had not seen yet. I woke up sometime in the early hours of the morning. Despite lying in a tiny corner of the bed, fully clothed and without switching off the light, I had slept well and dreamed. I looked for my phone. It was still connected to the net and there were a few new notifications. None of them from the unknown number that had sent me the snippet of the poem, even though, before falling asleep, I had sent a smiley in reply.

My eyes fell on an email notification. Without getting up and going to the bathroom to get ready for the busy day ahead, I opened it. A long email, from Mudritha.

ANIRUDDHAN'S NOTEBOOK – PART 5

The first email from Mudritha:

Aniruddhan,

Have you ever heard of a river that killed itself? (*Mudritha had used the word 'nee' for 'you' – a word one would use to address someone who is your equal or younger – and apologized for it.*) I suppose you might think of the river Saraswathi, but I am not talking about her. Saraswathi performed an anthardhanam – a going-under. I believe that each going-under is an act of suicide, an annihilation of the self. As someone who has annihilated herself several times, I am able to say this with a great deal of certainty.

We all know the scientific explanations about Saraswathi's disappearance. Relentless movements of the earth's crust that cause, over millennia, changes in its natural landscapes. I, however, do not believe that Saraswathi ceased to exist because of geological changes. It is widely assumed that all rivers are female. Perhaps that is why I have always thought that Saraswathi was destined to annihilate herself from the moment she was born. That, after all, is the fate of at least some women. Those movements, they happened in her life, and so she had to make herself disappear.

Devastree – women of divine birth – attain youthfulness as soon as they are born. This particular devastree, the beautiful

Saraswathi, had a strange fate awaiting her. She was destined to be the victim of her own father's romantic love. 'The victim of romantic love'– there is something awkward in that construction, no doubt, but we must use that phrase for all love that is illicit, forbidden. Some of us, accursed, become victims of love when the rest are subjects of love. Do you know that Saraswathi has many names? The one I like the most among all of them is Shataroopa. If I had a daughter, that's what I would have called her – Shataroopa, one who has a hundred forms, one who cannot be contained within a single form.

And yet, her own father, Brahma, the God of Creation, was overcome with lust the moment he saw Saraswathi. To escape him, she tried to swerve to the right, but Brahma sprouted a face on his right to see her better, to ogle at her. No matter which direction she moved to avoid his lustful overtures, her father sprouted another face in that direction. She even tried to escape into the sky, it seems, and there it was, another face on her father's body, looking upwards. Every time I heard this story, I felt an intense sorrow. Imagine the depth of the helplessness she must have felt … The sprouting heads are, well, only a metaphor obviously, a metaphor for the violence a lecherous man is capable of. Perhaps he uses not only his penis but his head, too, as a weapon of rape, violating, penetrating, with his whole body.

She had to surrender, finally, or was forced to surrender. How desperately sad … And then she had a son. Shataroopa was the first girl to be raped by her own father, and he kept on using her. There is no word other than 'use' to describe it. No wonder no one worships Brahma despite the fact that he is the creator of everything. There are only a handful of temples with his idol.

Well, her miserable story does not end there. When the fire of Shivan's ire threatened to burn down the world, Brahma ordered Saraswathi to carry it to the sea and destroy it. The merciless father, the cruel mate – he would have, by then, wanted to get rid of her. Weeping, she carried the fire away. Legend has it that it was

Vishnu's blessing that kept her from being burned herself. I don't believe that. Badavagni, the fire-spitting creature that was Shivan's anger, was not hot enough to burn a woman who had already been burnt to a cinder. That's the real reason. Will any woman, who has endured as much as she had, miss an opportunity to put an end to it all? It is life that was unbearable to her, being alive was the punishment. I remember another tragedy she had to endure. The sixteen thousand wives of Sreekrishnan took their lives by jumping into her waters. She had to drink their tears, too, and she, Shataroopa, became a long, long cry. It is said that she is still flowing underground, in the womb of the earth. Not dead even after death, not gone even after annihilating herself. Whenever I read about efforts to bring her back to the surface, I say to myself, no, she will not come back, ever.

But it is not Saraswathi I began writing about; it is about another river that killed herself. Her name is Chandrabhaga, a sacred river that flowed near the Sun Temple in Konark. She was beautiful, her waters plentiful, and she coddled and cooled the roaming Sun even as her own waters boiled in his heat. It would have been from her that the Sun gathered the energy for the day's meandering. His cart, horses and horsemen would have bathed in her waters before setting out on the long journey.

Let me tell you about a problem that all men share. If a woman were to show them some affection or care, they mistake it for romantic love or for carnal desire as though they have decided that every woman who is not theirs has only these two emotions. Not only that, they also think women who are theirs – by which I mean women they think they have proprietorial rights over – do not possess these emotions. For example, if you have a sister and if she is in love with someone you don't approve, you will be the first one to try and destroy that relationship at all costs. Am I wrong?

As for sexual desire – well, what can I say? It is men who decide the level and intensity of women's desire. Like sticking price tags on things in a supermarket. Fixed price, no discount, no bargaining. Anyway, what I was getting at is Chandrabhaga's love. The Sun misread her concern, her friendship, took the tray of soothing water droplets and the fragrant breeze to be offerings of love. Wondered why she wasn't declaring her love for him and so, took it upon himself to declare it. Meanwhile, all Chandrabhaga was trying to do was serve him as well as she could, he who was witness to all that was the world. She was not in love with him, did not desire him. Besides, she was already in love. Even her name was an indication of how she had already become part of her lover, body and soul – Chandrabhaga, part of the Moon. But the Sun did not understand any of it. Dawn to dusk, he cast fiery looks at her. Expressions of love that began tenderly in the morning, that intensified as the day progressed and as she refused to comply. His looks burned her, boiled her until, by evening, as she lay exhausted, he reduced their intensity again. Day after day, it went on, this threat of total destruction unless she changed her mind, complied. Chandrabhaga began to thin, to dry out, and yet she tried to hide it from the Moon who came to frolic with her on chilly nights. Not that there was much he could do even if he knew – the opponent was powerful. And as he came to her during high tides, he did not notice how emaciated and exhausted she had become.

That is a problem with all men who are lovers. They might notice the physical exhaustion of their beloved, but they don't know how to look into their minds and find the reason for the exhaustion there. And even if they did, it is unlikely that they would be able to find the reason. She held back her tears and pretended to enjoy the night with the Moon. As dawn arrived and it was time to part, she must have held on to him, drenched him in her tears, whispered, in a trembling voice, 'Don't go…' He would not have understood any of it. He would have patted playfully on her cheek and said, 'Don't be silly, I'll be back tomorrow.' That is all lovers can do. They don't know how to read beyond the words uttered, to find the meaning or the vision beyond mere words.

We have almost finished Chandrabhaga's tale. The Sun was at the end of his tether. He had tried patience and persuasion, threats and tenderness, and yet Chandrabhaga's beauty remained unattainable. Furious, he came down to the earth, resolute now to take her by force. His blazing rays pulled her to him from afar, and smelling danger, Chandrabhaga ran out of his reach, threw herself into the ocean and killed herself to save her dignity. In the story, it is said that she killed herself to save her chastity. That is not what I think. Rape destroys a woman's dignity, not her chastity or her fidelity to her man. Those are descriptions men have attributed to her pride, her sense of self. Self-worth is described as dignity for men and chastity for women. So many such hilarious things exist in our language!

Saraswathi could not escape abuse. Her abuser was strong; he was the creator himself. And it was domestic abuse; it happened in her own home. As for Chandrabhaga, she escaped her abuser, but she could not survive. The Sun returned as though nothing had happened. The waxing Moon would have come looking for her. Her absence would have puzzled him. But soon, they would both have returned to their concerns. Poor Chandrabhaga – the river that had to take her own life…

You once suggested a package to me – Konark, Puri, Lingaraja temple, and so on. I remember responding to you angrily, saying that we will decide where we want to go ourselves. I feel bad about it now. I was scared that you might even decide not to go ahead with our trip. Still, I had told myself right from the start that no one else would decide where we would go on this journey, even if it meant that the journey would not happen.

If you ask me why pick Odisha – it used to be Orissa, remember? – I have only one answer. Our trip is not for visiting temples, not a pilgrimage. Odisha is the land of Chandrabhaga. Isn't that a strong enough reason? And I have no desire to see Konark; neither does anyone else in our group. It is the place where she used to flow, where she was destroyed. The emptiness would scare us. It would hurt us.

Have you ever seen the face of a woman who has died by suicide? Usually, dead bodies are washed, dressed in silk, and strewn with flowers before being sent off to their final resting place. But the one who dies by suicide … She is brought straight from the post-mortem table, swaddled in a piece of white cloth. Forget silk clothes, she probably won't have any clothes under that white cloth. The cruelty and neglect she had suffered all her life – she would have suffered it once again on the post-mortem table, with double the intensity. No one would have remembered, as they cut into her, carelessly, without love, that this body was alive until recently, that this was a person. Only in order to discover what everyone knows already – that the woman who had taken poison had died of poison; that the woman who had hanged herself had her cervical vertebrae broken and died of asphyxiation. No one would discover *why* she died; no forensic surgeon would find out the extent of the pain and anguish she suffered.

I am digressing again. The face of a woman who died by suicide … There would be a harshness on her face. She would have her teeth clamped tightly. All that life had done to her, as well as the effect of having been mercilessly hacked into on the post-mortem table, would settle heavily on her face. Usually, we look at dead bodies and say, oh they look like they are asleep. But we will never be able to say that about the dead body of a suicided woman. She would be truly dead, all her beauty, all her grace gone out of her. It is better not to see her at all.

This is not the only reason for not wanting to go to Konark. It is the Sun who is worshipped there. The falling-down temple is known by the name of the violent, lustful god. Don't you think that is reason enough for us to avoid the place?

Tomorrow, we begin our journey, and for a few days after that, we, who are total strangers, will be together. Do you remember how many arguments we've had so far? I am sure you will be feeling anxious about this journey, an anxiety, I can imagine, that is mixed up with trepidation as well as curiosity. It might sound strange, but that is exactly what I feel. I have been on so many journeys, but this one … Still, I will not avoid it for any reason whatsoever.

It was forty-five days ago that I called you for the first time. It was afternoon, well, around twelve. The reason I remember it so clearly is because that morning, as I stepped into the yard outside the kitchen, I slipped, twisted my foot, and almost fell over. I applied some kuzhambu and massaged it, hoping that the pain would go away, but it only intensified. By the time I went to the vaidyar, I was in agony. I was sitting in the taxi with my leg stretched out on the seat, trying to swallow my pain, when I saw that old building. I studied in that same college, used to get off at that bus stop to go to the college. And that building used to be there in those days, except that it was in its youth then, and it had been the tallest building in that area.

A student procession, accompanied by drums and singing – it must have been the victory celebration after college elections or something – and all the vehicles had to be pulled to the side to let it pass. The pain was intense, and I watched the building in a bid to ignore it by conjuring up some old memory from my college days. The building stood before me, empty, tired as though it would topple nose-first into the dust any moment, as though it had itself forgotten its proud old days. Regardless, I raised my head and looked up, stubbornly, and read the faded white letters on a blue board hanging there: 'Himadri Tours and Travels'.

In my sudden amazement, I forgot my pain for the time being. Yes, the pain was forgotten, not lessened. All the pain I have endured in my life – none of it has ever lessened or gone away; I have learned to forget it on occasion, to pretend that it has ceased to exist. On a falling-down building, the signboard of a travel company, hanging on as though stubbornly declaring its refusal to give up. It amused me. What arrogance even in the face of imminent destruction! Where were its owners, I wondered. Why didn't they take the signboard along when they abandoned the endangered building and left? I could guess it was the remnant of a failed venture. Still, as my taxi began to inch forward, I wrote down the telephone number on it in my hand. At that moment, there was no thought of going on a journey in my mind. I was only looking for something to occupy myself with in order to ignore my pain, to laugh at it.

As usual, the vaidyar's place was busy. I say 'as usual' as one says as a matter of course; I had never actually been there before. The vaidyar was famous, a physician who healed the consequences of careless moves and missteps with a few manipulations that might seem simple to us. I had to wait because there were others who had come before me waiting for their turn, and the vaidyar took his time with each one of them. My pain asserted itself again. I could not sit still, but I could not walk around either; I had had to support myself on the taxi driver's shoulder even to get up to the vaidyar's veranda. So, I sat there, my eyes overflowing, biting my teeth. Quiet! I told my pain. I am the empress of my body, so I command you, do not make a sound.

Time passed. Somewhere along, I saw on the palm of my hand the number I had written down. It was beginning to rub away in the tears and sweat. Hurriedly, I picked up my phone and dialled the number. I was not sure why I did that, neither did I think someone will pick up. But you did. I might have expected a rough, male voice. Your voice was not rough or heavy. It was calm, and it reminded me of a young mango sapling wet from the rain, somewhat battered by the raindrops. A voice that held back sobs … I don't know if you will believe me, but in that moment, I felt the urge to embrace you.

I told you a lot of lies that day. Well, not complete lies, but half-truths. You listened to me and agreed to everything I said. I was feeling guilty, so I ended the call saying I will call back later. I had no plans for a journey at that time, but I think I told you about Odisha and Chitrotpala. Anywhere in India would have been the same to me at that point. It did surprise me that it was Odisha that came to the tip of my tongue unbidden.

There must have been a journey through lemon orchards in my dreams. A dream I might have forgotten, but it had not forgotten me. Chitrotpala, a tributary of Mahanadi. A beauty who flows quietly, calmly, her waters touching both of her banks. And on her banks, dark green orchards, sprawling tamarind trees. I used to know a person who would place a plastic cot in their shade, one that could be folded and carried, and sit or lie down on it, reading, dreaming only of light. A student at the Utkal University in Cuttack. He used to write long letters to me, at least one a week.

Like the Brahmaputra, Mahanadi is also an angry river. Every year, she floods Cuttack. They say that was why the capital was moved to Bhubaneswar. His university was by the banks of the Mahanadi. The water came up the steps when least expected. On holidays, he travelled for kilometres looking for a calm shore. All these are old stories. I had stopped thinking about them. But when I called you, when you picked up the phone immediately, somehow all of it flowed back into my mind. I can't explain it any better than that.

The email ended there, abruptly. Puzzled, I wondered why Mudritha had sent this incomplete message to me. It was almost dawn. I lay back down, but when it was clear I couldn't fall asleep again, I decided to get up. I had a shower, changed my clothes, and began packing my bag. I was hungry, but the thought of running into Chechi and Amma together in the kitchen made me feel exhausted. Better to wait until Chechi left for her office, I decided, until Amma was on her own. A soldier alone lost some of their valour; it was better to face them then.

The packing was over in a matter of minutes. A ten-day journey, four to four and a half days of which would be spent in trains. A couple of pairs of clothes, a few underclothes, soap, toothbrush, toothpaste, a towel … A few bits and pieces … What an impoverished way to get ready for a journey, I thought to myself. I had picked up my phone and sat down on the chair unlocking it when Chechi came into the room with a cup of tea in her hand. Her unexpected arrival threw me – she never came into my room. We never met other than in the shared spaces of our home.

'Here, drink your tea,' she said, leaning against the table. I obliged.

'You'll be gone before I get back from work, so I thought I'll say goodbye now,' she continued. 'Be careful. Pay attention. You don't know the place or the language. And your companions are all women. Look after them well.'

I nodded, mechanically. This advice, care, they were unusual. Even going on a ten-day trip made one special!

'Packed everything necessary, haven't you? ID proof, ATM card? If you've finished, give me the cup. Amma has gone to the temple. I'll be off now. Your food is in the casserole. Go and eat if you're done with your preparations. Do you need money?'

She continued standing there. As for me, I was beginning to feel bored with this unfamiliar show of affection. I reminded her that I was going on a business trip and that I wouldn't have to spend my own money, handed her the empty teacup, and waited for her to leave.

'All right then,' she said. 'I'll see you when you're back.'

The stairs creaked quietly as she went down.

On my phone was another notification – another email from Mudritha.

ANIRUDDHAN'S NOTEBOOK — PART 6

The second email from Mudritha:

Aniruddhan,

I don't know whether you read the email I sent yesterday, whether you even saw it. I was twisting and turning in my bed, unable to sleep, when I remembered I had a few things to tell you and started writing it. There will be that much less to talk about when we meet, I thought. I have never been able to sleep the night before a journey. Not just long journeys, even the prospect of going to a wedding or a trip to the hospital would excite me. And with my sleep-deprived, puffed-up face and eyes, I would make myself miserable on the actual journey. My head would hurt, and I would feel nauseous. Usually, I take a Valium and make myself sleep, but it didn't work last night. So, I began writing to you. Somewhere along the way, I fell asleep and didn't realize until this morning that I had hit 'send' on that incomplete letter. I don't like starting or leaving something halfway, but weirdly enough, life always seems to make me do things that way.

The reason I started that letter yesterday was to tell you about our journey, but I guess I digressed into other things. That day, sitting on the vaidyar's veranda in unbearable pain, I called you and told you things that I had no idea I would tell anyone.

Amazingly, by the time I ended the call, my pain was almost gone! And I sat there quietly enough until he called me in.

The vaidyar massaged my ankle, and when I least expected it, pulled it back into place. If you have ever been to these healers, you would know. We will be crying out in mortal pain, and he will distract us, saying things, asking questions, massaging the injured area as though he is sponging out the pain, and in the soothing coolness of oils and kuzhambu, we believe he is indeed doing so.

And then comes that moment, utterly unexpected, when he straightens the twisted joint back into place. The pain will make us see stars! It is difficult to respond mildly when pain is inflicted upon you, but in this instance, all you can do is thank the person who tricked you into it. Still, I was soothed by the fact that he left his hand on my foot as I rode the pain until it subsided. I know there is nothing crueller than hurting someone and leaving them to the pain.

Sometime later, when I was able to open my eyes, the vaidyar, a young man with a thin face, was still sitting beside me, his oil-smeared hands still gently stroking my ankle. I smiled at him for the first time. He applied herbal potions to the injured area, bandaged it, and instructed me on how to take care of it. As I left the room, it felt as though I had been inside it for over a century.

On the bench outside sat a young boy dressed in a school uniform, screaming. He must have arrived when I was inside. Two women sat beside him, trying to calm him down and patting his head and shoulders mechanically. Comforting without affection … Must have been his teachers. In the midst of some energetic game during lunch break, a bench or a desk might have fallen on his leg, or he might have twisted his foot while running down some steps. I wished one of his teachers would take him in her arms, hug him to her chest and console him. When I sat there only a few minutes ago, how I had wished I was consoled that way … There is nothing more fortunate in this life than having a shoulder to lean on in times of pain and hurt. At the very least, they could have called his father or mother on their way here.

I began to feel angry towards those women who continued to pat him on his shoulders as though playing a rhythm while looking impatiently at their watches and at the vaidyar's door. Perhaps they had missed their lunch. After teaching one class after another all morning, tired and hungry, they might have just opened their lunch boxes when the accident happened, and abandoning their lunch, they might have rushed the boy to the vaidyar. They might have moved their post-lunch, first-period class, exchanged it with some other teacher. Or they might be teaching Class 10 and still had a lot of the syllabus to cover before the board exams. Perhaps, worn down by all these worries, there was only so much love they could spare for this child who was not their own, I argued, my mind this time advocating on their behalf. By then, my taxi arrived. On my way back, too, I watched that old building. There was not much traffic and the car was travelling at speed, and yet I stuck my head out of the window and tried to read the word 'Himadri' on the board.

I had assumed that I would fall asleep quickly that night, what with the pain and the medication. But the snippet of a poem kept bubbling inside me. Don't misunderstand me, I don't write poetry. I used to read a lot, but that was a long time ago.

> I don't know what to do – I am of two minds
> I don't expect to touch heaven

I cannot tell you why, but that night, these lines kept repeating in my mind, making me teary, breathless. Lines by Sappho, a Greek woman who had lived almost twenty centuries ago, a poet who was described as Lady Odysseus. She was a worshipper of the Greek goddess of love, Aphrodite. Well, why am I telling you all this? You are a teacher giving PSC coaching. You would know all about Sappho.

Perhaps it was the condition of my legs that made me think of those lines. There was a time when I tried translating Sappho from English to Malayalam. I guess, by now, there are several translations. I am not sure if the lines I remembered were my translation or someone else's, but I kept reciting those lines over and over again. At that moment, I was scared there would be no more journeys for me. Where would I go with these legs? My journeys had barely begun, the places I wanted to visit left unseen. I cried, loudly, shamelessly. There are advantages to living alone. One can express all one's emotions in their rawest forms, without the fear of disturbing others, without the fear of being seen. A chance to leave aside all considerations for others – that is not a small thing.

It did occur to me that I should call you and apologize, but I didn't. I talked to you about a journey that might never happen, and you listened to me as the representative of a travel agency that did not exist. Lies, yes, but transparent lies as clear as water. There is an irony in the phrase 'transparent lies', isn't there? Can any lie be transparent? And if it were, would it be a lie? But this lie – I felt it had made both of us happy. Still, instead of calling you, I continued weeping thinking about my helplessness, and fell asleep somewhere along the line. I slept until your call woke me, and all night in my dreams, I travelled through various places.

To tell you the truth, I didn't expect you to call me back. I didn't think you would have the courage to take on an all-women tour, donning the false identity of the director of a travel company that didn't exist. At the same time, in all honesty, I hoped you would call. And when you did, I told you more lies. By then, I was determined that we will go on this journey. I say 'we', but at this point there was no 'we'. I was yet to find the other nine members of my group.

You told me about the successful tours you had organized, and I am sure you were telling the truth, but you didn't tell me that they were a long time ago or that it had been years since you last organized one. Instead, you told me that you were teaching at the institute with the strange name because there weren't that many trips as it was the off season. Are you teaching fairy tales to your students, I asked. You laughed, but I am not sure whether that was because you found my joke funny. I found it hilarious and couldn't stop laughing, and you waited patiently for me to finish. Anyway, by the time we ended that call, our journey was almost decided. I was fully aware of the lies you said, but you had no idea about my lies. I had, by then, decided that it was not a pukka tour company doing a deal like any other business deal that my dream journey needed, that it was someone like you who should accompany us.

Will you believe me if I told you that, after our phone call, I sat on my bed until I found our co-travellers, all nine of them? It was not as hard as you would imagine, but not so easy either. I posted a message in one of the women-only groups that I am part of on Facebook – a closed group, called 'Lesbos'. So far, I have only been a passive member in that group. I don't know anyone in Lesbos personally. The group had three hundred and thirty members when it began, and I still don't know who added me to it. Don't let the name mislead you. It is not a group for lesbians as some might think. It is named after a poem by Sappho. Its profile picture is a photo of the poet and these lines:

> You will remember
> We, too, did these in our youth
> Many and beautiful things

What name other than Lesbos for a secret group of women who celebrate youth and all its joys and excesses! It is a dangerous island with rock clusters covered in slippery moss, sugar-sand beaches, plump vines clambering up magnificent trees, and countless creeping, crawling things. It has only one season, always – youth. I hope you understand that this does not mean we are, all of us, young women.

In my first post, I asked whether anyone would be interested in going on a trip to a land with many women-centred festivals such as Yama Puja, Karthika Purnima, Pausha Pournami, Dhanu Sankranti, Magha Sapthami and so on. 'Who's with me?' I asked. To my utter amazement, within half an hour, there were eighty-four positive responses. What festivals do we have for women in our land? Thiruvathira, Pongala … that's it! But I don't think the mention of women-centred festivals was the only reason for the interest. I think all women yearn to travel. The desire to slip away, anxious that their lives don't end in its everyday confines. That is why so many people responded even though they did not know where this place was. If those who were offline at the time had also responded, the number would have been much higher.

There was no way all of us could go together. So, I had to do some screening. I sent my second message to the eighty-four who had responded. It said: 'The old Kalingadesham with a rich diversity of India's indigenous people. Famous in the annals of history for its temples as well as economic deprivation. A journey to this land, avoiding all its usual tourist spots.' I called it a journey to its underworld.

I have read that Odisha's heart beats in its tribal lands. A people of great inner strength, who have proved their courage at least twice in history. One was the unsuccessful war waged by Chandragupta Mauryan against Kalingam. He had already conquered the rest of the land, and conquering Kalingam would have made him an unchallenged emperor. But the tribal communities came together to resist his advent. Chandraguptan found out that his well-trained soldiers and modern warfare were no match for them. Their weaponry was ancient, their army untrained and their warfare unscientific, and yet the indigenous people of the land proved that these too could win a battle when backed with integrity and unadulterated valour. This is something we women understand only too well. After all, our small wins are very similar.

This is history that repeated when Emperor Ashokan attacked Kalingadesham. The entire tribal population, including women and children, resisted him. The blood that flowed stained the water and the sandy shores of the river where the battle took place red. I am certain this river was Chitrotpala although all the history books call it by some other name. We have been taught that Ashokan turned to ahimsa and became an advocate of non-violence because of this war that affected his very soul. I often think that there is nothing more indecent than preaching non-violence and peace after plunder and war.

Many places in this land have found their way into the World Heritage list. It has lakes, like the Bindu Sagar which is sanctified by the waters of all the sacred rivers in India, hundreds of temples built in granite. Still, tourists tend to avoid this state, except for those who have a keen interest in history. There are many other, more beautiful places for those who like long journeys, or if one's interest is in spirituality, they can choose a journey to the Himalayas.

This, in short, was my second message, and it did not put anyone off. And when one of them posted a note about a festival called Agni Purnima, the interest multiplied. It is, apparently, a festival that marks the end of winter when, all across villages, in the night, people gather in a piece of land in the outskirts, build a bonfire of straw, set light to it, and sing and dance around it.

Imagine the joy and energy in coming together around a fire on a cold night … It would certainly untie the knots inside us, make our bodies flexible like never before. It would unleash the songs and stories suppressed within us, set our lips singing sweetly, bodies dancing, stepping and swaying in their own individual rhythms. Reading that message about Agni Purnima, written by a woman named Shashwathi, each one of us would have hummed a little tune. Even I, with my damaged foot, felt the urge to forget the pain and dance a little. All of us wanted to be part of it. And since almost all villages celebrated Agni Purnima, this would not be difficult. Someone suggested getting together at a specific place, and everyone agreed. People's interest increased when Shashwathi said that the occasion was also a faith-based ritual – apparently, the coming year's crops would be decided based on the direction in which the bonfire of straw leaned.

It has to be said that Google has turned every person into a mini encyclopaedia. The moment the possibility of a journey to Odisha was mentioned, the group was inundated with pictures of women from rural Odisha in brightly coloured clothes. They wore intricately designed nose studs that covered almost half their faces, so unlike the tiny white or red stones that women here wear. And they wore plenty of bangles, metal bangles with pointy studs on them. Unlike the glass bangles that break when a hand is grabbed, these would pierce the skin of anyone who dared. They had large hairdos adorned with flowers, complex tattoos on their arms and legs. From our various locations, we would have gazed at those women in the pictures as though they were from another time. People began talking about the metal bangles and the nose studs they intended to buy while in Odisha.

Then, one of the group members – her name is Sarvaranjini – told us about a custom that used to be practised among the Khonds of Odisha, a specific kind of human sacrifice in order to please nature. You've probably heard of it. The intended victim, called Meriah, was killed inch by inch by inflicting a thousand deadly cuts. The belief was that the more the pain inflicted on the victim, the more pleased nature would be. Wasn't it similar to our own lives, Sarvaranjini asked. The practice was banned in Odisha a long time ago, but in the privacy of all our homes, it still continues. Tiny cuts, flowing blood, excruciating pain … The Meriah would die within a few days. But there are still sacrificial victims in most houses who die much slower deaths, spread out over years, crying incessantly, hurting endlessly. Sarvaranjini's message made us all sad.

It was past 10 a.m. and yet we went on chatting. I hadn't even left my bed yet, and my leg was beginning to throb. I wanted a cup of tea but there was no one to bring one to me in bed. Living alone has some such negative sides too. Still, finding the nine people to go on this trip was more important than tea. Do you know why I hesitated adding more people to the trip? Because I thought it would be too much for you. You have only arranged relatively easy tours for college students, and that was years ago, and you have no one else to depend on. How would you then take a group of women to an unfamiliar place? Seeing the interest in the Lesbos group, I so wanted to take them all with me. But I had already given you the number 'ten' when we talked first, when I had no real plans in mind, and I didn't want to change that now. I can tell you one thing: if this tour goes well, you will most certainly receive more requests. May be from our group itself. Which means you can leave your job at the coaching centre, and, instead, become an eternal traveller with people who love to explore the world. I keep feeling that this is a better job for you.

Anyway, that morning I sat there wondering how to decide who to include and who to exclude out of the eighty-odd people. So, I continued screening – don't ask me how, I barely know what I did – to reduce the number. I chatted with the remaining, assessed who most needed to be on a journey, who absolutely had to go on a journey, until I had the group of ten, of which one, of course, was myself. Thus, finally, by around 12 p.m., our tour group was ready, and I was exhausted.

I don't remember all their names. I have forwarded their ID proofs, names, addresses and other details to you by email. And I have given them your mobile number.

We, people who come from many different places, will all meet in person for the first time this evening. I am excited about that. As I told you, all except four will board the train from previous stations – one of them would be already in it now, she is the farthest. Three of us, including me, will be at the station by 4 p.m. The remaining person will get on board at a later station. We don't really have to be at the station that early, but why not avoid unnecessary anxiety? It is great fun to roam around the platform as though one has nowhere to go. I have often wanted to sit on a bench at a railway station platform for a whole day, watching the trains come and go … Quietly, contentedly, amidst the rushing multitudes … Today, I will sit like that, at least for a while.

You asked me why we didn't take a flight instead of the train. I know those who have the means do that these days, and to be honest, it would not have been a burden for any of us. But, flying never gives you that sense of peace that train journeys do. It is all a rush at the airport – check in hours in advance, go through security clearance, and once you are in the plane, before you've fastened your seat belt and taken a breath, it is time to get off. Standing around the conveyor belt waiting for my luggage upsets the rhythm of my heart, I feel.

In the train, the journey lengthens over day and night. It is like a sweet that is eaten slowly, bite by tiny bite, savoured in order to make it last, its taste lingering. By the way, Odisha is well-known for its sweets. Chhena poda, rasagolla, shrikhand … The Bikalananda Kar confectionery in Salipur is old and famous. I have only heard of it. My mouth waters at the thought of shrikhand but I have never eaten it.

No one in our group has been to Odisha before, nor do any of us know a word of Odia. Now don't go searching for guidebooks on spoken Odia. I am sure we will manage with Hindi and a bit of English, and of course, that universal language – gesturing. In any case, Odia learned from a book might come handy at a railway station or in a restaurant, but it will be useless for us in our journey to the underworld, or in understanding the dialects we will encounter in the villages. So, best not to worry about it. We will travel, and communicate, whether we know the language or not.

I have only told you that we will be staying in Salipur. What we have in mind is not a sightseeing trip – spending the day wandering around temples and museums and coming back to the hotel to sleep. We want to go into the villages, spend a night taking part in the Agni Purnima ritual, go on treks. One of India's gharial crocodile breeding centres is in Tikarpada – something I found out on the internet. I want to go there but not to see the crocodiles. To reach Tikarpada, we have to cross the Chitrotpala, and it seems it is better to come back crossing the Mahanadi. So, we will take boats across two rivers. As it is winter, we can hope that Mahanadi is not too tumultuous. For me, this is a journey to recreate another time. The realization of an old dream, much longed for but never fulfilled.

It is late. I am yet to prepare and pack for the journey, and there are many things to do with the house which will be left unattended for several days.

I will see you in the evening. I am so grateful to you because I feel that this is not just a business trip for you either, that you have taken this little trip of ours to heart. I may be wrong, but that is what I would like to believe. So, thank you. I am sure you will be on time. Us older women get anxious when there is any trouble. So, try to be there before us and wait for us.

Bye for now,

Mudritha.

VANITHA

I have taken on the responsibility of looking into Mudritha's disappearance because I found the case intriguing. I'm not going to conduct a criminal investigation like in those Mammootty films about the CBI, that's not what I mean. A civil policewoman does not have the powers to conduct such investigations, especially on her own. This is just a missing persons case that no one seems particularly interested in. Even Aniruddhan, who filed the case in the first place, has never met this woman. He doesn't seem to be particularly invested in finding her; he did not even get in touch later to see whether we had made any progress. I called him to say that he could come to the station the next day on his way back from work and pick his notebook up. But he said he wouldn't be able to come, and so I brought it home with me.

That night, I sat up and read it again, especially Mudritha's emails, and I felt the rising urge to speak to her. I sent a message to her email ID, just a 'hi', and a reply came promptly stating that it was an invalid address. That was the moment when I decided not to return Aniruddhan's notebook. Those notes and emails are all I have to go on. He wouldn't have any use of them. I also decided not to file it in Mudritha's casefile and resolved to investigate this case that no one else wanted. Will I succeed in finding her? I am not sure.

When women go missing, the usual process is to continue investigating until they are found. Unlike missing cases involving men when the investigation is ended after three months. Is this because men are incapable of remaining invisible for more than three months? I often think that men are a mixture of intense self-love and ego. They cannot remain hidden. It would be too much for them to stay away from others, not to reveal themselves, even for three months. But women – they are capable of keeping themselves out of sight like a tiny caterpillar. Not because they dream of metamorphosing into a beautiful butterfly, but just to remain a pupa, unseen and unrecognized by anyone … Perhaps this is why we are required to keep looking for them when women go missing.

Normally, though, these cases are abandoned after faltering through some inquiries, and then filing a report saying 'undetected' in court. It is easier for us, too, especially in cases where no one is interested, no one comes to ask about the progress made. In this case, we had already conducted inquiries as part of filing the FIR, and we had all the necessary records to prove it. After six months, we could say that we have investigated this case and ask the court's permission to conclude the case, and file it away as soon as we are given an order to drop further action. And if anyone comes inquiring after the case later, or if the missing person turns up, we can, of course, open it again. I feel that Mudritha's case will have a lifespan of six months. She will not exist after that – in fact, I don't actually know if she still exists. Will anyone remember her after that?

And so, I feel I have to continue investigating her case, that I have to find her. I don't know who I will take her to when I find her, to declare in proper filmy style, 'Here she is, take her.' For all I know, Mudritha could have made herself invisible precisely because she has no one. In which case, going after her to make her visible again would be unconscionable. I know that there is no one who feels self-hate as intensely as those who have been abandoned. They prefer to remain hidden. And even if they come out, they are covered in a thick outer skin, a carapace that is too heavy, too restricting to be able to see what is in front of them clearly, too cumbersome to move around properly. And yet, if it is removed, they become naked, exposed, like a shelled shrimp.

Whether I find her or not, I have to know more about Mudritha. My desire is not to single-handedly investigate her disappearance, solve the mystery and cover myself with glory. It is, simply, to know her. Most likely, in about six months, I will leave the police and join another government department. That gives me just enough time to wind down the investigation, mark 'undetected' on the file, and close it.

Mudritha … Even the name is strange, uncommon. It makes me think, for a while, that she is not a Malayali. Besides, can a Malayali woman erase herself just like that one fine day? Even if she desperately desires to disappear, it will be impossible. There will be countless roots and branches that will reveal her. Frayed roots, yes, and broken branches, wilted leaves, and still, they would speak up, point out her hiding place. Yet, here she is, a woman who has disappeared without a trace, her disappearance noticed only by a man, Aniruddhan, and that, too, not because of any personal, emotional connection, but just because they had a business transaction. Even if she is never found, it will not really matter to him.

As I read her emails again, I feel that I am walking along a barely visible hillside covered in a thick, encompassing fog that makes it difficult to see even what is right in front of me.

A trip planned by a woman no one has met. A bunch of sad, dissatisfied women who decide to go with her, who put enough trust in a Facebook post to transfer, in advance, the money for the trip to her account. It is easy to conclude, in these days of rampant online fraud, that she made away with their money. That would at least give a solid reason for her disappearance. But I can't conclude that is the case because she transferred that money to the travel agent, and he, a man more honest than most, is trying desperately to return the surplus money – the ten thousand rupees that had not been spent on the tour – to her. I could even imagine a scenario where the woman who organized the trip and the travel agent were in cahoots, but that is not the case either. Only the organizer has disappeared. And the tour went ahead without hitches.

I tried discussing the case with Thomas sir and Renji. I hoped that Thomas sir, with his years of experience, might be able to shed some light on it. A similar case he had investigated in the past or a general rationale behind such cases – anything would be useful at this stage, I thought.

'Just leave it, Vanitha, let it go,' was what he said, with obvious disinterest. 'When that house was demolished – or maybe even before that when she couldn't live there any more – she went elsewhere. It's possible she has a husband and family, isn't it? That area is full of affluent people. Old money, prominent families with relatives living abroad. She may even have gone abroad. And this trip, women-only groups … just what ladies with money to burn do to pass time. Wait six months. Then file an FAD and close the case. What else!'

'Further Action Dropped' … As I said, the final report on challenging or complex cases that generally gives us peace of mind, saves us from further investigation. But in Mudritha's case, even the thought of filing an FAD scares me. I have to find her, at the very least find out where she is or what is happening to her.

Renji Kuriakose and I made the selection list together and trained at the police academy in the same batch. His first posting was to this station, meaning he has known this area for four or five years longer than I have. Has he ever been to the area where Mudritha's house used to be? Does he remember any incident associated with that area? I asked him, pushed and prodded him, but for Renji everything is a joke.

'My dear Vanitha, that woman pissed off somewhere, that's all,' he said. 'No relative of hers has come looking for her or filed a complaint. So why should we dig this up? Last year alone, 7816 women went missing in Kerala. Not to mention the unreported cases where no complaints were filed.'

'But this one was reported, a complaint filed, and we did a preliminary investigation. We didn't find out much about her, true, but that doesn't mean we should close the file, does it? Shouldn't we give it at least six months?'

'Great! Are you mad, Vanitha, to go after a case that no one cares about? Especially at this station where we are so busy and don't have enough staff? If it was a young woman, we could have gone after her mobile phone ... and at least got an interesting story in return. This is not like that, is it?'

'So? What, we shouldn't investigate because she is not young? What if she has had an accident? Or someone has harmed her? Don't we have a responsibility to the man who filed the complaint?'

'Ah, him!' Renji laughed loudly. 'I've had my suspicions about him right from the start. Not that he has harmed her – I don't think he's capable enough to do something like that – but that he's cooked up this whole story. "Mudritha", "women-only tour", "disappearance" ... are these even believable? There's no Mudritha and no disappearance, I'm telling you. He's made it all up. Did you take a good look at him? Didn't you feel there's something off about him? He, his mother, his sister ... they're all a bit weird!

Renji launched once again into the story about Aniruddhan's father. It had happened the year he joined the station. He wondered why anyone with even a semblance of self-respect would continue to live in the same town after such an incident. And when he went on laughing at them, calling them 'mentally ill', I stopped trying to convince him and left him be.

The accident must have been embarrassing for Aniruddhan and his family, of course, but they are not responsible for it, nor is it right to paint them 'mentally ill' for what they have endured. I recall the sadness in Aniruddhan's eyes, and his mother who had looked at us dazed, as though she had forgotten how to smile.

Days pass in the confusion of trying to figure out where to look for Mudritha. Then, suddenly, as I am searching for an important file in the dusty, dark records room, my nose red from sneezing and barely able to breathe, a few lines of poetry come to my mind.

> Artful goddess
> Weaver of snares
> And so many
> Who follow her

By the time I locate the file I am looking for and leave the records room, I have recited these lines many times. And as I look in the mirror in the restroom and dust cobwebs off my hair and wash my face, they begin to trouble me. Whose lines are they? Were there more? Or did I make them up myself? Like a grain of sand inside an oyster, they begin to grate against my mind.

By evening, I connect those lines with Mudritha. Artful goddess, it was her, the goddess who wove butterflies or dreams out of enticing words, gently breathed life into them and set them free. Others followed her like supplicants unable to resist. Those lines explain, I begin to be convinced, why so many women agreed to go on a journey with her based solely on a Facebook post. Find them, and they might take me to Mudritha, or at the very least, help me understand her better. I am aware that Mudritha did not know these women before. But they were connected, for over a month, because of this journey. A connection that has frayed since. Still...

I need Aniruddhan's help to contact them, so I call him. His first question, when he answers the phone, is whether there has been any development with the case. And, assuming that I had called him about his notebook, he apologizes for not picking it up yet. I put him at ease, tell him that we are still investigating, and ask him for the telephone numbers of the other women in the group.

'None of them knew Mudritha personally, madam,' he tells me. 'They didn't have even as much of a relationship as I did with her. They only knew each other as members of a social media group.'

I sense he is being reluctant, so demand, in proper police style, that he give me their details. He explains, helplessly, that he doesn't have them.

'As I have already explained, I only spoke with Mudritha. There was never an occasion to speak with the others before the journey. We did talk on the phone a few times during the trip, but I haven't saved any of their numbers. It would be difficult now, after six months, to scroll back through the call log and try to identify whose number is which.'

Reluctantly, I accept that I have no other option than to believe him. As I think about my next step, Aniruddhan himself comes up with the solution. Mudritha had forwarded the emails they sent her with proofs of identity for booking tickets. He promises to look for them as soon as he is back home from work and to send them to me.

Back home from work myself that night, I go straight to my bookshelf. Those lines of poetry which seemed so familiar as though I had read them many times, felt so personal as though my mind had spontaneously composed them … I want to know if they are real. My hand hovers over a lean book with a beautiful woman on its cover. This is it, I realize with a shiver, the poem is in this book.

It is a collection of Sappho's poems in translation, my favourite book at one time. I find the lines in it. And simultaneously, with a shudder, I remember the name of the group Mudritha and the women had belonged to: Lesbos.

Coincidence, I think, amazed, and I am consumed with a certainty that I will, after all, get closer to Mudritha. Why else would I remember these lines out of the blue, these lines written by Sappho.

Instead of having a bath or attempting to cook dinner, I take the book to my bedroom and lie down on the bed reading it. My reading had gone downhill ever since I joined the police department. All I read these days, in my desperate desire to leave the department and get a new job as a college lecturer, are guidebooks for the PSC exams. I hope to be on the rank list and to get an appointment as soon as possible. I might be able to return to books and my lapsed reading habit then. I sigh hoping fervently that I would, at the very least, have the opportunity to ruffle through books.

It is late by the time I finish all my chores, sweep and mop the kitchen, and stare at it one last time from the door. I don't like waking up to a dirty kitchen that looks crossly at me. Everything has to be in order, not even a spoon out of place, and it should welcome me enveloped in the fresh fragrance of soap as though it has just had a bath and changed its clothes. I am aware of the inordinate amount of time I spend ensuring this, and of my family making fun of me saying I have OCD, but I can't stop it.

Not wanting to disturb those who are sleeping, I take my phone to the sitting room and switch on the TV with the volume lowered right down. If Giriyettan wakes up, let him think I am watching TV. Not that he will bother getting up to check on me, and if he did, he will make his displeasure on seeing me with my phone clear. Won't say anything directly to me, but there will be expressions of annoyance and meaningful grunts in the morning, and a secret inspection of my phone.

I switch on the phone, and as I had expected, there are messages from Aniruddhan on WhatsApp. Nine email ids, each tagged with the owner's name, not that it is hard to figure out from the ids themselves.

Over the course of the night, I send nine emails. After introducing myself as the civil policewoman investigating Mudritha's disappearance, I tell them I am not looking for information about their journey or about what happened after that, only about what transpired while the journey was being planned. What led to such a journey, for example, and what they had discussed with Mudritha, their own thoughts about her, and anything else that they might know about her.

Emails sent, I continue sitting there because I can't sleep. The TV plays one programme after another without me glancing at it even once, as though it is consoling me, telling me that I am not alone in that dark night, by singing, crying, laughing, trying to make me laugh.

In truth, I am not alone. My nine letters have gone in nine different directions searching for nine women. Soon, they will join me in my search for Mudritha who is somewhere else, hidden. Life is not a riddle to be solved, but a mystery to be revealed, a search for an answer yet to be found. I remember reading something like that once, and lean back in my chair. I will reveal this mystery. I am on the path to do so.

I have let myself be caught in a trap which is of no personal or professional use to me. All this investigation will do is suck my energy and use up my time. I know this, and yet, surprisingly, I don't feel the half-heartedness or laziness that one usually feels when pursuing something that brings no discernible gain. Instead, I feel upbeat, full of energy.

And so, from the next day, I start waiting for replies to my emails. It is not a comfortable experience. Some don't bother responding, while others who do respond make me wonder whether they had actually read my email. Other than a cursory expression of sadness, they don't give any indication that the news of Mudritha's disappearance touched them in any meaningful way. A woman they didn't quite know, or had known for a brief moment in their lives, who they might never see again … what is there to really worry about such a person's disappearance? The only person who offers help is a woman named Sarvaranjini. She suggests that she post something in their group. I agree on the off chance that there might be someone in the group who knows Mudritha personally.

Ranjini may have made the post, but so far there has been no response. Meanwhile, I have persevered, communicated back and forth with the nine women, and I have been able to put together some notes about the day of their trip and about the days leading up to it. Or it would be more precise to say that I have put some notes together about their lives, based partly on what they have told me and partly on what I have deduced. Will these notes help me find Mudritha? I don't know. I used the notepad on my phone to write these down and kept them locked. These are people's lives. I am adamant that no one else see them, not even by mistake.

I open them every now and then, edit them, make corrections. When I was a student, I used to take part in creative writing competitions. That experience may have come in handy. Anyway, I have decided that, once these notes are complete, I will send each document to the woman it belongs to. I won't be able to be the keeper of their lives forever. I have to believe that I will find some information about Mudritha by then.

I wish I could gain entry into Lesbos, their group. But none of the women I communicate with are admins of the group, and so it hasn't happened. Since my official position is not all that important, and since the investigation is not solely my responsibility, I don't try gaining entry that way. But that closed group and its name bother me, keep tempting me. What these women have told me – they are not just stories; they are their lives. And as I try to arrange them into an orderly narrative, I keep thinking about another woman who had lived centuries ago. A woman who had written a clutch of poems that blazed like fire, who had loved as fiercely, and after many departures and many more abandonments, had thrown herself into the sea. Sappho … Legend has it that she was only thirty years old then. For a woman, any age is the perfect age for suicide, so much more than it is for living.

SARVARANJINI

The blind sage, Deerghathamas, was the husband of a woman named Pradweshi. They had a whole bunch of children. Instead of supporting his family, Deerghathamas neglected them and got himself involved in pointless pursuits. All he did was make their lives miserable. Fed up, finally, Pradweshi told him, 'A husband is one who looks after his wife and provides for his household. You don't do that. Instead, I'm the one who looks after you and the children. I'm sick of all the work I do, and I don't intend to continue.' Deerghathamas was enraged and cursed all women everywhere. It is not clear what the curse entailed. Come to think of it, being a woman in itself is a curse.

Pradweshi, in any case, was a smart one. She didn't bother falling at Deerghathamas's feet, bawling and begging to be released from the curse. Instead, with her children's help, she built a raft, loaded the blind sage on to it, and sent him floating down the Ganga. The king of a land named Odaradesha saw the raft floating past down the river with a scared looking man sitting on it. He had it pulled to the shore. This king, he had heard of Deerghathamas. He was a renowned sage after all. It is usually like that – those who don't look after their household, don't take care of their wife and children, are nevertheless well regarded by the rest of the world, have great standing in society.

The king decided to make good use of the great personage who had arrived at his kingdom. That is fair enough, but what is weird is the way he put the sage to use. He requested Deerghathamas to produce children with his wife, the queen Sudeshna, children who would seek the path of virtue and wealth. It is unclear whether the king already had children. What is clear is that, pragmatic as he was, he was not about to let a sage who had literally floated in go unused. There was nothing to gain financially from this poverty-stricken sage, so why not have sagely progeny at least in return for food and board. Maximum manpower utilization theory, full use of human resources leaving no source of energy unused. He was a king after all, bound to know theories of economics and management.

Men in those days seem to have been far more open-minded than today, enough to temporarily let another man have a go at their wives. Husbands who said to their wives, 'Go, lay with him, his sperm is special, much better than mine,' as though they were sending their wives to a fertility lab where eggs and sperm would be mixed in a test tube. But no, not really. What the king requested of the sage, and ordered Sudeshna to do, was to engage in good, old-fashioned sex. Of course, he didn't ask for Sudeshna's permission or whether she was willing. That was not the done thing, there was no need for that.

Sudeshna did not fancy laying with the ugly, old, blind sage, so she sent her maid in her place. It is not quite fair to call her a cheat. Women often become cunning like this because they have no other option. Perhaps if the sage was young and handsome … Who doesn't like a change every now and then?

By the time she writes this much, Sarvaranjini is unable to hold back her laughter. Ever since their trip had been planned, she was spending all her free time digging up information about Odisha, and had chanced upon the fact that Odisha was once known as Odaradesha and that there was a story behind it.

Why Odisha? Why not some chilly hill station, she had wondered. Sarvaranjini is convinced that all cold places are beautiful. Odisha gets cold too, but it is seasonal, summer, rainy season and winter come and go. Cold places are cold all the time, even in the summer.

Her love affair with the cold had started with a college trip to Kodaikanal. The tourist season had just begun, only a few honeymooning couples around the lake and in the pine forests. She and her friends had watched their love-filled antics and then looked away shyly.

'Soon enough, you girls can come here too and do all these things,' their teacher, Subaida, had said.

'If I come to Kodaikanal again, I will never go back,' Sarvaranjini had told herself then. 'I will live here forever. We'll have a beautiful house in the valley, with a gorgeous garden.'

The 'we' was made up of herself and someone else, but she had not known who that might be. It was not important.

Beautiful flowers would bloom even on thorny bushes in her garden. In the backyard, a strawberry patch. She would run a homestay rather than look for a job, set the ground floor of her house aside for the guests and live in the wood-panelled upper floor. In her spare time, she would knit woollen shawls in myriad hues.

Draping a shawl woven with peacock and sapphire blue yarns over her shoulders, she would walk to the market. Bending a branch of the orange tree by the gate, she would pick a fruit, its green skin barely giving way to golden. She liked her oranges slightly sour. And she would walk sucking on its segments. It would be fun if she had girlfriends on this journey. How wonderful it would be if the 'we' was made up of herself and a girlfriend!

Ah, what mad dreams she had in those days ... And caught in the rush of that madness, she had applied for admission to a Masters degree at the Mother Teresa Women's University in Kodaikanal. All she had to show for it were the letters exchanged with the university. She had wanted to study social work, which would have allowed her to leave the campus on fieldwork.

The off-season started with the rains. She had imagined walking alone along the paths mangled by the footsteps of tourists. Most of the roadside shops would be closed, and the lake, placid now that the tourist boats were gone, would shiver awake again as raindrops touched its surface. The most beautiful sight would be at Suicide Point, where threads of rain fell unbroken into the bottomless chasm. To walk under an umbrella along quiet, deserted lanes, to sit on a bench when the rain let up, to shiver in the cold, and to drive it away eating warm peanuts from the carts ... Oh, how she had yearned to do all these things!

But to what end? Girls didn't need unnecessary degrees, her family had declared; what was important was to find a proper job. So, they doused her dreams and sent her to Palakkad to study for a BEd degree. Her only consolation was that Kodaikanal was a mere four or five hours away from Palakkad, even though she never went there again. When marriage proposals began arriving, she hoped, secretly, for someone working in Russia or

Ireland. Sitting at the reading table in the hostel after everyone went to bed, she began to scour the matrimonial pages in Sunday newspapers, searching among the 'ready to marry' men.

A handful of black letters utterly devoid of human feelings, cut down to the barest minimum of words in order to reduce the cost of advertising. Behind those words, an ocean of emotions surged, thousands of dreams, hopes. Every time she picked up a Sunday newspaper, Sarvaranjini shivered in anticipation. He was in it, the man who would take her to Iceland and to Antarctica. There they would build an igloo and walk together in their slippery yard. But there was barely anyone from Ireland in those ads, and no one at all from Russia. And even if there were, the chances of them being from the same religious and caste backgrounds were miniscule. Besides, she could predict how her family would react to any proposal she herself took to them.

There was the time she had fallen for the advertisement from a twenty-nine-year-old man who claimed to love travelling, said he had not settled down anywhere and would not do so any time soon. He did not care about caste or religion, he claimed, looked only for broad-mindedness in his life partner. She had noted down the post box number with the ad and written to him, her heart beating loudly as she posted it. Weeks passed and there was no reply. She was relieved even as she grieved. What if he had replied! A man from a different religion, a vagabond, and above all, a man she had found for herself. There would have been murder in her family.

Still, even now, she thought of him occasionally, with a deep sense of loss. Had he found his dream partner? Were they still travelling around? Why did he reject her, she wondered sorrowfully, or had she made a mistake in the post box number? It embarrassed her even now to recall what she had written, that when they had travelled enough and were ready to settle down, they should do so in Siberia. She should not have been that forward, she thought now, in that first letter. She should have held back, sent a more formal letter with only a few details – her name, address, qualifications, skin colour, height and so on, like the biodata for a job application but with a little embellishment. Instead, her letter had few such facts and a lot of subjective nonsense. It would not be surprising if he took her to be a silly, foolish girl. Whoever heard of the woman herself replying to a matrimonial ad instead of her father or an uncle? Even the broadest-minded travel-lover would look askance at a rude girl who blurted out requests to be taken to Siberia. Besides, all he had said in the ad was that *he* liked to travel; he had said nothing about looking for a life partner in order to go travelling together. It was she who had read this intention into it.

Perhaps he was looking for someone to wait for him when he returned from his travels, someone to wash his dirty clothes, to cook him tasty food, to sleep with him if he so desired. Sarvaranjini has never come across travel-lovers who take their wives with them, and perhaps she never will. She has read a lot of travelogues – by Megasthenes, Ptolemy, Ibn Battuta. What did their wives do when they went away on their travels? There was no guarantee that they would return, no letters or phone calls in between, just the waiting, endless like the oceans into which they set sail.

It was good, in the end, that she had not ended up married to that travel-lover, she told herself often, consoling herself, and yet each time the memory surfaced, she remembered how insulted she had felt by the snub.

It turned out to be the first and last time she tried to arrange her own marriage. If she were able to express her desires or take an independent decision, Sarvaranjini would have told her family that she did not wish to be married, that she wanted to live her life making friends and travelling. The dream of running a homestay in Kodaikanal was never forgotten. And when it became clear that she had no other option than to get married, she had hoped, desperately, that it would be at least someone of her own choosing.

Instead, keeping up with the customs of all typical marriage proposals, Venumadhavan came to see her in the company of the marriage broker. All she had been told when her mother telephoned her to summon her home was that 'the boy' worked abroad. A polar bear woke up inside her mind, shaking snow off its fur, and until the day of the pennukaanal, when the prospective bride and groom met for the first time, she did not ask for more details. Let the polar bear stay alive and hopeful in her mind until then, she had mused.

On the day of the pennukaanal, the polar bear melted away to nothingness, or, perhaps, went into a deep, endless hibernation. After the customary 'seeing' of the would-be bride, it was time for the orchestrated show that allowed 'the boy' and 'the girl' to talk to one another. And that was when she discovered he worked in the Gulf.

'In Kuwait. You must have heard … it is the hottest country in the Gulf,' he told her as though boasting of some great achievement. 'Don't expect the temperatures to go under 45 degrees often. Offices, flats, everywhere is air conditioned. You'll burn if you go out in the sun.'

As Venumadhavan talked, sitting in her room that opened on to a veranda where white flowers bloomed on sankhupushpam vines, Sarvaranjini felt that she was burning to a crisp without going out into the sun. There was nothing she could do to escape from this marriage, no way to protest. Instead, she decided firmly that she would never go to Kuwait with him, not even if her life was on the line. Let him come to her. He had a month's leave each year. That would do. She would not go to him, to Kuwait, no matter what.

After the wedding, before going back to the Gulf, Venumadhavan told her smugly that he was eligible for a family visa and would take her to Kuwait within three months. 'Why not mark me with your signet ring?' Sarvaranjini thought derisively. 'I'll sit here waiting, fingering the etching.' But she was careful not to voice her derision. She ignored the official procedures required for applying for the visa, left them undone until Venumadhavan grew impatient. He accused her of having a secret love affair, quarrelled with her over it. Why else would any woman choose to be separate from her husband, that too in the honeymoon period of their life together? What other woman would turn away from the opportunity to live in an air-conditioned flat, to travel abroad, to see new sights, experience a new life?

Sarvaranjini felt that all men, especially husbands, behaved as though they had the undeniable, God-given right to reach such conclusions if women showed even a little reluctance to follow the habits and traditions that were expected of them. If she had clamoured to be taken with him, cried over the telephone and written teary letters, she would have been considered normal, adjudged to be a kulastree, woman well born, goodwife. How happy he would have been then! But she did not mourn the parting, did not shed copious tears.

'I'm not coming,' she said instead. 'I have my school and my students. I can't just leave it all and sit closeted in a flat in a strange country. You come here, as often as you can. People live like that also, don't they?'

Words that only served to strengthen his suspicions. And so, even before they began their life together properly, a man, a stranger, pulled up a seat between them and sat on it, never to leave ever again. The thought made Sarvaranjini laugh. She, who didn't really like men, only put up with Venumadhavan because she had no other choice, was being accused of having another man as her lover!

Venumadhavan did not give up easily. Within six months, he found her a job at the Indian school in Kuwait and had her transplanted. Then followed twenty long years of life in that flat, with Venumadhavan constantly sniffing around her like a police dog after a culprit. A life in the same, slow rhythm, year in, year out. Other than the two-yearly trips home, she never went anywhere, not even to other Gulf countries, and spent all her days between the flat and the school.

Life was punishment for a crime she had not committed but had been proven beyond the shadow of doubt, without being given an opportunity to protest her innocence. Instead, she found herself regretting actions that she had not done. It was on one such day, when the guilty conscience from crimes she had not committed threatened her very existence, that she bought herself a smartphone.

Unnecessary, growled the police dog, but for her, that phone became a shade tree with a hundred branches, some that bent to the ground and some that soared into the sky. She climbed on to them, sat on them and changed places as she pleased. Artificial reality, two words that she muttered lovingly, more real to her than reality itself. Her life changed as though she had now sewn herself two wings. Not ordinary wings, but tender, transparent wings strewn with vines and flowers that she sewed more carefully, lovingly, than the baby frocks she had made for Vinnie. Now she could fly even when Venumadhavan was around, and he would not notice, would not be able to see her wings. He could accuse her of spending too much time on the phone but he would not be able to find out how far she travelled through her phone. If he ever came to know, it would hurt him. More deeply than it had hurt her when, all those years ago at the beginning of their life together, he had accused her of refusing to come to Kuwait because of 'him', her non-existent paramour.

And it was as she travelled aimlessly through online skies that she came across Lesbos, and later became part of Mudritha's travel group. She did not know who else was in the group; she had assumed she was part of the group right from the beginning. She was an active member, entertained the other members with jokes and games and little competitions. Not because she set out to entertain others or to make them laugh, but because she herself wanted to laugh and have a good time. 'Laughing, loving and making friends to find my own existence,' she wrote on her status. No one who read her posts or watched her energetic presence would imagine that Sarvaranjini was a highly strung woman with a face that seemed about to break into tears. Artificial reality.

Every time she looked at her reflection in the mirror, Sarvaranjini rubbed her face hard trying to get rid of the ingrained sternness and the sadness, the shadows that were not on her face when she first came to Kuwait but had, over the years, spread across her skin like black marks, never to fade away.

Odisha was not quite what she had in mind when she had wished, yearned, to be able to travel. It didn't matter, she told herself as she reconciled with Mudritha's unilateral decision; she would welcome the opportunity and go, even to hell. She did not know who Mudritha was, did not recall seeing a single post or comment from her in the group, did not know whether she read other people's posts or even saw them. But there she was suddenly one day, with a tantalizing proposal and a question, 'Who's with me?' A crisp question like freshly fried kaipakka kondattam, hot, spicy, crunchy. Sarvaranjini found it irresistible.

And so, she began collecting information about Odisha. That winter, she had to come home to Kerala unexpectedly to deal with some matters relating to the family property and inheritance. Complex dealings involving several claimants including dead ones, an old civil case, and other complications that dragged on, forcing her to extend her stay several times. Since they were also set to receive a considerable portion of the inheritance, the police dog could not growl.

Each time he called, Venumadhavan told her how sad he was to be away from her, complained that she, on the other hand, had forgotten all about him. She choked on phrases like 'Miss you' and 'Love you'. To tell Venumadhavan that she was bored without him, that she could barely breathe without having him near … how horrible! And even if she said such things, would he be soothed? Would he even believe her? She did not know. She was on parole, for the first time in over twenty years of marriage. Even when she gave birth to Vinnie, she was not allowed to go home. Instead, her mother was brought to Kuwait to look after her.

She enjoyed those days of freedom, hoped that the property related issues would not resolve quickly. Still, one night, reluctantly, grudgingly, she typed a message – *Miss you*, followed by a string of heart emojis – and sent it to him. An unstoppable urge to wash her hands gripped her immediately, and when she went to the bathroom, scrubbed her hands with soap and came back, there was a reply waiting for her.

What are you doing online so late in the night? Who are you chatting with?

Rage and laughter rose inside her simultaneously. He didn't deserve a 'Miss you', not even a bogus one. She blocked him on WhatsApp – she would unblock him in the morning – so that he would not see she was online, and spent the entire night scrolling through porn sites.

The thought that she would not have been able to go on this tour if not for her serendipitous presence in Kerala at the time sent shivers through her. She has resolved not to tell Venumadhavan about the trip until the last possible moment. Telling him beforehand would certainly put an end to her plans.

She would tell him today, the day of the journey, when she is on her way to the railway station, or better still, when she is in the train. She is all set, bags carefully packed and ready.

There is still time before setting out to the railway station, and that is why Sarvaranjini begins writing something she had read about Odisha to post in Lesbos. Everyone would enjoy it, she is certain, but she is finding it hard to type as tears of laughter stream from her eyes.

Ah, Deerghathamas … Would he have felt shame? Or anger that the king had looked at him like a handy tool? Or did the king's request make him happy? After all, the opportunity to have sex with a woman, even if it came with strings attached, was something to seize upon, wasn't it, especially when that offer was made by her owner? And for a man who had been rejected by his wife, it would have presented the tantalizing prospect of revenge. Sleep with one woman to get back at another. A declaration of victory!

Man's victories, in one way or the other, revolve around the six-inch-long organ he possesses. It is an obscene fact. Women are not excessively proud of or sing praises of their reproductive organ, even though, to be honest, it deserves praise. But men's reproductive organ, that only knows how to excrete urine and the slimy liquid full of slithering sperm, makes them think so highly of themselves! Just look at this old, useless man, banished by his own wife and children. Even he gets invited into the inner halls of a palace in another country! Look at the arrogance with which he holds his head high and saunters into another woman's bed … Well, maybe not his head but his penis held high.

That first time, Sudeshna saved herself from this ignominy by sending her maid in her place. Perhaps the blind sage couldn't tell whether it was the queen he had sex with or someone else. But the king … he knew, because it was the maid who became pregnant and not his wife. He wasn't about to give up though. Coaxing and threatening, he sent Sudeshna again to Deerghathamas, and this time she could not escape because the king stood guard outside the bedchamber, sword in hand. Come to think of it, there is nothing astounding about two bodies copulating without love, without desire. It is what happens in most bedrooms.

In the end, as the king had desired, Sudeshna gave birth to five sons. It is unclear whether it was all in one go, or at five different times. And so, there they were, the sons – Anga, Vanga, Sunga, Kalinga and Pundra. Kalinga became the ruler of Kalingadesham, which, later, would be known as Odisha.

Sarvaranjini started writing this story she had found while diving into the history of Odisha as a joke, but by the time she reaches the end, she is overcome with a great sorrow. Did the king continue to honour his wife as his queen consort now that she had given birth to another man's sons? Would she have, at least in private, spat in his face? Did the old sage who, in the end, was only a tool for impregnation, continue to live there, or did he go away? Who did Kalinga and his brothers call 'Father'? Did Pradweshi ever hear about any of this? Hundreds of such questions clamour inside Sarvaranjini's mind. That is the problem with the puranas – the story concludes swiftly and unceremoniously, with no exposition of the characters' thoughts or mental states. Everything is resolved without acknowledgement of the emotional trauma, the conflict, the complexities. If Sarvaranjini had been the narrator of this story in the puranas, she would have told it from the perspective of the nameless woman who was forced to stand in for the queen only because she was a maid.

There is no more time now for storytelling. Her train is on its way, and she has to be at the station in an hour to catch it. Another five hours, and she would get to meet Mudritha, her fellow travellers and their tour operator. She has begun to feel, for no particular reason, an attachment to this young man. There has been no contact between them other than a couple of emails exchanged while organizing the trip. Mudritha had sent her – all nine members in the group – his phone number yesterday, just in case something came up and they had to go ahead with the journey without her.

Last night, Sarvaranjini had made an overture to connect with him and sent him a snippet of a poem. His response was a lifeless smiley, and she had given up when she saw it. The language of emoticons annoys her. He could have, at the very least, shown enough curiosity to ask whose lines they were. Those were her favourite lines, about pure, prayerful, ethereal love, written by the Sufi poet Zeynep Hatun. She could not forgive the offhand way in which he had treated them.

What she really wanted to do was to send it, adding a few more lines, to Mudritha.

> I am a traveller
> You are my road
> I go from You to You
> I am a spring
> You are my water
> I flow from You to You

Is there anything more Sarvaranjini could do to show Mudritha what is in her heart? Mudritha had never shown her any special liking, a fact that had hurt her. She wanted it, that special place in Mudritha's heart, desired it. When they finally meet, would she tell her that she is not satisfied with an equal share of her affection? Not Sarvaranjini, no, because she is a woman who knows, with complete clarity, what she desires, and yet has lived all her life accepting what was given to her, pretending she is satisfied. Perhaps Mudritha would understand what is in her heart without being told.

On the night before the journey, another member of their travel group, a woman named Madhumalathi, contacted Sarvaranjini. She had asked a question to which Sarvaranjini did not know the answer. And she had resolved to find the answer before they met.

As she sits in the taxi that will take her to the station, she deletes the story of Pradweshi and Sudeshna, and types out a single line, 'Meriah – an endless scream of hurts', and posts it to the group. It contains everything she wants to say – about Sudeshna, the nameless maid, Pradweshi, Sarvaranjini and all the women who had ever lived on earth.

The first comment to her post is a series of questions. 'Why, Sarvaranjini? Why are you sad? Aren't we going to heal all hurt? Isn't that why we're going on this journey?'

The comment is from Sancharini Deeptha. 'Sancharini' – sojourner – was a description that she had attached to her name, perhaps because it suited her better as a columnist in a travel magazine.

Before more 'likes' and comments come in, Sarvaranjini logs off and sits looking at the sights outside.

SANCHARINI DEEPTHA

Deeptha's day turned out to be extremely busy.

The previous day, her editor, Shishupalan, had called her in to his office to give her a hefty assignment, even though she had told him, nearly a month in advance, that she would be on leave for ten days. Apparently, the editorial board had decided to do a series of features on the yogini temples in India. The first instalment was scheduled for the next issue, which left barely a week before the magazine had to go to the printers.

'I simply can't do it for the next issue, sir. I can try for next month's,' she said to him and continued muttering silently, 'I don't care how important it is, I won't do it, I can't do it now, I'm going on a journey tomorrow, I told you a month ago…'

'Do you know anything at all about yogini temples?' Shishupalan asked. The smile on his face did not fade.

Questions that began with 'Do you know…' always embarrassed her. She had heard of 'yoginimata' and so on, but knew nothing about these temples, not even that they existed. Thankfully, Shishupalan's phone rang, and as he answered it, Deeptha typed 'yogini temple' into Google Chrome. The connection was slow, and all she could see before he hung up was the first two search results, one about a temple in Madhya Pradesh and another in Odisha. There was no time to read the details.

'Write the feature before you leave,' Shishupalan said. 'Photographs to accompany the piece are ready. Sumanth, as you know, has been travelling across north India taking photos. It's his idea, really. Our readers know practically nothing about these temples, so they'll find it informative and interesting. Let's not delay this. What if some other magazine gets the same idea? Opportunities don't present themselves twice, Deeptha. So, it's important that we use them at the right time.'

Deeptha worried that he would launch into one of his usual Bhagavad Gita style lectures. Shishupalan was not just her editor, but the editor-in-charge, four or five years her senior, the darling of the management, and most importantly, a shrewd man. She would never become the editor-in-charge, not even if all the seniors at the publication were to die all of a sudden. Senior sub-editor – that was as high as she could hope to reach before retirement, and only if she didn't walk out of this damned job first.

'Sir, I did tell you … I have an unavoidable trip and I'm on leave from tomorrow. This last-minute assignment … I'm sorry, sir, but I have to decline. Please give it to someone else. Or, better still, we can start the series in January?'

'No, you will do it. I've emailed you the photographs from Sumanth. Have a look at them, and I'm telling you, the words will just come to you. They are that good! So evocative of another time … Get going then, go look at the photos and start writing. Your train is in the night tomorrow, isn't it? You can still go on your trip.'

As though to underline he had nothing more to say on the matter, Shishupalan turned to his laptop. Deeptha was familiar with these tactics, and knew that he would not say anything more, or even look up, and would pretend to be immersed in other, important things, denying her the opportunity to say anything more either. Those who pretend will continue to do so until the curtain falls and the audience applauds. Shishupalan, too, would continue with his act until Deeptha left the room, or he was acting so that she would be forced to leave the room.

And Deeptha left, not wanting to sit there, a silent spectator of his performance. 'You can still go on your trip,' he said, meaning she will now have to hunker down and write through the night and all day tomorrow. She could plan the word count only after looking at the photographs. Shishupalan's praise aside, Sumanth's photos were not always that good, often showing shadowy, falling down granite structures, that required embellishment through the words that accompanied them. Not an easy task. Sumanth was an eccentric who trampled through back-of-beyond forests and wastelands, took photos, and sent them to Shishupalan. And he would look at them and exclaim, 'Oh!' and 'Wow!' and 'Wonderful!' and order Deeptha to write copy. 'Just looking at these photos makes you want to write, isn't it, Deeptha? Get on with it. You have twenty-four hours.'

Sumanth was barely at the office, travelling around almost three quarters of the month. In preview and review meetings, Shishupalan spoke very highly of him as though Sumanth single-handedly provided the matter for the entire magazine. It drove Deeptha mad. The photographs were mostly his, of course, but those alone didn't make the magazine, did they? It also required the hard graft put in by Deeptha and the other writers. Did anyone mention that? No! Instead, they exclaimed, 'Oh, what wonderful photos! Almost as though we are right there!'

'In my next life, I will be Sumanth,' Deeptha told herself in those moments. 'I will work in this same magazine, travel all around on company expenses, taking photos and not writing a single line.' When she talked about this to Sumanth, he stroked his beard and smiled. That smile, she had to admit, was attractive. He was an attractive man with his long hair, thick beard and dark skin, and on top of it all, he was an actual traveller.

'You just have to wander around taking photos,' Deeptha complained. 'It is the rest of us who have to suffer the consequences, working our asses off writing copy. And yet, only you get the credit!'

'But I'm writing too, aren't I, with the camera? What you're doing is translating it into words. And frankly, no one else translates my photos as beautifully as you do. No one else can find the words to match my visuals.'

'Bullshit! It's not translation. I'm writing about things I haven't seen! Details I don't even know!'

'I see them for you, Deeptha. It's enough one of us sees them, isn't it? One person sees and the other person writes.'

One stone is gold and the other is the touchstone that determines its value. Deeptha recalled learning something like that in an Eastern Theory class, words some literary expert said about the talent of the writer and the reader. His photos were gold, and she was the touchstone. What if she didn't want to be his touchstone any more, she thought rebelliously even as she knew such thoughts were of no use. Her fate was to produce words on demand without even the hope of a byline, with the sole purpose of making his photographs attractive to the reader. He had once won a runner-up prize in a National Geographic photo contest and that had endeared him to the editor-in-charge and the management. Famous travel photographer! About to win the Goenka prize for photojournalism! That he hadn't won it already was not his fault, but the incompetence of the jury!

Deeptha had no awards to recommend her, nor any hope of ever winning one. To be even considered for an award, she would first have to write something under her own byline. She was a travel writer who never travelled or had a byline. What else could she expect when she worked for an editor like Shishupalan who believed that women did not have many skills. She was certain that, when the magazine was launched, she was the only person who had written in requesting to join the team, prompted by her desire to travel and hoping for opportunities to do so. She had been confident that she would be able to write well about the sights she saw and took in until they were etched in her mind. Not the quickly disappearing landscapes seen from the window of a bus, but the mountains and valleys and deserts that lay waiting to be written about by her, only her.

Those hopes had been short-lived. At first, she was given assignments to write about 'Ten things to keep in mind when packing a travel bag' and 'Traps to look out for while travelling'. Articles that did not require her to step out of her office cabin, that she could write sitting at her desk. Who didn't know that they should keep essential medicines in their travel bag or should not accept food from strangers? Who, in fact, read these things! And yet, Shishupalan wanted her to write only about such things.

'Only because I'm a beginner,' she had told herself, and hoped that soon she would be given assignments that required actual travel. A few years passed, and she was released from the cage of these assignments, but not to travel. Instead, she was given the work of creating lyrical content to accompany the photographs taken by those who did travel. And still she thought this was part of her training, that soon she would be asked to go travelling with the photographers to see, to experience, what she was asked to write about.

And now, after so many years, she knew it was never going to happen. Recession, decrease in subscription, the rising price of paper, a new generation of travel enthusiasts who found it easier to go places than to read about them in magazines … The company had many such reasons to cut costs so that its financial problems did not affect staff salaries. Shishupalan read her the gospel every time she worked up the nerve to ask him.

'Besides, this is more convenient for you too, Deeptha,' he would say. 'You don't want to haul your bags and get into trains and buses, do you? Put up with the heat and dust? You can do your work in the comfort of your own cabin, at your desk. You're lucky, you know, if you think about it. All because we have someone like Sumanth to do the dirty, difficult work!'

Mockingly, in the privacy of her mind, she thanked Shishupalan for his generosity. He was indeed the right person to be the editor-in-charge of a travel magazine like this one. Had he ever ventured beyond the familiar paths between his house and office? His body and body language showed it was unlikely. The bodies of those who have travelled, those who loved travelling, were carefree, naturally relaxed. They walked as though they were flowing, their eyes filled with the wonder of the sights they had beheld.

That is why she liked looking at Sumanth, had the urge to touch his face to feel the remnants of the wonderments left behind from his journeys.

Deeptha had not been to an airport in recent times. But at the railway station, at the bus stand, she was able to recognize people like Sumanth among the hundreds of travellers she saw every day. Travel bags, feet encased in trainers on legs carelessly stretched out, headphones, eyes that glittered from beneath deep shadows … She knew without talking to them that they were not going home or to work, but were setting out on journeys, that their faces had these special expressions because they were thinking about the sights they were about to see. Deeptha wanted to write a feature about such people, but that would only be possible if Shishupalan ever left the chair of the editor-in-charge. When she saw them sitting relaxed on the station platforms and in the bus shelters, she wanted to go and sit with them. She had never seen any women among them. All the women she saw in such places had exhausted, tense faces that looked out anxiously for the arrival of the buses and trains running late.

Every time she thought about it, her body shuddered awake, screaming, 'I want to go too! I too want to see the things I haven't seen yet, experience the tastes, smells, touches I've never known.' Shishupalan did not hear her screams. No one heard them except herself, and she had learned to ignore them or chastise them to silence.

When she had started in this job, she had added 'Sancharini' to her name and opened a Facebook account with it. Sancharini, sojourner, traveller … How ironic! Perhaps she should change it to 'Sancharikkatha Deeptha' – Deeptha who never travels, the un-traveller.

Back in her cabin, Deeptha switched on her desktop and clicked open the email. She thought of calling Sumanth and asking him what these damned yogini temples were and how in hell he had ended up visiting them. But she only spoke to him because she liked looking at him, and speaking to him on the phone meant listening to his somewhat effeminate voice without that benefit. She was not convinced, despite what he said about her words translating his vision, that he read what she wrote to accompany his photos.

But, as she looked at the images attached to Sumanth's email, the hairs on Deeptha's arms stood up. They were from Odisha! The very place to which she was travelling tomorrow! Was he still there? Not that it mattered because hers was a different type of journey. Still, she entertained herself for a while imagining running into him in an orange orchard by the banks of the Chitrotpala and him taking some beautiful pictures of her group. How shocked he would be if that happened … running into someone he had only met in the corridors of the office in the lanes of a faraway village…

'My day will also come, Photographer,' she would tell him if that ever happened.

Sumanth's photographs were from the Chausath Yogini Temple in Hirapur. Deeptha quickly checked the posts in Lesbos to see whether the place was mentioned as part of their travel itinerary or in the discussions, but found nothing about either Hirapur or yogini temples. Never mind, Deeptha thought, smiling to herself, there is still time to add it to the itinerary. After all, they did not have a strict timetable to adhere to. She posted some of the photos to the group. Let the others have a look too and be tempted.

It was not the artistry of the images that attracted Deeptha. Sixty-four yoginis, demi-goddesses, who had taken birth from the various aspects of Goddess Durga. Stunningly beautiful, they adorned the inner walls of the temple, each one alone, even though they were in a group. In the silence of nights, did they step off the walls and sit together in a circle? Did the clink of their bangles, the chime of their anklets, and the much sweeter sound of their laughter echo within the walls of the lonely temple in the middle of the woods? Over ten centuries had passed since they had been carved into the stillness of black granite. And yet, their faces reflected tenderness and joy, not the hard coldness of stone, perhaps because they had each other to spend time with, to laugh and play with.

Deeptha zoomed in on the images. Full, firm breasts, shapely waists, long, flowing limbs … They were centuries old, and yet here she was, about to write their stories, bearing a body and mind that felt much older. If only someone had carved her too in stone a long time ago…

She brought up Google to search for information about them. Sumanth had captioned some of the photos but those were not sufficient for the article. She had to find information with good references and had very little time to look for them. Still, expanding bare minimum facts into a full-fledged article was not a new game for her.

The website of the Archaeological Survey of India yielded some information about the history of yogini temples. They were built mainly between the ninth and twelfth centuries when tantric Buddhism was popular. Rulers who were goddess-worshippers would have had them built, given them patronage. There were only four yogini temples in India. Was that because there was a reluctance to worship women? In these temples, it was not just the goddess idol that was worshipped but the sixty-four other women who had taken birth from the goddess – from her nose, forehead, cheeks, lips, ears, thighs, thumbs, womb, voice, sweat and anger. Who could be asked, laughed Deeptha. It was hard enough to acknowledge a single woman, let alone worship sixty-five of them!

As she made a list of the names of the sixty-four yoginis, she wondered which of them had taken birth from the goddess's anger. Chamunda? Jwalamukhi? Ghora? Agneyi? Running her cursor down the list, she hovered over a name – Umanarayani. She was going to meet a woman with that name tomorrow, and they might even visit this temple together! Deeptha had not seen a photograph of Umanarayani yet – her DP on the Facebook page was a flowing river. The thought of going on a journey with complete strangers did not worry her; it was those she met and talked with daily that she found to be strangers, people she could never understand.

Among the yoginis was a woman with braided hair piled high, an embroidered belt around her waist, and eyes that looked mellow. On a whim, and not because she had found any solid clues, Deeptha identified her as Umanarayani. And for a lark, she sent that photograph to Umanarayani with a note that said, 'We've already met!' Only then did she notice that one of the breasts of the statue had fallen off. An ottamulachi, a single-breasted woman. Tantalized by the rest of her beautiful form, Deeptha had not noticed it. For a moment, she worried that Umanarayani might be offended, but then decided not to dwell on it.

The office was deserted by the time she collected enough material for the article, picked up her handbag and laptop and left the cabin. Even Shishupalan's room was dark. She had planned to do some last-minute shopping, but the evening had slipped away from her. It wasn't all bad, she told herself; she had just had a fruitful, interactive session with the yoginis. The goddess and the yoginis preferred offerings of glass bangles, she had read, and she resolved to buy a whole lot of them and to wear them after making the offering. Aeons had passed since she had worn glass bangles and gone around with noisy forearms.

As she waited in the late evening for an autorickshaw to take her home – it took almost twenty minutes to find one – she tried to come up with a suitable title for the article. Isolation, mystery, a temple that was centuries old, connection to tantric practices, and above all, sixty-four lascivious women carved in stone. Men were barely present, except for the handful of dwarapalaka figures standing guard at the doorways. A circular temple only of women who, in her imagination, came together in its inner courtyard in the dead of night. She struggled to come up with a title that captured all of this.

'Yogadeepthi in the wilderness', 'Secret gathering of spiritual sensuality', 'Mystic magic in the middle of nowhere' … She typed such inane titles into her phone, romantic nonsense that Shishupalan usually preferred. Let him select one or find a better one himself. But this time, she would insist on a byline: 'Text by Sancharini Deeptha'.

For the first time in her life, she was going to visit a place she had written about. It should have been the other way around; she considered herself lucky that she would get to see it at all this time.

Deeptha sat up late into the night and wrote the article following the usual style the magazine preferred. An introduction complete with every possible cliché: the usual complaints about the crowds in Bhubaneswar and its dusty, fly-infested streets, and the journey through the village road with the swiftly flowing Chitrotpala on one side and fields of tamarind, guava and orange on the other. Greenery, peacefulness, tranquillity, bullshit. Roadside eateries with palm-leaf walls; spicy daal-bara crisping up in oil; strong tea laced with buffalo milk; innocent Odia girls looking into the vehicle with pots balanced on their heads; old women in brightly coloured saris selling guavas under shade trees; the plentiful tattoos – enough artwork to fill the walls of several galleries – on their arms adorned with metal bangles; haggling with them over the guava chunks dusted with salt and chilli powder; the soothing, cool taste of the fruit in their mouths. Followed by the body of the article made up of the information gathered earlier and the description of the photos, all embellished to the maximum. Finally, a conclusion that described a return journey, with a mind dazed by the brief sojourn into a time way back in the past, imprisoned in the quietude of granite.

Deeptha went over what she had written, made some minor edits, and sent it off to Shishupalan's email. In the early days, Shishupalan would suggest substantial changes to her articles, even make her rewrite the whole thing sometimes. He didn't do that any more; only cut out a thing or two, just enough to wield his power as the editor, or make inane suggestions like changing a red sari into green or a guava into a mango.

Before going to bed, she checked her phone to see if there were any messages in her travel group. There was a personal message from Mudritha with the telephone number of the tour coordinator. There is something strange about this lady, she thought as she saved the number into her contact list. Still, she would always be indebted to Mudritha for planning a trip like this and including her.

Sleep eluded Deeptha, and after tossing and turning in bed for a while, she got up, made herself some tea and took the mug to the balcony. She realized, as she sipped her tea and watched the slowly brightening sky, that she had not been up this early since she moved into this flat. Before moving here, she had never had the luxury of sleeping in until she was ready to get up, hectic as her mornings had been having to leave home early enough to take two or three modes of transportation in order to get to the office in time to punch in at half past nine. Moving nearer to the office was not an option then, caught as she was in knots of hometown, family, relatives and friends – knots that were not hers but her husband's, although, as in most lives, she had assumed they were hers and that they were as strong and unbreakable as iron chains. It had taken much longer, until she had actually done it, to realize that they were, in fact, weak enough to be broken by tugging just a little hard.

It was a friend of hers who had added her to Lesbos. She had since left the group, but Deeptha remained, 'liking' a few posts and occasionally sharing links to articles, remaining, mostly, invisible. 'I have polished myself up, cobwebs removed and the debris washed off. I am determined not to allow dust and dirt to settle again.' That was her reply to Mudritha's invitation to join the tour. She must have liked it. 'Women become dusty because they barely move,' she had responded. 'We have to keep moving, as though caught in a constant breeze. Alongside the boring, unavoidable journeys to the office, the grocery store, the vegetable market, we must find time for the occasional, unexpected journeys, to keep ourselves amazed. How wonderful that would be ... These journeys, they need not be to faraway places. Get off the train two stops ahead from your usual stop one day. Don't ask why or what for, or worry about the half-day leave you might lose. It will give you a chance to think new thoughts, see new things, boost your energy even if it is for a short while. And if that is not possible, journey with your mind ... keep on going.'

Deeptha was aware that Mudritha was not responding to her alone, that she was sharing these thoughts with the whole group. And the only response she got were a few emojis – thumbs-up and clapping hands. Everyone seemed to be in awe of her, kept their distance as though from a stern headmistress.

And today, finally, she would meet her. There was something intriguing about the woman, the journalist inside her told her, something mysterious in her character that could be the subject of an investigative feature.

Deeptha switched on her phone and found a message from Umanarayani.

Thank you, kutty. I liked the photograph and what you posted in the group about the yogini temple. Let's hope we'll get to visit this temple. And thank you for telling me that I share my name with one of the yoginis.

Every time I see your name, I think of a shlokam by Kalidasan: 'Sancharini deepashikheva raathrau.' A flame that travels onward leaving darkness behind and lights up what is ahead. I have wondered whether it is your penname, that perhaps you might be a writer, but how can I know for sure! It doesn't matter, to be honest, I just love the name.

Did you notice that the sculpture in the photograph you sent me has lost a breast? I looked up the temple on Google and saw that all the other sculptures had both their breasts intact. I began to think that it wasn't by accident that you decided that her name was Umanarayani and sent it to me. And that strengthened my hunch that you are a writer.

Please don't think that I am hurt or angry. For those who have been ravaged completely, the missing left breast on a centuries-old statue is nothing.

Anyway, see you this evening.

The message saddened her. She should not have sent that picture to a woman she did not know on an impulse. And she had not been able to follow it up with an explanation because she had been distracted by a phone call from the office. It will be all right, she consoled herself, they will soon meet in person.

THE REST OF the day sprouts wings and flies swiftly. She packs her bags, pops into the office, makes the corrections Shishupalan had requested on her article and sets out well in time to reach the railway station by the time Mudritha had specified. Only to find herself stuck in traffic!

For almost an hour, her autorickshaw has been imprisoned in a massive stream of vehicles. A stream that has stopped flowing, Deeptha thinks, and quickly corrects herself – that which has stopped flowing should not be called a stream. Good thing Shishupalan is not around; he would have wielded his editorial pen and scolded her for not reading books on stylistics. The thought makes her giggle. But her mind is not in Shishupalan's office, and mentally flinging his stylebook away, she resolves that she will call it a stream if she feels like it. Indeed, right now, she is in the midst of a stream that has stopped flowing.

As the traffic jam continues, Deeptha begins worrying whether she will reach the station on time. The cause is a procession of women, all of them dressed in mundu-veshti or set-sari in the colour of sandalwood. They seem to be divided into groups, each group differentiated by the colour of their blouses, each colour perhaps, she thinks, representing a different district. She had read about the plans for the procession – a protest against the recent decision to allow Hindu women of all ages entry into the Sabarimala temple which had, traditionally, denied entry to women between menarche and menopause. The road had turned into a sandalwood-hued sea. She watches as women, with flushed faces and sweat darkening the armpits of their blouses, red, green, blue, orange, and of every other conceivable colour, pass by. They chant mantras, not in unison, and not even the same mantra; the only uniformity seems to be in the marks drawn on their foreheads with sandalwood paste and the sandalwood colour of their saris. Most of them have their hair held back in the kulippinnal half-braid. And as was routine for any public demonstration by women, men guard the groups, insinuate into the lines shouting commands and directions.

One day, when she finally has the freedom to pick her own topic, she will write about these women, Deeptha resolves. Women who denied themselves the right, the opportunity, to travel, who had declared that they were refusing the new avenues opened for them to travel. Cool, shaded avenues leading through lush green landscapes, and forest paths that had never known the footsteps of women in their prime.

The driver of her autorickshaw has, by then, extricated his vehicle and, like a magician, turned it into a side alley. Speeding through back lanes, he seems more worried than her that she will miss her train. The stream of sandalwood is left far behind.

UMANARAYANI

I was nine years old when the American space station, Skylab, fell to earth. I cannot remember now whether it was because it had finished its assignment or because of some technical fault. It was the biggest and most sophisticated space station NASA had sent up, a direct challenge to the progress in Soviet Union's space programme, and because of it, its six-year-long journey was fuelled also with politics. Everything I know about Skylab's fall I learned by eavesdropping on the conversations Acchan had with his friends through most of 1979, half of which I did not understand at the time.

I loved the shiny pages and the pictures in the *Sovietnaadu* magazine, but my real love was reserved for America. So, I prayed, fervently, that Skylab would not fall back to earth, that America would not fail before Soviet Union. I wanted Skylab, which looked curiously like the little toy aeroplane that I bought for Chinnu at the weekly market, to fly around the skies forever. When I grew up, I would go up to visit it, I told myself. Already people had visited it three times. But what if it fell before I was all grown up? So, I prayed some more, put all the money I received as kaineetam on the day of Vishu from my elders in the donation box at the Krishnan temple, believing, with all my heart, that if anything went wrong, Krishnan, an avatar of Vishnu the Protector, would guard it. He was immensely powerful, after all, had even lifted Mount Mahameru.

That year, even at school, all everyone talked about was Skylab. When Acchan and his friends read the newspapers and discussed it, my sister, who was born thirty minutes before me, and I sat on the veranda with our legs dangling. She would listen quietly for a while, then poke me, 'Come, let's go play Sat.' But I wouldn't budge, no matter how big the temptation, especially when our neighbour Bharathan maman went on praising Soviet Union's spacecraft, Soyuz, comparing it to my Skylab which he considered inferior. Everyone contested his claims – Acchan cited evidence after evidence – and this made me happy. And because he defended Soyuz, Bharathan maman would become my sworn enemy forever. How right I had been in my estimation of him, I thought, when he grabbed me in the darkness of the corridor in the southern side of the house and tried to do the dirty. I was studying in Class 9 then. 'Oh, Uma…' he had breathed, trying to squeeze my body to his, which angered me even more. I scratched him viciously and ran away, shouting, 'Piss off, you dog! I'm not Uma, I'm Narayani!'

It angered my sister when I continued sitting there on the veranda, listening to the elders, refusing to go play with her. 'Come if you want,' she would mutter, 'I'm leaving.' Sliding off the veranda, her skirt would ride up exposing the edges of her red knickers. If it happened at any other time, I would have made merciless fun of her, but not when Skylab was being discussed. I wanted to hear every word. So, I would sit there as she skipped to the gate – just a prickly fence and bamboo style. Climbing over the style, she would turn back and call me, once again, 'Come on!' and I would pretend not to notice until she walked down into the lane. I would be reminded of the ballerina in the pages of *Sovietnaadu*, and it would make me jealous.

Our family dealt with us in two ways:

Pointing at me, our elders would say to my sister who could never sit still, 'Look at Narayani here … Look how well-behaved she is … how quiet … Can't you be more like her?'

And to me, who sat listening every time the adults discussed things, they would say, 'Look at your sister, Narayani. Look how active and energetic she is. Don't just sit around all day. Be more like her.'

We were confused about which of their contradictory instructions we were supposed to follow. It took many more years of growing up to finally understand that there was no need to mould ourselves to the demands adults made according to their moods and fancies. Until then, my sister and I rushed back and forth between 'quiet' and 'energetic' until we were breathless, and it created a rift between us, a rift that only deepened as we grew older. We had never had the unity or the intimacy usually shared by twins. I took great care not to like anything that she liked, and all my likes were her dislikes.

We were not identical twins, nor were we born at the same time. Between twins, thirty minutes are more like the difference of thirty years between ordinary siblings. Up until she gave birth, Amma was not aware that she was carrying twins. Even the experienced hands of Radha doctor, the gynaecologist at Menon Clinic where we were born, had failed to find this out. All through her pregnancy, as her stomach grew and as four legs instead of two kicked her, Amma would have stroked her tummy and said, fondly, 'So naughty! If you're like this inside, what will I do with you when you come out!', and Acchan and other family members would have nodded along, laughing, expecting just the one child, preparing everything for it.

The joylessness of going where one is not expected, not wished for, is something that is known only when experienced.

Amma and Acchan were happy to have just one child, not at all prepared to accept a second, unexpected one. Amma was only twenty-two years old, not capable of handling the two of us at once. We took turns to cry, allowing her barely any sleep at night, gave her no peace during the day, clamoured together for her right breast, rejecting the left which had less milk.

I understood how all this must have felt only when I had twins myself. In my case, it was not unexpected; I knew I was carrying twins and was prepared mentally. Still, when they arrived, each one with their own demands and likes, I was overwhelmed.

When Amma was admitted at the clinic – her pains had begun two weeks earlier than her due date – Radha doctor had chickenpox and was on leave. She – my sister – came out with the help of the duty doctor and the nurses, without giving Amma too much trouble. By the time I was ready to come out, they had, happy that the delivery had progressed without trouble, even stitched up the cut they made in my amma's perineum. I was late, always, everywhere.

Amma's pain did not subside. At first, everyone tried to console her, told her it was not unusual and so on, but soon they were all concerned and confused. It must have been then that they considered the possibility that another child might be clamouring to come out. And she, protesting that she had been ignored, refused to be born on her own. In the end, Radha doctor had to be called in, chickenpox or not.

And thus, I arrived, thirty minutes after my sister, via caesarean section. By then, even the small similarities we had as two people who had shared a womb at the same time had faded away. She, firstborn, a fair, plump, healthy child, had already made her mark, taken her place, before I, second-born, dark and scrawny with not even the required body weight, made my presence known. Most importantly, she had already been given the name Amma and

Acchan had picked out in case they had a baby girl. A beautiful name – Umamaheswari. They had no more names picked out and ready for their second, unexpected, child. And to add to the misery, on the fourth day of our birth, Amma and I caught chickenpox. Umamaheswari was safe while I had to make yet another return from death's door.

In the midst of it all, no one had the time to find me a name. Neighbours and relatives identified me as 'the thin one' or 'the dark one', while Amma called me Kunju or Malu or other generic pet names reserved for girls as the mood took her. Finally, when I was three and a half years old, when they took me to enrol me at the balavadi and they asked for my name, it came out, after a moment's hesitation, from Acchan's mouth – Umanarayani. Just a name that sounded nice next to Umamaheswari, Acchan might have thought. Narayani was also my grandmother's name, but it did not go well with 'Uma'. Umamaheswari embodied in itself Ardhanareeswaran, the complementary forces of the male and the female, conjured up the age-old, legendary, fierce love between Uma and Maheswaran. Umanarayani, meanwhile, sounded illicit, adulterous.

The teachers and children at the balavadi called Umamaheswari 'Uma', so my name was shortened to Narayani and Naru. Since then, until yesterday when Sancharini Deeptha told me about a yogini by the same name, I have hated it. Deeptha also sent me a photograph of my namesake. It took forever to download it on my old, slow phone, and when it finally did, there she was, a beautiful woman in the dark hue of the granite she was carved in, shapely, perfect except for her missing left breast. It was only natural that she had sustained minor injuries, given that she had been carved centuries ago and left to the mercies of the elements. Perhaps it was because of that single imperfection that I fell in love with her. Deeptha wasn't to know, but I, who had also lost half of me, shared that imperfection with the yogini … For the first time, my name sounded sweet in my mouth, and I kept saying it over and over – Umanarayani.

All that time ago, with no inkling that one day I would come to love my name, or that my namesake, a beauty with an imperfection, would be waiting for me in a small town called Hirapur in Odisha, I sat in that veranda watching, with a tinge of jealousy, Umamaheswari run across the cold, rain-drenched yard, while also listening, greedily, for more stories about Skylab. Adult gatherings had a problem. Often, the talk slipped into jokes meant only for adult ears, used words unsuitable for young ears. A nine-year-old sitting nearby, latching on to every word that was said, was an annoyance to them.

'Go on, child, go and play. Tell Uma not to wander too far, and come back before it starts raining again.'

Acchan's words were not to be ignored, so I would step reluctantly into the mud in the yard. Not to go after Umamaheswari; she could come back whenever she pleased. In those damp evenings, I skulked under the pavizhamalli tree by the gate, listening intently for snippets from the veranda, watching the sky and wondering, fearfully, whether our house was in Skylab's orbital path. My fear was justified. Our science teacher had told us that Skylab could fall out of the sky at any time, and since no one knew exactly where it would fall, it could well be on our roof or in our yard. The children had taken to scaring one another, and such anxieties were voiced even in the discussions in the veranda.

'If it falls, nothing will remain. Seventy-five thousand kilograms it weighs! Our whole district will burn to cinders. It will already be burning when it hits, wouldn't it, when it comes down from such a height, carrying such a weight … A laboratory in the sky – that's what America had in mind when they sent it up. And the thing is like an apartment with all the facilities! They should have made sure it never came down before sending such things way up there. Even a small piece of it could cause untold damage!'

The speaker was Suku maman who lived in Bombay. He had come home with his family even though his daughters, Pridha and Medini, had school. I had overheard Sreela aunty telling Amma the reason.

'Pridha's acchan is scared! Newspapers there reported that it was likely Skylab would fall in Bombay. Why die in a foreign land, he said, and brought us all here. If only this thing would fall already! The children are missing classes…'

Unlike Suku maman, Sreela aunty was brave and did not consider Skylab to be much of a threat. All the while, Medini annoyed her mother, scratching and pinching, perhaps because she felt slighted by the construction 'Pridha's acchan' that did not include her.

Sreekumaran maash, who taught us English and Maths at the Madhava Menon Memorial Lower Primary School, would agree with Suku maman. The fingers on his left hand had nails like the sharp fangs of the yakshi, and they left blood-red designs on our forearms whenever we made mistakes in maths problems.

'Laughing at gravitational force, aren't they, when they send these things up?' I heard him say. 'Gravitational force is as real as the day is bright. They can fool it for some time but not all the time. What's gone up will come right down, doesn't matter if it is American or Russian!'

No one took these comments seriously, but they terrified the nine-year-old listening to them. I went around anticipating a deathly danger that could fall on us from the sky above at any time. No matter how much I tried, Umamaheswari took neither me nor Skylab seriously. When I told her not to leave the house and run around all the time, she called me a coward. I doubled my prayers at the Krishnan temple. I had no more money to put in the donation box, so I promised to bathe early and pray at the temple every day in the month of Karkidakam. I had heard my grandmother make such offerings.

Every day, there were stories of Skylab in the newspapers, accompanied by photographs from various angles. Those black-and-white photos were not as attractive as today's multicoloured ones, and it was difficult to imagine Skylab as an apartment although my acchan and his friends constantly described it as one, going on and on about the people who resided in it, how they cooked their food and so on. Not permanent residents, but people who went up and came back. It was in those days that I began entertaining the hope of visiting Skylab one day, and to answer the question, 'What do you want to be when you grow up?' with 'An astronaut.' And why I prayed so fervently that Skylab, which had left its orbit, did not break through the stratosphere and fall back to earth.

And what a name it had! A name that combined the vast, open, blue sky and a confined, locked laboratory fitted with test tubes – I imagined it to be like the one I had seen in some movie. No other name has attracted me as much. My favourite person in those days was my baby cousin, my elayamma's child who was one and a half years old. I called her Skylab, and every time she heard me, she cooed happily.

If, despite all my prayers, Skylab were to fall, I hoped that I would find at least a piece of it, even the tiniest piece that I could look at from time to time, show everyone, treasure.

I still remember clearly the peculiar mental state I was in, terrified that Skylab would fall in our yard or on our school, and at the same time, wishing it remained in the sky. Much later, I came to understand that it was possible to wish intensely for the safe and continued existence of that which caused equally intense fear, that I was capable of embracing the thing that I had hated only a moment ago. It has always been one of my weaknesses.

In the end, rendering my fear and anxieties pointless, on the evening of 11 July 1979, debris of the burned Skylab fell in Australia, in Perth and the sea beside. A holiday was declared, I remember, and we didn't have to go to school. As the predicted time of Skylab's demise neared, there was akhandanamajapam at the Krishnan temple and Muthassi went to join the throng of devotees chanting, uninterrupted for the whole day, the God's name for protection.

'Come, children,' she invited us along. 'No Skylab will dare touch the God's abode. We'll chant His name and be safe there.'

'You mean America's space station can identify exactly which yard is the God's and adjust its course accordingly,' Acchan said, laughing loudly. 'My dearest amma, it's a blazing ball of fire that is falling down from the sky above. It doesn't care about gods or temples!'

'Don't you mock me, Kutta,' Muthassi said. 'You'll see. Nothing will happen to the temple. And even if it did, we'll die with the God's name on our lips.'

Umamaheswari went to the temple with Muthassi while I hung around near the radio listening to news broadcasts. A whole lot of interesting things ended that day. My ardent prayers to keep Skylab in its orbit, my terror of it falling in our village and the possibility of death, the secretly nurtured, intense wish that I would find a piece of it to treasure forever … The discussions in the veranda also ended, and evenings went back to their boring routine.

It was not until the festival at the Krishnan temple later that year that I thought of Skylab again. I was in the bangle shop, watching Umamaheswari anxiously searching through the glass bangles on display as though she wanted to buy up the whole shop.

I hated wearing bangles, my thin forearms were always bare, while Uma collected bangles in all the colours that matched her clothes, strung them on colourful threads and hung them on the wall. So pretty they were to look at, and even more so when they were on her fair, plump arms. I was beginning to get bored but could not leave without her. We were sent to the festival ground with admonitions to never leave the other alone. We were flush, having received gifts of money from all the aunties who were visiting. Nothing in the shop tempted me, but when Uma asked me for my money so that she could buy more bangles, I refused.

As I stood there disinterestedly, the shopkeeper beckoned me. 'Come and have a look, kutty,' he said. 'See, these are Skylab bangles. Brand new fashion! Remember that helicopter America had sent up? The one that burned down the other day? These are made with pieces from the wreckage. You won't find these anywhere else.'

I looked at the bangles. They were the colour of melted sunshine, not the eye-splintering colours Uma usually bought, and like sunlight, they were almost transparent. I bought as many as I could with my pocket money. They were pricey, but they would be, I told myself, given that they were made of pieces of Skylab that were brought all the way from Australia.

'You don't even wear bangles, so why did you buy so many?' Uma asked on our way back home. 'You'll give me some, won't you?'

I just shook my head. One more bunch of bangles strung on a piece of thread went up on the wall of our room. I never wore them, but took them down whenever I could and fondled them, enjoyed looking at them. Some broke as I played with them, and when they did, I put them in an empty ink bottle until, over time, all the bangles were broken and the ink bottle was full.

By then, significant changes had happened in our lives too. I was a below-average student and so my desire to become an astronaut was only something that everyone made fun of. Umamaheswari excelled in her studies and scored high marks in all the exams. After the school leaving exams, I joined the teacher training institute run by the management board of our school. By the time Uma was in her second year at the engineering college, I had a job as a teacher at the M.M.M.L.P. School where we had studied. Amma was more adamant than everyone else that I should have a job, perhaps because she wished for the security of a regular income for her child who was far behind in everything else compared to her twin. I have always thought that Amma carried in her an unnecessary sense of guilt. Was it for not realizing, until it was too late, that I too was in her womb? For unknowingly directing all her love and affection towards her, my sister? I don't know. Muthassi, too, carried the guilt for not having realized, despite all her years of experience with pregnant women and their growing bellies, that Amma was pregnant with twins. Would my life have turned out better if they had? Who knows!

Every year on our birthday, Amma set aside a pavan – about eight grams – of gold for each of us, a custom she had started on our very first birthday. It was usually in the form of a kuthirappavan, a coin embossed with the design of St George on horseback, or, very rarely, as plain bangles that took little extra cost to make. We didn't get to wear these often; they sat at the bottom of Muthassi's clothes-trunk, wrapped into two separate bundles in pieces of cloth torn from her old red-bordered neriyathu. But we did get to open the trunk and have a look at them on our birthdays as another coin or bangle was added to each bundle, marking another year added to our age. Finding the money for the gold was not easy, but they, the two women, managed enough to buy two pavans every year, adding up what they made from selling the little paddy they secreted away from everyday use, the tiny portion set aside from Muthassi's pension, the occasional cash gifts from Amma's family...

Twin girls were twice the burden, complicating matters for their parents by getting to marriageable age at the same time. They had to be sent away with gold on their hands and around their necks, just a little, just enough so that no one criticized their family. Finding them suitable husbands, assembling wedding saris – everything was twice the expense. Acchan paid scant attention to these matters, but Amma was only too aware that it was not as easy as buying two sets of schoolbooks every year.

Still, when the opportunity for a job came up, Amma took out the bundle set aside for me, sold some of the gold and found the one lakh rupees the management demanded as a pay-off for the job. She then redistributed what was in my sister's bundle to make both bundles equal again. How it must have troubled my parents, the knowledge that the dark-skinned, not-pretty twin needed the extra attention, the extra preparation on their part to secure her a good future ... They seemed to have an increasing anxiety in everything concerning my life in those days, and went around as though they were carrying a heavy weight that they yearned to set down.

I was married before Umamaheswari finished her studies. It turned out to be not that hard, in the end. There was no expectation for someone special to come along, so I was married off to the first person who said he liked me, the third man who had come to see me. Things are simple for those who do not have too many choices, no confusion, no seesawing between this and that, no what-ifs.

More of the gold set aside for Uma was turned into ornaments – a nagapadam necklace and a kaappu bangle – and given to me for my wedding. Each time we went shopping for the wedding, I looked for Skylab bangles. They were nowhere to be found; no one had heard of them. How I had wished I would wear them for my wedding along with a Kanchipuram sari in the dark magenta colour of the vadamalli flower…

Within a couple of years, my marriage formed a skin on top as naturally as would a pot of boiled, cooling milk. Like most women, I, too, took it to be a part of cohabitation, and gently blowing on the crust to move it to the side, made use of what was underneath as and when required. I gave birth to two sons, twins who entered my life together, and I tried to rekindle my life like a wood fire that had gone out, blowing on it until my eyes and throat burned from the smoke and ash. Every now and then, an ember would burst into flame. I was happy with that, did not need it to blaze high as long as it did not die down again. But before long, it became imperative that I picked up and patched together the pieces of my life, that I showed everyone that I, at least, had a good life. It became my responsibility, my duty towards my amma and acchan, because Umamaheswari, my sister, my twin, died.

Until her death, no matter what happened in my life, I could find solace in the fact that she was there to make up for it, that she could compensate for all my failures, even my death. But her death took that safety net away. In death there are such losses too. I lost the choice to think about divorce or suicide or, even, running away. Now I had to have a constant smile on my face, show the world that I had a happy life. I was annoyed with Umamaheswari. In death, too, she had obstructed my path, just as she had done at the time of our birth.

It was on the day of her death that I thought, for the first time in years, about gravitational force and about Skylab. Uma had finished her MTech and found a dream job, and had married a classmate of hers she had been in love with. She died on the fourth day after their wedding. It was vacation time, and I was home with my six-month-old twins who filled my life with stress and strain. Busy with the wedding, no one had the time to help me, not even to take them off my aching arms for a brief while as they cried non-stop, disturbed by the bustle around them. As a result, I didn't have the opportunity to go anywhere near the wedding dais. The silk sari, in my favourite green colour, that I was given to wear at the ceremony, sat in the almirah. I did not know then that I would never wear it. I could not take part in the nallavathil ceremony either when the bride's family accompanied the bride on her first visit to the bridegroom's home, and sat listening dejectedly when they came back bursting with descriptions.

Three days after she went to her husband's home, the phone rang bringing us the news about Uma's death. It was around 10 a.m. I had bathed one child and put him to sleep and was breastfeeding the other. Even today, thinking about that moment sends a shiver up my spine. The ringing of the phone woke the sleeping child, and he began screaming. As I sat there trying to soothe both children at the same time, I heard Amma's scream. Something unimaginable had happened, I was certain, and in that moment, bizarrely, all I could think of was Skylab and the utter vulnerability in flying so high, disdaining gravity, only to catch fire and fall back down to earth. How cruel, the comparison! The realization that I had nurtured such extreme intolerance towards my sister's accomplishments filled me with intense self-loathing.

Uma, too, came back burnt, entered the wedding pandal that had not been fully dismantled, and lay on the long veranda of our old home, the same veranda where I used to sit all those years ago, eavesdropping on my acchan and his friends discussing Skylab, where I used to let myself be terrified for its safety and of mine. I thought I could hear Suku maman's hateful voice warning everyone how a single piece of its burning wreckage could destroy the whole land. Umamaheswari left us burning forever, not to be turned to ashes at one go, no, but to smoulder, slowly, painfully, eternally.

Police case, investigations … all that went on as they were supposed to. The police were convinced that it was suicide. We, her family, did not believe it, wanted to know, understand, why she would have done such a thing. All these years later, we still don't know. Muthassi repeated, even on her deathbed, 'My child was murdered.' 'Must have been an accident … Why else would my Uma…' I remember Acchan muttering to those who came to pay their respects. Amma, meanwhile, had no words, only silence, and took to staring into my life, watching, observing. And unable even to breath freely, I began to suffocate.

When Nikesh installed WhatsApp and Facebook in his old phone and gave it to me, it was Umamaheswari's photo that I chose as the wallpaper. Fourteen days after she died, the photographer had come home, reluctantly, with the wedding photo album. What was he to do, it was his livelihood, and he had to be paid for his work. I remember Acchan accepting the album and silently handing over the money. No one opened it and looked at it; it lay abandoned on the bottom shelf of the almirah. The photo I set as the wallpaper on my phone was the one on the first page of that album, taken the day before the wedding, in the attire she had worn while going to the Krishnan temple. It is still in my phone.

I had assumed that it was one of my colleagues who had added me to the women-only group named Lesbos, until I realized much later that none of them were in the group. I have been in this group from the time I first got on social media, on Facebook, from the time Nikesh gave me this phone. Always only a silent observer, sometimes neglecting to pop in for days.

The only person I know in the group is a woman I have named 'Jaratkaru', after the character from the Mahabharatham. We only became acquainted because we had, by accident, chatted with one another. I haven't seen her since, but I know she is also part of our travel group.

Every now and then there were cleansing rituals in the group to get rid of inactive members. I have remained safe so far, somehow. 'Saved' is the word to use, really, because had I fallen victim to the cleansing ritual, I would not have heard about the journey Mudritha planned or had the opportunity to get to know these women, strangers who spread light around me. My journeys were always confined within a small circle – school and teacher-training college close to home, a job at the same school where I studied, and a marriage to a man who lived close by. None of them journeys that took more than ten minutes on the bus. The occasional school tours where I accompanied the students were all one-day trips to small cities not too far away. We have never been on a trip as a family.

When Mudritha posed the question, 'Who's with me?', this is what I replied: 'I'll be there, most certainly. A long time ago, my wish was to become an astronaut, and I had prayed desperately that a space station would remain in orbit until I was grown up and could travel to it. But I have, so far, not even been on a train.'

I told my family about the journey only after it was confirmed. My sons, Nikesh and Pratyush, were shocked, but not by my decision to go on a journey on my own.

'You mean you've really never been on a train, Amma? Unbelievable!'

'No! I've seen trains from far away but never at a train station. Forget about getting on one!'

'You must go. Absolutely! I'll take you to the station myself, Amma,' Nikesh said.

There was an unnecessary tinge of guilt in his voice. Before Mudritha's message, even I had not actively thought about the fact that I had never been on a train.

I took Nikesh's hand in mine. 'Do you know, there was a time when I wanted to be an astronaut,' I told him. 'Your valyamma used to make fun of me. Well, not just her, my entire family. And especially when we got our answer sheets back after exams. Too big a dream for someone who barely gets pass marks, they would say…'

Nikesh didn't seem to quite understand what I was trying to say. 'Don't worry, Amma,' he said, patting my back. 'We'll get you on an aeroplane. Come back from this trip of yours. Your next one will be in a flight.'

'There's no need for all that,' I said, laughing. 'Let me get through this one first.'

Our journey will begin this evening. I am glad that Deeptha told me about the yogini temple. Now I have one more reason to go on this journey. To see Umanarayani, the woman who had remained rooted where she had been placed, who had, just like me, sat in the same place getting mouldy, her body parts falling off … I touch the empty space where my left breast used to be before the mastectomy. Now when my emotions get the better of me, I am afraid that my heart will escape out of my ribcage, too conscious that there is no extra padding to keep it in.

I also have another thought that I cannot quite shake. Surely there is another yogini there, one whose name is Umamaheswari, who is shapely, unblemished … I could ask Deeptha, but I know I won't do that. Instead, I will let myself smoulder, imagining, hoping, that she would be there, waiting for me.

BABY

Baby had spoken to the woman named Umanarayani twice, both times on Messenger and only for a few short minutes. When she discovered that she had been added to a Facebook group called Lesbos, she had been confused, miffed, altogether uncomfortable. She had bought her smartphone in a moment of excitement when she had come into some money after winning the lucky draw of the chitty, the subscription lottery she was part of. Nimisha had helped her download WhatsApp and Facebook on to it, and she had felt great carrying the phone around, dressed in its little red cover. But her enjoyment was short-lived; on the tenth day of being a proud phone-owner, her son Agasthi took it away from her.

'What do you need a phone with so many features for, Ammachi? Let me have it,' he said. 'Here, you can have my phone, it's much simpler to use.'

Baby was used to having old things – clothes, books, umbrellas, pens, food … In one sense, it was better to use old things. Scuffed or patched up already, they didn't demand the care that new things did, removing the worry of carelessness or breakage. Agasthi's phone was only two years old, but it was already damaged. Unlike the new phone that needed just a gentle touch, its cracked touchscreen worked only if one pushed down hard, as though its nature had been irreparably altered by his rough, unkind behaviour.

'You'll get used to it soon enough, Ammachi,' he said. 'I've been using it, haven't I? Nothing wrong with it except, yes, you need to press a bit harder on the screen. Tell you what, just get the screen changed when you have some money. It'll do until then. What do you need a mobile phone for anyway except to make and receive calls.'

And off he went with her new phone. Baby downloaded Facebook on to the old one he left behind. Then she discovered that she had been added to this group, the one with the weird name that had no one else in it that she knew. Nimisha told her that it happened quite often on Facebook, that people added others to groups without seeking their permission.

'But, well, best if you leave, Chechi,' Nimisha said. 'It's a women-only group. I don't know, I feel something is off. The name – well, it feels like it is a group for *those women*.'

Baby's heart missed a beat. She assumed *those women* meant women who, unlike her, went to work in the evening and came back home in the morning. A different type of women who did a different type of work. She could not fathom how she had ended up in such a group, who had added her to it. Did she give out vibes that she was one of *them*? Truth be told, in times of grave crisis when she had no idea how to keep going, she had herself thought of making such a living. But getting into the business was not easy for a woman like her, she had found out. It needed someone to help, to encourage, men willing to pay money and use her.

So, she had not become one of those women – that was all she had ever thought about it. But now, at this late stage in her life, at this age, someone had included her in their group. Having never known the difficulties of such a job, or its possible joys or the financial gains, she did not want this special membership.

It had taken Nimisha a while to disabuse Baby of her assumption, to convey to her what she meant by 'those women'. 'Homosexual', she said, and 'Lesbian', and yet she could not come out and say what she meant.

'Is that all!' she exclaimed eventually when it sank in. 'The way you were going on about it, I was beginning to think it might be a terrorist organization or a Maoist group or something! You scared me for no reason.'

Shocked, Nimisha stared at her, wondering whether the Babychechi she had worked with for the last four or five years was, in truth, a lesbian. The thought scared her.

'But, well, since I don't have such a leaning … best to get out of it, no?' said Baby. 'Still, I wonder who added me to this group…'

Nimisha, still scared, deleted Baby's profile picture. It was a photo she had taken herself with great enthusiasm on the day she was helping Baby set up her Facebook page, a selfie of them both. At the time, she had only been concerned about picture quality and pixels of the camera on the new phone. But now, Nimisha saw something untoward in their posture, their arms around each other and their faces close together. They had so many selfies like that, hugging or standing with their bodies pressed against each other with the sewing machines and bolts of fabric in the background. Their breasts were almost touching, Baby's lips almost on her face. And the expression on her face … Nimisha felt they should never have taken such pictures. Anyone would get the wrong idea. And now, if Baby became a member of this lesbian group and someone saw this photo … Especially now that her marriage was almost fixed … Nimisha deleted the photo and replaced it with a picture of Baby and Agasthi that she found in the photo gallery.

'This one is better, Babychechi,' she said. 'Besides, Sajeevettan doesn't like it when I post photos of myself on FB.'

Sajeevan was the man who might marry her. 'Might' was right, all she could say at this stage, because Nimisha herself talked about how he was always suspicious of her, scolded her all the time. Still, she hoped to marry him. All day he picked fights with her, made her cry, but at the end of the day, just before bedtime, he apologized, 'Nimi, my love, I can't live without you, forgive me.' This had become like a sleeping pill for Nimisha; she couldn't sleep without it. And the moment she heard it, everything melted away, her anger and her annoyance, and she lulled him to sleep with kisses and cuddles over the phone so that he could wake up the next day and do it all over again to her.

Foolish girl, that is what Baby thinks of her. See how she deleted a perfectly fine photo because of him, scared that people might think she and Baby were in love with one another. Poor thing!

'You deleted it because you thought they might add you too in the group. Nimisha, my girl, find a photo of me on my own. I'll post that as my profile picture.'

'No, chechi. When women use FB, it's best to post a picture with a man so that people will know you have someone to take care of you. And it will stop people from adding you to groups like this one.'

Baby told Nimisha that she liked being on her own even in pictures but did not pursue the matter further. She also thought of leaving the group to which she had been added without her permission. Not because she thought women loving and desiring one another was wrong; she truly believed that it was down to each person to decide how they lived their lives. The truth is, she never had all that many opportunities to explore her own bodily joys, nor had anyone helped her pursue it. It was difficult for her

to believe that her somewhat dark, skinny body held secret sources
of pleasure. It had only ever given her pain.

Baby was thirteen years old when, in the screw pine thicket by
the side of the canal near her house, she was raped. Her amma
was at work. Baby had gone to the canal in the afternoon to wash
clothes. In the noontime sun, under the clear water of the canal,
pebbles sparkled and sand glittered like sugar. Minnows swam
up to her and kissed her toes. Baby loved seeing this shiny face
of the canal, visible only at this time of day. At other times, in the
mornings and evenings, it had the expression of a sober-faced
woman who held back secrets. So, on days when there was no
school, Baby came to the canal in the afternoons.

That day, he came to the bank of the canal and called her
'kochey' – child. She had pulled her skirt up to her chest, tied it
over her breasts, and was soaping the clothes sitting in the water.
The mundu and chatta that Amma wore when she went to work
were dirty and strewn with a hundred different stains that refused
to budge even after boiling in soda bicarbonate. She soaped them
again and left them to soak. Water foamed white around her from
the soap and the bicarbonate. She would get rid of the stains,
rinse them in kanji water to starch them and spread them on the
rock, and they would be dry by the time she finished her bath.

He must have been watching her before calling out. She
had been feeling uneasy for a while now, as though something,
someone's gaze, was piercing into her. His voice startled her and
when she looked up, she could not see him immediately. He was
squatting on a rock behind a sprawling coffee bush. He could see
her clearly, but she had to strain to be able to see him. There were
men who came and sat on that rock to watch grown women bathe
in the canal. But Baby – she was only a child. It did not occur
to her that someone might sit there watching her. The women
ran the men off, unleashing a string of abuse that burned like

acid, most of which, to Baby's consternation, would be words that badmouthed their mothers. It is men who behave badly but it is their poor mothers who are abused.

But now, here was a situation where she, too, would have to use some of those swear words, yet nothing seemed to come to her tongue. Perhaps she should just say, 'Poda pattee, get lost, you dirty dog!' As she turned this over in her mind, something else occurred to her. The peeping Toms who came to watch the women bathe did not attract attention to themselves and sat there quietly taking in the scene and sometimes pleasuring themselves. So, why did this man call out to her? In the confusion, the 'poda pattee' lay unvoiced, stuck in her throat.

He stepped out from behind the coffee bush and said, 'Kochey, could I have some water to drink?'

She glanced at the flowing water of the canal and the old kanji water she had brought along in the bucket to starch the clothes. Neither was drinkable. Why was he here, at the canal side, asking for water? If he climbed over the style and walked a bit through the rubber trees, there were houses there, including hers, and someone would give him something to drink, fresh kanji water perhaps, or perhaps even a meal.

As she continued her silence, he came closer. She had never seen him before, a stranger in these parts. She noticed the thick hair, like that of a bear, growing on his thighs, dark under his tucked up mundu.

'It's lovely to sit in the water in the sunlight, isn't it?' he said.

She was terrified. It was difficult to move quickly in her wet skirt, the drenched cotton weighed double and threatened to trip her over. She had hiked it up and tied it over her tiny breasts, but it refused to sit there and kept sliding down. She pulled it up with both her hands.

'What do you want?' she asked. 'I came to wash clothes. I don't have drinking water. Go to Thekkel over there, they have a well.'

He ignored her and untucked his mundu. 'I'll show you how to be more comfortable than sitting in the water. Come on up here.'

Baby dived into the water. She had known this canal from the time she was a newborn. The year she was born, the water in their well had dried up in the drought, and her ammamma had brought her to the canal, laid her in an areca nut spathe, oiled her tiny body and bathed her in its water for twenty-eight days. It would not forsake her.

But he came after her, grabbed her by her hair and dragged her through the water. When she cried out, water filled her mouth and nose, suffocated her.

'Stop playing with me, you little slut!' he shouted.

And then he raped her as though he was doing her a favour, in the process wounding, deeply, not only her body but her mind. He flung her on to the bank and lay on top of her, kneaded her breasts and laughed at their smallness, bit her lips and spat saying that they were nasty. Fifteen minutes that would forever soak Baby's life in acid that corroded every surface it touched.

It seemed to Baby that he was trying to insert a red-hot iron poker into her. In her terror, she could not do as he asked and lay there frozen, granite-like, which made it hard for him to have his way. But every time he met with resistance, he pushed harder, tore her open, bit her lips, pulled at her nipples as though he wanted to fling them off, put his hand over her mouth and nose to keep her from crying out, suffocated her, and finally satiated himself somewhere half-way into her. As he got up to leave, he kicked her into the canal and cursed, 'Nashichu po!' It surprised her that, after assaulting her, after all that he did to her, he had cursed that she would come only to ruin. Shouldn't she be the one to curse?

Baby lay in the shallow water trying to soak away the pain and the insult. She lay there until the sun began to weaken, until women began to arrive to wash clothes and bathe. As she gathered up her own laundry, some washed and some half-done, she realized that her amma's mundu and chatta had floated away. That evening, Amma beat her with a switch cut from a coconut palm leaf for losing them.

That was how Baby learned to put up with pain without letting anyone know she was in pain. For days after, she experienced a burning sensation when she urinated. The wounds on her breast festered. She kept the injuries that could be covered with her frocks hidden. As for the wounds on her lips, she lied to her amma that she had tripped on the roots of the coffee bush and fallen over. Amma scolded her even as she put a bit of sugar over the wounds. Wet from her tears, the sugar tasted of salt.

Baby never saw the man again. Her terrified eyes looked for him everywhere, even now, after so many years. She expected him to appear in front of her suddenly, jumping out from a corner or from behind a screen. She would not recognize him if he appeared; she had not paid attention to his face, had kept her eyes screwed shut as he lay over her. But his bear-legs covered in bushy hair – those she remembered still. She worried more when she was with Agasthi. What if he jumped in front of them and started abusing her? It would shame her like it would if she lost all her clothes in public. Baby thought that it was to mark her life with darkness that he had come into her life. Just the one time, but that one time blackened everything, covered her life in soot that no amount of scrubbing would get rid of. A pervading darkness that only she was aware of.

It was in a rainy season when the river rushed into their home with great pomp and swagger that Baby met the man who would become Agasthi's appan. Most years, the canal flooded when there were mudslides far away in the eastern forests, something that happened at least once in every season of rain. The water came up to the bottom of the style into their front yard and retreated a couple of days later. And when it did, venomous snakes that floated into the canal, which usually accommodated only harmless keelbacks, would come exploring into the compounds, hang from the rafters or hide under palm leaves. That year, the water did not stop at the style. It came up the steps and into the yard and waited there as though making it clear that it would not hesitate to come into the house itself. Baby and her amma had to accept that they had to vacate and go to the disaster relief camp set up at the church school. The camp was another disaster, one that they tried their best to avoid.

That year it seemed inevitable. Amma asked Baby to pack up a few necessities and went to dig up the little tin, her safe that held her savings. The old Cuticura tin was hidden in a somewhat deep hole dug into the floor of polished cow dung in front of the kitchen fire, under an old box made of softwood. It held a few currency notes and coins, and a little gold – nothing much, just a chain in the thara design, two thin bangles, and an ear stud that had lost its screw. Amma had had to struggle to keep even this much aside. Baby's wedding – that was a dream she held deep within, and she wanted to be able to give her daughter something for the occasion. She would have cursed her too for turning out to be a girl, for being a child whose father had died the same year she was born. If it were a son, she could have asked him to provide for her, not the other way around. Meanwhile, in the unsafe house they lived in, she had needed to dig out a hidey hole to keep her little treasures safe. Amma tied it all up in a piece of cloth and slid it inside her blouse, and hid the Cuticura tin in the firewood and dried palm leaves stacked above the fire.

The disaster camp at the school was hell. Those who arrived first pulled benches together as makeshift beds and slept on them. Others had to sleep on the floor, on mats if they had brought them along. They were lucky if they were given anything to eat or drink. But Baby did not mind any of this. What she dreaded were the toilets that stank to the high heavens, and by the time they went back home, Baby would have made herself sick by refusing to use them, by holding back. So, they waited until the last possible minute to go to the camp. They had stowed their pots and pans, clothes-trunk, and pillows higher up and were locking the door when they were startled by the sight of the man standing in the water in the front yard.

'Who are you?' Amma asked. 'What do you want?'

It began to rain again.

'I'm from the east,' the man said. 'It's all under water there, all gone. I'm really hungry, pengaley. Something to eat … kanji … water…'

He had a bald head and a tall, thin body. Looking at him standing there drenched in the rain, Amma asked, her voice replete with sympathy, 'How did you come this way?'

He did not respond except to ask for water again. Did he float down the canal, Baby wondered. Why else would he come to this impoverished house by the side of the canal, far away from the road where there were so many better households? The memory of another man who had accosted her asking for water made a heat rise through her body from the underside of her feet.

'Let's get going, Amma,' she said. 'The school will soon be full, and we won't find any space.'

As though she had not heard her speak, Amma invited the man on to the small veranda. She gave him one of the boxes of food that they had packed for their lunch, and as he sat on the low wall of the veranda and ate it, Baby stared angrily into the rain. When he finished, he came to where she stood, washed the aluminium box in the rainwater, rinsed his mouth, and gave the box back to Amma. As though he had no intention of leaving, he sat back on the wall and took out a rain-soaked beedi he had tucked behind his ear. He will want matches now, Baby thought, but he did not ask them for it, perhaps because he knew he would not be able to light the beedi even if he had a burning torch. He threw it into the water in the yard instead. Baby watched as the beedi bobbed and floated away.

'I'm thankful to you, pengaley. May Karthav bless you,' he told Amma. And then to Baby, 'Come off from the edge, kochey, you're getting drenched.'

Irritated, Baby itched to tell him to make himself scarce now that he had been fed.

'Edee, Baby, did you not hear? Move away from the edge,' Amma scolded her.

Angrily Baby walked to her amma and whispered in her ear, 'Finished with the hospitality, haven't you, so let's go. The school will be crowded by now.'

'You were on your way somewhere, weren't you?' he said. 'That's all right. You go ahead. I'll just rest here for a while and be on my way.'

Amma stood there, consternation writ large on her face, as though she had picked up a snake off the fence and draped it over her shoulders. How could they go away leaving this stranger here in the veranda of their home? The door only needed a push to be opened. Not that there was anything valuable inside, except all that they had was valuable to them, even the leaking aluminium pot and the fish chatty with its broken edges that they had not thrown away.

'You get going, chetta, only then we'll go,' Amma told the man, pressing the bundle of clothes in her hand to her chest. 'We're on our way to the school, worried that the house will be flooded soon. Don't stay here. Why don't you come with us?'

Baby did not like that her amma invited him to come along to the camp. Still, that would get him away from their house. Amma and her confounded sympathy! Now they will have to share the one box of food left. Who knows whether they will be given anything to eat in the night.

He stepped out. The rain had stopped, the water level had risen again.

'Give it here, kochey,' he said, pointing to the bundle in Baby's hand, 'I'll carry it for you.'

She refused.

'She'll carry it, chetta. It's not heavy. Just a few clothes and such. Don't know how long we'll have to stay there,' Amma said, as though to save him embarrassment.

'Let out the cows and hens, haven't you, pengaley?' he asked Amma as though he was the head of their family.

Baby told him in an irritated voice that they had no cows. They had let the few hens out of their coop in the morning. Would they survive, or would they find them dead and rotting on their return? Who could tell. The rooster they had not killed even for the church festival, letting it grow a bit more … The eggs they had not eaten, setting them aside to incubate and hatch into chicks … All gone. Baby's amma was on the brink of tears. Setbacks of some kind or the other, every year, year after year. The loss of things nurtured, scrimped and saved for, and now they would have to start from the beginning, all over again.

And to top it all off, this girl, the daughter who was well beyond the age of marriage. She was Baby's amma's biggest worry.

It was to see the wedding minnu tied around her neck that she struggled like this, day in, day out. But all that came looking for her instead were floods and more hardship.

'Everything has its own time, Chinnachedathi. Karthav will let it happen when it is time. He will bring you the man for your daughter. The Lord is my fortress, my shield, my stronghold – isn't that what it says in the Psalms? Put your faith in Our Lord, He who is like the new rain that makes grass sprout. Pray to Him. You'll find a way.'

Advice often repeated by neighbours and the kapyar, the verger of the church, who everyone called 'mic vizhungi' because of the loud voice in which he spoke, like he had swallowed a mic. Amma listened to them and the duration of her prayer time increased – three hundred repetitions of the Apostles Creed, standing on her knees, a hundred Hail Marys, crawling. And she scolded Baby for not joining her.

'No wonder you're not married, you Maramkeri-Maria, going about unruly, unladylike. One has to have the fear of God. He's like new rain that makes tender grass sprout from dried up earth, do you know? There's nothing He can't do.'

Not new rain, more like a deluge that wipes out everything that exists, Baby would think, laughing inside. She was relieved that she was not married, and she was not going to recite even one extra prayer for it. In fact, every time someone brought an alliance, she offered special secret prayers that it came to nothing. Thoughts of marriage made her nipples hurt as though they were being torn away, made the place where she urinated from burn. She did not want to experience any of it ever again, but she could not talk about it. For a while, she went after the people at the convent hoping to become a nun, but even Karthav did not want her as His bride, she who was from the waste land by the side of the canal.

She would continue like this on her own, she had decided, and she had a trade to provide for herself. She had learned tailoring, embroidery and other decorative work from Jyothibhavan, the home run by the nuns, and she worked there and made enough to get by. Not that she has been able, yet, to save up some money and buy a sewing machine. Amma took any money that was saved and bought gold with it. 'For you only,' she would say.

That year, the rain continued, relentless, and they who had gone to the camp at the school hoping it would only be for a day or two had to stay there for over a week. By then, Amma caught dysentery and had to spend three or four days at the General Hospital. After about a week and a half, as Baby worried about taking Amma back to the house that had flooded and drained, he arrived. He had tried to help them, despite Baby ignoring him studiously, while they were at the camp and at the hospital. 'You wait here, I'll go and see what state the house is in,' he said, took the key from Baby and went away. That evening, when Baby brought Amma home, everything was spick and span. Usually, after being flooded, the house stank for days. But he had worked hard to clean the place up. The smell of bleach and phenyl made Baby wonder whether she was still at the hospital. He sat proudly on the low wall of the veranda and smiled at them.

'So nice of you,' Amma said to him, and in the same breath, to Baby, 'Make some coffee.' She sat chatting with him until Baby scolded her gently and told her to go and lie down. Such a lovely man, Amma kept repeating even after he left.

Baby had not been able to guess what her mother was thinking at the time. Nor did she know whether, had she been aware, she would have been able to avoid what happened. She was under such immense pressure. The sisters at Jyothibhavan, and even the parish priest, spoke to her, cast hooks baited with a hundred reasons – her mother's ill-health, their penurious situation, the need for male companionship … With nowhere to escape, Baby was trapped. Amma had, by then, stopped calling him 'Chettan' – older brother – and started using his name, and he gave up calling her 'pengaley', sister. It turned out that his name, too, was Baby. Baby learned soon enough that when Amma called out the name with love, it was him she was addressing, and when it was used with irritation, she was the one being addressed.

That year, the day before the twenty-five-day fast – the fast before the Nativity of Our Lord – the man, who was at least twenty-five years older than her, and whose family and whereabouts they knew very little about, tied the minnu around her neck. Despite all she tried to avoid it, the tiny piece of gold lay entrapped around her neck.

And it continued to doze between her breasts at the end of a thara chain, worn out and about to break, made of one-and-a-half pavan-worth of gold. She could have taken it off, but it lay there without reminding her of its presence, forever weary.

Baby does not remember much about their married life. They lived in her house for a while, for about two rains. She could not love him, could not bear his thin body that had already begun to age, or his endearments. At night, all nights, she pushed him away, smug in her youth and the arrogance that it was her house. She did not learn, from their relationship, that there were sources of pleasure deep within her own body.

As his rough fingers caressed her breasts, as his beedi-smelling lips brushed against her face, she felt nauseated. On occasion, biting her lips, holding in her distaste, she allowed herself to lay beneath him, frozen as though she were dead. Much as he tried to pleasure her, tried to tell her that this was not how it was done, she did not relent. In the end, he would do what he could and pull away, and she would open the door and run to the toilet.

Then, one day, from one of those incomplete efforts, Agasthi was seeded in her womb. He had gone away by then. He would not have known about it. Even she had become aware of it only after he had gone away.

A terrible pregnancy that was. She threw up and lay exhausted all through those nine months, and her amma, despite her ill-health, went to work to be able to provide for her. Even the smell of boiling kanji made Baby vomit violently, so Amma took to cooking on a fire out in the yard. As Baby became increasingly weak from not being able to eat properly, Amma cursed the man who had taken off after getting her daughter pregnant, complained to the parish priest. The priest wrote letters to the churches in the east with a description of the man, but they could not find him. No such man existed, Baby thought. He was only a ghost, a malignant spirit that had come floating in the eastern waters just to make her suffer, and he had disappeared having done his evil deed.

When it was time to give birth, she could barely stand up. For months, she had been living on glucose water alone. Anything else made her vomit. Amma lamented that what he had deposited in her womb was a piece of burning ember, cursed that he would come to ruin wherever he went, the bastard.

Baby's contractions started on an afternoon when the Edavappathi rains began in earnest, finally ending the scorching heat of the summer. She did not tell her amma when she returned, exhausted from her work, that evening. But by the next morning, she could not bear the pain. She was taken to the General Hospital, but she did not give birth immediately. For three days she floated in an ocean of pain until, finally, her womb was cut open to bring Agasthi out. The stitches did not heal, got infected and painful. From the time of her pregnancy until Agasthi was five or six months old, all Baby knew was pain. So, what could she do except laugh if someone told her about women who sought bodily pleasures!

BABY'S DECISION TO leave Lesbos was based on her assumption that she was not suited for such a group. Her body did not know how to be joyful, how to conjoin with other bodies, male or female, for its pleasure. She was ignorant, too, of the pleasures of the mind. But she would not display her wounds to anyone, not even to Agasthi. She kept them covered instead. She did not wish to parade them, show them to those who would not know how to heal them, and watch the sympathy or the revulsion that was sure to reflect on their faces.

But before she pressed the 'leave' button, she wanted to have a quick look at the other members of the group, and somehow ended up chatting with a woman named Umanarayani. She disabused Baby of the idea that it was a group for lesbians, and encouraged her to stick around, to read the posts and comments, told her that she could do this without having to post anything herself. An interaction that Baby, too, had been longing for, like a tree to lean against when life's pains and uncertainties seem inexorable. Think of it as a place to regroup, Umanarayani told her, to simply sit, like a statue on a seashore, letting the waves wash over, purify. Water does not hurt, Umanarayani said, it only cools, cleanses.

Baby thought that Umanarayani might be a teacher and took to heart everything she said. As expected of all new friendships, she asked Uma about her family, not because she was curious but because she thought Uma might be offended if she didn't ask. But all Umanarayani told her was not to call her 'Uma' and promised to explain some day. Baby found that strange.

And when Umanarayani asked about her, she told her that she had a son, and that the father of her son had the same name as her.

'That's so funny,' Umanarayani replied, attaching a string of smileys to it. 'This Baby, he's not with you now, is he? Tell you what. I'm going to call you Jaratkaru.'

Baby had no idea who Jaratkaru was, and Umanarayani signed off promising to tell her later. A woman that kept everything for later! Baby felt somewhat irritated. Besides, how did she know that the man she married was not with her any more?

It was Nimisha who told her about Jaratkaru. When Baby brought the name up as they sat sewing, Nimisha did not know who it was, but the next day, she came armed with the story, having read up about it. Jaratkaru was a sage who, after being celibate for a very long time, decided to get married so that his ancestral spirits could find salvation. But he was adamant that he would only marry a woman with the same name as his, and he spent quite a while searching for such a woman. Vasuki, the king of the serpents, heard about him and went to him with his sister. It was her bad luck that her name, too, was Jaratkaru. Vasuki was happy to have found a man to palm his sister off on, and the sage Jaratkaru was happy that he found a wife just as he had wished for. No one asked the woman what she thought. The marriage took place. The sage warned his wife that he would abandon her if she did anything to displease him, and it was in the shadow of this threat that they began their married life. Some time passed, and one day, as he had threatened, the sage left her for no fault of hers. She cried, begged for his forgiveness, but to no avail. He just took off. She was pregnant at the time, and gave birth to a son, Asthikan, whom she brought up on her own and with great difficulty. And through this child, the sage Jaratkaru's ancestral spirits found salvation.

'Just like your own story, chechi,' said Nimisha with a sense of awe.

But she never cried and went after him begging for forgiveness, Baby told her, irritated. She held her son, Agasthi, close to her heart, brought him up despite adversity, and not because he could save the souls of his father's ancestors.

That day, she sent a message to Umanarayani telling her that she now knew Jaratkaru's story. Her response was to ask her whether she was going to Odisha with them. Confused, Baby logged on and looked through the messages in Lesbos, found that a trip to Odisha was being discussed there, organized by a woman named Mudritha. Me, too, she raised her hand. A journey without a clear reason, with nothing to accomplish, no one to visit. In that moment, she felt there was nothing purer than such an endeavour, one that cleansed the mind like the yearly confession before Easter, that took away the weight of everything.

Baby did not find it hard to come up with the money for the trip. She sold the thara chain. The dozing minnu went with it. She did not bother letting Agasthi know. She rarely saw her son who came to her or called her only when he needed something. He would not even notice that she was gone. Besides, Baby was adamant that all her journeys now would be without asking for permission. Like water on a flat surface, let it flow where it wants to.

It was off-season, so the tailoring shop also did not pose any problems. She cut the fabrics for some immediate jobs; Nimisha would do the sewing as long as that man of hers did not create problems. If he didn't perform the apologizing ritual in the night, she tended to have a headache in the morning. In any case, they were not as busy as they used to be. These days, everyone relied on readymade shops like Trends and Max, or bought online. Even sari blouses were readymade, and very few people wore saris.

Sometimes it seemed as though they might soon have to shut up shop.

THE DAY BEFORE the journey, Baby hands everything over to Nimisha. She still has some shopping to do. She has never been on a journey like this, so she has, in discussion with Nimisha, made a list of things to take with her.

As she is about to leave, Vennila, a Tamil woman they are familiar with, enters the shop in a hurry. She is a home nurse looking after a woman who lives somewhere nearby, and comes in to have the blouses and kurtis she is given altered or resized. To Nimisha's annoyance, she has never brought them anything new to tailor. She takes them to the city, complains Nimisha, and brings us only things for alteration, and Baby pacifies her, telling her that Vennila, perhaps, has nothing new to tailor.

'Akka, please, do these today itself,' says Vennila. 'I am going on a trip tomorrow.'

Ignoring the irritation on Nimisha's face, Baby hands the churidars to her and leaves hurriedly. Tomorrow, at this time, she will be in a train. Her first train journey, her first ever holiday trip. With a surging sense of affection, Baby thinks of Mudritha, the woman who is making it possible for Baby to step outside her own little piece of the earth.

VENNILA

Vennila lived with a woman named Philomena. Seven years ago, when she left her faraway village near Karoor with her appa and arrived at Philomena's house, she had been a broken, defeated woman. Exactly a month before that, her husband Kalainayakam had run away with her akka. Or perhaps it is better to say that Akka had run away with the man who was her brother-in-law.

Their appa, who had studied Tamil literature in college, had lovingly named his daughters Manimekala and Vennila. Manimekala was older, educated, a teacher in a school in Tiruchirappalli, and had decided against marriage. Up until the day she ran away with her husband, Vennila had assumed that Manimekala had decided not to get married because of the life they had known in their own home growing up. Their parents had fought all the time. Appa came home drunk and beat Amma for no reason. Amma beat her breasts and wailed, sometimes hit him back. They had witnessed such scenes throughout their childhood.

Vennila had worried that, like the original Manimekalai, the celebrated daughter of Kovilan and Madhavi from the *Silappatikaram*, her akka, too, would become a sanyasini. Manimekalai had, despite being beautiful and wealthy, and despite having a king like Udayakumaran to pursue her with promises and temptations, followed the path of Buddhism. With her magic begging bowl, Amritasurabhi, in hand, she had wandered the earth seeking an end to world hunger, engaged in philosophical discussions.

Vennila's akka was not all that beautiful – at least, everyone said, not as beautiful as Vennila herself – or rich. Still, she decided not to get married, pontificated about matters beyond Vennila's comprehension. But there was one thing that she said that Vennila remembered still: 'Aakamalavai arivanoolaar pokapuvanam undu enappulankollal.' According to great scholars, there were other worlds above and below this world where one could experience pleasures that would put to shame those of this world, extraordinary pleasures and unearthly comforts. Reciting the line melodiously, Manimekala had explained its meaning to Vennila.

And yet, she had, in the end, stolen the tiny begging bowl of happiness from Vennila's impoverished world. Vennila despaired trying to make sense of why she would do such a thing, why she would forego the pursuit of otherworldly happiness and settle for Kalainayakam.

Manimekala had hated being at home after it became motherless, where Appa was always lost in the mire of alcohol, where only want and penury existed. As soon as she finished her studies, she went to Trichy, did odd jobs for small salaries until, a little later, she joined the Kannimatha Girls School as a Tamil teacher. Once she also became the resident tutor at the school's boarding house, she rarely came home, even for Deepavali or Pongal. Appa went to her for money every now and then. He was proud of his daughter who had studied Tamil literature in college and had become a teacher. He too had dreamed of being a teacher, had completed the first year of a BA degree. Then he got a job as a railway gangman, and that put an end to his academic ambitions. He could never reconcile with the difficult life of a gangman, trundling along railway lines that burned red-hot in the daytime sun and froze up in the cold of the night. It made him a sad and frustrated man, and he meted out only sorrow and frustration to all those around him. He was generous with it too, for we can only be generous with what we possess, Vennila would think, and her appa did not possess joy or comfort.

With Manimekala's departure, it was Vennila who suffered. By then, Appa had lost his job. Vennila was not particularly keen on her studies, but she went to school every day because she did not want to be at home. She had to finish all the household chores before going to school, fetch water from afar, cook the day's food. Appa would sleep till noon, and by the time she got back from school, he would be gone, and she would have to sit alone and scared at home till midnight. They had to vacate the railway quarters after he was dismissed, and the only rental property they could find was near a burial ground – where else would they find a house for such low rent! Don't leave me here alone, she begged her appa and akka, but she was left alone, always. The sanctuary of school was also lost when she failed her Plus 2 exams.

Once, Vennila asked Manimekala if there was something they could do to stop Appa from drinking so much, some medicine, or perhaps a special prayer at the church attached to her school. Appa drank day and night, and sat huddled on the cot in the yard, barely conscious, until keeling over and falling asleep.

Manimekala had laughed at her question. Prayers are of no use, paappa, she told Vennila, neither are medicines. Appa won't stop drinking until he himself decides to do so. Impossible to advise or persuade an alcoholic because they are never in their clear minds. Besides, trying to make them come to their senses is like searching for a drowning man under water with a lit lamp, pointless. Vennila was angry. There were no solutions, not even in books; only a load of useless philosophy, and banal utterances about how those who indulged in alcohol embarrassed even the Goddess of Shame. Even if there were solutions, Vennila did not know what they were. Besides, how was she, who had failed her Plus 2, had never been anywhere farther than Srirangam that one time, to find out!

On such days, Vennila would think about her amma. The last time she saw her, Amma had crossed the railway lines in front of their quarters to the canal on the other side to clean fish. She walked across them many times a day. They had no running water in the quarters; only a well, as deep as hell itself, that served all the households. Drawing water from it was hard, especially in the summer when the water level went down even further. So, they used it only for drinking water. For all other needs – washing pots, cleaning fish, bathing and washing clothes – they depended on the canal that was as wide as the four-line railway track it lay parallel to, its water never going below waist-deep even in the hottest summer.

Vennila was in Class 8 when it happened. Cleaned fish in hand, Amma was hurrying back home from the canal. Appa came home for lunch, exhausted from walking along the railway tracks in the blazing sun. If, by that time, the rice, meen kulambu and a kondattam of sun-dried chundanga were not ready and waiting, she would be beaten. In her haste, Amma only looked in one direction, watching out for the inspector's trolley. If it was returning to the station, the gangmen would be walking right behind it.

The train that came speeding from the other direction and smashed into her was running out of schedule. Vennila was at school when it happened, and so did not see her mother strewn all over the railway tracks. All she saw, when she got back, was the mat in which they had bundled up her remains. No one helped her see her amma's face even, one last time, and for years after, she cried over it. What did she look like in death? She did not remember looking at her face when she left for school that morning, or in the preceding days, and now, when she wanted, desperately, to see it one last time, it was denied to her forever. Manimekala, seven years older than her, held her close and sobbed. With Amma's death, Appa began to drink even more, stopped going to work regularly, and ended up getting suspended and then dismissed. By then, Manimekala had gone away. Vennila had to swallow all that came with it, the hardship and the heartache.

It might be possible to fall asleep within a blazing fire, but to rest properly in the fire that is poverty, that is impossible. Something Vennila's appa said often, and yet he did nothing to assuage the flames that engulfed them. He spent almost three quarters of the money Manimekala gave him in the arrack shop, leaving only the rest for household expenses. Many were the times when Vennila ate old rice with water poured over it, with not even a chilli kondattam to flavour it. After she stopped going to school, she thought about finding some work, but every time it was mentioned, Appa hugged her and cried, 'En kolandai…' The only job that was available in that area was construction work, breaking stones under the searing heat of the sun. He could not think of sending his child to do that job.

It was during that time that Kalainayakam came into her life. He was the new pointsman, from Madurai. He was acquainted with Appa, and one day when he fell over after a long bout of drinking, Kalainayakam took pity on him and carried him home. The lonely house next to the burial ground and the helpless young woman stranded there invoked a deep sympathy in him. And the next day, he persuaded Appa to move into his quarters with her, and he moved himself into an empty cabin. Being back near the railway station was like a breath of fresh air for Vennila, the noise of the trains and the bells, the shady tamarind and elanda trees near the platforms, the canal across the tracks ... The tracks themselves used to make her heart bleed, but now she felt only relief.

Kalainayakam requested that she cook for him too and brought home the groceries. For a year after, Vennila and her appa lived on his charity. And before the next Deepavali came around, he tied the wedding thali around her neck at the Ammankovil. He wanted his quarters, which he had given to them as a temporary arrangement, back. And her cooking, well, it did not quite satisfy his Maduraikkaran tastebuds. Still, why spend money on a cook, he might have thought, and should he not be compensated for taking on their upkeep? Why not take the payment in the form of a nightly companion. He was, after all, looking for someone to marry and settle down with.

That Deepavali, as a new bride, she went to Madurai armed with clothes and sweets for his family. All she remembers now from that time is the dark green of the sugarcane fields and the water channels flowing through them. She spent most of her six days there in this coolness and greenery. Kalainayakam's family showed her no affection. His mother, her maamiyaar, scolded him in front of her, beat him with a length of sugarcane. He took the beatings silently, without protest, sending angry looks at Vennila. And she escaped into the sugarcane fields. No one came looking for her, and she spent hours alone, leaning against the sugarcanes, dangling her feet in the cool water.

Her Thalai Deepavali, when she, as a new bride, should have been pampered by her new family, turned out to be a damp and icy one instead. She was given the paniyaram and modakam and murukku made in their kitchen, and a not too shabby Kanchi silk sari, none of it with any affection. Gestures of cold-hearted charity had only ever suffocated Vennila, so she, who did not own many saris, never wore that yellow silk, and stuffed it into the bottom shelf of her almirah.

In those loveless days in Madurai, Vennila understood that the thali around her neck was also charity. It did not symbolize affection or love, only pity. It made her suspicious whenever Kalainayakam behaved affectionately towards her, and yet she tried to keep him close by being more and more submissive. Whatever he desired, she strove to make ready, be it food or anything else. In the six years they lived together, Kalainayakam did not have to ask her for anything; she would have it ready before he could ask. Vennila would register even the smallest sign that he wanted to sleep with her, and those nights, before he could voice his desire, she would be waiting in bed, her clothes removed and her body perfumed. No need for persuasion or foreplay; all he had to do was enter her body in whatever manner he desired.

And until he ran away, Vennila had assumed that he was happy, content. He had never expressed any dissatisfaction; if he had, Vennila would have given her life to find a solution.

Appa, by then, had liver cirrhosis and had cut down his drinking substantially. Most of the time, he sat huddled on the cot under the neem tree in front of the quarters, occasionally glancing through a tattered book from those Manimekala had abandoned, *Thirukkural* or some such. Kalainayakam took care of his needs – medicines, treatment – and Vennila was forever indebted to him. If she had a tail, she would have wagged it non-stop in front of him.

Manimekala had come to attend Vennila's wedding, slid a kaappu bangle of two-and-a-half pavan-worth of gold on to her wrist as a gift. Women who treated their husbands like gods and bowed at their feet every morning had the power to summon rain with their words, she said, and joked with Vennila that she could now have it rain as and when she pleased in the hot season. Vennila felt a deep sense of guilt. Manimekala was older; she should not have allowed herself to get married before her older sister. She felt that she had snatched something away from her sister.

On their first trip to Srirangam after their wedding, they visited the Kannimatha Girls School where Manimekala worked. Getting off the morning train at Trichy, they spent several hours in the dark coolness of the Srirangam Kovil. In the space between the pillars, laying his head in her lap, he, who had done the night shift the day before, even had a nap for a couple of hours as she sat watching over him, her eyes wide open. In the afternoon, they bought lemon rice and Mysore pak and had their lunch right there. When the sun goes down, we will visit the Ucchi Pillayar Kovil, he said. She had never been there before.

But it was to the boarding house where Manimekala lived that they went, with an armful of sweets and strings of jasmine buds. It was he who had asked whether she didn't want to see her akka after having come all this way. Vennila nodded and sat waiting for Manimekala on the rickety bench in the visitors' room like a culprit awaiting trial. Kalainayakam stood outside, chatting with the watchman. Her akka arrived, dressed in a pretty pink outfit, and was surprised to see her, hugged her, and asked, repeatedly, 'Endee shollaamal! Didn't tell me you were coming!' She stepped outside and chatted with Kalainayakam – he was her age – and called him, lovingly, 'Kolunthanaar' – brother-in-law. Just call him by his name, Vennila whispered in her ear, while Kalainayakam smiled shyly, but she continued calling him, stubbornly, Kolunthanaar.

Then, after changing her clothes, Manimekala went with them to the Ucchi Pillayar Kovil. As they climbed up the steps, she described the view of the city from the top, decked out in lights, told an enchanted Vennila that nights were the best time to visit the temple, to sit on the still sun-warm rock and watch the sprawling scenery below. No other sight to match it, paappa, she said, one that is never forgotten once seen.

But, by the time they got to the top of the steps, the gate was locked. Never mind, Kalainayakam consoled Vennila, we'll see it on our next visit. Manimekala, meanwhile, continued to talk about the sights ahead that were lost to Vennila – steps carved through tunnels, the coolness within, the kovil with its many deities, the aarathi, the fragrance of camphor. Vennila did not know then that she would not visit the kovil ever again.

That evening, they had coffee and snacks in a hotel. Then they went shopping. Manimekala bought a silk sari for Vennila from a shop named Sharada's, and a red-bordered veshti and shirt for Kalainayakam. When Vennila selected three cotton saris for Manimekala – they were better for daily use, for going to the school – she was worried that Kalainayakam might be annoyed, but he smiled and paid for them promptly. In that moment, Vennila felt a deep love for him.

They dropped Manimekala back at the boarding school and took the night train home. Vennila would never forget that journey. With the package of jalebi they had bought for Appa from Mahalakshmi Sweets, a shop next to the station, in her lap, she sat with her head leaning against the bars of the window, watching scenes of dark and light flashing away outside. Her man sat next to her, his head occasionally resting on her shoulder as he slept. That was the day she recognized herself as the happiest woman on earth. She had no inkling of what would happen, what was to come in the future, but in that moment, she was fulfilled, secure. The magical night slipped away as soon as they got off the train. And the day after, they went to Madurai.

In the summer of the year Venilla lost her baby in the seventh month of her pregnancy and spent days at the hospital and at home unable to do anything more than weep, Manimekala came home and spent her vacation with them in the quarters. Appa was not quite well, and Kalainayakam had to go to work, so

Manimekala took over everything. She experienced, for the first time, what it meant to run a household. It must have been then that she began to enjoy the sweet languor it entailed, savour its sour-bitter taste. Its lackadaisical uncertainties must have seemed tempting to her whose life was ordered and codified according to the ringing of bells.

All assumptions that Vennila came to later. In that moment, she did not suspect anything, her heart was as empty as her womb. She had gone across the railway tracks to the canal to bathe and was on her way back when she tripped on her wet sari and fell, hitting her seven-month pregnant belly on the tracks. Her cries had brought people running from the canal and from the station, and their quick actions saved her from being run over by the Thirukkural Superfast Express, although, later, she would wish that she had been left there to die. The life that had sprouted inside her a full six years after her wedding, each year a long, burning stretch of waiting. Her maamiyaar called her machi – sterile – to her face, but she had been more scared by Kalainayakam's silence in those moments. And when she was pregnant, finally, how careful she had been. The path to the canal and back was so familiar, and yet.

'You shouldn't have gone there, paappa,' Manimekala said at the hospital. 'It's where Amma died. I think she was pulling you to her.'

An older woman overheard her and agreed with her. The soul of a woman who had died without having finished living. She must have reached out with so much love when she saw her pregnant daughter. After Vennila was brought back home from hospital, they had the Neerkalaayam and Sooniyam vekkal ceremonies done. The spirit had to be pacified and sent back, the evil intentions of others driven away, otherwise this, such a disaster, could happen again. Vennila watched them go about it with eyes overflowing with tears. Her amma would not do such a thing to her, not even by accident. Amma had not caused this, her own foul fate had.

And that fate took away not only her happiness but Kalainayakam too. Manimekala looked after her well in those days. She did not have her child, but she was still a woman in the post-pregnancy phase, who needed her body to be cared for, its health restored so that she could try becoming a mother again. A paati, an old woman who was a distant relative, gave the necessary instructions and Manimekala followed them. Even now, when she recalls how she was fed balls of neem leaves ground with jaggery, Vennila feels like throwing up.

The vacation was over and the school reopened, but Manimekala took more leave and stayed on with them. She sat beside Vennila, her paappa, and tried to give her courage, reminded her that no matter how much we yearned and how desperately we desired, all we would ever have is what destiny had parcelled and set aside for us.

Destiny had set aside Kalainayakam for Vennila only for a few years. In the next parcelling up, he became Manimekala's. She had gone back by then, and after a few days, he too left for Trichy. He had been transferred there, he told Vennila before he left. Two days later, Manimekala called Appa to tell him that Kalainayakam would not be coming back. Vennila did not cry and complain. In fact, she was not quite able to understand what was happening in her life at the time.

Appa was the one who had to shoulder the problem. Kalainayakam was gone, so they could not stay on in the railway quarters. But where would he, with his infirm body and health issues, take his daughter who was physically and mentally distraught? He decided to bring Vennila to Philomena. All night on their journey, as they sat on a piece of cloth spread on the floor of the unreserved coach in the Tea Garden Express, Appa rebuked Kalainayakam. Vennila assumed it was rebuke; what she heard were lofty philosophies. All she could remember now is the statement that Appa had kept repeating: A man who, without contemplation, leaves his wife for another woman, is undone no matter how fortunate he is. Perhaps there was nothing in Appa's books about the consequences for a woman who steals another woman's husband. Vennila's tears, which had been brought under control, began to flow again. The train was filled with the fragrance of jasmine. Women sat on the seats, dozing and stringing garlands at the same time. All of the flowers to Kerala crossed the border on that train.

The next morning, when she reached that big house, her eyes swollen from lack of sleep and weeping, and her head throbbing from the smell of flowers, Philomena, the woman they had come to see, was well enough to receive them. Appa had been acquainted with her dead husband, Samuel sir, when he had been the station superintendent – a long time before Vennila was born. Both Samuel sir and Philomena had been fond of Appa, and he had come to her putting his faith on this tenuous relationship. Philomena was alone now and was in need of help. Was he getting rid of her as a servant in this house, wondered Vennila, but before the thought took root, Philomena looked at her and sent her to one of the rooms to sleep.

She slept, lost to the world, until evening, until Appa woke her to say goodbye. He was taking the night train. Vennila did not ask him where he was headed because she knew that he would not have a reply for her. 'Nimmathiyaa iri, kolandai,' he said and kissed the top of her head. The tenderness of that kiss still calms her whenever she thinks about that moment.

Philomena told her that she was not looking for a servant but a companion, and instructed her to call her Philo. Vennila had been wondering how to address her, and was reluctant to call a person so much older than her by name, but Philomena insisted.

Vennila took over the housework. In the beginning, because she was not too keen on the Tamil taste of Vennila's cooking, Philomena helped out in the kitchen. Vennila learned all her likes and dislikes very soon. Philomena's was a life that saw her debilitated and bedridden for almost half the year. In the rainy season and in the cold, her legs gave out, became so painful that she could barely sleep at night. And then suddenly one day, she would be up and out of the bed again, as though having thrown off the shackles of pain, and be all around the house filling it with her energy. She could walk by herself then, although with a slight drag to one leg, would call the driver to take the Ambassador car out of the shed, and they would go to shopping malls, to the beach, and to the cinema. Philomena would buy lots of saris and churidars, and when she was bedridden again, she would give them to Vennila.

'You take these,' she would say, sorrowfully. 'Where am I going to go now wearing all this?'

They were not in Vennila's size, and she became a regular at the tailor shop nearby where she took them to be resized. She liked one of the tailors, a thin woman named Baby, but she had not talked to her, nor had the woman asked her about anything other than the measurements of the garments. Still, Vennila felt an indescribable sense of calm when she saw her.

Philo spent most of her days on her phone in an effort to keep her pain at bay. The worlds of wonder that the phone opened up – WhatsApp, YouTube, Facebook – amazed Vennila. Manimekala and Kalainayakam had phones like Philo's, but Vennila had never dared touch them, terrified that she might drop them or break them somehow. She kept her distance from Philo's phone too in the beginning.

Come nighttime, unable to sleep with the pain devouring her, Philo would throw the phone on the bed and demand, 'Talk to me, Vennila.' And Vennila would sit leaning against the wall, on a mattress spread on the floor beside Philo's bed, and begin speaking. At first, not entirely sure what she was supposed to talk about, she would go quiet, and Philo would prompt her, 'Tell me about you.'

So, Vennila walked along the paths of her childhood once again. The same railway tracks; the tamarind tree; the plastic-meshed cot under the neem tree in the yard of the railway quarters; the trains that rushed past quaking the earth; the canal that never dried; swimming in the river Kaveri at the far end of the eucalyptus plantation with Manimekala and their friends, and the games on its vast sandy shore; sitting on the veranda of their quarters stringing jasmine into garlands to put in their hair before rushing off to the Ammankovil; watching movies at the theatre after begging money off Appa; getting spanked by Amma for breaking the plastic pot trying to imitate the karakattakkaran who could dance with pots balanced on his head.

A good listener, Philo paid attention, tried to imagine village scenes through Vennila's words, consoled her when some memories brought tears. The day she told her about Kalainayakam, Vennila had resolved not to cry, but broke down inconsolably. Ignoring her hurting legs, Philo left her bed on her own, sat down next to Vennila.

'Don't cry, my child,' she said, stroking her shoulder. Alcohol only affects those who drink it. But lust, it affects even those who stand by and watch,' she said. In that moment, Vennila thought of Appa and Manimekala, both of whom could preach from lofty heights great big things found only in books, while she, with no learning or wisdom, standing way down below, could understand nothing of what they said.

'We should never trust anyone without due diligence, without testing them,' Philo continued, holding Vennila close. 'Wisdom of our elders. But we … the moment we like someone, we decide that's the person for us and do our best to overcome all barriers to make that person ours. And the moment that's done, we start doubting them, suspecting their loyalty. This is the greatest sorrow of our lives. Let me tell you, I feel sorry when I think about your akka's life. Do you think she will ever be able to trust him? No! She'll spend every waking moment wondering whether he will go off with someone else like he left you and went with her. And that, right there, is her punishment. And his punishment is that he will now have to live the rest of his life with a woman who will never trust him.'

Vennila, sobbing, thought that she did not desire to see Manimekala and Kalainayakam punished. Let them live happily as a family, have worthy children who will bring them joy for seven births. Her mind was full of such virtuous considerations, but her heart did not stop raining sorrow.

That night, Philomena told her a story from a faraway land. She told it to her as though she was telling it to a child, holding Vennila's head in her lap and gently stroking her shoulder.

There was an ancient Greek king, Tereus, who married a princess named Procne. After a few years of marriage, one day, Procne expressed a wish to see her sister, Philomela, in Athens. Why travel all the way there, I will bring her to you, said Tereus, and went off to fetch Philomela. On the way back, unable to contain his lust for her, he took her to a cabin in the woods and raped her. And to keep her from ever telling her sister about it, he cut off her tongue and left her locked up in the cabin. Over time, Philomela wove a tapestry that told the story of what had happened to her and sent it to Procne. An incensed Procne rescued her sister and set out to exact revenge on her husband.

To this day, Vennila cannot reconcile with what happened in the story at this point. Even though she knows, only too well, what women are capable of, what cruelties they are capable of, if pushed into extreme states of anger and helplessness.

Procne exacted her revenge by killing their son, Itys, boiling his flesh and feeding it to her husband. It was only half-way through the meal that Tereus realized what had happened. He chased the sisters wanting to murder both of them. They called desperately to the gods to save them, and they did: they turned Procne into a swallow and Philomela into a nightingale. And Tereus, they turned him into a hoopoe. A sad end to a wretched story.

The story only intensified Vennila's sorrow. There was no conceivable parallel between the story of Procne and Philomela and Vennila and Manimekala. Neither was Kalainayakam Tereus. So, why, she wondered, did Philomena tell her this story?

'Everyone who experiences sorrow thinks that theirs is the worst,' Philo continued, smiling. 'If we hit the floor in anger, we'll only end up hurting our hand. And so it is when we beat our chests in times of intense sorrow. It is best not to hurt ourselves more. This much we can try. Forgetting, well, that might be hard, but we can try not to hurt ourselves again and again by remembering. We can teach ourselves to think of it as something that happened to someone else. "The Vennila who was betrayed by her husband and her sister – that Vennila is not me; it was never me." See, you should train yourself to think that way. Then you can separate memory from sorrow, from heartache, dry its tears. That's what I did, continue to do still because I have not mastered it fully yet. The mummification of an ache, a handful of memories, a whole life itself, so that it is no longer alive, nor is it going to rot. We just transform into pyramids that move about.'

All that night, Philomena talked to Vennila, while Vennila's mind was taken up with one question: Who was Philomena?

Was she Procne in the story or Philomela? It was clear enough who Tereus was. Vennila had not seen a single photograph of Samuel sir anywhere in that house. Once, curious to know what he looked like, she had asked Philo, and she had said something about not wanting to imprison the dead on walls, or some such.

After that night, their relationship solidified and became stronger. On one of her good days, when she was able to move around, Philo told Vennila that she was going on a ten-day trip. Vennila could go to her village if she so desired, she said, or stay on here. She was going on this trip with some other women, not quite strangers although she had never met any of them in person. Vennila was concerned whether Philo would be able to travel alone.

'Not alone. I told you, there are ten others with me,' Philo said. 'I'd take you too with me, but these are all women over forty. Too old for you. You'll be bored!'

The tune she was humming flowed out of the room into the open.

'Now you know,' she said, 'I'm the nightingale that sings, not the swallow that chirps quietly.'

The answer to the unasked question that was frothing inside Vennila. She did not know what kind of bird a swallow was, but she thought she could be the bird that chirped quietly, that caused the death of its own child by its carelessness. The difference was that she only knew about the betrayal after she had done the deed.

Days went by with preparations for the journey. Busy days until, two days before the journey, Philo collapsed.

'Too much excitement!' Philo said. 'It's always like this with me. Miss out on tasting things just as they are about to reach my lips. Tongue throbbing with the anticipation, eyes half-closed, mind trying to guess what fruit juice it will be and how potent ... And the next thing I experience will be the sound of the glass slipping and shattering on the floor, the juice spilling everywhere!'

Her doctor scolded her for planning to go on this journey, for forgetting that she was in no physical condition to undertake such trips, that her remissions were just temporary respites.

'Why don't you go?' Philo asked Vennila that night. 'You've never been anywhere. They are not your age group, true, but they would also have experienced what you've experienced in life. You'll fit right in.'

A journey with some older women who were different from her. She was only a home nurse, from a poor background, one who did not possess even a smartphone, while they, she assumed, were educated women from a higher class. She did not want the charity or happiness that chance brought her. Still, faced with Philo's relentless persuasion, she agreed. Philo told her that the journey had been organized by a woman named Mudritha and showed her photographs of some of the women going on the trip. One of them, named Hannah, had a slight resemblance to Manimekala, and Vennila felt an instant attraction towards her. We will become friends on this journey, she told herself. Hannah seemed younger than the other women. Vennila herself was only thirty-two.

Philomena considered whether she should let Mudritha or the tour operator know about the change of plans. Then, thinking about the complications it might entail, she decided against it. Let no one figure out until they were well on their way that it was not Philomena but her home nurse Vennila who was with them. With a mischievous smile, Philo gave the outfits she had bought for the trip to Vennila.

THE DAY BEFORE she is to set off on her trip, on her way back from the tailor shop after getting the clothes resized, it occurs to

Vennila that she has not been on a train since that journey, seven years ago, on the Tea Garden Express. Like pages in a moth-eaten book, the old days flutter in her mind, days when her life was set to the rhythm of trains and a train station. The railway tracks visible from the old quarters and the trains that rushed over them, the neem tree in the yard, the tattered *Thirukkural* that Appa read. Tears fill her eyes as she thinks of her father who she has not seen since then, perhaps never would again.

The following day, as she gives some final instructions to the temporary nurse who has come to look after Philo in her absence, kisses Philo on her forehead, and leaves, Vennila's heart leaps. She is on a journey even if as a last-minute stand-in for someone else. A journey all of her own. 'Aakamalavai arivanoolaar pokapuvanam undu enappulankollal,' she whispers. But she is not going to other worlds in search of pleasure. This world, right here, held joy, and she is going discover some of the paths to it for herself.

HANNAH

The Lord kills and brings to life;
he brings down to Sheol and raises up.
The Lord makes poor and makes rich;
he brings low, he also exalts.

… the Lord is a God of knowledge,
and by him actions are weighed.

Valyamma, reading the Song of Hannah from the Old Testament. I know she is doing it in such a loud voice because she wants me to hear it. Little does she know that I, lying here quietly in an easy chair in this room, know it word for word. Rufeenamma sister at the boarding school in Ramapuram taught it to me all those years ago. Nithyagarbhini, we used to call her – perpetually pregnant – because the poor woman had a belly that stuck out from her plump body. The older girls in the high school made fun of her and disobeyed her all the time. And when, at the evening prayer, after the fifty-three Hail Marys, Rufeenamma sister handed me the Old Testament and said, 'Go to the Book of Samuel and read the Song of Hannah, loudly now,' she was actually addressing them.

I told myself that she gave me this job not because my name was Hannah Maria but because I was good at elocution and singing. And I would oblige happily, a bit arrogantly as well, and open my throat and read:

> Talk no more so very proudly,
> let no arrogance come from your mouth;
> for the Lord is a God of knowledge,
> and by him actions are weighed.

As I read, Rufeenamma would glance at those unruly girls. And they were angry at me, not her. It has taken me years to realize that I am destined, always, to be punished for inadvertent mistakes. If I were woken up from my sleep and asked to recite the Song of Hannah, I could do it perfectly, even now, but I suffered their wrath. They pushed me out of the early morning queue for the bathroom, emptied the bucket I had painstakingly filled with the thread-thin trickle of water from the tap, jostled me as we washed our plates in the mess hall. 'Go complain to Nithyagarbhini, why don't you?' they needled me, but I said nothing because I was scared of Rufeenamma. Although she singled me out to read the Bible at the evening prayer, she showed me no affection. If I dozed off at study time, she pinched my arm as hard as she could with no consideration for the fact that it was 10.30 in the night and that I was only eight years old.

And now here is Valyamma, trying to upset me by reading aloud the Bible passage that I had read almost every single day at the age of eight. Not a chance, Valyamma, I mutter, smiling. Outside, the eleven o'clock sun shimmers gently.

The window of my room opens to the southern veranda. There was an elanji tree there once, and every morning, as soon as I woke up, I would run to it, pick up the flowers strewn on the ground and put them in a coconut shell. In the late afternoon, my amma and kunjammas would sit on the veranda, chatting and stringing the flowers into long garlands. One for the Virgin Mother in her glass case at home, another to give to Polly sister at the morning Qurbana to put around the neck of the Virgin Mary at the church.

Valyamma would scold them for sitting around stringing garlands. Cut some grass for the cow instead, feckless women, she would scold, but she loved it when they gave her a string of the flowers. She would hold it in both her hands, inhale its aroma, and place it at the bottom of her clothes-trunk. In those days, all her clothes smelled of elanji flowers.

Now, sitting here staring out of the window, I imagine that the breeze still carries that scent. I flare my nostrils, inhale deeply, trying to take it in. Foolishness, I know, because that elanji was consigned to memory a long time ago. There would never be another one in its place.

It is not just the elanji that has disappeared. My old house is almost gone too. Each time I come home, I feel I am looking at a different house with newer and newer extensions added to it, turning the old house with its wrap-around veranda and elegant pillars into an ugly thing. That is how things are, I think. It is risky to tear down the old and build the new in its place; easier just to tack on appendages. And if it does not work, blame it on the old and wash your hands off it. Still, on every return, I am confused, wonder where my old house is. I tell myself it doesn't matter what shape or form the house is in because it doesn't exactly affect me. It was never mine; I have done nothing at all for it.

'… a land with fine, large cities that you did not build, houses filled with all sorts of goods that you did not fill, hewn cisterns that you did not hew, vineyards and olive groves that you did not plant…' I recall the passage from Deuteronomy. Experience everything to its fullest and turn back. Leave aside sentiments about the elanji tree and the old house with its elegant frame and proportions.

It has gone quiet. Valyamma seems to have put her Bible aside. It is time for her insulin shot, a task she insists that I do when I am around. Her arm is a scatter of veins, a bickering, squabbling tangle. I love running my fingers over them and use the opportunity to massage them, trying to coax and cajole them apart. Each time, Valyamma holds her arm out readily enough and then hangs on tightly to me, begs me to be gentle, and swallows the pain as the needle goes in. She has had these shots for almost thirty years now, but her fear of needles has not diminished. I remember her eating jackfruit, the fruit pockets stuffed with grated coconut and sugar. How she loved sweet things ... And now, for years, it has been a life devoid of sweetness.

I collect the vial and the syringe from the fridge, but when I look for her, she is not in her room. I call out, and finally find her in my room, sitting on the easy chair. She holds out her arm as soon as she sees me. I run my fingers over her forearm, rubbing along the veins.

'Do you remember the elanji that used to be here?' she asks, looking out through the window.

I am surprised that she is also thinking about that tree.

'Such sweet-smelling flowers it had,' she continues. 'Never seen the like of it anywhere else. When I first came here, it was only a sapling. *He* brought it back from Wayanad, you know, when he came up for our engagement, and by the time we were married, it had taken root, standing out there all smart and lively. Even the name of our house changed because of that tree – from Kuzhikkattil to Elenjikkal. That tree has been in my thoughts since last night.'

She stops and looks sternly at me. 'Aren't you about to do it wrong? The shot goes in the shoulder, not in the vein! Supposed to be a big-shot nurse from England and all – look at you!'

I don't tell her that I am well aware that it is a subcutaneous injection and that I was only indulging myself playing with the veins on her arm.

'That was lucky for us,' I say, instead. 'Kuzhikkattil – jungle in a ditch – what a boring name! But Elenjikkal – even the name invokes the fresh fragrance of the flowers.'

Usually, this is the time Valyamma uses to advise and admonish me. She sits quietly until I finish giving her the shot, then pulling at my arm, makes me sit down next to her and starts talking about stuff. I am bored most of the time, angry too at times, but I let her go on and sit there patiently, quietly. Who knows whether she will even be alive when I come for my next visit? So, I let her words in through one ear and out through the other. Words we do not absorb, take to heart, are like leaves and flowers on the water's surface. They will float away, eventually.

'I don't know what's going on, but for the last couple of days, I've been having all these memories,' Valyamma says. 'Forty-five years since he's been gone. I never thought I would live this long without him. Doesn't even feel like it has been that long – not that his being around did me much good. And the elanji tree. I've been thinking about that too, and the fragrance that would waft out whenever I opened my clothes-trunk. I'd give anything to smell that again.'

As she talks, Valyamma is staring out of the window. Perhaps she does not want me to see the nostalgia reflected on her face. She doesn't seem to be in the mood to impart advice today, I realize, and that puts me in a better mood.

'Don't worry, Valyamma,' I say. 'You know Ancy from Mutharathil? There's an elanji in her husband's house. I saw it when I went there the other day. I'll ask her to bring some flowers over.'

'O, no need for all that. I don't want flowers from someone else's tree. The fragrance of the elanji from my own yard, planted by my own man … On the day I came to this house for the first time after our wedding, he gave his mother the slip and came to me. Do you know what he said? This sapling is his wedding gift to me, he said, and that I should take good care of it. And I did. Whenever he went off to Wayanad, he didn't come back home for months. I took care of that sapling like it was my own child. I wanted him to be happy when he came home and found it thriving, putting out new shoots and branches. Well, our lives were always about making other people happy…'

This last statement surprises me. The person who always admonishes me, always anxious about what other people might think, is changing her tune now. What if I had heeded her words and changed my mind!

I knew her story. Appappan was already dead by the time I was born. There used to be a picture of him on the wall, one that someone had hand-drawn based on a tiny, old photo. A young man with a sorrowful face and dark eyes that looked like they were lined with kanmashi. A romantic artist from an older era. 'Are you sure he hasn't written a memoir titled "My Life as an Artist",' I would tease Valyamma. Restless journeys and meandering paths, that was the sum total of his life; never settling down, never finding purchase anywhere. Slipping away farther the more one tried to hold on.

He had been given a piece of land in Wayanad and was sent off to look after it – his family's way of extricating him from some unsavoury relationships he had developed, relationships that were formed in the world of music and drama that he immersed himself in, short-lived yet enough to tarnish the family reputation. But there had been no dearth of music, theatre, even love, in the new place he was banished to.

The land and the fields lay mostly fallow as he pursued this world. When he did cultivate the land, he was called away at crucial times of weeding or fertilizing, and by the time he came back, days or even weeks later, everything would be spoiled. On rare occasions, he managed to stay put until the crops matured, then went away suddenly, returning to find it all run to seed, lines drawn in water. Still, the land did not forsake him, did not send him into penury. Gathering up what was left provided enough to make a living. The incredible kindness of the good earth. It extended a welcoming bounty to all those who claimed it, perhaps because it did not want them to forsake it.

When his family realized that his life was still disorganized, they got him married. Only two traditional remedies for wayward men, for disciplining them, in Nasrani Christian families: Make them responsible for a spit of land, and if that does not work, get them married. If that, too, does not work, write them off; they are already in their grave, of use to no one.

Valyamma looks dejected, and that makes me sad. I like it when she is chatty and full of beans.

'Sing that song, no, Valyamma?' I say in an effort to make her smile. 'The one you sang when you first came here after you got married and got thrashed with a tapioca stick by Appappan.'

An old story that she liked to narrate with glee. It was in 1959 that Valyamma got married, a time of great political upheaval and agitation in the state. Back in her place, she used to attend, along with her fellow parishioners, including women and children, meetings organized in the compound of the school attached to the church. The parish priest insisted that everyone attend, threatened, in the middle of the Qurbana, to expel those who did not, to deny them burial in the church cemetery.

After the meeting and the speeches, there would be a procession. The song was what they used to sing as it proceeded. Slogans, really, that turned into a song when several mouths uttered them in unison, melodiously, with sincerity.

Thekku thekkoru deshathu
Thiramalakalude theerathu
Far away in a southern land
By a shore of ocean waves
In her husband's absence
O, Sarkar, you shot down dead
A pregnant lady, pretty Flory
If the blood in our veins
Like your flag is coloured red
Avenge her we will, rest assured

Valyamma sings this song all the time even now, hums it under her breath as she goes about her chores, mourning the fate of poor Flory. All those years ago, still in their honeymoon days, Appappan had not returned to Wayanad. On the fourth day after she came to the house as a new bride, as they were clearing out the tapioca bed alongside some day labourers, she hummed it under her breath. Valyamma was bent over, pulling out tufts of grass when she was whacked with a tapioca stick, right on her back. She straightened up in intense pain, and there he was, her brand-new husband looking at her with fiery eyes. The labourers watched, stunned. Beating one's wife was ordinary in those days. In fact, it was considered peculiar if one didn't beat one's wife; embarrassing for the wife if she wasn't beaten occasionally because that would mean her husband was not showing her enough attention. For Valyamma, though, it was a big shock. She always said how she had wished that, in that moment, the tapioca bed had split open and swallowed her. Still, what had scared her, shocked her, was not the beating itself but the thought that her husband might be a communist, a godless, churchless, unclean soul bound straight to hell. Sixteen years old she was at the time, an age at which one believed anything. But she figured him out soon enough, that he didn't put too much faith in anything, oscillated, changed colours like a chameleon, be it politics or personal relationships.

When we were little, the song, in her sweet voice, used to waft in the background, unobtrusive, as she weeded the yard, chopped the tapioca, or picked nits off our hair. By then, it had lost its sharp edges and sounded more like a hymn; nothing that could be recognized as political slogan was left in it.

'Ah, let it be, child, I've forgotten it,' she says now, deftly avoiding my bait, and asks, instead, 'When are you going back?'

I haven't decided. I have an open ticket valid for a month. I could stay on till the end of my leave or go back early if I was bored. A flexible itinerary unlike the other times when I have had to cramp everything into fifteen days, rushing around from the time my plane landed and not finding a moment's quiet until I was back in it. This time, all I have done so far is go to church a couple of Sundays and go for a ride with Ancy yesterday after church.

Ancy is an old friend, and my second cousin. She invited me home, but because I couldn't bear the thought of making small talk with her family, a dead smile fixed on my face, I refused. Let's go for a ride then, she said. In the beginning of our drive, she was anxious, muttered about not having told the family, about how they seemed incapable of having lunch on a Sunday unless there was beef roasted with coconut slices, about how her husband would be angry for not asking his permission. Then, gradually, she calmed down, declared that they could all be damned.

We enjoyed the drive, chatting away and singing songs one after the other at the top of our voices. I think we went almost as far as Alappuzha. Ancy wanted to get out at the beach, but I declined. We were not madammas to frolic in the sea getting burned in the midday sun, I said. On the way back, we stopped in Karimbinkalayi, and had a big meal with fried karimeen and crab roasted in banana leaf, washing it all down with cold toddy from an earthenware pot. After that, Ancy was worried about driving, so I took over. You're drunk too, she said, and we cackled when I retorted that I was not the type who gets drunk on a bit of coconut toddy. They don't usually stop women drivers during the day at traffic checkpoints.

On the way back, we stopped at my old school – St Augustine's. Should we, really, in this state, Ancy worried, but I insisted. It was a Sunday, no one will be around, and we will only be a minute, I argued. We parked the car by the side of the road and went into the compound through the wicket gate. There was no watchman to stop us. Several buildings lay scattered within the compound – schools, each teaching a different syllabus, a working women's hostel, a convent, a chapel, and a park. I felt I had entered a different world. There used to be only a small school building with an attached boarding house, and the convent and the chapel, with green spaces full of trees in between.

As we walked towards where I guessed my old boarding house used to be, I told Ancy how we used to make fun of the weird names the nuns had in those days – Sister Dressless, Sister Sulfuricacid ... She scolded me, asked me to be quiet. She was scared because her daughter had been a student here and she knew many of the nuns personally. Then I told her about a bishop we had named, while in college, Reverend Syphilis mar Gonorrhoea. This made Ancy really angry, and the tip of her nose turned red. She does not approve of making fun of priests or the thirusabha, the holy church, obedient little lamb that she is.

'Lay off the silliness and I'll introduce you to a sister with a lovely name,' she said. 'I think she's here these days.'

She took me to the working women's hostel. I couldn't help thinking that our old boarding house used to be in that spot. It used to be a two-storey building with a long veranda with round pillars. When it was achaar-making day at the mess, after supper and prayers, the nuns would sit us on the veranda and make us peel garlic. There would be no study time on that day, so even though we didn't like peeling garlic, we would get to it enthusiastically. The tips of our fingers, with their nails cut very short, would burn from pinching at the garlic cloves. Still, it was lovely to watch the creamy white buds emerge out of their plasticky skin. At the next prayer time, Rufeenamma sister would reward the person who peeled the most garlic. Only a rosary or a little crucifix, but receiving a reward was a matter of great pride. And we were allowed to sing, tell stories, or recite poems – on that one day, Rufeenamma did not object. 'Anayaatha-manivila-kkazhiyaatha-kumkumappo-ttanivaadaamalarmala-yavanikkival…' I imagined I could still hear Suma's sweet voice reciting the poem from our fifth-standard textbook. I wondered where she might be these days – Suma Cherian, the thin, dark girl with long hair. Would she still be reciting poetry in her beautiful voice? She would not remember me; I was the one who had worshipped her silently.

The new building, which did not have a veranda, looked like a concrete almirah. No one seemed to be around; it was a Sunday afternoon after all. As I wandered around thinking about the old, tile-roofed, two-storey building, a nun, dressed in a saffron sari, came out asking what I was doing. She might have seen me through a window, standing near the panineer chamba tree, and assumed that I was about to pick its fruits. Rufeenamma sister used to be like that too, suspicious of our intentions as soon as the tree began setting fruit. She would rush out to tell us off the moment she saw us near the tree, forgetting that we were small children and could not even reach the fruits on it.

Ancy took me by hand and led me to the nun. She was very pretty in her saffron – almost a pinkish orange – sari, much like a panineer chamba herself. I began chatting with her, disregarding the pokes and pinches Ancy gave me, warning me to watch my words. Let her wallow in deference and decorum, I thought, I had no use of it. The nun told me that her name was Marianalini. Nuns had such beautiful names these days, didn't they, I said. Whatever happened to Sister Petteneetta – 'just given birth', our childish parody of the name Petunia – or Sister Hydrochloric? As I laughed at my own joke, Ancy stood there mortified. I did not feel like addressing the nun as 'Sister'. I would call her Nalini, I said, and not Maria because my name also had a Maria in it – Hannah Maria.

It was when there was some trouble with Appappan's land in Wayanad, and Papa, Mummy and Valyamma had to relocate there for a year, that I ended up in the boarding school. That one year became longer and longer. Initially, they had thought that Papa could go over and sort things out, but it turned out that the problems were too knotty, emotional tangles that were difficult to undo. There were people living in the house Appappan had built, helping themselves to the produce from the land that ran into acres, people who could not be written off as illegal tenants or encroachers. They had emotional ties with Appappan, much deeper connections than Valyamma and his own family could claim.

These days, I, too, am aware that illegitimate, improper currents are more powerful and run deeper than expected, accepted ones. What flows is not blood, but a liquid thicker and stickier than blood. In the end, Valyamma went over to Wayanad, armed with copies of their marriage certificate from the church, proof to be submitted to the police and to the Party. How feeble those were, I would think later, evidence that remained only on paper. I imagined her standing before them, mortified, faced with evidence written in hearts and minds.

Anyway, I remained at the boarding school through classes four and five, until they sorted out the problems, sold all the property in Wayanad and came back home. I told Sister Marianalini about my time at the boarding school. She had not heard of Sister Rufeenamma. She must be dead by now, in any case. Even in those days, it had been difficult to guess her age – she seemed neither young nor old. Marianalini told us about a convent specifically for elderly nuns, but I was not about to go looking for Nithyagarbhini. I didn't have the time. Nor did we have that close a relationship. We chatted some more and left soon after that.

Back in the car, Ancy told me that Marianalini was quite famous. In what way, I asked her, but she would not come out and say it.

'She was in the papers. I've been wanting to see her, you know? Damn, we forgot to take a selfie with her. Could have posted in the family WhatsApp group and got some kudos. She's here on a punishment transfer. Will be expelled soon, I heard. Like she can take on the ecclesia and win!'

She went on saying such things that made no sense to me.

An older woman, waiting for a bus at the gate, knocked on the car door. 'If you all are going into town, just drop me off near the big church,' she said as she opened the door and let herself into the back. 'Been waiting for the wretched bus for almost half an hour.'

With her in the car, I could not press Ancy for an explanation. She dropped me off at home and went away, and as I walked in, I realized I had forgotten to ask her to bring some elanji flowers next time she came over. Valyamma disapproved of these spontaneous trips of mine. 'Women from good families don't go gallivanting about without telling anyone' and 'Only women who refuse to submit to manly discipline do such things.' Before she could start on me, I told her I had a migraine and escaped to my room, emerging only this morning, into the sound of her reading the Song of Hannah.

'Didn't you hear me?' she says, now, tapping my shoulder. 'I asked, when are you going back?'

'Soon,' I said. 'I have three more weeks.'

'How come you haven't been to your mother's house yet or to visit your uncles? Three weeks is not much time. They will disappear in the blink of an eye.'

Papa and Mummy were in Texas, visiting Bennychettan, my older brother. Hasn't Valyamma figured out that I had come home when they were away because I didn't want to spend time even with them? Mummy is upset with me, but not enough to come up to Ireland to see me, so I am not too worried. There is a limit to the amount of advice and telling off they can send over the telephone. I am not about to visit my relatives only to collect sacks full of advice, to take them back and preserve them like so many china-clay jars of spicy, salty pickles. No matter how carefully their mouths are wrapped with pieces of white cloth, the red oil leaks. I have decided not to carry these harsh, pungent words back with me. I have declared myself to be a traveller with no permission to take any baggage with her, and I will go back with my mind as free and unencumbered as my hands. I don't say any of this to Valyamma.

'Call Aanimma and ask her to come back,' I say, instead. 'I'm going on a trip the day after tomorrow. I'll be back after ten days.'

Aanimma has been Valyamma's home nurse and helper ever since Papa and Mummy went to Texas. After I arrived, we had let her go home for a week. I could look after Valyamma during that time, and as for cooking, she did it herself even when Aanimma was around. What Valyamma really needed was someone to do the dishes and wash clothes and take care of the house. And someone to talk to, well, not really to engage in a conversation with, just to listen to what she had to say.

'What trip? Where? Ten days? Child, you've only just got here after a long trip, and have to go back in three weeks. Can't you spend the little time you have visiting your family and catching up?'

I don't answer her questions. This trip, I think to myself, is too important to me. I want to go back renewed. To start over once again from scratch, to look for a new home leaving behind all my savings, foregoing mortgage payments already made on my current home. My beloved apartment in New Ross ... Beyond its white-curtained windows is a rose garden beside a green lawn. An enchanting view, but one I have not gazed at to my heart's content, never having had enough time between shifts at the hospital, working overtime, catering to Joe's sentimental requests to eat tapioca and fish curry, and collapsing, finally, into the bed at the end of the day. And on sleepless nights, there was only the grey darkness outside. All the while, longing to sit on that tiny balcony one day when all commitments were met, when I was not rushed off my feet. No hope now.

'Where are you going? Tell me. Who with?' Valyamma asks again.

I answer only in my mind. I don't know who I am going with. All I know is that it is a bunch of women from a Facebook group that I am a part of. Women from many different places, who love to travel but have never been on a journey for themselves. Odisha, as a place, holds no special interest to me. In fact, I don't care about the destination, or if they change it at the last minute. What is important to me is that I am part of that travel group and that we will go on this journey.

It was about a year and a half ago that I joined Lesbos. Those were days when I joined several women-only groups on Facebook and wandered through them on quiet mornings at the end of night shifts at the hospital. Everyone else made use of those unexpected moments of quietness to catch up on sleep, laying their weary heads on tables. Not me, I was going through a period of sleeplessness, and I couldn't sleep even after three consecutive night shifts, even if I hadn't slept during the day. Instead, I spent all my free time on my phone. I am, perhaps, alive today because of my phone. Spending a free day at home with Joe in those days was unthinkable. Home was full of secrets that revealed themselves even when I did not go looking for them, an oven in which I baked like a cake.

Lesbos was quieter than the other groups, calmer. I was part of another group, Penlokam or some such name that meant Women's World, that had organized a programme to demonstrate women's power and had promptly split into four. The admins of all four splinter groups had added me to their groups, but I left them all. These groups, for me, were places to escape the turmoil inside me, and then to be faced with more turmoil only worsened my headspace. I had never managed to make any deep connections with anyone in these groups and had only shared random things – photos of the indoor plants in my apartment, vehicles and crisply ironed saris on hangers, a few stories from the hospital, that sort of thing. My silly posts seemed to have a good reach, and so I posted more.

I had posted a couple of things in Lesbos too but had not paid much attention to it. It was its tagline that had attracted me – 'You will remember / We, too, did these in our youth / Many and beautiful things.' In those days, my own fading youth had begun to scare me. I had begun to suspect that Joe's infidelities had something to do with it. It was easier to think that; I did not consider other reasons.

I noticed Mudritha's invitation only a couple of days after it was posted. I put my hand up immediately. I am a long way away, I wrote, but I have been prepared and waiting for just such a journey for quite some time now. And the day after tomorrow, we begin this journey, which, fortunately, is happening while I am here. A journey to unfamiliar places with a group of people I don't know, or barely know from online chats.

Valyamma will not understand any of this and will not let me go. I don't really need anyone's permission, but I would rather not upset her. So, I tell her that it is a trip with some family friends from Ireland who also happened to be here on holiday.

'To Odisha?' she asks. 'What's there to see there?'

I take my phone out and show her pictures of the Sun Temple and Bindu Sagar. She examines them with interest.

'He used to tell me he would take me to Wayanad,' she says. 'Train to Kozhikode and from there in the bus. When the bus climbs up the ghat and you feel nauseous, just smell your hair, he said. It's a different world up there, he said, fields and rivers and forests and the cold. So many tempting things … and so what! He would go away once again and not come back for another year. Sent letters saying he was busy – it's the harvest, the planting season, and so on. Not all the time, mind, I'd have to wait and wait for a letter and for him to come back to me. All my life I spent waiting. Oftentimes, I've sat up all night with the wick of the lamp turned low, but he wouldn't turn up even after he promised. I gave birth to your papa, and he didn't see his own child until he was a year and a half old. Never took me to Wayanad in the end, not when he was alive. You were in Class 4, weren't you, when I finally went up there for the first time.'

I feel sorry for Valyamma. She has never known fairness. Would she and Appappan have spent even thirty days together in all? Four or five days every once in a while, four or five such trips, a son – that is the sum total of their married life. A life like the smouldering, suffocating wick of a lamp with the oil running low, and yet without the courage to blow it out. Women in those days didn't have that courage. Smoky lamps spread their noxious fumes all through their lives, and yet they waited for their bridegrooms, watched as other women, holding brightly burning lamps, went into the bridal chamber with them and shut the door.

'Fetch the Bible and read a bit,' Valyamma tells me. 'I don't feel bad about not going to the church any more. Your papa has ordered that I should sit here and pray, hasn't he? Still, I feel better when I read the Bible or listen to it being read aloud, like I'm closer to our Karthav. But I read a bit and my eyes hurt. Aanimma reads to me, any which way, mind, and only if I beg. The godless woman is interested only in watching those serials on television!'

'I'm hungry, Valyamma,' I say. 'I didn't eat anything last night either.'

'And whose fault is that! You know what all special items I made for you yesterday? River fish cooked with ilumbi fruit, jackfruit seeds and mango curry. Is it easy to find jackfruit seeds and green mangoes at this time of year? I persisted only because I thought, well, the girl loves it. And what did you do? Went off gallivanting with nary a word! Impudence! Well, it's all in the fridge. Heat it up in the oven and eat.'

I hug her, decide to wait till lunch time, settling now for a glass of water and an avalosunda from the glass jar. I fetch the Bible, its pages so delicate that a careless touch would rip them. It falls open on the Book of Samuel.

'There was a certain man of Ramathaim, a Zuphite from the hill country of Ephraim, whose name was Elkanah…'

I begin but am immediately stopped. Valyamma wants the New Testament whereas I like the stories and songs in the Old

Testament. The nuns at my nursing college hostel did not let us have the Old Testament. All copies containing it were confiscated, and we were under strict instruction not to read Song of Songs. Why include things that should not be read in the Holy Book, we would mutter, and read it in secret anyway, copy good lines into our notebooks. Eighteen years old we were, an age at which we were overflowing with the idea of love, a time when we pined for an unknown someone – 'Let me see your face, let me hear your voice…' I feel jealous of that old self of mine.

'…they made me keeper of the vineyards, but my own vineyards I have not kept!'

Valyamma recites out of the blue, and I marvel at the synchronicity of our thoughts. I tell her this, and she laughs saying that she is talking about herself.

'They had him marry me and brought me here to make me the keeper of the family's esteem and traditions. And while I toiled and tanned under the sun, I did not realize that the vineyard of my love was burning down to a crisp. I suppose my destiny was to turn the Kuzhikkattil house into Elenjikkal.'

I understand what she means, but I wasn't aware that she could talk so poetically. A bride to discipline and corral the wayward son of the family. He continued following the paths of his waywardness while she became the family servant, welcomed him wholeheartedly on the rare occasions he returned home, bore him a son to maintain the family tree. What if, instead, she had gone to Wayanad with Appappan? Tried to keep a vineyard of love? At the very least, left him to his waywardness and returned to the safety of her own home? None of that happened. She stood watch over someone else's vines while her own orchard of love lay parched, untended, until it perished.

Valyamma takes the Bible from me, puts it in her lap and, holding my hand, begins speaking in a low tone. This is how she used to tell me stories when I was little. In the night, after prayers and supper, she would sit on the wide, low wall of the veranda, leaning against a pillar. And I would cuddle up to her demanding a story. Most of her stories were from the Bible. Fireflies flickering in the darkness of the rubber plantation would scare me a little, and I would press even closer to her. And as we sat there, we would see the light of an approaching torch – Papa returning home from his shop. The memories bring tears to my eyes.

Valyamma is narrating another story. With her eyes half closed, her hand holding firmly on to mine, she is lost in the world of the story.

'Elkanah had two wives – Hannah and Peninnah. Hannah had no children while Peninnah had given birth to five. Every year, Elkanah went to the city of Shiloh to worship the God of War and make sacrifices, and he would give a large share of the sacrificial offerings to Peninnah and her children, while Hannah received only a single share because God had sealed her womb. Peninnah harassed her at every opportunity, said hurtful things. And when Hannah wept, Elkanah would console her saying, "Hannah, why are you weeping? Why are you so miserable? Am I not better to you than ten sons?" One year in Shiloh, Hannah prayed fervently to the God of War, begged him to bless her with a son. Watching her moving lips as she prayed silently in her heart, people assumed she was drunk. But God heard her, and in time Hannah became pregnant and gave birth to a baby boy. She called him Samuel because, she said, "I have asked him of the Lord." And when he was weaned off the breast, she gave him to God as his servant.'

'But if she was going to give him away to God permanently, why bother asking for him in the first place?' I interrupt Valyamma.

She gives me an angry slap on my shoulder. 'You don't

understand the indignity of not having a child, or the sheer joy when you have one,' she says. 'It's a mercy. A lifesaver.'

I can only laugh in response. My papa is named Samuel. Valyamma wanted him to become a priest. But he fell in love with Mummy when they were both still at school, and refused priesthood even if it meant certain death. I know all these stories. I am familiar with Peninnah too, but knowing Appappan's character, she is likely to be several people, not just one person.

And it was Valyamma who named me Hannah, she who was brave enough to demand what she wanted from the God of War himself. I have asked God for nothing; I don't want anything. Instead, I threw away the little I had, left it to Peninnah, and walked away. Elkanah's endearments – 'Am I not there for you?' 'Am I not enough?' – these, too, I discarded in the wastebasket. I don't need any of it ever again.

'Our generation ... unlike you, we didn't even dare think about things like divorce. What right do we have to separate what Karthav in His wisdom has brought together? But your generation – something happens and the next moment you go your separate ways. No thought, no worry even about what people will think!'

I get up, pick up the Bible resting on her lap and help her up. 'Let's eat,' I say, and as I lead her to the kitchen, I put my arm around her shoulder and whisper in her ear.

'I am Hannah, you know. Just as I know how to demand what I want from Karthav, I also know how to say "no" to His handouts. You are the one who gave me this name, remember?'

Playfully, she pulls my nose. A slight smile flits on her face as she serves me the food. I can see she is proud of her granddaughter. Midukki, she thinks of me – I can read the compliment in each of her movements. My vineyard, too, wilted in the sun, but I am not going to keep vigil over it and waste my life. I will plant another one instead, no matter what it costs me.

Later, as I pack the things I need for the journey, I feel I am walking back to the beginning, to the clarity and purity at the source. And with this journey, I will transform into someone else, something else. I say a silent word of gratitude to Mudritha.

Valyamma's voice rises from the other room: 'My vineyard, my very own, is for myself...'

Song of Songs, again. I grin and repeat it to myself: 'My vineyard, my very own, is for myself. I will never let anyone take it from me.'

SHASHWATHI

Shashwathi remembers, constantly and fearfully, something she had once read about suicidal tendency being handed down genetically. She has often thought of killing herself. In her younger days, the thought came when she didn't do well in exams or when someone told her off. There were plenty of people in her house – a big family of people with not so big hearts – and always plenty of altercations. The children, including Shashwathi, bore the brunt of it, were punished for the tiffs and tensions between adults. The fate of children everywhere, not just in her house.

At the end of a heated argument between her acchamma and amma, Amma would knock Shashwathi on the head with the montha before handing it to her, shouting, 'Don't just stand there gawping. Go, fetch the milk.' Not fully aware of the all-out war that had just ended, Shashwathi would wonder, as she cried from the pain, why she had to be knocked on the head with the metal milk pot. She was slapped also when her amma and her chittammas were in the middle of their regular cold wars. Amma never used her hand, but lashed out with whatever she picked up. Sometimes, in the height of her rage, these attacks would turn lethal. Once, as she sat chopping vegetables, she swung the knife at Shashwathi to scare her, the remains of an earlier quarrel fresh in her mind. The knife slashed through Shashwathi's forearm, cut open a long gash that bled profusely. Even Amma must have been scared that day.

After these incidents, unlike most children, Shashwathi did not think about running away. She thought of hanging herself, and she tried, too, many times, and failed because of her ignorance and inexperience. The moment would pass and she would wonder, what did I just do! What if I had died! No more Shashwathi; the loss only hers. Her quarrelsome Amma might feel a fleeting sorrow, and then redirect her endless ire towards her younger sister, Bhaswathi. That would be all. Even those closest to us deal with our absences ever so easily.

That was something Shashwathi learned when her acchan died. She was very young then, but she noticed how, after the seven days of rites and rituals, everything began to return to normal until, by the tenth day, it was difficult to say if such a man had ever lived among them. One less person among the newspaper readers in the front veranda in the mornings. One less command – 'Bring me some tea' – tossed into the interior of the house. That was all.

The shops and fields Acchan had looked after were not his own. They belonged to everyone, and so, her chittappans took over the responsibilities. But the huge debt that Acchan had built up in the process, that was his alone, and his wife and children were to carry the weight of that responsibility. It turned Amma into a full-time kitchen maid catering to everyone's needs. Still, she continued trying to enact the role of the eldest daughter-in-law of the family even when no one else acknowledged her as such. Throughout her childhood, Shashwathi's fate was to suffer the consequences of the tensions that arose from the situation.

They continued sleeping in the same room where her acchan had hung himself from the rafter. There were no other rooms to move into, except for the lean-to, a space with no proper doors attached to the outside of the house. Amma knew very well that if she stepped out into that space, she would never find her place back inside the house again. So, they hung on to the death room. It scared Shashwathi. Bhaswathi was only a baby then. On the day Acchan died, Bhaswathi had woken up crying in the early morning hours. Amma had fed her, put her back to sleep, woken Shashwathi up and gone downstairs with her. Acchan, who usually came home after she had fallen asleep and woke up only after she had already left for school, had barely been a presence in her life. But he died leaving an everlasting impression. It was she who discovered his swinging body. Bathed and ready for the balavadi, she had run into the room to get dressed. She had not understood what Acchan was doing hanging from the ceiling like that, but she found her frock and put it on before going downstairs to tell Raju chittappan, who was reading the newspaper, what she had seen.

The second suicide she had known was of her aunt, Ramani. By then, she was grown up enough to understand death, and had already tried to kill herself several times. Her biggest problem in those days was waking suddenly from sleep to see her acchan's lifeless legs swinging above her head. How she wished she could leave that room and sleep elsewhere. But it was not to be because she was not a child any more, and there was no use hoping that all the male members of the family would behave appropriately towards her. It didn't matter what had happened in that room, or even if a real dead body was still hanging from its ceiling. It was more important that it had doors that could be bolted from the inside.

Ramaniyappachi died on her wedding night. The family had an upper primary school and Shashwathi's muthachan, her paternal grandfather, was its manager. Most of the children, including Shashwathi, went to that school. When Muthachan died, the school should have gone to his wife, her acchamma, but it was not to be. Sometime after his death, in the May of the year two of the teachers retired, a woman, quite young, came along claiming to be his wife. She had a son, she said, and that they had a legitimate claim over the school. Muthachan had dabbled in the alcohol business at one point, and had met the woman at a toddy shop where she was a cook at the time. Shashwathi recalled seeing her once before when she had come to the family home to talk to her uncles. Sitting firmly in a chair in the front room, she had, in a strong voice, spoken about property shares and such things. Shashwathi had not understood any of what was being said, but she remembered hanging around in the vicinity, looking at the woman with the solid, sculpted body and wondering what she was supposed to call her. Kunjacchamma – younger grandmother – seemed appropriate but the woman looked too young to be a grandmother.

Acchamma sat in an inside room, her head bowed, as though she were thinking about the husband who continued to disrespect her even after his death. Her usual belligerence was gone, and she did not move when the chittappans called her outside. Ramaniyappachi sat beside her, wearing a dark scowl on her face. She had completed her teacher training course and had been waiting, for several years now, for a vacancy to open up at the school. Meanwhile, a few marriage proposals had come her way, but none had turned into anything. Ramaniyappachi did not want to leave home and go anywhere far. She did not like Amma or any of her other sisters-in-law, and preferred to spend all her time in Acchamma's room or in a room upstairs reading her books. She went to the temple occasionally, but the only place she went often and willingly to was the library. Shashwathi had always felt that she found the children of the household irritating.

The following years were taken up dealing with the cases Muthachan's second wife had filed. The vacancies at the school remained unfilled. Ramaniyappachi's face grew darker and her scowl fiercer. She stopped going to the library, perhaps because she had already read all the books there. It was during this time that Shashwathi heard, for the first time, about the condition called 'depression'. Once, when Maya chittamma complained, 'Her Ladyship has not deigned to come downstairs to eat yet,' Raju chittappan scolded her.

'Shut your mouth,' he hissed. 'She has depression. She needs a doctor and treatment.'

The word was a new one for Maya chittamma as well. Her husband's anger scared her and brought tears to her eyes. That same week, they took Ramaniyappachi to a doctor in Thrissur. 'Let go of me,' she screamed at Raju chittappan as he forced her into the car. Maya chittamma whispered that 'depression' was just another word for madness. 'Ha, I've been saying all along that she was crazy,' Shashwathi heard her amma mutter, standing at the kitchen door.

Medication and mantras followed that incident, and Ramaniyappachi remained at home, sometimes bright and lively and oftentimes steeped in a broody darkness. Shashwathi remembered that when the court passed the judgement that finally ended the dispute over the school, Ramaniyappachi was happy. Acchamma also sighed with relief that the shadow cast by the spectre of the second wife was finally removed. And in those days, it was she who emerged victorious from the arguments and altercations that exploded in the kitchen. It seemed certain that Ramaniyappachi would be able to join the school as a teacher in June when the new academic year began. And in April, she received another marriage proposal, this time from an old classmate of hers who was aware of her personal circumstances. Concerns about the financial and social status of the bridegroom's family were set aside when Ramaniyappachi agreed to the alliance.

Shashwathi remembered, even now, that the muhurtham, the auspicious time for Ramaniyappachi's wedding ceremony, was in the morning, and that it was to take place at the Shivan temple on the other side of the river. Ramaniyappachi bathed and tied a knot at the end of her long hair, and someone threaded a length of jasmine mala through it. She drew a kuri with sandalwood paste on her forehead, and persuaded by Chittamma, added a small pottu underneath it, and lined her eyes with a touch of kanmashi. As she left the house, dressed in a kasavu-bordered mundu and veshti, she took blessings only from Acchamma, bowing and touching her feet. 'Ahankari,' Amma muttered, angrily, and the chittammas must have agreed – they were all bursting at the seams to be seen blessing their troublesome and arrogant sister-in-law.

Wearing one of her nicer skirts, Shashwathi followed. There were other children too in the wedding group. The sun was not strong yet, still Maya chittamma walked alongside Ramaniyappachi holding aloft an umbrella, following the men at the front of the group. Shashwathi had never seen such a colourless wedding party. She had overheard the chittappans discussing the 'ill-timed' wedding and deciding on a bare minimum ceremony, but she had not expected it to be so joyless. The river was running dry, and they crossed it walking on long stretches of sand and across the few, feeble water channels that remained. A few more steps across some fields and they were at the temple. After the thalikettu ceremony, they sat on the veranda in front of the cash counter where people paid for poojas, and someone handed out idli and sambar served on a piece of banana leaf and tumblers of coffee. A little kadumpayasam followed, sweet rice cooked with jaggery and banana, leftover prasadam from the pooja someone else had paid for.

There were only around thirty people in the whole wedding party. As she watched Ramaniyappachi with the tulsi garland around her neck, Shashwathi thought that the bride did not look pretty at all, just ordinary, like she was hanging out at home. She had only ever seen resplendent brides, sparkling from head to toe in saris of deep colours and gold ornaments. Appachi looked as though all the colours had drained off her. But her new husband was handsome, a slim man with a thick moustache, his eyes and face brimming with kindness. Shashwathi, a teenager then, had decided that this was the type of man she would take for a husband. How tender his gaze as he looked at Ramaniyappachi, what love in his eyes. In that moment, she even felt jealous of her aunt.

His house was close to the temple. Shashwathi watched Ramaniyappachi walk away with the bridegroom's party. Her own people had already turned back, and she had to run to catch up with them. The return journey was not as comfortable as in the morning. The sun was high and the dry riverbed hot. She had assumed that they would all be going to the bridegroom's house. She wanted to see the place where Ramaniyappachi would spend the rest of her life, to see whether there was a room on the top floor of the house where Appachi would sit reading, a room with windows opening out to the fields and the river beyond, allowing the wind, the rain, the sun and the moonlight to come rushing in. She imagined that it would be in that room that *he* would kiss Appachi for the first time as the moonlight of the month of Medam took a quick peek inside.

The thought made her sad, and she was relieved when she heard Maya chittamma say that it was a small house with just the one floor. When the school reopened, Ramaniyappachi would have to walk across the river or take the ferry in the rainy season. The work on a bridge across the river had only just begun. Ramaniyappachi's husband had been in love with her for a long time, Shashwathi heard, but had not had the courage to tell her that or to ask her family for her hand. Now, at a time when Appachi was beaten down and broken, he had decided to let his wishes be known. What love, to have waited for her for so long, and how wonderful that she now had a chance at life. Shashwathi did not feel the distance or the heat as she walked back home listening to the adults discuss such things.

'I just hope my child will have a good life now,' Acchamma said when they returned, looking up from where she sat massaging her legs with kuzhambu. 'May Bhagavan look after her. They'll come here tomorrow, won't they, both of them?'

'We didn't really discuss that,' Shashwathi heard Sree chittappan answering. 'I'm sure they know the conventions. Why won't they come?'

But on that day itself, just as it was time to light the evening lamp, Ramaniyappachi returned, alone. Sitting in front of the house, they watched her come in, walking too fast, panting. She was still in the kasavu-bordered mundu and veshti she had put on in the morning, and her hair was swept up into an untidy knot with the jasmine mala, now limp and wilting, still in it. 'What! What has happened?' asked everyone, but she did not respond. To Acchamma's question whether she had come alone, she answered, calmly, that she just wanted to be home, and went inside the house. The chittappans stepped outside the gate to see whether her husband was following her, and began discussing what to do.

'Did she just run away? Won't they be worried? What shall we do?'

In that moment, everyone would have concluded that Ramaniyappachi's life was never going to prosper. Shashwathi, however, was thinking about how heartbroken *he* would be right then, knowing that he had lost the woman he had finally made his own after waiting for such a long time. What nonsense was that, the morning's wedding procession she had been part of!

Ramaniyappachi was dead even as the anxious discussion about her future continued in the front of the house. It just took her family a little while to realize it. Declaring that he would take her back before people heard about the fiasco, Raju chittappan picked up the torch, and Maya chittamma went upstairs to fetch Ramaniyappachi. Her screams reverberated through the house. Shashwathi, who had followed her into the room, saw it too. Ramaniyappachi had taken off her veshti and hung herself with it. Her mundu had come undone and had fallen off, her thighs partially visible through the underskirt she had torn to shreds in the throes of death. Inside her cream-coloured blouse, her breasts were pointy. Her face was contorted, terrifying.

Shashwathi would never forget the sight. And she feared that if, one day, she succeeded in one of her attempts to take her own life, she, too, would display herself in such a grotesque manner. She never saw Ramaniyappachi's husband again. Did he have the chance to kiss the woman he had made his own after waiting for so long? Would he have found the privacy for it in that small house filled with people? Or did he wait, patiently, for the night? How it would have hurt him to know that the bride, one who meant so much only to him, had run away.

These were the things that the sixteen-year-old Shashwathi thought about when Ramaniyappachi went, with no loud, heart-wrenching wails to accompany her, to her funeral pyre in the southern compound of the house. She wanted to hold him close to her, console him. She resolved, many times over during that period, that as soon as she turned eighteen, she would run away to the house across the river to be with him and never come back. She yearned for affection, for love as fierce as his, the kind that made one wait for years for one's beloved, that undid one when it slipped out of grasp.

When Shashwathi joined college and became friends with a girl, Preethi, from across the river, it was about that house she asked her first. Preethi knew the family and had heard the tragic story. People had talked for days about the woman who had run away back to her own home and killed herself on her wedding night. The man, her husband, had refused to come out of his room for days, not even to view the dead body. Preethi did not know what had happened to him after that. Shashwathi had heard, when the marriage proposal had come, that he worked in Rourkela.

He must have gone back, she imagined, got married perhaps. Faced with the trauma and embarrassment of his first marriage, he would have told no one, perhaps, and married some Odia woman. A village woman with green tattoos on her hands and a nose stud that covered half her face. She had seen pictures of such women. That woman would have given him love, given him everything that Shashwathi wanted to give. The thought made her jealous and she felt like crying.

He would not even have noticed the ordinary, unremarkable girl who was in his wedding party, or if he had, not given her a second thought. But she had, for years after, spent so much time thinking about him. In those years, she forgot to die. In moments of great personal turmoil, she did not think about dying but about running away to look for him.

Still, by the time she finished her degree, Shashwathi forgot all about him. That one-way love had been like a wild plant that had sprouted in a dry corner. It tried, as much as it could, to sink its roots firmly into the soil, but in the end, it wilted, disappeared as though it had never existed. Good thing, too, Shashwathi would think sometimes, because even if it had survived, it would not have set buds, flowered. It would have had to spend every moment of its existence hiding in fear of being uprooted and chucked away, its desires buried deep inside.

Spectres of the two suicides followed her everywhere, the haunting hard to overcome. Many were the incidents that she survived because of the sheer will to live, and for some bizarre reason, her life kept presenting before her such occasions constantly, relentlessly.

Shashwathi got married, and then waited, year after year, for a child. She knew she would never become a mother and yet she waited. Her husband stood by her, consoled her, but she did not want his ministrations. What she wanted was a child, she declared stubbornly, not willing to give up. And he, unaware that his empathy was only making her more sorrowful, was generous with it.

Her delicate womb was incapable of hosting an egg, but it nurtured fibroids, fed them lavishly. On long days of bleeding and abdominal pain, caught in self-loathing, Shashwathi died several deaths. Even more were the occasions when she wanted to die, and she tried too, many times. Women are more likely to die from a suicide attempt than men, and yet all of Shashwathi's attempts failed.

Then, one night, an unusual, profuse bleeding from her fibroid filled womb soaked the bedsheets and mattress. Shashwathi lost consciousness and fell on the bathroom floor. That night, she lost her womb for good.

At the hospital, the doctor scolded her husband. 'So much bleeding! Haemoglobin count is only four! What amazes me is that this woman is still alive!'

Her husband took the scolding with his head bowed. He had not been aware of the extent of her suffering. How was he to know if she didn't tell him? How was he to know that this woman with the sad face, who spoke very little but exploded in an occasional rage, was carrying so much physical pain? On certain specific days, she came to him to mate. In those days, she smelled faintly of sandalwood. The sprig of tulsi she wore in her hair would fall on the pillow as she lay down on the bed to receive him, and he would enter her, sometimes with desire but mostly as though it was a chore he was expected to do.

A ritual that lasted ten minutes, no more. In those minutes, Shashwathi did not feel like kissing him or holding him close, but she did it anyway. So that he might be aroused, so that he would sow in her his most energetic seed. She calculated her ovulation days carefully. What if it happened this time, she would hope. She knew from all the fertility clinics she had consulted that the problem was with her womb that could not nurture the egg. Still, Shashwathi did not give up hope. Miracles did happen, sometimes.

And yet, on every twenty-eighth day, she became a river of blood. For ten days she flowed, strongly at first, and then just a trickle, until, at the end of it, she became a desert. It was to this desert that she invited her husband. It was painful for him, too, and yet he obliged, for her sake.

With the loss of her womb, the ritual ended forever. Shashwathi survived those days with great difficulty, spent almost forty days in bed. Her amma stood watch over her through those days. She was not young any more. A lifetime of toil as the kitchen maid of a large household and the relentless battle of words she fought in order to survive had sucked away her energy and her health. But she had succeeded in giving her daughters, Shashwathi and Bhaswathi, an education, in getting them married off, without fanfare, to men who had jobs, however small. No one foresaw her needs and provided for them; she had to wrench it out of them, beg for them, even. She had waged an unrelenting war that went on for weeks for the sixteen pavan-worth of gold and the small feast for Shashwathi's wedding.

All through these times, Amma cursed Acchan who had mercilessly abandoned his family and gone away without a word, leaving behind only debt and disgrace. That one day had changed her life, made it worth nothing. It was as though someone had taken away the staircase that led from the top floor to the bottom, and this woman – Lalitha, that was her name – had had to jump, with her two daughters in tow. And when she landed, she stood up immediately, ignoring the injury from the fall. If she had not, she would have been trampled to the ground.

It was only now that she allowed herself to truly feel the hurt of those days. Shashwathi was aware of this, and in order not to add to her mother's burden, she swallowed her own sorrows and pains. Those were days when she could not even cry out loud. Having already experienced extreme pain, she will never feel pain again, she tried telling herself. Body and mind become accustomed to pain and immersing in it will help overcome all situations without shedding a single tear. Nevertheless, she felt it, all of it, and shed copious tears whenever her amma was not around or was asleep. She wanted to be rid of her life like a snake shedding its skin. She had read it in some book. A gentle suicide, without looking back, without regrets.

She would not have let them take her womb had she been conscious. No one asked her, took her permission, no one waited until she regained consciousness. It was a disease-ridden thing, but she had loved it intensely. How many years had she put up with the bleeding, the excruciating pain, hiding it all from everyone? Countless were the nights she had sat up massaging her aching legs. Even her husband, who slept in the same bed, had not known – she had not wanted him to know. Even if she could not bear a child, she had been proud of the fact that she had a womb that bled at regular intervals. They had plucked it away, the doctor and her husband.

Shashwathi stewed in a constant rage at everyone and everything. It was in one of those days that her amma talked to her about adoption. Lying next to Shashwathi in her bed, she brought it up as though it was the most natural thing in the world. It was dark, so they could not see each other's faces.

'You must get up, get your strength back, and think about it,' Amma said. 'I'll talk to Ravindran. Not someone's child from our extended family, but a child that will be yours, yours alone.'

Shashwathi had turned over, hugged her mother and wailed. That was the first time, as far as she could remember, that she had touched her amma so fully, deeply. In the hopeful verdure of her amma's words, Shashwathi recovered, healed. Years passed after that, and yet there was no child in her lap. It took forever to convince her husband, his family and relatives. Insisting, arguing persistently until she got what she wanted, was not in her nature. It would have been faster that way. She was the type who waited, silently, and it took time before people knew her mind.

Her husband had assumed that she had abandoned the idea after he had opposed it the first time it was brought up. It was only later that he realized that the desire had intensified within her, and by that time, it had become a thing that could not be let go of, that would swallow her whole. In the end, he joined her, looked up the Central Adoption Resource Authority's website, registered their names, went with her to the orphanage run by the Deenasevana Sabha.

Shashwathi wanted a little girl, an infant no older than two or three months, so that by the time the child was old enough to be aware, she would think of her as her mother. There were no children of that age at the moment, said Sister Pavithra at the orphanage. She held Shashwathi close and told her that she would let them know. The sister had seen many such women over the years, those who came to them with a flame of hope still burning in their eyes dry from weeping, those who hoped to search among the children to find the one that would be held close to their hearts for the rest of their lives. We can't just show you the children like that, Sister Pavithra would tell them, as gently as she could, that it was not a supermarket where they could browse until they found what they liked. The women understood; so did Shashwathi. How cruel to pray that a newborn would be abandoned by its mother so that she could have it. She did not make that prayer despite her fierce desire.

This, too, did not come easy, they realized soon after finishing the process of registration. Many of the requirements for adoption were beyond their means – home ownership, stable financial situation, savings. A child was a dream that had to be deferred, again. Those were the days when Shashwathi attempted suicide several times, had nightmares about Ramaniyappachi's grotesque face and pointy breasts, finally understood the true meaning of depression. She experienced it as a gathering grey fog that swallowed up the greenery as she watched, until it hid everything other than itself. Caught in the fog, she gasped for air, felt that her life was ebbing away, wanted to bang her head until she was dead.

Shashwathi was in the hospital recuperating from another attempt at suicide – an overdose on her antidepressants – when her husband gave her a new phone. Something to divert her mind, to pursue new things and relationships. Perhaps her doctor had recommended it as a way to help her out of the fog of depression. A smartphone, in the place of something else precious that he was unable to give her. A child was not the only thing that could change a life; a smartphone could do it sometimes too.

And it did change her life. She began to brush away the fog that had shrouded her, and the thoughts of death, just as she had done in those long-ago days when she had fallen in love with Ramaniyappachi's husband. WhatsApp and Facebook apps were installed, but Shashwathi spent most of her time on the phone reading and listening to new things. What she learned, she recorded in a diary. With equal enthusiasm, she wrote down the recipe for the chana masala made in the Saravana Bhavan restaurant style, the strange rituals in different parts of India, and interesting games from around the world. She could not explain why she was doing this – she had no intention of trying out the new chana masala recipe. Her husband joked that she was cramming up on general knowledge as though she was planning to sit for the Public Service Commission exams, and she shrugged him off with a vague rejoinder that it was not a crime to learn new things.

One afternoon, she was searching for clinical reports about suicide on Google. One of the links that came up directed her to a music band. The only reason she ended up listening to one of their songs – 'You Can't Bring Me Down' – was because the band was named Suicidal Tendencies. She could not remember ever listening to an English song willingly, but this song, by a band with such a negative name, she played again and again, and each time she felt more and more energized. A wild, unruly song, a headbanger, so removed from her personal tastes. It surprised her that she liked it so much.

Her life, she realized, had begun to change, become more tolerable and interesting. It was in one of those days that she noticed a message about a journey posted in a private group on Facebook. She had not been aware that she was part of this group until then. Something stirred awake inside her when she read that the journey was to Odisha – the memory of her early youth that had been consumed with the love for someone who lived there. A love that he had never known about, that, even if he had known, would have come to nothing. She had dreamed that she would soothe his hurt with her heart. The memory, even after all these years, transported her to the girl she had been then.

Quickly, before she could worry about anything else, she dashed off a reply that she wanted to join them. She told the group about Agni Purnima, sharing details that she had recorded in her diary a while ago. The dance, on a misty night, around a blazing haystack. No studied steps, no mudras, no disciplined, coordinated routines, just simple, organic movements. That night, in the group, the discussion went on for a long while.

Shashwathi had expected that her husband would forbid her from going on a journey with a bunch of strangers, but he surprised her.

'Go, of course, and come back refreshed,' he said. 'Go happily.'

Tonight, Shashwathi will get on the train with nine other people and the tour operator. There is much to do before going away for ten whole days, and as she gets on with her chores, she hums, 'You can't bring me down…'

And when she gets back, they will go to Deenasevana Sabha once again. Her husband's ancestral property, that had been mired in disputes all these years, has finally been divided up amongst all the beneficiaries, and the family house, although old, has become his. There has to be someone still at the orphanage, someone who could not come to her earlier because they did not own a house. Shashwathi and her husband are older now and can only adopt children above the age of eight. It does not matter. Shashwathi will give her all the love she has held on to all these years. She does not know who that might be or what she might look like, but she is there, waiting, and now the distance between them is shorter.

And perhaps she might see him, too, on this journey, Ramaniyappachi's husband, her first love. She can no longer remember his name, but how will she ever forget those eyes that brimmed with love! She does not consider the fact that Rourkela is not on their itinerary, or that it is quite possible he has retired from his job and returned home. She waits for the evening, happily humming, 'You can't bring me down…'

MARIANALINI

Yesterday – or was it the day before – Ancy came to the hostel with another girl. I don't really know Ancy except through her daughter who had been a student here. I still remembered her, so when she introduced herself as Rachel's mother, I said, 'Ancy.'

The person with Ancy was not a 'girl' really. She was at least as old as Ancy, but looked much younger, perhaps because she was very thin. Watching her body language, I suspected she lived abroad, and I was right.

They didn't have a purpose to their visit, nothing I needed to worry about in any case. The woman said she had been a student, a boarder, at the school when she was in classes four and five, and had come to have a look around. I could have let them get on with it, but I really couldn't allow strangers, however consumed with nostalgia, wander around the compound, especially when I was charged with looking after the place. They didn't come into the visitors' room, so I went out to meet them.

It had gone past noon. The ground beneath the panineer chamba in the yard was a carpet of flowers. As Ancy introduced the woman as Hannah, her cousin and best friend, she picked up a flower, smelled it and said that she remembered the chamba that was in this exact spot all those years ago. The building from that time, a handsome, two-storeyed structure with shapely pillars, perhaps constructed during the time of the British sahebs, was long gone. I had only seen it in photos. The current one was only a concrete cage.

'On Sunday afternoons, Rufeenamma sister would go to the convent next door and return only at dusk. Treesa chechi, who ran the mess, was in charge then. Sundays were less strenuous in the kitchen – we were given bread and eggs in the morning, pulisseri and meat curry for lunch, biscuits with our evening tea, and pulisseri again for supper. So, Treesa chechi would use the free time to catch up on sleep while we children made full use of the time playing boisterous games. The best one was going up and down the wide wooden staircases that produced loud, echoey noises under our feet. We would stamp harder and harder to make louder and louder noises, and wouldn't stop even when the senior girls upstairs came down to scold us!'

Hannah talked without taking a breath. Chatterbox, I thought, smiling to myself. I like people who talk a lot. Through the chinks in their unrestricted flow of words, they reveal deep, secretive things. They are like lamps, not just shining themselves but illuminating everything around them. See, for instance, how this woman brought me out of my noontime stupor and energized me? She seemed to have a clear memory of her childhood, even of the events from when she was only seven or eight. I suppose she tells people these stories now and then.

I, on the other hand, don't quite know how to speak. I go through life more or less wordlessly, damp and huddled into myself. What did I eat when I was in Class 4, I try to recall, and a path that ran through rubber trees, with several styles across it, and the taste of upma eaten on the school veranda come to mind. The upma left an oily fragrance on my fingers that did not disappear even after washing my hands. On evenings when Appan came back home early and took out his drunkenness on the pot of kanji, and everyone went to bed hungry, that fragrance was all that sustained me. A regular occurrence that Amma tried to mitigate by feeding us half-cooked kanji from the pot that was still on the fire before it was dark outside. Dried mullan fish roasted on the coals, a little crushed kandari chillies, or something similar, was all we could afford as accompaniments. The taste is still on my tongue, and it makes my mouth water, but I will never be able to narrate those stories as entertainingly as Hannah did.

'It's been about thirty years since they tore down the old building,' I told her. 'This building now, we celebrated its silver jubilee the year before last. Now this is also a working women's hostel. Schoolchildren don't stay in boardings any more.'

Hannah bent down to examine the potted plants, walked around as though searching for old memories. Would she find remnants of a time gone by? Why did she need them? Me, I don't want anything of the past. I dust those memories away as though cleaning an old almirah, wiping its shelves and sprinkling ant repellent powder, getting rid, even, of the old smell.

'They picked so much fruit from this panineer chamba,' she said. 'We children would stand around watching as Mathayichettan filled sack after sack with it. But Rufeenamma sister wouldn't let us have a single one. Maybe that's why I still have such a hankering and nostalgia for panineer chamba.'

I didn't tell her that this was not the same tree, that it might be the daughter, or granddaughter, even, of the old one. All convents have fruit trees lovingly nurtured by nuns who breathe life into them with water and fertilizer. And perhaps that is why they always produce such copious fruit.

'Bindu and I were the only Class 4 students, the youngest of all of us boarders. We used to wonder what the sisters did with all that fruit. There were way too many, they couldn't be eating them all! Then the chechis from Class 10 told us that they made wine with it. They said each nun had a priest, a special someone they were intimate with, and that they would drink this wine with them. There was this overweight priest who came to officiate the prayers during Lent. How Bindu and I laughed imagining him to be Nithyagarbhini's boyfriend! That was our way of getting back at her I guess.'

As she spoke, a sour smell emanated from her, and I realized they had drunk toddy. I pretended not to see Ancy pinching her, trying to tell her, in a hushed voice, to stop talking.

'Sorry, Sister, I'm a little excited and it just came out,' Hannah said. 'We were young and didn't know any better. How else do children take out their frustrations? Maybe it is because we can behave that way that we are less frustrated when we are children. Then we grow up, become more and more guarded. Things frustrate us and we have no way of letting them go – only entrances remain and all the exits close.'

I gave her a smile to show that I agreed with her. They left soon after. As I watched them walk away, hand in hand and giggling about something, I felt happy and jealous in equal measures. The end of Hannah's sari, dark blue strewn with stars, and her hair, cut to skim her shoulders, danced as she hopped down the steps. The sight was beautiful to behold, and I stood there watching them and did not go back to my room until they disappeared from my sight.

The office room is small. In the lethargy of the remaining afternoon, I feel it looks staler and greyer than usual. With its chequered tablecloth in light blue and curtains in the same colour, it would induce boredom in anyone who worked in here. I had, in my first or second day here, arranged a couple of money plant vines in a bottle lined with pebbles, filled it with water, and set it on the windowsill. But the woman who came to clean the room, Emily, had knocked it over as she dusted the window carelessly with her broom. It shattered on the floor, and she looked a little worried, but I consoled her, told her it was all right. It was an old, pretty wine bottle, round and green, that I had picked up a long time ago from Alexi's house, and I did, in fact, feel sad that it was broken. But so many more important things have broken, I told myself, and helped Emily clean up the shards of glass. I knew what she would tell others when she went back inside, how the sister had not scolded her for breaking the wine bottle, probably because she had many more such bottles in her possession. Not just bottles of wine but of whisky and brandy, and probably not even empty!

The thought makes me laugh. I have read somewhere that bad words are like feathers flung into an open space. They will fly away where the wind takes them. It was pointless going after them, trying to collect them all. Let them go where they want. I don't care. I am not the words in other people's mouths.

Emily still displays an unnecessary guilt over the broken bottle, and I give her consoling looks. I know that I won't be around for long, so I haven't made more attempts to decorate the room or make it more inviting. To correct, to rebuild – these are beyond me, I know now, and that I have wasted too much energy trying to do that. All I need now is a place to be, to live in peace, and I have already found that. She, the one who left before me, has promised such a place for me too. But I have promised myself that I won't run away like her. 'The Lord will cause you to be defeated before your enemies; you shall go out against them one way and flee before them seven ways.' It was about bad people that Karthav said this. I haven't done anything bad; I am pure of soul, and so also, I am not prepared to flee in secret. That is why I sit here in this tiny office room, accused of countless crimes and ostracized by everyone, my only job to keep track of visitors. The only people who talk to me are Emily and the chechis at the mess, and that too not out of love. Every morning, without fail, I attend the Qurbana. None of the sisters I see in the chapel talk to me or have even a semblance of a smile on their lips. In the eyes of the priest, too, all I see is hostility. I stopped receiving the Eucharist a while ago, a decision I took when there was talk about how those who did not seek the sacrament of penance should not take Holy Communion, and that no priest was willing to hear my confession. I may, I think, even have to stop attending the Qurbana. It is with my whole heart that I pray, at the end of each Qurbana, that I may yet be able to attend the next one.

The church and the Qurbana could be, at any moment, forbidden to me, and I think of these words of Karthav: '… you shall be continually abused and robbed, without anyone to help … You shall build a house, but not live in it … Your ox shall be butchered before your eyes, but you shall not eat of it. Your donkey shall be stolen in front of you, and shall not be restored to you.' Punishment for disobeying the Lord's commandments. I have not broken any of them and yet unjust punishments have been bestowed on me. And precisely because of it, I have sworn not to give up, to submit.

The evening crawls into the room, a dusk greyer, duller, than the afternoon. A few inmates of the hostel who had gone home return, sign the register on my table and go to their rooms. Their faces show the fatigue of their journeys, the despondency about the week to come. Still, if I look carefully, I can see the sheen of contentment the two or three days at home have given them. Home … some magic that can only be found there has given them joy, the energy needed to spend another work week here.

I watch them knowing that I don't have a home to run to any more, to recharge like them. I will never again have such a place. I had an amma, older brothers, an older sister and a younger one. They are all still there, but they won't welcome me any more, or be there to support me. Write a letter of apology and stay on in the convent, they tell me, don't cause us more embarrassment. People at the convent also tell me this. I will not. They are asking me to disrespect the Lord's commandments, trying to persuade me with the temptation that, in doing so, the blessings of this earth would be bestowed upon me, that it will be my enemies who come at me one way and flee in seven ways. It reminds me of the hero in a movie I had seen a long time ago, a superhuman who fights singlehandedly with his enemies and scatters them in all directions.

The image of my home nestled in the shade of rubber trees comes to my mind often, and each time I am filled with a sense of loss. We didn't own those trees, only the hut that stood on the tiny piece of land between the treeline and the road. Water in the rainy season and sunlight in the summer lived in the hut with its seven inhabitants. The roof of our hut, made of coconut palm fronds, had to be replaced regularly as it disintegrated, and every two or three years, Amma would go begging to the parish priest. And he would, through the church committee, instruct the parishioners to allow us to collect palm fronds from their trees. We would go from house to house, drag the fallen leaves back from their yards and soak them in the canal. For the next several nights, Amma would come home after a whole day's labour and sit up late braiding them in the light of the kerosene lamp. When the lamp ran out of oil, starlight came to her rescue. We had to finish rethatching the hut before the rains came. The begging would start months in advance, but the priest always made us wait until the last possible minute. The braiding of the leaves would go ahead without a hitch as long as Appan didn't show up drunk. We would help, too, until we nodded off.

Thatching day was like a small festival. Appan would come along with his friends. Amma had to prepare enough tapioca and meat curry for them and provide toddy to drink. When they dismantled the old roof, snakes and centipedes would scatter. Our home would be laid bare, its penury exposed to the world. But once the new roof was in place, a renewed sense of security would settle in.

A tender, green scent would envelope our home. Those who did the thatching would complain that the leaves had not been soaked and dried properly, and that it made it hard to lay them well. But I loved that smell and would inhale deeply, filling my insides with it. The green fragrance of the coconut leaves combined with the smell of the newly repaired mud floor polished with cow dung ... How I wish I could experience it once again. Home, for me, is that little hut by the roadside encased in that fragrance. But it is long gone, never to be reclaimed. So, I don't hesitate when I say that I have no home.

The bishop had summoned me to the palace. There, the father who was his private secretary and the father who did counselling advised me for over an hour. Retract the complaint and I would be allowed to go home – that was the gist of their advice. There would not be further actions and proscriptions, they said. I could take off my habit and return home, become part of the lay apostolate, they said, lead a family life, even. 'I have no home to go back to,' I told them. 'I left it all behind when I became the bride of Christ.'

Father Counsellor's face showed the anger that their words had as much effect on me as water poured over a downturned pot. The bishop did not say much, except, 'Please don't embarrass the church, my child.' Perhaps Father Private Secretary had already told him of my stance. I listened with my head bowed. He did not offer me his hand to be kissed as I wished him grace and left. 'My soul, go forth in courage,' I kept muttering to myself – an incantation I had taught myself as a way to deal with the fear induced by centres of power and the unbreakable rules and demands set by them. They have all strayed far away from Christ's path; they deny God by praying at the altars of self-interest they have built. I follow Karthav, Our Lord, and no one else. I may be able to forgive those who trespass against me, but I will not forgive those who trespass against Him.

It was in the May of the year Appan died, falling into the deep well near the church kitchen, that I felt the desire to become a nun in the service of God. My younger sister and I were to have our first communion that year. We spent our days at the school next to the church, learning all the prayers and getting prepared spiritually. Jobina and I kept quiet while the other children talked about the new clothes and shoes they had bought for the occasion. Amma had half-skirts and blouses made for us from cheap cheetty cloth, the expense of which was still more than she could bear. Chrysantha sister offered to give us the hair ornaments and net scarves. They were not new, and we were to return them after the function. As for footwear, well, we were not allowed to wear them inside the church anyway, so let the boasters talk about their gilt-covered shoes and sandals.

We were at the school when we heard the commotion. We ran towards it with everyone else and watched as they dragged Appan out from the well. He had climbed in to rescue a cat that had fallen in, and was on his way back after sending the cat up in a basket at the end of a rope when a step collapsed and he fell back in. There was not much water in the well. He hit his head on the rocks at the bottom. As they loaded him, bleeding profusely, into Father Kappalumakkal's jeep and took him to the hospital, all Jobina and I were concerned about was whether our first communion would be cancelled if something happened to him. We had so many dreams about the day, perhaps the brightest day of our lives, and we were worried that it, too, would be darkened.

Appan died on the seventh day after the accident, but our first communion went ahead anyway. Father Kappalumakkal summoned Amma to the church. The children were prepared and ready and there was no point in postponing it, he told her. As she left the church, Chrysantha sister called after her. 'We'll take one of your daughters, Elichedathi,' she said. 'We'll send her to school till Class 10, and if she hears the call of God, we'll make her a nun.'

Amma was jubilant when she came back home and told us this. 'I won't go,' said Jobina in a small, scared voice, secretly pressing my hand. It was clear pretty quickly who was to carry that responsibility. Jobina was the baby of the family; Amma would not want to let her go. I would have to, instead, I knew. Having one of her girls taken off her hands was no small thing to Amma. Normally, girls from poor households could not become nuns. They would have to take the vows of chastity, obedience and poverty like everyone else, but they would not be given a habit. Instead, dressed in a white sari, they were delegated to work in the kitchens and surroundings, to live out their lives suffering abuse and neglect. Servants to the brides of Christ. But Chrysantha sister had promised she would make me a nun. I liked the thought of going about in a snow-white habit, just like her.

I changed a lot in those days. I began to pay attention to the prayers and lessons I had learned by rote until then, to take in their meaning. And when I prayed sincerely, when I received the Holy Communion for the first time, I thought I could feel the touch of Eesho. I felt electrified. I know now that His presence, His touch, is truly felt when I am able to focus my mind, to think only that which is good, to yearn for Him. It is not like the touch of a human being; it is a touch that is felt on the inside, that is deeply felt. I did not know any of this then, and remember boasting to my sister, 'Edee, Jobina, Eesho touched me,' and so on. When His

Excellency the Bishop came to the Qurbana and implored us in his sermon to be kind to the poor and the destitute and to become brides of Christ so that we may know Him in our heart, I took it all in earnestly. I will become a nun, I decided, that was my path.

By the time the new school year started, I was far away from home, living in a house called Snehasadanam. What a name, Snehasadanam – House of Love – which had not an iota of love to be found anywhere. All of us who lived there were poor or orphans, and many were the indignities showered upon us. I put up with them all purely because of my intense desire to become a kanyastree, a woman dedicated to God. We had no homes to go back to, no one wanted to leave either.

After Class 10, I went to a convent farther away as an aspirant. It was the first step towards becoming a nun, and I had to beg and plead with the sisters and fathers in Snehasadanam. Recently, Mother Superior raked up those stories when the order to demote me from my post of the vice-principal to that of hostel caretaker arrived. 'What do you expect if you put a leech on a silk bed? Slither away it will, what else!' she said. I was the snake, rescued from the pigsty of a home to become Christ's bride, that bit the hand that fed it. As she said these things, there was not a drop of empathy in her eyes, only hostility. 'As for me, I would seek God, and to God I would commit my cause,' I would recite, words that I had learned precisely for such situations. 'For He wounds, but He binds up; He strikes, but His hands heal.' I took refuge in these words throughout my aspirancy and my postulancy, at the Ranigiri convent, which was a time of torture that passed for tutelage under a nun named Guruthiyamma. Horrifying years that almost convinced me to leave it all behind and escape, that made it seem impossible to stay on.

'Becoming a nun is not easy! You think it's easy to be God's bride? Endure. Endure!'

Guruthiyamma repeated these words all the time. I had to have something to find purchase, to find solace in, so that I could endure. To wait out the years until I was given my tunic and coif and my new name. None of my family came to my confirmation. Amma wanted to come but she was bedridden with a sprained back. But the families of my fellows were there, and it created a festive atmosphere. I did not feel alone at all.

Memories of those days still bring me joy and pride. No one forced me to become Karthav's bride; I chose it for myself, and I am not going to listen to people who tell me to take off my habit and leave, as though that was a tempting prospect. It is almost certain that the ruling on the complaint I have filed in the sabha's court will be against me. I filed it to prove to myself that I object, that what happened should not have happened.

At the trial – a farce, really – they only had one thing to ask me: 'Can't you withdraw this complaint?' I did not respond to that question; I have no idea what they decided to read into my silence. Three men sat in a row making up the bench of judges and interrogators. It was the eldest of them who began to speak.

'We've already begun action against you for filing a false complaint and demeaning the thirusabha, the holy church, and one of its most respected priests. The process is not complete yet – you're still wearing the holy habit and living and working in one of our institutions. The sabha is undoubtedly showing you, one of its members, mercy, even though you have done inexcusable damage to it. Forgive seventy times seven, said Karthav, and it is His words we are trying to follow. You still have time to atone. You've called a press conference before – a clear breach of protocol that was, as you know. So now, call another one, this time with our permission. Or we can arrange one for you. And this time, you only have one thing to say. That your allegations were baseless, that in doing so, you had been influenced by the Devil, and that you apologize unconditionally to the person you besmeared and to the sabha. That's it, that's all, and this whole thing will end. And afterwards, if you don't want to leave the church, we will send you to another state. We have many institutions, many convents. You can continue rendering services if that's what you wish.'

The eldest man had begun speaking on his own, but by the end of the speech, the other two had joined him. They had no questions about my complaint, not one. It left no doubt in my mind about its fate.

'I've been receiving plenty of advice and instructions, and I'm not here to listen to more of it,' I told them. 'If you have any questions about my complaint, I'll be happy to explain, provide details. I want justice, not these offers. I want to know why the person who wronged me is safe in another country while I'm being hounded. He was provided all the support he needed to escape abroad. Bring him back. If the sabha can't deal with him, the laws of the land will.'

My words upset them, and they asked me to step outside.

The next time I was summoned, it was only a nun who spoke with me. This, too, they called a trial. She asked me if I weren't ashamed to call myself a nun after losing my virginity when I had taken the vows of celibacy and chastity. It amused me. I did not choose to lose my virginity, I told her. It was rape, by a man who was a priest, who had also taken the vow of celibacy. And then he ran away out of the country when I filed a complaint and continues to be a priest. Bring him back, I told her, interrogate him.

The nun was much older than me. She called me arrogant under her breath, then raised her voice to remind me that I had also taken the vow of obedience. He is someone of great stature, she told me, a man of quality who would not fall into such temptations. She has known him for over thirty years, she said, and could vouch that he was truly a representative of Jesus Christ.

Not Jesus Himself then, only His representative. I had no intention of being his bride too. I did not say this to the nun. Arguing with her was pointless.

'Yours is a fake complaint,' she said. 'Sexual harassment is only a ruse to embarrass good, upstanding men that women who are whores – I'm ashamed to use this word but there is no other word for it – use routinely these days. Nuns doing that to our most saintly priests – it's a deadly sin! You'll be undone. God will punish you until you're destroyed, pour down torrents of rain from the sky, and fire and brimstone. Have you not read the edict that a woman who illegitimately touches the privates of a man shall have her hands cut off? And here you are! Are you admitting that you, a nun, did this act? An ordained priest, if he commits a crime, he can atone by sacrificing a young bull in the name of Our Lord. Meaning, it is that easy for them. Haven't you read the Old Testament? But you, your sin is unatonable.'

As she spoke, her face seemed to narrow and sharpen like the faces of evil witches in stories. She panted like a wild animal hungry for blood. Without saying anything else, I got up and walked away. She must have recorded that I did not cooperate with the proceedings. I have decided that I am not going to cooperate with any more of these trials when they have already decided upon the verdict. I will not attend if they summon me again. I will wait for the final decision, and on that day, I will leave the convent. The bishop is in Rome. The copy of the verdict, signed by him, will arrive by registered post only on his return.

And it will read like this: *Marianalini, who, by making baseless accusations against an anointed priest of special standing in the thirusabha, tried to bring disrepute to the priest and the sabha, and made serious breaches to the church's disciplinary protocols, is hereby expelled. She is no longer deserving of the title of an ordained nun.*

They would want to mark me, hang a garland of slippers around my neck, and send me out of the convent sitting astride a donkey. But I will not wait for it. I will leave as soon as I receive the copy of the verdict. Those who want to cast stones are already doing so. I do not intend to hang around for more. Still, I will go out fighting even if I lose.

The night after the encounter with the nun, much as I tried to still my mind, I found myself agitated. Prayers did not calm me, so I switched on my phone. After I made the formal complaint, when the media and the world outside the church began to discuss my case, I had felt the need for a smartphone and an internet connection. I still have no idea what salary a vice-principal of a school is paid, had always just signed the salary register without paying attention to the numbers in the columns. It was hard to live on the seventy rupees the sabha gave me as an allowance. Food, clothing, accommodation – these were primary needs and were provided by the sabha, but that is not all that is required to live. It is hard, but I have managed so far by earning a bit extra by writing study guides, proof reading, and working at the school public exam evaluation camps that took place once a year. Poverty is a constant penance for those who come from families in dire financial circumstances, not a special vow one has to make. These means of making a meagre living are closed to me now that I have been demoted from the post of the vice-principal. The convenor of the Action Committee that took up my case, Neha Joseph, told me to install Facebook and WhatsApp on the phone. 'Be ready always,' she tells me often. 'This is a purification. Like Jesus did all those years ago at the Temple of Jerusalem. People should feel the pain.' Only twice have I gone out into the world with her. And both times, I did not make speeches or sit on the dais like an exhibit. Let the church investigate, I told these people, strangers who were ready to agitate on my behalf. I had believed then that the church would take the necessary action, and I did not want to wash my dirty linen in public. But when he escaped, sneaked off into a foreign country, I had to call them, organize a press conference – my most unconscionable breach of discipline according to the church.

I don't usually carry the phone around with me or connect to the internet. The only people who call me these days are Vimala sister and Neha, and they usually do that in the night. That disquieting night, after my session with the nun who heaped accusations on me, I switched on the phone. And as I wandered through the colours and celebrations on Facebook, I came across a message, only a few hours old, about a journey, in a group that I was a member of. Possessed by an indescribable urgency, I sent the woman who had posted it a personal message. I would like to be part of your journey – that is all I said.

My body awakened at the thought of a journey not through the usual tourist spots in Odisha but through its villages, rivers and forests. I yearned for a change of scenery, to be away from this cursed place for a short while at least. Soon, I will be leaving this place for good and heading to a village like the ones described in the message. Vimala sister, with whom I had shared my novitiate, was in Bihar now, in a remote village named Champa, where she ran a small school and an ashramam. She had left the convent seven or eight years ago of her own volition, with no complaints or accusations. All she had told me, in a letter she wrote, was that if she stayed on, they would kill her. She never told me who 'they' were, but now, after all these years, I know who they are and how dangerous their wrath can be.

A roof to shelter under … Vimala sister has promised me that much when I am ready to leave this place. 'And perhaps a life like the one we had dreamed of during our novitiate, one with no lies, nothing imposed. A life that Karthav approves, where we can provide solace to those who need it. There are others here, too, with the same dream. It will not be easy, of course, but nothing is impossible for those who have dedicated their lives to Him. He will be with us, always, He will not forsake us. There is nothing to worry or to be frightened of.' This is what she wrote to me in her letter.

I don't know why I wanted to go on another journey before this final departure, but I found myself craving it when I saw the message in our group. Life as an ascetic demands abstinence, the suppression of desire, and it is what I have become accustomed to. And yet my heart insisted that I needed this journey. Perhaps because I wanted it so much, my message to the woman who organized it went unanswered. This, too, I am used to, so I did not give up hope and continued checking the posts in the group every day. Finally, at the end of a whole week, I received a reply. I had been accepted, but only because someone had dropped out, she said. The journey had to have ten people – no more, no less.

Some uncertainty remained until the dates for the journey were fixed because if the verdict on my complaint came before I left, it would have spoiled my plans. It has all been cleared now. The bishop will return from Rome only towards the end of my ten days away. By the time he signs the document – after reviewing it or probably not – and sends it to me, I will be back to receive it. And I will leave for good a week or so after my return.

This, too, is a trial. I did not give Mudritha any details about where I lived, and she did not ask me, and gave my official name for booking tickets and so on. As far as I can tell, my fellow-travellers are all family-women. What if they found having a nun along, especially a notorious one like me, inconvenient? So, I decided not to tell them beforehand. I didn't want to be ousted from the group, hence this harmless silence.

I told Neha about my plans. She asked me that I take an active role in the Action Committee protests once I am exiled from the convent, that I don't run away to Bihar or some other such place, that we make him come back and face the consequences of his actions.

'I'm not running away,' I told her. 'I've been a nun for twenty-five years, but I have not served Our Lord. I want to be able to do that now. If not now, never! There are so many more like me suffering silently in the convents. Continue your agitations for their sakes. I'll be with you, always, from afar.'

Making him come back – I know that is not easy given how influential he is. Still, I hope that this ember of protest continues to glow. Come back he must, some day. All those women just like me ... He said that too, on that night.

I had gone to see him to seek clarification on some official documents pertaining to the school. They were confidential papers, which is why I, the vice-principal, was sent. I had booked an appointment and yet was not able to meet with him during the day. He sent word asking me to come to the convent in the night, that we could have an uninterrupted discussion. Our meeting in one of the convent guest rooms began normally enough. He looked through the documents, clarified some of the issues, and I sat opposite him, taking notes. Suddenly, unexpectedly, he reached over and touched my hand. Then he stood up, came up behind me and drew me into a forceful hug. I recognized the smell of alcohol on his breath.

'Shall we have some fun?' That was what he asked. And as I struggled and tried to push him away, he said, 'Why? What's this show for? This is natural, isn't it? We have physical needs, too, don't we? Everyone does it – you must know that after all these years.'

He covered my mouth, first with his hands and then with his lips, so that I could not scream. I have, at times, wondered how a man entices a woman to mate with him. And there have been times when my body has betrayed me and become aroused, and I have repented with a hundred Hail Marys and the Lord's Prayer. Natural responses of a body denied its physicality, yet I have strived to overcome these lapses through spiritual means. But there he was, telling me that the physical body needed to be sated with physicality, that it was natural and not wrong.

The room was on the ground floor of that convent, off a long, dimly lit and deserted corridor with doors opening to other guest rooms, the visitors' lounge and the mess hall. In that small room, he overpowered me, hurt me until he was sated. As he left, he picked up the papers and told me he would deal with them by morning. A nun appeared, perhaps from the top floor, to open the grill gate at the end of the corridor for him.

My body felt as though it was caught in a hurricane. When I was able to stand up, I called out to that nun. Sister Rosalinda – that was her name – came into the room, shock writ large over her face, helped me into the bathroom and to tidy myself up. Be calm, she told me, wait for morning, and we will deal with this. She woke up Mother Superior and another sister and told them what had happened. They came, sat with me, and prayed. The Litany of the Blessed Virgin. All through the night and the next morning until it was time for me to go back, they were by my side. And when it was time, they did not let me go alone. A senior sister accompanied me, and all along the journey back, she stroked my hand, talked to me about patience, about sufferance. It was only when she handed the file containing the official paperwork he had taken away to the principal sister that I remembered them.

I believed, truly, that Rosalinda and the other sisters were protecting me, supporting me. But they forsook me at the crucial moment. At the trial, Rosalinda told them that I was the one who had initiated the incident, and that she had opened the gate for the angry priest who, having resisted my temptations, wanted to leave. My one and only witness became my betrayer.

That was when I realized I should have gone to the police, had a medical examination. Neha thinks so too. But in that moment, in the mental state I was in, it was hard to think clearly. Back at my convent, they treated my wounds and comforted me, but no one talked about the man who had done the wounding or acknowledged that such a man existed. It was only when I watched him go about his business, safe, respected, that I decided to file a complaint. My hope was that the matter would be resolved internally, that the sabha would punish him appropriately.

MY LIFE HAS been extremely uncomfortable from the moment I handed the white sheet of paper in which I had written my complaint to Mother Superior. What amazes me at times is not that I have survived and not wilted under the pressure, but that I am still alive.

And tomorrow I will set out. I have written to Mother Superior informing her that I will be away for ten days. I, who have never been on a sightseeing trip, am about to go on one with some women who are strangers to me.

Tonight, though, I am trapped in a line from the Book of Numbers:

'The man shall be free from iniquity, but the woman shall bear her iniquity.'

All holy books say this, only this. The women who will be my fellow-travellers tomorrow, would they also be bearing the consequences of their sins? And Mudritha, what might have persuaded her to plan this journey?

Before I go to bed, I pray for all of them; I pray to St Christopher, the patron saint of travellers.

MADHUMALATHI

What is the name of Draupadi's mother?

It was Roshanara who had asked that question. How long ago was that? Madhumalathi could not remember. Four or five years, at least. When she had stood up in the classroom and asked that question, Roshanara's thattam, the scarf she wore around her head, had slipped and partially exposed her hair gathered into a high bun. Unlike the other students, Roshanara did not wear a hijab, choosing, instead, a chiffon thattam the same colour as her salwar, wound carelessly around her neck and head so that it slipped off every now and then. But Madhumalathi had watched her fix it in place with hairpins when it was time to go home.

Madhumalathi had not known the answer to her question. She had said, 'Let me ask the Malayalam teacher,' or 'I'll find out and let you know,' something vague like that. It was not her class; she had only stepped inside because of the noise the students were making, left as they were without a teacher. On her way to the canteen for a cup of tea, it had started to rain, and not wanting to walk all the way across the yard and down a steep flight of steps without an umbrella, she had turned back to the staffroom when she heard the cacophony from the classroom. And she went in only wanting to frighten them a little, quieten them, but the students would not let her off that easily. So, she stayed, and they had a lively discussion on topics beyond what was in the syllabus. She, too, was one of those teachers who struggled, even after conducting extra classes, to cover what was in the textbooks, but still tried to make the time, in each of her classes, to discuss interesting things and allay the boredom of the students. Madhumalathi's subject was history, and there was never a shortage of stories and facts to discuss.

These students were energetic and asked her to sing them a song or tell them a story. She found telling stories easier, and when someone wanted to know the meaning of her name – Madhumalathi – she used it to sneak them into the world of the puranas. She could not remember if there was a puranic character by that name, but she did know that it was the name of a flower.

As a child, she had found stories from the puranas intriguing. Every day after school, she would go to her neighbour Indrani teacher's house and wait there until her amma returned from work. Indrani teacher, a wispy, old woman with thinning grey hair, was well into her retirement. She did not offer Madhumalathi a glass of milk or some biscuits. Instead, she gave her books containing stories from the puranas. Until Amma came to pick her up, Madhumalathi sat there devouring them. On days when Amma's train was late, she remained in the world of stories as the evening lamp was lit and the teacher sat next to her reciting her prayers, the dancing flames reflecting on her forehead with its mark of bhasmam. Madhumalathi would move closer to the lamp to see the pages of the heavy Puranic Encyclopaedia in her lap better. And then her amma would arrive and call to her from the gate, and she would place the book back on the table, pick up her schoolbag and run to her. The disrupted story would vex her all through the night. No matter how much she pleaded, Indrani teacher would not let her take any of the books with her.

Back home, Madhumalathi would suddenly be aware of her hunger and thirst. Who denies a child a drink of water, her amma would exclaim, and Madhumalathi would wonder why she was saying such things about Indrani teacher. She had not wanted a drink. All she wanted were the storybooks, and the teacher gave them to her with such love. She did not tell her amma that, every day, as she sat leaning against a pillar on the veranda in Indrani teacher's house, she would pray that her train ran late. Instead, as she blew into the glass of hot Horlicks and drank it slowly, she would tell her a story that she had read that day. Amma would barely listen, but would let her continue until she would tell her to go wash up and read her schoolbooks. Madhumalathi would abandon the half-finished story and run off to do as she had been told. All her evenings followed this pattern until she reached Class 7.

That year, Indrani teacher died. The house that she had taken good care of, the books, the trees in the compound, the flowers, everything lay abandoned. Jumping over the gate, and later opening it fearlessly, children went into the compound to pick mangoes. Thinking about the books and stories that were imprisoned inside the house, Madhumalathi felt a deep sorrow. After the funeral, Indrani teacher's son had locked up the house and gone away. She did not know whether he would return, and even though they were neighbours, they did not have his address. If he did come back one day and open the house, she would ask him for the books, make them hers, she told herself.

In the years that followed, as Madhumalathi watched, the house disintegrated, termite-ridden and the compound overgrown. No one went inside any more, not even for the honey-sweet mangoes that fell off the trees. And finally, in the rainy season of the year she started college, it collapsed.

One evening, when she got back from college, the screaming rain was falling on a pile of roof tiles over a mound of dirt. It was foolish to look for books among the decaying household goods buried under. Even today, stories invoke that image in her mind – a house made of stories, crumbled in a heap.

Back in the staffroom after the class, Madhumalathi remembered the answer to Roshanara's question. Draupadi and her brother Dhrishtadyumnan were not born of a mother. They were born out of the sacrificial fire of the yajnam that the sages Yajan and Upayajan had performed for King Drupadan. When the yajnam was finished, Yajan had summoned Drupadan's wife, the queen, to receive the havyam, the offerings of the yajnam. Wait a little, she said, for she wanted to wash and cleanse herself before receiving it. Whether you come right now or not, the havyam will take effect immediately, the sage replied angrily, and put it back in the fire. Draupadi and her twin brother took birth from that fire. Madhumalathi did not remember reading the name of the queen who had missed the chance of being the mother of such legendary and valiant children because she wanted to take a few minutes to wash herself.

If she were to tell Roshanara this story, she would laugh. 'It's not like it is immediately going to be ineffective, is it, or how would test tube babies be born?' she would say. 'It is possible to freeze the sperm and the ovum, fertilize them outside, and deposit it in the womb, isn't it? That sage! Way too hasty he was!'

The new generation's interpretation of the puranas. Telling them that it was havyam and not an embryo would only make them laugh some more and argue that it was all the same. Madhumalathi also had a girl of Roshanara's age, but she was not interested in stories from the puranas. Still, if she heard these stories, she, too, would respond similarly. As a young girl, these stories had inspired awe in Madhumalathi, and she had never subjected them to this sort of rational analysis or felt the need to connect them to the present. For her, stories were just to be enjoyed, to be marvelled at.

Madhumalathi did not have another opportunity to speak to Roshanara until the last day of school, on the send-off day for their batch – the one day the students were allowed to wear civilian clothes, making the school bloom in colour. On all other days, the school looked as drab as the grey uniform they were obliged to wear. Roshanara, however, was in her uniform, which made her stand apart in the sea of colour. It made Madhumalathi uncomfortable. She had not taught Roshanara but had heard so much about her from her teachers – a smart, young woman with a mind sharper than her contemporaries.

So, when she came into the staffroom, Madhumalathi could not help asking her why she had chosen to wear her uniform on that day.

'Well, Miss, soon I'll be wearing nothing but colour dresses,' Roshanara said, laughing, pulling the thattam over her hair. 'Lehenga-choli, salwar-kurti … all with expensive embroidery and jewel work, like the sultanas in stories. And on top of all that, a burqa. I have very few days left to wear my school uniform.'

Madhumalathi did not understand what exactly she meant until, later that day, Roshanara's class teacher showed them the invitation to her wedding. 'Such a smart, intelligent girl,' she exclaimed, holding it up in the staffroom, 'there goes her future!' Everyone who knew Roshanara felt a mild sadness at her fate, thought that she did not have to get married this early, that she could have built a future of her own, that she was not someone who should sit unnoticed in the shadow of another's charm and wealth.

'If not immediately, in a couple of years for sure. Why else do you think many of us feed and fatten our girls?' Mumtaz, the

Arabic teacher, whispered in Madhumalathi's ear. 'Best to get it over with sooner rather than later. That way, there will be fewer hopes and dreams to wither and die.'

Madhumalathi knew a little about the battles Mumtaz herself had to fight to be able to sit in that staffroom with them.

On the day of the send-off, Roshanara did not give any direct indication of her impending wedding. What she did say indirectly, Madhumalathi failed to understand. She had walked into the staffroom saying, 'You're yet to give me an answer to my question.' Madhumalathi told her all she knew. That the king Drupadan wanted a son who was valiant enough to kill Dronacharyan, his one-time friend now turned sworn enemy. He did not have much hope in the sons he had with his wife, and so he went to the sages Yajan and Upayajan. But it turned out that his wife was unable to receive the havyam that they created out of the sacrificial fire. She was, instead, destined to watch Draupadi and her twin brother come to earth by other means. Madhumalathi still could not remember reading her name anywhere, this ill-fated woman.

'Ah, she must have thought she could redeem herself in her husband's affections by giving him some better, braver, children, right?' Roshanara said. 'The ones she had already produced were no good. And then she squandered that opportunity too! Stupid woman!'

Her response shocked Madhumalathi. The way young people these days thought!

'I love stories,' Roshanara continued, blithely. 'Stories from the Quran and the Bible, and those from your holy books, Miss, which are even more interesting. I checked out the prose translation of the Mahabharatam from the library. I'm well into it but haven't finished it yet. We have to return all the books today. And anyway, I don't think there'll be much time for reading now. But, Miss, there are a lot of nameless women in these books.'

Madhumalathi did not correct her and tell her that the Mahabharatam was not a 'holy book'. She might still think of it as a storybook, but she was well aware that it was in the process of being elevated to the stature of a holy book, and the people would soon read it with self-centred devotion rather than with the awe and amazement its stories inspired in her.

'Come back after the exams,' she told Roshanara. 'I'll check it out from the library for you. Read during the vacation and bring it back.'

'There won't be time for reading now,' Roshanara said in an off-hand way. Reminding Madhumalathi to let her know if she recalled the name of the woman who was Draupadi's mother, she left with her friends who had come to fetch her. Madhumalathi did not see her again.

The exam results were announced during vacation time, and when the school reopened, Madhumalathi heard that Roshanara had not collected her mark list. Her transfer certificate and conduct certificate sat in the office with no one coming to ask for them. She is married now, and living abroad perhaps, so why bother with mark lists and TC, etc., someone said in the staffroom. Madhumalathi tried to find out about Roshanara from some of her batchmates, but they had no idea what had happened to her. The PTA of the school organized an event to felicitate the students who had scored A+ in all the subjects, and they had come to attend the function. Roshanara should have been here with them too, thought Madhumalathi sorrowfully.

'She'll be on her honeymoon right now,' Mumtaz said to her in the canteen. 'By next year, she'll have a child, by the year after another, and yet another after that. Then it will be all about getting them into the best schools, arranging extra tuition, trips to beauty parlours, shopping, tailors, festivals, fasting, weddings, feasts, and in the middle of all this, frequent trips to the Gulf ... This is the life of young Muslim women from wealthy families. And they will bring up their children just like them and get them married off as soon as they turn seventeen. I bet Roshanara's umma is not even forty yet.'

The indifference in Mumtaz's words shocked Madhumalathi. The hijab hid the full beauty of her shapely face. She had seen Mumtaz's hair only once and only for a few seconds when, in the washroom of the hotel they had stopped at during a staff tour, Mumtaz had taken the hijab off to rearrange it.

Caught in the grind of admissions, new students and busy schedules, Madhumalathi forgot about Roshanara. Years went by before she appeared again one night, suddenly, as she sat up trying to prepare for the class in the morning. Reading books for the sole purpose of teaching was a tiring experience, so Madhumalathi allowed herself to be distracted by her phone. Events, dates, wars, kings, nuggets of boring information to be imparted, history written down in acceptable formats. There were no human beings in it, only supreme rulers and superhumans, no emotions other than hostility and violence, no experiences other than battles and conquests.

If she were to write a textbook, it would be a book about human beings, Madhumalathi was certain. A book about ordinary people from various time periods, and about the ordinary experiences of those who ruled them. An unrealistic dream, she told herself as she set the prescribed textbook aside, the same book she had been teaching for many years now. She knew its contents well, without having to refer to it. She tried, as much as she could, to make her classes more interesting by bringing in stories and events that were outside the scope of what was in the textbook. History, she felt, had become an old, overgrown mausoleum, and her task was to clear away the weeds and vines covering it. It should not be etched in the students' minds as a neglected relic but as a beautiful garden. Let it bloom with white flowers, spread a delicate fragrance, inspire admiration instead of inducing fear. So, she looked for stories outside of the prescribed textbooks, outside recorded history, that spoke of the ordinary lives of long-ago people.

But these days, more and more, she is confronted with students who told her, 'Just teach us what's in the textbook, Miss. What you're talking about will not be asked in the exams.' A generation of students who were focused, their gaze pointed only at their goal. Madhumalathi was afraid of them. It is not enough to see the bird as the destination of the arrow, she believed. One has to see the branch it sits on, its leaves, flowers and fruits, the bird's nest on the branch and the chicks nestling in it, the tree and the forest it is part of. And if one learns to look, to see, to envision, in that way, they would not want to shoot an arrow at a bird ever again, would recognize that birds are not things to be shot down from trees. But her students these days focused only on the birds, found joy in shooting them down. The young person in her own home was exactly like them too. Still, if there was even one student in her class who, with wide, interested eyes, sat expecting stories, she strived to include them. By the time this tribe became extinct, she would have retired from her work as a teacher.

The next day's class was about the Mughal dynasty. Running her fingers across the spines of books, she stopped at one about Jahanara Begum, the Mughal princess who was also a poet and scholar. Jahanara Begum had helped her father, the emperor Shah Jahan, in governance and political matters, strived to attain unity between Hindus and Muslims through her work. She was the lover of the Bundi king, Duler. Madhumalathi decided that she would tell her students the story of the downfall of the Mughal empire through Jahanara's story. What better story than hers to tell when speaking of the greed for power and the violence that transcends even ties of blood!

Her phone pinged, announcing a message on WhatsApp. It was from an unknown number. It read: *Miss, not sure whether you'll remember me if I told you my name.*

Somewhat irritated, Madhumalathi wrote back: *Tell me your name. Only then I can say if I remember you or not.*

Every so often, students sent her these random messages. They had all the free time in the world and assumed that their teachers did too.

I'm Roshanara, Miss, came the reply. Surprised, Madhumalathi sent back: *Oh, you!*

Yes, me, Miss! After a long time. An emoji smiled at her.

Roshanara did not seem to share the excitement or eagerness that Madhumalathi felt at hearing from her after all this time. She chatted for a while, asked after her teachers. Switching to voice messages, she made a simple request: She wanted her mark list and her TC because she wanted to enrol for a degree with the distance education department of a university. So many years had passed since her school exam, and the mark list would have been sent back. When Madhumalathi told her that it might take some time and some convoluted correspondence with the education department, Roshanara was quick to let go of the idea, although she sounded downcast.

It occurred to Madhumalathi then that Roshanara might not have contacted her for this purpose alone, and that she might have used it as a way to begin a conversation. But what could she want from her, Madhumalathi could not guess.

Before she said good night and signed off, Roshanara asked, 'Do you know the story of a woman named Sudarshana, Miss? Somebody who prayed that she wanted to be born as a woman in her next birth too, or some such?'

Nothing came to Madhumalathi's mind, not even a vague memory of having read something like that. Helplessly, she gave her the usual excuse that teachers give to students. 'I'll find out and let you know.'

'That's okay, Miss, just tell me later. I don't have any books here where I can look this up. How come you are up so late, Miss? I had your number all this time and wanted to message you also. Then I thought, would she remember me? Would she have the time to chat with me? But today when I saw you were online, I thought, why not! And I wanted to know more about this story. You must be up reading … What are you reading right now?'

Madhumalathi told her that she was reading a book about Jahanara.

'Oh, Jahanara,' said Roshanara. Her voice sounded tired. 'She had a sister, didn't she? Roshanara – my namesake. "Light of the world" it is supposed to mean. But she got herself sorted and wealthy by spying on her sister and helping to betray her. Lived a happy, comfortable life while Jahanara rotted in prison. No light, that one! Dark she was, just like me.'

Roshanara sounded like a mature, old woman with not even a trace of youthfulness in her voice. To Madhumalathi, it sounded empty of hope, of vigour. She had assumed that Roshanara was in the Gulf somewhere and was surprised to know that she actually lived quite close to the school. She evaded questions about herself, changing the subject each time Madhumalathi asked something.

Madhumalathi invited her to come to the school for a visit. 'We can look into getting you your mark list and certificates. And I'll check out books for you. Don't waste your time doing nothing.'

Roshanara sent a string of laughing emojis in reply.

'I'm reading a book that will never end,' she said in the voice message that followed. 'The only book I'll read now. I didn't want to forget what I have already read though. That's why I asked you that question. I feel I should remember the things I have read, at least to keep my mind sharp.'

'Aha! What book is that then?'

'Life, Miss, what else! And as for books, there is the *Ihya Ulum al-Din* and, of course, all the kitabs. Not sure if you know of these. You don't need to, I guess. All in Arabic. Nothing else is available here, not that it would matter even if they were.'

And then, without giving Madhumalathi the time to ask more questions, Roshanara said good night and went offline. Madhumalathi saved her number and examined her profile photo. Her face was fully covered. Even her eyes, which were behind a black net, were a vague outline when she zoomed in on them. Were they the same eyes that used to be beautifully outlined with a gel liner, lively eyes that reflected the confidence to win the world and an intense desire for knowledge?

Sorrowfully, Madhumalathi put the phone down and looked for the prose translations of the Mahabharatam to search for the story of a woman who wished to be born a woman again. It took a while, but she found her eventually in Anushasana Parvam – Book of Instructions – the thirteenth of its eighteen books. But this woman was not named Sudarshana. Nor was any other name given to her. Yet another woman who was not shown the courtesy of a name that could identify her.

To be perfectly clear, she was not a woman by birth, but a man, a king named Bhangaswanan, who had become a woman. Bhangaswanan goes into the forest to hunt, and while there, he is tricked by Indran, the king of the devas. Indran was angry with Bhangaswanan because he had conducted the Agnistuta yajnam, a sacrifice to cleanse himself off the sin accrued from earlier births so that he could father good and prosperous children. And he had failed to offer the prayers and rituals required to please Indran, focusing his devotion only on Agni, the God of Fire.

Bhangaswanan loses his bearings in the forest, and as he wanders around trying to find his way, he takes a dip in a pond and turns into a woman. He – she – does, after much trouble, find her way back to the palace, but Bhangaswanan's wife and his one hundred children are not able to recognize him. She tells them who she is, instructs her children to rule the land, and returns to the forest. There, she marries a sage and gives birth to a hundred children. She returns to the palace and hands over her new children to the children she had fathered while she was a man. The two hundred children get along and rule the land according to his wishes. This annoys Indran who still bears a grudge against Bhangaswanan. He interferes and causes strife between them, and in the end, Bhangaswanan's children destroy themselves by killing one another.

Bhangaswanan – now a female sage – is heartbroken, and as she wails, Indran appears before her and reveals that it was he who had caused all this to happen. She apologizes to Indran for the wrong she had done him. Pleased, Indran tells her that he will bring a hundred of her children back to life and asks which of her children she wants back – the ones she had when she was a man or the ones she gave birth to as a woman. She chooses the ones she gave birth to as a woman. Surprised, Indran asks her why.

'A woman has more love,' she says. 'A man does not feel the excess of love. Let my children who I gave birth to as a woman live.'

Her honesty pleases Indran, and he lets all of her children come back to life. Indran also offers to restore her masculine form, if that is what she wants, assuming that having known what it is to be a man she would choose to regain her masculinity. But she chooses her current feminine self.

'It is women who experience more pleasure, more joy, from sexual congress,' she says. 'I am content in my feminine self.'

'May you remain a woman and be joyful, in this birth and in those to come,' blesses Indran and takes his leave. And the king Bhangaswanan becomes a woman forever.

Perhaps she was given a name then, Madhumalathi thought, and looked for one. But the story ended there, without ever naming her. It was a story that Bhishmar told Yudhishthiran to establish that women experienced greater pleasure from the act of sex with men. She sent Roshanara the gist of the story, explaining, also, that it was not the story of a woman named Sudarshana.

Sleep evaded her that night, thoughts of the nameless woman occupied her mind. The story was right about its representation of a parent's love for children. No father would have as much love for his children as the mother who gave birth to them, so it was no wonder Bhangaswanan chose the children he gave birth to as a woman. Men only had a passive role in the birthing of children. In fact, they were only involved indirectly in all that followed the act of sex. But the idea that women experienced more pleasure from sexual intercourse – Madhumalathi could not accept that. If that was the case, wouldn't women be the ones clamouring for sex all the time? She has heard men, including her colleagues and friends, talk authoritatively about how men were naturally inclined to polygamy and were intrinsically incapable of being satisfied with just one woman. Rationalizations presented as jokes to justify their own trespasses. And as they pontificated, their eyes would gleam with a greed that made her flinch. If it were true that women received so much pleasure from sexual intercourse, how come they were not constantly searching for more and more of such pleasure instead of being contented with a single partner?

'Contented' – a word that annoyed her. 'Act contented', more like. If indeed such pleasure existed, it was not something

Madhumalathi had ever experienced. Perhaps there had been a sense of joy in the early days of her marriage, the desire to touch and to be touched, and then, if it led to sex, it did make her happy. But that was nothing deep, only a fleeting pleasure, and she had known then, too, that it was he who derived more satisfaction from it. As time went by, she had had to work hard even for that feeling, focus her mind and body on the act, thinking sexual thoughts, and for what! For a momentary sensation that was nothing worth talking about. She had then started acting out orgasms. He would not stop until she was satisfied – he was at least that democratic when it came to sex. She was adept at it now, in putting up a convincing act, before it went on and on, that she had reached that special sensation. She did not even have to focus any more, and could let her mind wander where it pleased.

Madhumalathi was convinced that most women dealt with sex in this way, so why would that nameless woman say what she did? Or was it Bhishmar who misrepresented her? That night, before slipping, finally, into sleep, Madhumalathi remembered another character – one who was born a woman but had to live in the body of a man. Shikhandi, Drupadan's son whose mother was another unnamed woman, the one from the Draupadi story.

The next morning, Madhumalathi woke up with a headache induced by the lack of proper sleep. Managing to finish her morning chores, she left for school, and then took a half-day leave. Mumtaz had her first period free, so they went to the canteen together. A Crocin washed down with a cup of black tea seemed to calm Madhumalathi's headache.

'Look at you!' Mumtaz said. 'On leave but still don't want to rest at home.'

It was impossible to rest at home, Madhumalathi told Mumtaz in a tired voice, and laid her head on the table.

Mumtaz stroked her forehead, and suddenly Madhumalathi felt much better. A loving touch can console the mind too and loosen the veins of hurt.

Raising her head, she watched Mumtaz drinking her tea. Mumtaz did not usually go to the canteen; she was here now only because of Madhumalathi. Should she tell her about Bhangaswanan and his comments about women's sexual pleasure, Madhumalathi wondered. Would Mumtaz have anything to say about it? Probably not.

Mumtaz got married when she was still in Class 10. Not 'got married', was 'made to get married' would be more accurate. It took her a long time and a fierce battle to be able to continue her studies, to regrow her life that had wilted away. Everyone around her, including her family, seemed determined to pour hot water over the tender plant her life was, but she, ever vigilant, protected it fiercely. Even now, Mumtaz talked, completely devoid of emotion, about the number of times she had tried to end her life. What use, then, asking her about sex and its pleasures when all she had to remember were instances of aggression, of force, right from her wedding night. Her husband's way of trying to prevent her from doing her post-graduation was to get her pregnant, but she dragged her big belly and went to her exams. When the child was born, her studies got disrupted again because she had no one who would look after the child while she attended classes. Still, she fought her way to a BEd course. Her husband threatened to divorce her, and her family demanded that she obey her husband, stop going to classes and stay at home. Yet, stubbornly, she persevered and completed her course. Her husband married a second time without divorcing her.

Mumtaz's husband was a teacher of religion in a mosque quite far away from their home. It is possible that he has more wives. He came to Mumtaz when he needed money, and on each visit, abused her physically and sexually. The children, all four of them, needed their uppa, Mumtaz would say, and putting up with his abuse for a couple of days a month was worth the peace she had the rest of the time. Two days of sufferance and a little money – the price she paid for the dignity of having a husband, a father for her children.

'Month after month, we put up with intense pain during our periods, and yet we don't think about excising our wombs, do we?' Mumtaz would say. 'This is like that too. It'll stop, eventually, on its own, like the periods.'

Asking her whether it was men or women who experienced the most sexual pleasure … Well, Mumtaz might slap her, Madhumalathi thought, smiling. She told her about her chat with Roshanara instead.

'Ah, her, Roshanara from the commerce batch.' Mumtaz remembered her, but she did not put much stock on what Roshanara had said about wanting to continue her studies. 'Most unlikely,' she said. 'I think she is from an orthodox family to begin with and has married into an even more orthodox family. Sometimes it feels like there are more and more people like that these days, especially in the new generation. Everything in the extreme. Women who only want to pursue religious studies, go about covered from head to toe, always concerned only about akhir, the hereafter. They have no interest in songs or stories or poetry!'

Madhumalathi recalled an incident from the book about Jahanara she had read the previous night. Aurangzeb, her brother, had banned music in his empire. Musicians of the land mourned, carried their musical instruments in a funeral procession to be buried, a symbolic protest against the death of music. Bury them deep, said Aurangzeb when he heard about it, so that they are never resurrected. Jahanara wrote in her personal papers that the emperor's diktat could not silence the flow of music in her heart, her internal music.

Roshanara, too, would have music flowing inside her, music of the soul that cannot be silenced by commands and censures. So, why was Mumtaz, who was herself the shining example of triumph over odds, so adamant that it was unlikely she would ever return to retrieve what she had lost?

'It's simple. I'll explain it to you,' said Mumtaz. 'Roshanara is wealthy. The person she is married to is even wealthier. Money combined with extreme religious belief is double trouble for our women, like a person struck by lightning also getting bitten by a snake. It wasn't like that in my case – we were lower than lower-middle class. Those without money also have religious sentiments, but they have more opportunities for compromise, for manoeuvre. Like a veranda screened with an old mat – it is screened, yes, but it also has many holes and chinks that let in breeze and light, that allow the view of the outside. But Roshanara ... she is behind a wall of granite. She can't see anything, nor can anyone see her. That's the difference.'

Mumtaz stopped and sat silently for a while. Then she said, 'I remember the old days. We were brought up ready for the cattle pound. Covering up awrat, living with iman ... "Aarante adukkale kerendathaa," we were reminded constantly, that we are meant for other people's kitchens. So, watch yourself, behave. All we were allowed to read were kitabs and hadiths. After the maghrib prayer, Valyumma would sit leaning against the wall and recite the Nafeesath Mala by Nalakath Kunjimoideen Saheb. Everything we needed to know, to fill our lives with light, was in it, we were told. And so beautiful it was, too, to listen to. Cook, serve, mate, reproduce, work like beasts of burden, obey. This is what we were taught, using kitabs and hadiths to give these lessons a spiritual authority, a divinity. Something we realized only when we grew up. God forbid we women should read something else and have our minds expanded! To tell you the truth, I didn't realize until I began reading Arabic literature how beautiful it all could be – Gibran, Yazid, al-Masudi … Do you know that the Quran is not just a holy book but an exquisite work of literature? The light in it, the dignified way in which it describes women – that's what we miss out on, a whole world of beauty, because we only engage with the hadiths.'

Mumtaz's eloquence was a rare occurrence, and as she listened to her, Madhumalathi recalled the book Roshanara had mentioned in their chat.

'*Ihya Ulum al-Din* – Roshanara said she was reading a book by that name. Do you know it?'

'Hmm, chances are she will get to read only books like that now,' Mumtaz said. 'Islamic instructions – customs, diktat, deeniyat, amliyat, soul, the hereafter … It is not easy to escape. Even the mildest attempt to break free will be dangerous. Did she tell you anything at all about her children? It's been, what, five, six years? I bet she has at least three children. Some people believe contraception is haram. I think she's married to someone like that. Poor Roshanara…'

Mumtaz had to leave soon after because she had a class to teach. Madhumalathi continued sitting at the table until, at the mid-day interval, her colleagues began to come into the canteen in groups. Before leaving, she had another cup of black tea in an effort to banish the headache that had begun to reassert itself. She checked her phone often, but there were no more messages from Roshanara. Perhaps she had not seen Madhumalathi's message … She yearned for a response – at least a 'Thanks', just a word to tell her that she had seen the message. Madhumalathi imagined, for no reason at all, that she was cutting a channel so that Roshanara, imprisoned within a dam, could flow outwards, even if as a trickle.

It was while sitting in that badly ventilated room in the canteen, set aside for the teachers, that Madhumalathi saw the post about the journey in the Facebook group, Lesbos. She was a regular follower of the group, kept up with the jokes and games and the occasional writing competitions there. She did not recognize the woman who had made the original post, but Sarvaranjini, who was actively engaging with it, was familiar to her. Madhumalathi guessed that she was a teacher too. Her posts, with weird tales from the puranas and mischievous questions, exhibited her intense love for stories, which is what attracted her to Sarvaranjini.

Overcome by a sudden urgency, forgetting that she did not know any of the women who would be going to Odisha or that she had no real desire to go there, Madhumalathi shot off a message. 'Can I come too? There is a twenty-four-year-old in my mind, the same age as my daughter, who needs new paths pointing outwards. I can no longer bear the weight of her inside me. This journey, it will do us both good.'

But when she found herself included in the travel group, her anxiety grew. She found journeys boring, dreaded having to use public toilets, especially in trains. She was one of those people who liked to sit somewhere quietly in peace. Now she had committed to this journey with a bunch of strangers who had some mad, wild plans. She even thought of withdrawing, but when she told her daughter about it, she encouraged her.

'Go, Amma, have some fun and come back,' Arpana said. On the video call, she looked thinner than usual. 'It sounds wonderful. And it is a group of women, so there will be no one controlling you all the time – "Don't go there" and "Come back here" and "Not that, this will do", and so on. Even I'm getting excited!'

Memories from old family trips that her daughter still carried, Madhumalathi thought, smiling. She wanted to tell Arpana about Roshanara, but decided against it. Arpana, who had had the freedom to plan and pursue her education, and now worked in Bangalore and lived by herself in a flat, would not understand. She was comfortable letting go of what she didn't want and go after what she did. Life, for her, was a list of endless choices, and it made her believe that compromising with obstacles was unnecessary. How could she understand that a young woman of her age, her contemporary, lived the way Roshanara did?

Still no messages from Roshanara, and Madhumalathi began to wonder whether the message to her had been delivered at all. She suggested to Mumtaz that they might visit her at her home.

'For what?' Mumtaz asked, unenthusiastic. 'If we go there, I bet she'll welcome us like a happy, contented wife, mother, daughter. She didn't even invite us to her wedding. How would we explain our visit after all these years? She won't tell us what is hidden in her mind, and we, well, we have nothing to do, no role to play.'

Mumtaz's response saddened Madhumalathi. The real disappointments in life were ones that went unvoiced. Her own life was testimony to it. Her colleagues, even Mumtaz, thought of her as a happy, lucky woman. But many were the dark corners in her life that no one knew about, that no one would know until she chose to speak about them.

On the day before the journey, in the midst of packing and other tasks she had to take care of, Madhumalathi sent a message to Sarvaranjini. What was the name of Draupadi's mother, she asked in the message, correcting, immediately, the word 'mother' into 'stepmother'. Let's talk tomorrow in person, said Sarvaranjini in her reply.

IN THE TRAIN the next day, one of those two women, similar in age and profession, will say the name of that unfortunate woman, queen consort of King Drupadan, the woman who could not give her husband the children he truly desired, and had, instead, given birth to Shikhandini who was both woman and man and neither man nor woman. That name is Prishati, daughter-in-law of Prishatan, not really a name of her own. Madhumalathi will send this answer to the girl who had asked the question, so many years after she had asked it. She will not know whether that girl would ever see the message.

VANITHA

I have now communicated with all nine members of Mudritha's tour group, mostly through emails and not in person. I had imagined, in the beginning, that this process would unveil their entire lives to me. These strangers who lived elsewhere in this world did tell me something about themselves, and not only because I am a policewoman – I have not enforced the power of my position on them.

I had asked them for information about the few days before the journey and about the day of the journey itself, and of course not all of them disclosed any more of their lives than was necessary to answer my query. Some of them did tell me about the circumstances that led them to go on this trip. I must admit that I was a little disappointed because, in my mind, I was talking to them as though I were a friend, but they responded to me as they would to a policewoman doing her job. Perhaps it is just my imagination. There is a greedy person inside me, someone who hankers for more and more when it comes to knowing about other people's lives. I try to keep her hidden, but she reveals herself whenever I am alone.

I made elaborate notes out of all the information I received. Some of the emails I received were clear and complete without me having to tinker with them, while others needed a bit of organizing. I now have the lives of ten women locked safely in the notepad on my phone. More than ten, in fact, because in each of their stories are stories of other women. Aniruddhan's amma, Vennila's sister Manimekala, Hannah's valyammachi, the dead Umamaheswari, Roshanara, and so many more. I want to know more about them, but there is no possibility of doing so, not any more.

Of course, the person I was really hoping to find out more about was Mudritha. Some clue, something that would point me towards her – that is the only reason I began this inquiry, taking personal risks, staying up late night after night after my regular work and commitments, reading what they wrote and preparing notes. Watching me busy with my phone at every chance I got at the station, Renji has been full of innuendos. How easily, flippantly, he asked whether I had 'a new line', a secret affair. His comments are, sometimes, unbearable. He will make a sympathetic comment about the dark shadows around my eyes from the long nights, and then bite his lower lip and add in a low, insinuating voice, 'Chatting all night, weren't you? Or was it video call? Your Giriyettan is useless. If it was me in his place…'

Difficult to laugh off, these comments, but I am also careful not to fall out with him. Even the time he said, 'Will you pick up if I made a video call tonight? Fancy and the children are not at home,' I only brushed him off gently. I will leave this department very soon, so why make enemies in the meantime. Men tend to get wounded if we respond sharply to these innuendos, and they will not forget that even in death. It is better to show disinterest. The smart ones will leave you alone after that.

Those were busy days at the office. We had several new cases to deal with in addition to all the routine work. Most of them were boundary disputes, motor vehicle accidents and petty theft, but each had complex rules and regulations associated with it and required a tonne of paperwork, evidence gathering, and trips to the sub-jail and the court. I was bored stiff, especially with the boundary disputes. We try, as much as possible, not to register these complaints and to get the parties to compromise, pointing out the long time it takes civil courts to settle these cases. So much more effort on our part just so that we can avoid the paperwork. The mediations are filled with much jargon and tedious talk – survey, re-survey, settlement deed, sale deed, land usage rights, ownership rights … Thomas sir loves this work, and as long as the disagreement does not escalate into actual physical altercation, parties involved in boundary and financial disputes are called in for mediation.

'It's all about the land, Vanitha,' he says. 'It should not be left untouched and uncared for while people go after courts and cases. So, we must try and resolve the issues as quickly as possible. We humans have a special bond with soil. Just look at how we fight over it, forgetting even the strongest of blood ties, how we don't hesitate even to kill. But the land, it only likes some people and wants to belong to only them. People's love for land, and land's love for certain people – I only have to talk to them to understand it.'

Out of his earshot, Renji mutters that Thomas sir is mad. I am, meanwhile, required to sit in on these discussions, especially if there are women present. Every now and then, Thomas sir will look in my direction and say, 'Isn't that so, Vanitha?' and I will nod or make some agreeable comment.

Still, to this day, I myself have not been able to glimpse the love of the land that he talks about in the eyes of any of these people. All I see is greed and the stubborn determination not to give an inch, even in those fighting over tiny pieces of land, just one or two cents. I often think about an old dispute that escalated out of hand, one where the mediation ended with the parties declaring that not even enough land to stick a pin on would be relinquished. It must be said that Thomas sir is often able to tame the initial sentiments, hostility and rage, into something softer, more pliable.

One day, Thomas sir told us why he was so invested in mediation in these cases. We were involved in a case that had exploded again after the parties had been placated and sent away. One householder was in the hospital with a head wound and the other had gone into hiding.

Renji was busy with some other case, so it was Thomas sir and I who dealt with this one. It was a scorching day, and by the time we finished collecting evidence and talking to all the witnesses, we were exhausted. The thunderous expressions on the faces of those involved made it clear to us that neither household was in the mood to extend hospitality. So, on the way back, we stopped at a roadside shop for refreshments, desperate for some lime soda. The little shop was under the sprawling canopy of a wild njaval tree. We – there were four of us – sat on the rickety benches in front of it. A large mud pot covered in a layer of precipitation looked invitingly at us, and when we were told it contained morumvellam, all of us changed our minds and opted for it instead of the lime soda. As we sat sipping the buttermilk, cool from the pot and fragrant with the lime leaves crushed into it, Thomas sir began to speak.

'A dispute about right of way – that's what made me a fatherless boy at the age of five,' he said. 'The way to our house was through our neighbour's front yard. One day, for some silly reason, they decided to close it off. A fight ensued, of course, much pushing and shoving, and the local parish priest called us all in for a mediation. The matter was settled, the neighbour agreed to take down the fence he had put up in the morning. But that night, my appan got drunk, broke down the fence and walked across their yard. I guess he would have stood there for a bit, challenged the neighbour, sang some silly song. Appan liked to sing and could make up funny songs on the spot. The neighbour got riled, came up behind him and stabbed him. I still remember the crowd that gathered and all the commotion. Appan was laid up in hospital for a few days and then he died. Amma was nine months pregnant when it happened, and she gave birth to my younger brother the day Appan died. He, my brother, never had the chance to meet his father. The neighbour was punished and sent to jail. After he served his time, he came home and apologized to us. And the family sold everything and went away. So now, when people come fighting over land and property, I can't help thinking about the grave loss that we suffered.'

I can still recall the black road, deserted in the noonday sun, in front of the shop, the morumvellam, cold even without ice cubes, us sitting there on those rickety benches, and Thomas sir's sorrowful face. And the wild njaval that held its umbrella of leaves, moving in the gentle breeze, over us. The scene is etched in my mind like an unfinished, abandoned painting by a talentless artist, its drawbacks displayed in smudged colours and shaky brush strokes, yet with the simplicity and innocence innate to art created not for competitions, exhibitions or sale, without the polish or embellishments meant to attract viewers. A still life that was washed away like brush strokes in water when Thomas sir's mobile phone rang. It was the sub-inspector, and he asked us to get to the hospital immediately.

'I think it's gone out of hand. To think what those two families will have to suffer now…' Thomas sir muttered as he got into our jeep.

We honked the horn to alert Shali and Mukesh who had gone to pick njaval fruits. Shali had a leaf bowl full of the purple fruit which she held out to us.

'If there was a bit more time, I'd have climbed up on the tree and picked more. It's loaded with fruit!' Mukesh, who had joined the police through the sports quota, said with a tinge of disappointment.

I didn't see him eat a single fruit. In fact, I heard him say, somewhat disgustedly, to Shali, 'I don't like this bitter fruit.' Thinking, with a mild feeling of jealousy, about youthfulness that made one want to take risks even for the things they did not like, I savoured the bittersweet taste of the fruits as my fingers dampened with its purple juice.

It was late by the time I finished the formalities at the hospital. Having not eaten on time, my hunger seemed to have died down. The jeep had returned to the station with the others, so I stepped out into the road through the back gate of the hospital to look for an autorickshaw. There were none to be found, so I decided to walk along the quiet road until I came upon one. It was a pretty road that led to the beach, with bungalows in the traditional style of architecture along both sides, and an old church that withstood the test of time, remnants of a long-ago glory. This used to be the main road of the city, its only road in fact before it grew and expanded beyond recognition.

Abandoned now for the most part, the road still retained an air of grace with the old houses and the poovaka trees that burst into flame-red flowers in the summer lining its verges. Most vehicles avoided it as it took a meandering route into the heart of the city. I decided to walk along it for a while, perhaps go to the beach which I had not seen for a long time, or to the old church which was built during colonial times. Unlike other churches, its interior echoed not with silence but with the sound of the sea. It had low walls at the back that invited people to sit and gaze at the sea. I thought I might sit there for a while, thinking about the woman who was still hiding from me. She, too, had lived in this city, I thought, and immediately corrected myself – she, too, lives in this city.

I realized quickly enough that none of it was possible. I was on duty and had to return to the station as soon as possible because the papers relevant to the case were still with me. Abandoning the flitting dream of walking along the road strewn with poovaka flowers to the church to sit gazing at the sea, I turned into a narrow lane off it that led to another major road connecting to the main road where I hoped to find an autorickshaw. But as soon as I turned left from the lane into this road, I had an overwhelming feeling that I knew this place, that I had been here before. And then it came to me – it was here that I had come looking for Mudritha's house.

I came up to a florist – Meena Flowers – and remembered stopping there to ask for directions to the house named Mullapparambil. It was in an old building, and the young man who was in the shop at the time had not been able to help us. I walked past the florist to the spot where we had found a tree-filled compound within a gate. The rusted gate had disappeared, and all the trees had been cut down, the timber piled up alongside more piles of sand and gravel. It was clear that construction was about to begin on the piece of land that now seemed replete with light with the trees gone. I could tell from the look and demeanour of the few young men who were around that they were construction workers from out of state and that they would not be able to help me.

Had Mudritha sold this place? Or did she still own it and was getting something new built?

For a while, I stood there lost, and wondering who to ask. I was anxious too. I had arrived, completely by accident, at the spot where Mudritha's house used to be. It had to be now that I found some clue to her whereabouts – if not now, never! During my earlier visit, the dark, brooding compound had held back its secrets. The only sign of life was the twittering of the plentiful birds on the fruit trees, although the thick undergrowth would have hidden a haven for creepy-crawlies. But now, it was alive with people and activity. If the land had been sold, whoever bought it was bound to know something about Mudritha. I decided not to lose the opportunity to find out more.

On my way back to Meena Flowers, I noticed the billboards by the side of the road advertising a well-known construction company and gathered that they were building a shopping mall on the land. As I noted down the telephone numbers on the billboards, I was aware of the somewhat anxious glances aimed at me, a woman in uniform, from the shops around. A policewoman was still something of an interesting sight for the people of this land. A snippet of a poem came unbidden to my mind: '… the dead injure me with attentions…' It was not only the dead who engaged in such harm, I thought, and when I remembered that the woman who had written this line had taken her own life, my anxiety increased. Unnecessary attention injured me too, just like her.

I could have, quite easily, questioned any of the workers in the shops around, walking into the shops or summoning them outside. I could even have threatened them, put the fear of authority in them for a little while. Those were the privileges that the uniform gave me. It did make me sad to think that I would soon lose these privileges, and that I would become just another teacher, one among thousands. I tried to console myself with the romantic idea that I would then have authority over the minds of my students. All thoughts of someone who is about to leave behind a difficult profession to take up one that is comparatively easier, financially better, and held the promise of well-defined working hours. Things that attract me to it, I thought guiltily. I will do the job with the same dedication as I do the policewoman's job, I told myself. That is all there is. Only that.

An old man sat in Meena Flowers, and he rose reverentially when I entered. How long had the shop been in this spot, I asked him, and he told me, somewhat fearfully, the history of the shop. It was his father who started the shop fifty-odd years ago, in Venus Corner at first, but they had to move when rents increased after the road was widened and a new mall was opened. After the move, in the initial phases, they did not do very well as it was quite a way away from the main road. But it survived, and was not doing too badly now after ten years or so, he said.

All irrelevant information, except for the last part, that the shop had been there in that spot for over ten years. I asked him about the Mullapparambil house.

'The boy told me the police had come before also,' he said, suspicion glittering in his eyes. 'Why? What is the matter, sir?'

'It was me that time too,' I told him. 'The matter is not to be discussed with you. Just answer my question.'

'To tell you the truth, I just come in the morning and open the shop,' he said. 'We sell flowers, don't we? If they wilt a little, it's all over. Fish or meat, you could ice it or put it in the freezer and so on, but flowers … So, I barely have time to stand still. The flowers come in the West Coast train in the morning. I have to go and pick them up. Then I have to make garlands and wreaths and bouquets as the orders come in. And the biggest job – watering them. Just enough to keep them fresh and not one drop more, or they will rot. Always in balance and on time. Even if an earthquake happens in the middle of all this, I am bound to miss it, sir.'

'And where do the flowers come from?' I was not quite sure why I asked this garrulous man a question that had nothing to do with my case.

'From Trichy and Coimbatore, sir. Why? What is the problem?'

I remembered Vennila's story. It was Philomena who talked to me about her. Flowers from Tamil Nadu came to Kerala on the Tea Garden Express, the same train Vennila had taken when she arrived, bathed in the fragrance of flowers and suffering from a headache, at Philomena's for the first time. Some of the flowers were unloaded from the Tea Garden at Palakkad, and they then travelled in a different train to reach my city.

'So, you have no information about this house or the woman who used to live there?' I asked before the old man could break into a treatise on the travel trajectories of the flowers.

'No, sir. I know there was an old house there, but not sure if anyone lived there. No one from there has ever come to buy flowers from me. If they did, I'd have known all about them. You say a woman lived there? Can't be, because she would have bought flowers from here, wouldn't she, while going to the temple or to a wedding. Now they are building a new mall. There will be a movie theatre also, it seems.'

Without saying anything more, I left the flower seller behind and jumped into an autorickshaw that was passing by. As we sped towards the station, I thought of what he had said about women and their journeys – to the temple or to a wedding, with a sprig of flower in their hair. Such simple equations. Why didn't anyone know that women made other journeys too? Was it that they didn't know or were they pretending not to know? No one seemed to notice the unsafe, unpredictable journeys that we made, that promised the thrill of risky pleasures.

That evening, it was very late when I left the station and went home, and by the time I finished with my domestic chores, there was no time left for anything else. Two more days have passed since. And today, a day off after night shifts, I finally have the time to place calls to the telephone numbers I had noted down. The night shifts were hard with no time to take even a quick nap, and my eyes are sour with sleep. But the day is valuable with no one at home to disturb me, so instead of catching up on sleep, I get on the phone. One of the numbers connect me to the construction company's office. Another gets me through to their sales manager who assumes that I am a customer calling to book a room or an entire floor in the new building. She launches into a sales prattle peppered with 'Ma'ams' and sweet nothings, and I don't quite have the chance to ask her anything. So, with a vague promise to call later, I hang up.

Before dialling the last number on my list, I prepare myself with some lies. I introduce myself to the person who picks up the call as a businesswoman looking to rent a thousand-square feet area on the first floor of the building for a boutique. Although I have to suffer through a sales pitch involving carpet area, profit, amenities and so on, I manage to convince him that I need to speak with a managing partner of the company. He is not entirely convinced but gives me the number in the end.

My next call does not go smoothly. The person who picks up the phone has a mild manner that does not reflect the arrogance of his position as a managing director. Still, he refuses to tell me who he had bought the property from. All parties in a business deal are entitled to privacy, he says, and asks me on what grounds I was expecting him to divulge this information to a stranger. I have no answer to that. In the end, I reveal who I am and why I was making the inquiry, and he relents.

'It was a jointly held property,' he tells me. 'I think there were at least three quarters of a dozen interested parties, some living here and some abroad. The person who dealt with us on their behalf was a retired doctor. Perhaps he was the one who lived there? I don't really have all the details. I'll give you his number, but only because I am choosing to believe what you told me, that this is an official inquiry and that you are the police.'

As soon as we hang up, the number for the retired doctor drops into my message box. I dash off a reply thanking the managing director profusely, and immediately dial the number, barely able to contain my excitement. Here I am, finally, so close to Mudritha. Like the women in her travel group, I, too, long to meet her. My assumption, when I began the inquiry, was that they would not feel a sense of intimacy with Mudritha. And their initial responses had underscored this assumption. But in the course of our interactions, I have come to realize that it is not so and that they like her at least as much as they like themselves.

There is one request all of them have made: that I inform them if I am successful in finding Mudritha or knowing more about her. If I find her, and if she is willing, they want to meet her, and they are willing to come together one more time for this, even the ones living farther away in Ireland, Kuwait and Bihar.

They are, each and every one of them, convinced that their trip would have been different had Mudritha been with them. Many of the plans they had made together had to be abandoned, many sights left unseen while other sights not in their initial plans included. They are all ready for another trip if Mudritha would go with them, once again to Odisha, where they will visit the places they missed out.

The phone rings and is picked up at the first ring.

I explain who I am and why I was calling, and the doctor offers to meet in person if I could go to his house right away. Otherwise, it will have to be a week later, he says. I agree, without hesitation.

His house is not far from the city, and I have no difficulty finding it. It is a big house, painted green. In the yard are a large number of potted plants, all of them bougainvillea in an array of deep colours, pruned into compact shapes. The doctor himself opens the front door. He has a clear, bright face like many who retire while at the height of their profession. His talk is strewn liberally with English words and his manner impeccable.

I spend only a half hour in his company; it takes only that long for him to tell me what I want to know. Leaving a springtime of dark colours behind, I open the gate and walk out into the blazing two o'clock sun. Suddenly overcome with sleep and hunger, I am dizzy, and as I lean against the gate, I feel an urgent need to call Aniruddhan.

ANIRUDDHAN

When the policewoman Vanitha called me, I was in my class and my phone was on silent. I saw the missed call – I had saved her number – and I thought, naturally, that it might be to talk about returning my notebook. She had called me once before about it, but I was not able to go to the police station that day. And because I didn't relish the thought of being questioned or ridiculed for not being able to present myself when asked, I decided to ignore it and wait until she called again. So, this time, I returned her call, but what she told me has thrown me completely.

I told her that I wanted my notebook back. It contained profoundly personal matters, things I had written down in a state of excitement, which, if the circumstances were different, I would never have shared with anyone else. Mudritha's disappearance had worried me deeply. I truly feared that she might have come to harm and was only concerned about helping to find her as quickly as possible. I had never met her, true, but I knew her more than most people I had direct dealings with. A short interaction of only a handful of days, over the phone and by email, and yet she had managed to put her gentle finger on the disappointments and desolation etched within me, had told me, although not in so many words, not to despair. At that point in time, no one except Mudritha seemed to notice that I was falling to bits and needed support. I am thirty years old. At this age, overwhelmed by insecurities and uncertainties, and desperate to hide it from the outside world, a man puts on a stern, severe persona. She, who had never met me in person, understood this.

Take, for instance, how long Padmameghna, who saw me daily for almost a year, held her grudge against me. She left Grandma last month; she made the last grade list and was appointed to the Taluk office. As she went around saying goodbyes, she came up to me and offered me laddoos from a box. Her face was dark and heavy. My earlier self would have rejected that joyless offering of the sweet. But this time, I accepted gracefully, wished her well, told her that I hoped she would continue taking the competitive tests and find a higher-level job. I told her then, laughing, about the bangles I had bought for her. I had brought back four dozens in green, blue, black and red from a shop in front of the Jagannath temple in Puri.

'Aiyo, sir, my hands don't have the strength to wear them all!' Padmameghna laughed, holding out her thin arms.

'Only a dozen was meant for you, the rest is for someone else,' I said, laughing louder.

Perhaps there had been a flicker of disappointment in her eyes which she hid before proceeding to question me about who this other person was. In all this time, we had never talked like that, joking and laughing. I had changed, I felt lighter as though the dark clouds in my mind had rained away. I was less harsh in my classrooms too, not as cruel as I used to be, able to handle the lessons with a gentler disposition. These days, I am determined not to hurt anyone with my jokes and taunts. Earlier, if a student made the same mistake twice, I would, with no compunction, curse that they would never make anything of themselves. How I have mauled their hearts, as though I had sharpened the nails on my ten fingers for the sole purpose of clawing their tender flesh into tatters. The violence used to give me a demented pleasure.

All that changed after my interactions with Mudritha.

Even the journey she had me organize was a gift, I feel. All my lies were revealed, and she knew that Himadri Tours and Travels had been defunct for years, and yet she allowed me to organize the trip, brought together a ten-person group, paid me in advance. She approached me at a time when I had collapsed into myself. I found myself standing up straight again, able to look around, to rediscover the sprouts of inner energy that had lain dormant for so long. Mudritha had given herself to me, I think sometimes. Why else would she have disappeared without a trace?

I remember the day I passed by the place where Mudritha's house used to be. A close relative was in hospital in a serious condition, and I had gone to visit him one evening – an unavoidable formality. Hospitals, I find, are dispiriting places. I couldn't actually visit the patient as he was in the ICU, so I hung around for a while so that his relatives would know I had made the visit, answered a couple of questions and, nodding to no one in particular, took my leave. The meandering corridors took me to the back exit. Walking out of the hospital, my heart fell when I realized that I was on the road that went up to the beach. When I was in college, it was one of the regular routes for me and my friends. Was this hospital here in those days, or was it being built? I couldn't remember. But I did remember, vividly, the many afternoon walks down to the beach with Nithin, Ramit and Hari, laughing and chatting under the shade of the poovaka trees lining the road, sitting by the cemetery of the English church, gazing at the sea, and clambering down its stone wall to be drenched in the spray as waves crashed on the rocks. So many nights spent lying on the sand, staring at the sky.

The memories of those days and of my friends surged inside me alongside a deep sorrow, and I abandoned the road and turned into a narrow lane that veered off it. It opened into another road, and when I read its name I realized, with a sense of shock, that this was where the person I had been trying to contact for the last five months lived. Anxiously, eagerly, I began searching for the house. I should have come here sooner, I knew, but something, fear perhaps, or my innate sense of introversion, had stopped me. Destiny had brought me there anyway, and I felt certain that I would find her that day.

It was not to be. Until then, I had told myself that Mudritha was just playing with me. Not any more. I felt certain that something had happened to her, that there was something sinister in her disappearance. I thought about it all night and finally decided to go to the police. I was reluctant and anxious, of course, because I was no one to Mudritha and the information I had of her was limited. But the desire to find her trumped all that.

That day at the station, Vanitha interrogated me, made merciless fun of me. To the point that I wished I hadn't gone to the police, and hoped, when I was finally allowed to leave, that I would never have to see her again. But when she came home to follow up, I saw kindness in her eyes, and was convinced that she was genuinely trying to find Mudritha. Not fearfully and somewhat distantly like me, but with confidence. She could succeed too, I thought, if she had more information about Mudritha, her nature, interests, friends … She had come to me hoping to find out more from me. Unfortunately, however, all I had to give her was my notebook, a child's diary, really, and the couple of emails Mudritha had sent me. The affinity I felt towards Vanitha on that day was as fierce as the force with which my heart pumped blood through my veins. So, without thinking too much about it, I handed the material over.

I have regretted it ever since and felt embarrassed every time I thought about it. That notebook contained so many deeply personal things that were not meant to be read by anyone else. An attempt to write myself down, to pour myself into a different vessel when I felt full and about to overflow. The act of writing had given me solace. Thinking about Vanitha reading all that … I felt mortified, and so I avoided calling her or going to the station when she called. She called one more time after that to ask for the contact information of the other women in the tour group. I was reluctant to pass on their email addresses without their permission, but I did, in the end, hoping that it would help find Mudritha.

When I returned her latest call, Vanitha told me what she had found out so far. Unofficial, she said, prefacing what she was about to tell me. As I listened to her, I was gripped by an urgent need to get my notebook back from her – I felt I was not safe as long as it was in her possession. There was an undertone in her voice that I couldn't miss, which suggested that she thought I had somehow deceived her. I was leaning against the grilles on the veranda of Grandma talking to her. Students of the two o'clock batch, coming up the stairs, were staring at me. I was yet to grab some lunch before the next class started, but when I hung up, I was in no mood to eat and could only keep standing there overwhelmed by fear.

Now, over six months since that eventful trip, I can truly say that it has changed not only my life but my general outlook towards life. Significantly, I have come to realize how childish the ideas I had of my life were, of being a traveller, of building a career as a travel agent and tour guide. A mere fascination of a twenty-year-old, remnants of which had remained unwilted within me, like fresh sprouts of grass after the rain. With this trip, in one fell swoop, I weeded them all out.

On the day of the journey, I arrived at the station very early, determined as I was to get there before Mudritha. Mudritha and two others were to get on the train from the same station as me, while others would join from other stations along the way. The other two women arrived not long after. I had no trouble recognizing them; their lively faces reflected a mixture of joy, enthusiasm and nervousness. Together, we waited for Mudritha, wandered up and down the platform looking for her while I kept calling her. I was the one most put out by her absence, worried about how I would see this trip through on my own as she was the one who had made all the plans. I even thought of cancelling it but that was not an easy proposition given that most of the others were already on the train. Finally, as the train arrived, the woman named Madhumalathi said, 'Let's go,' and gave me courage.

Mudritha's absence, and the fact that we could not reach her on the phone, cast a shadow over everyone's minds. However, by the time it was dark, and as the ties of friendship began to strengthen, they emerged from under it. Throughout the night and the following day, I did not see any of them take a nap. They interacted not like people meeting for the first time but as though they had known each other for a long time. They listened to one another with great care and attention, something that only women are capable of, I think. Men are incapable of such interactions as far as I can tell. No deep wells or currents in their relationships, only a surface dampness that dries out upon the first exposure to sunshine. Jealously, I watched them, this group of women. Only one person, Vennila, stood a little apart from the group, perhaps because of language issues and because of her age. She was a last-minute replacement for Philomena who could not make the trip. We were lucky that the ticket examiner did not crosscheck the tickets with the ID cards.

Mudritha's plans included travel through the villages of Odisha and a boat ride down the Chitrotpala. But once we were there, we were faced with all the problems a group with no real leader faces. Could we, out-of-town tourists, manage to find our way to those villages without Mudritha? We had no idea where to begin or what to do first. Finally, the manager of the hotel we were staying at organized a tour guide for us, and he took us straight to Konark. Unlike us, he had no confusion. His stance was that he knew exactly what to see and where to visit in Odisha, and he would take us there. I tried telling him about Agni Purnima and so on, but he frowned at me.

'Country festival, sir, waste of time,' he said, scornfully.

In his opinion, such events taking place in uncivilized, deeply rural places were beyond what people like us could endure. Odisha's pride and grandeur were in its temple architecture, he said authoritatively, and there were more places than one could see in weeks. So, why waste the limited time we had on faraway, poverty-ridden villages? The Yogini temple was also struck off the itinerary because of the distance, not by us but by our guide.

'Nothing there. Far away in the forest. Very old temple,' he said, discouraging us.

We caught glimpses of the Mahanadi from the windows of our vehicle. At one point, he pointed to the fading course of a river and said it was the Chandrabhaga, the river Mudritha had sworn never to see. A few puddles of water remained, and those who had come to see the Sun Temple were trying to bathe in them. I could not have brought myself even to paddle in the dirty water. The saddest part of it all was that I never got to see Chitrotpala, the river that had come to me in my dreams so many times. I remembered, with a deep sense of shame, how she had cut channels of desire deep within me. I asked the guide about her.

'It's a river, yes, just another ordinary river,' he said.

He could not understand why we would want to leave the beautiful temples and travel a long distance to look at a river. As far as he was concerned, all rivers were the same. Let her remain in my heart, I thought, the river that nurtured orange orchards along her banks. Let her flow within me. Unseen sights, after all, are sweeter.

The women were very cooperative. Even as they enjoyed themselves, they made sure I was not put to any unnecessary trouble. Vennila, as I said, was the only one who seemed lonely occasionally, so I tried to talk to her although she did not always talk back much. Still, whenever she found herself alone, she sought me out and sat with me. I was alone too. She was only a couple of years older than me.

Back from the trip, we went our separate ways, naturally. Despite what Mudritha told me, I have no real hope that more offers for organizing such tours would come my way. This is a highly competitive field, hard to gain a foothold in, especially without an office and other infrastructure. Even if I could manage to find the capital to set it all up, it would be difficult to run such a business on my own. A love for travel is not enough; there are many boring and complex things to do before and after each journey, none of which is as satisfying or joyful as the journey itself.

There is another reason why I now desire a steady job and an income that would allow me to have a settled life. I have begun to think that something I had no hope for, something I thought would never happen in my life, might happen after all. I want to marry Vennila. She hasn't said much to me – not just to me, to anyone – and when I asked her about it, she said she was a quietly chirping swallow. Then, seeing the confusion on my face, she laughed and told me the story of Procne from Greek mythology.

Being with her was like sitting by the side of calm water with just the right temperature. It made me feel comfortable, peaceful. No deep silences or loud noises, only even, moderate sounds. It was while sitting together by the Chilika Lake that I realized this was exactly what I needed.

The lake was a dark blue. Vennila sat silently staring at it while her friends walked around chatting, eating guava from the women vendors sitting under the trees. I sat beside her and told her about the peace her company gave me. My language was inadequate, but my face and my voice would have revealed what I meant.

A few days after our return, Krishnanandettan called me to his shop and asked me whether I would be interested in becoming a business partner of the coaching centre Grandma.

'You won't need to invest anything money-wise,' he said. 'You'll be a working partner. Take over the running of the place. I barely have the time to take care of this shop. Besides, we have more and more students enrolling as the days go by. We might have to start a new branch soon.'

I didn't have to think long to accept the offer. I am almost sure that Vennila will agree to marry me. She has told me her story, and I realized, when I visited her at the house where she lived, that she did that to dissuade me. But her past is immaterial to me. I saw her for the first time in the train, looking out through the window with her head leaning against the bars. As far as I am concerned, that was the moment she began to exist, and so she has no past. I gather that there are no official records of her previous marriage, only the thalikettu ceremony at some kovil. So, we don't have to travel to the past even to get the marriage annulled.

The day I went to the house where she lived, I talked with Philomena. She is, for all practical purposes, Vennila's guardian. Philomena, too, thinks that Vennila will agree to marry me, and asked me why not arrange a formal pennukaanal ceremony when my family – my mother and sister – can meet Vennila, the proposed bride. I have their half-hearted permission, given only after the usual arguments and whatnot, and while I am sure they would concede to the pennukaanal if I pressured them, I have no interest in such formalities.

And now, Vanitha … Right before she hung up, she asked me whether Mudritha was a figment of my imagination, and told me that if I had made her up, I would be culpable of deceiving the police and the justice system. At first, I didn't quite understand what she was accusing me of. Why would she ask me if the person I had interacted with for over forty-five days, sent me emails, was someone I had made up? There was a sternness in her voice, and she talked to me like a policewoman interrogating a suspect. Why would I make up such a person, I countered, what would I gain from it? To which she responded irritably that she would make me tell the truth.

I told her to return my notebook. I can't help thinking that I should get rid of it or hide it somewhere where no one will find it That leaves the official complaint, the one that they had forced me to file. I had not gone to the police station that day with the intention of filing a complaint. All I wanted was to inform them of the facts, and I had been very clear about it too. I am determined to stick to my version of events if Vanitha tries to pull me into this again.

But what of Mudritha? Has she truly disappeared? Or was she like the breeze that quietly opens a window, comes into the room to chill it, to fill it with fragrance, only to go away as quietly? Just like the wind, I had not seen her even when she was around but had experienced her comforting presence. Left, now, with the fragrance and coolness, I don't really know when exactly she was lost.

My head aches. It is time for my next class and my students are peeping out of the classroom impatiently. As I walk in, I remember that it is not in my mind alone that Mudritha has left the imprint of her presence. She had entered the minds of those other nine women too, hung around for a while, and gone away leaving behind something joyful. So, how could she be someone I had made up? Did we all make her up?

Before I begin the class, I come to a decision. I will get my notebook back from Vanitha, but I won't destroy it. I will not delete Mudritha's emails either. I will keep them safe in memory of those few bright days in my life. They are markers of the time when my life began to clear away the weeds darkening its waters in order to flow freely again, caressing both banks. I don't care if I am punished for it, but I will always say, loudly, confidently, that Mudritha existed.

VANITHA

On my way back from the doctor's house, standing in the blazing sun waiting for a vehicle, I called Aniruddhan. I was livid with the embarrassment of having been deceived, the wasted effort I had put into this case, the unnecessary stress I was under. I remembered Renji warning me about him right at the start. In my anger, I said some things, but Aniruddhan's only response was to ask for his notebook. What a fraud! What did he think of the police? That we could be conned so easily with a story and some bogus evidence? By then, an autorickshaw arrived, so I ended the call, but not before making it clear to him that he hadn't heard the last of it and that I would see him again very soon.

By the time I got home, I was exhausted. I took a bottle of water and went to my room drinking it and spilling more of it down my top. Shutting the curtains and creating darkness, I fell on the bed. In that moment, there was nothing in my mind – no Mudritha, no Aniruddhan or those nine other women – except the desire for sleep. And I did sleep, a deep, undisturbed sleep.

And now, as I wake up after four or five hours, it is truly dark outside. There are noises in the house, but I don't think anyone has noticed that I am home. My working hours are all over the place, so no one really pays attention. If they don't see me, they just assume I am out on an emergency. I could be dead in here for a whole day before they would think to look for me. There will be no food-related crisis because I have, as usual, stocked the fridge with meals. And as I sleep in the guest bedroom, Giriyettan won't miss me when he goes to bed either. I marvel at the ease with which a woman's physical presence becomes unnecessary in her own home. All anyone needs is her services, not her.

If I don't get up and go out now, or even for the whole day, Giriyettan and the children will eat, get all their work done, lock up and go to bed. If any of the children say, 'Amma is not home yet,' Giriyettan would respond irritably, 'She never calls to say she's running late.' It will not occur to any of them to give me a call. They know that I have the keys and will come in without disturbing their sleep however late I am.

I sit up, reach for the water bottle, drink what is left of the water, and lie back down. Mudritha and the Missing Persons case slowly surface back in my mind, taking time to become clear given how tired I am after the untimely sleep and the stresses of the day. I have not eaten since morning, and although not hungry, I am exhausted. I don't feel like getting something to eat or pouring some water over my body to refresh myself. All I want to do is lie here in the dark, and so that is exactly what I do.

The first thing that becomes clear in my mind is the fact that I will never see Mudritha. It hurts even though she is someone I came to know of only because of this case, and only in the last forty-five days or so. I know it is foolish to feel so emotional about it. I have experienced, witnessed, events much more heartbreaking than this. Even a couple of days ago, I was in such a situation. The young man who had sustained a head injury in the property dispute died in the hospital. And I watched, bereft of emotion, as the wife of his killer – she was pregnant and was brought to the same hospital with labour pains – hugged the dead man's wife and wailed. They were neighbours after all, had exchanged coconuts and pieces of jackfruits and the occasional loans of money, had gone together to Kudumbashree gatherings, church festivals and the cinema. I am used to watching such highly emotional scenes with the stern detachment that is part of my work, and yet here I am, taking Mudritha's case so personally. The thought embarrasses me.

I recall, then, the meeting I had with the doctor who was Mudritha's relative. That was only a few hours ago in the afternoon, and yet it feels as though it happened many days ago. He invited me in, offered me a seat and went inside. There were several potted plants inside the house – I recognized coral bead plants, Chinese evergreen and money plants – giving it the feel of a small jungle. The wicker chairs around the room had no cushions. Items made of bamboo, both decorative and utilitarian, were artfully arranged around the place. The space next to the living room that I took to be a courtyard was, in fact, a small pond. Water lilies bloomed on the surface of the blue water that fell into the pond over a cluster of rocks. A small waterfall, no less. Despite my excitement, I found myself observing the interior carefully. Usually, I am scornful of the unnecessarily flashy interiors of the houses of wealthy people, but this house seemed to impart a sense of peace and calm. I could easily fall asleep there, I felt. How wonderful it would be to lay myself down on the slightly damp red oxide floor next to the pond, with the gentle breeze scattering droplets of water all over my body. I yearned for the pleasure.

Luckily, the doctor came back then with a glass of sambharam which was not artificially chilled but still cool, perhaps from a mud pot. It reminded me of the morumvellam I had with my colleagues at the shop under the njaval tree. I held the glass in my hand and began talking, but the doctor stopped me.

'First, drink, then talk,' he said.

I downed the sambharam, perfectly spiced and sour, in one go, only then realizing how much I had needed a drink. As it cooled my insides, the doctor took the glass from me and placed it on the teapoy.

'So, you're a police officer,' he began, 'and you want to know about a woman who used to live in our tharavad house?'

I leaned forward. Here I was, finally, about to hear all about Mudritha. In my eagerness, I forgot to correct him that I was an ordinary policewoman and not an officer.

The doctor began talking, but mostly about the glorious history of his tharavad, his ancestral family, which I had no use for. But I sat there feigning interest, nodding occasionally, because I thought he might be offended if I interrupted. It was an illustrious family from the sound of it, with matrimonial relationships with the historic ruling families in Kolathunad and Kadathanad, and extremely wealthy. As he talked, he got up, fetched a journal-sized book and handed it to me. Printed on good-quality paper with pretty pictures, it would have costed a good sum to produce. It was the souvenir of a gathering of the Mullapparambil family at what looked to be an upmarket hotel. I wanted to flick through it to see if Mudritha was in there, but I refrained not wanting to show distraction on my part.

'You can give it back,' he said, laughing. 'Just wanted to show it to you, that's all. I know how boring it is to look through other people's photo albums or family history.'

He took the book from me and put it back in the bookshelf. 'I've heard my father say that during his childhood, there were over a hundred members in the tharavad,' he continued. 'I was also born in that same house. By then, there were some disagreements about property, so we moved away to Mumbai where my father worked. I went to school there and worked there until my retirement. Came back here only about six months ago. The tharavad house was still in dispute. No one to look after it or get it sold, so I took the initiative, talked to everyone, and got it done. The house itself was in disrepair, a portion had collapsed. But a two-acre land in the middle of the city ... It was worth something and everyone got a good share.'

Where was Mudritha in all this, I thought, confused. The doctor knew I hadn't come here to hear about the history of the Mullapparambil family. I had made the reason for my visit very clear when I called.

'Sorry, Doctor, but I—'

He raised his hand and stopped me. 'I'm coming to it,' he said. 'Just wanted to tell you about the house itself first. The woman who used to live there, as far as I know, is a relative. Not a close relative, mind you, one of those "cousins" that are there in all big tharavads, people you don't always know personally. She was born after we moved away. I might have met her once or twice in my childhood, I can't remember. After her parents passed away, she continued living there with her brother. Just the two of them.'

Anxiously, I hung on to his every word.

'Neither of them got married,' he continued. 'The brother, I think, was the same age as me. He had some mental health issues that needed proper care. When the parents were alive, he was looked after. I guess things may have slackened after their deaths, and there were no other relatives to attend to his needs. That's the problem with big families. There are lots of people but no one to help or support in times of need. No one even knows if we need help.'

The doctor sat silently for a while, and then continued.

'Two or three years ago, he fell from the top floor of the house and died. Must have been an accident. There is a wide veranda on the upper floor with unbarred windows with glass panes. You saw the photos earlier. He must have opened them to look out perhaps, and slipped. I think she continued to live there for a while after. In any case, by the time I came back here, no one was living there.'

He stopped, and sighed as though he was done talking. I found myself in a quandary. I had come here confident, perhaps even a little arrogant, that I had found Mudritha, but what he told me was a blow to my attitude. He talked about her, yes, but there was nothing in it that I wanted to learn. Where would I go next? Who would I ask? He could have told me all this over the phone and didn't have to ask me to come all this way in this heat.

As I got up dejectedly, he began speaking again.

'Sorry, Officer, I know you are looking for her. But all this … this story that she disappeared from that house, that the house itself disappeared … all this is utter stupidity. She moved away when she had had enough of living alone in that house, or when the house became unfit to live in. That's all. Now, where she might have gone, I don't know. Fortunately, her branch of the family had no claim on that house or property because they had already been given another property. Good thing the deed to this effect was available, otherwise I would have had to hunt for that too. Perhaps she decided not to continue living in a place that she had no claim over.'

I nodded in agreement, apologized for disturbing him, and opened the door to leave.

'One more thing,' he said, then. 'You told me she had planned a journey and that the complainant was the tour operator? I think that is a big lie. There is no way she would have been able to go on such a journey. You see, she was born with a debilitating physical disability and was unable to go out without a wheelchair, and even then, only with help. She did go to college for a while – they used to take her there and bring her back in a car – but I don't think she completed her degree. Had to stop her studies when her father died. For all I know, those might be the only journeys she has been on in her whole life.'

This took me completely by surprise. I heard the words being spoken but nothing seemed to enter my consciousness. I couldn't make any sense of it.

Outside, the day burned like fire. The yard was full of bougainvillea flowers in garish colours. Drunk on the blazing sunlight, they seemed determined to hurt the eye. Why did this man grow only these flowers, I thought, and I began to feel faint.

'Are you okay? Are you feeling dizzy?'

The doctor took my wrist in his hand and checked my pulse, examined my eyes, and commiserated that I was anaemic.

I went back and sat down on the settee, thanked the doctor for his care, and explained that I was only tired after doing a couple of night shifts. He sat down opposite to me and began extolling the virtues of adukkalacheera leaves in increasing haemoglobin, and I began to wonder whether he was, after all, not an allopathic doctor. The thought made me smile even in my distress.

'Are you sure you're okay?' he asked again, and continued when I nodded, 'You told me her name was Mudritha. I don't think that was her name. Well, I don't know if that's her official name or something. I've talked to several of our relatives too. In fact, I was on the phone until you arrived. Nobody knows her by that name. But you said you saw her Aadhaar card, so maybe you are right.'

I recalled how unclear her name and photograph had been on the printout of her Aadhaar card. We had made the copy at the station from the email she had sent to Aniruddhan. The printer cartridge had been almost empty that day, I remembered, and the copy, from an already unclear original, had been far from readable. Did I convince myself to read it as Mudritha because Aniruddhan kept repeating that name? I was confused; I had to get back to the station and look at the document again.

'One more thing. I told you she went to college for a while. She never went to school. She was home-schooled and only went to write the public exams. So, the question is how she could have gone away now. My thinking is that she might have had help from a voluntary organization. I'm positive that she could not have managed without help. To be honest, I'm not sure if she is still alive. That property I told you about, the one she is the sole claimant of? It's near Venus Junction. Prime property, but it is lying abandoned. Let's see, I'll look into it after a while. It shouldn't be just left there being of no use to anyone.'

So, according to the doctor, even her name was not her own. But no other name seemed suitable for this woman.

Mudritha … The woman who had left a mudra, a mark, an imprint, on so many disparate people. Marks of affection, of joy, of love. She had marked herself too with these. And here was this man, now, talking, I felt, as though she was already dead. That was why he wanted to wait a while before looking into her property. Perhaps he feared that, if he looked for her and found her, he would be burdened with her care.

'That's all I have to tell you, Officer,' he said. 'Assuming, of course, that the woman you're looking for is the one who used to live in our tharavad house.'

'Sorry, Doctor, I have one more question,' I said. 'Did she have any connection with Odisha? The journey she had planned was to Odisha, and she seemed to have a really good knowledge of the place. In one of her emails, she talked about a man who used to write to her from Odisha regularly. Perhaps a friend, a lover?'

The doctor laughed. 'I told you already. She never travelled anywhere. She couldn't. This last journey – we don't even know where she has gone. And a trip to Odisha of all places? Strange, indeed! Still, we have Google now if anyone wants to find out about a place, and travel magazines and books. I know that she was an avid reader. There was a library in the part of the house that was on the verge of collapsing. So many books, a lot of it eaten by termites. I took the rest and donated them to the public library. Tell you what, let me give you the email address of a distant relative of ours. He might know more. He's in the UK. Write to him.'

Then, as though he was giving me permission to leave, he said, 'That's it, then. Happy to have met you.'

I felt that he was passing on my question without attempting to answer it.

'Officer,' he began suddenly again at the door as I thanked him and turned to leave. 'I think there is something really fishy going on here. Don't you think this whole thing could be a story that the travel agent cooked up? He might have seen the old, decaying house and let his imagination invent a lonely woman living there. My cousin is not called Mudritha, and she was not in a situation to go on any journey. I am certain that she cannot be the heroine of this fantastic story.'

I thanked him again and left, my mind hooked on to the last thing he said. If that was true, did Aniruddhan make up the other nine women as well? Everything that they told me, that I thought they told me, where they his own soliloquies? The embarrassment, the indignity, was more than I could bear. Overcome with anger, I called Aniruddhan and spoke to him as harshly as I could standing on that public road.

As I travelled back home in an autorickshaw, the doctor's message with the email address for his relative in the UK dropped into my phone. At first, I thought of ignoring it, then decided to try one last time. Sitting in the jostling vehicle, I typed out a message – a brief introduction and how I got the email address, then getting straight to the point. I did not use the name Mudritha and referred to her only as the woman who used to live in Mullapparambil. Any information he could give me would be useful as part of an official inquiry, I said. The word 'official' might prompt him to tell me what he knew, if he knew anything at all. Still, I was not hopeful of receiving a reply.

I think, now, that it would not matter if my email went unanswered. Aniruddhan … he was responsible for all this. It is he who invented these fantastic stories, and tomorrow, I am going to summon him to the station and make him confess to everything. But those other women … The emails from Mudritha … I don't want to believe that all of it came from Aniruddhan's imagination. They had felt so real when I read them, as though I were talking to real people, women, like me, always in search of hidden springs of joy amidst disappointment and discontent, and yet capable of keeping that search a secret. Women just like me.

The room is as hot as a furnace now. I toss and turn in the discomfort. For days now, there have been signs of rain and yet it has not come. I get up and quietly open a window, pull a chair over and sit down on it. Switching on my phone, I find several messages and three missed calls. These I ignore and go to my email, and to my utter surprise, there is a reply from the man in the UK. Anxiously, I click it open.

A gentle breeze with a touch of coolness enters the room. Pulling my legs up on to the chair, pressing my face against my knees, without knowing exactly why, I begin to cry.

> I shall never get you put together entirely,
> Pieced, glued, and properly jointed.

These lines beat a rhythm against my heart, repeatedly, like waves, and I remember, once again, that the woman who wrote those lines took her own life at the age of thirty-one.

SARVARANJINI

It has only been a while since I received Vanitha's email. I am reluctant to open it, frightened that it will contain unhappy news.

From our communication so far, I have gathered that Vanitha is a genuine person. She has always behaved courteously and without guile, and not only towards me but to all of us. Her interest in talking to us was official, but she never used the power of her position on us. I have shared with her so many personal things, many of them silly, even though I wasn't sure they would help with the investigation.

The fact is that I wanted to share those things with someone. And so, as soon as she asked, without thinking about it too much, I began telling her things. A kind of voluntary disrobing. Taking off layer after layer, like peeling an onion. It gave me such relief, and more than that was the joy I felt in having someone listen to what I had to say. Vanitha did listen, attentively. She told me that she has pulled together the contents of my three emails into a single document. I am anxious to read it, but when she told me she would like to hang on to it until the investigation is concluded, I agreed. I can't wait to see how another person has tidied up and documented my life.

We, all nine of us, have been touched, indirectly, obliquely, by Mudritha. Each one of us would have experienced it differently, and yet we had in common the solace and calmness it brought us. It is strange that we realized this only after the conclusion of our journey together. Until then, we were only curious, eager to meet her and get to know her. But she never showed up, and never answered our calls thereafter.

By the end of that journey, she had set deep roots in our hearts. Our parched hearts had become damp and moist enough by then for her to do so.

I still wonder how a person could erase themselves so completely after having tempted us so. After the trip, for a long time, all of us waited for some news, a message at least, from Aniruddhan, telling us that he had met Mudritha or received an email from her. We had hoped we would then call her, get her to join the new WhatsApp group that we made after our return. It is called 'Silence', but despite its name, the one thing the group is not is silent. It is always noisy, a chattering group of women. We had hoped we would plan another journey together and that, this time, Mudritha would not be able to get away from it, that we would not allow her to stay away.

But there was no message from Aniruddhan. Instead, it was Vanitha who contacted us, and from her we found out about Mudritha's disappearance. I was so sure that she would find Mudritha. Back in Kuwait, back to living my life as a series of ordinary days, without Venumadhavan's knowledge, I have also been living an extraordinary secret life. A world that only I knew about. Mudritha will be found, and when she is, I will go back home. I will hold her close and kiss her cheek. I, who, for years now, have been barely able to suffer through Venumadhavan's touch or kiss, will hug her so, so tightly. Lovers don't meet in the end, they have always been together, I will whisper in her ear. I am sure she loves Rumi as much as I do.

So, now, I am not sure I will ever want to read Vanitha's email. Something inside me is telling me that it will be disappointing. Perhaps later, a long time from now, when I am able to accept the possibility that Mudritha has not been found, or that she never existed, perhaps then I will open the email and read it. Until then, let her be in my heart. I will find her there whenever I need her. And at other times, let her hide in there. Venumadhavan need not know. No one needs to know.

I switch off the internet connection on my phone and type a message in our WhatsApp group. It will be sent only when I connect back to the net tomorrow. I have to send the same message to Marianalini, to her personal inbox, because she has a sporadic internet connection. I will do that tomorrow.

AND THEN, I cry. All through the night I cry until I am satiated.

VANITHA'S EMAIL

Ranjini,

I typed this on my Notepad wanting to send it to all nine of you. But when I was about to send it, I chose only your email. I don't have to tell you why, do I? I have gathered that, to you, Mudritha was not like what she was to all the others. And it was you who offered, when I first contacted you, to post a message about her disappearance in Lesbos. You were invested as much as me, or perhaps even more than me, in finding her.

Let me tell you, first of all, that my investigation has been a complete failure. I could claim that I have been able to find out, to explain, certain things, but it will be meaningless to do so. My objective was to find Mudritha, and in that I have failed. She is a crossword puzzle that I cannot complete with the information I have gathered. So, I have to let her go, unconditionally. In a couple of months, the court will grant the department permission to close the case, and that will be the end of that. Not in your mind or mine, of course, but in official terms.

I was so eager when I began this investigation, and when I contacted each one of you, I was keen to know how you, members of the travel group that she brought together, got in contact with her. The emails Aniruddhan shared with me had made this clear somewhat, but I wanted to check whether it was true. I thought I might get some clues from what you tell me about your personal relationships with her. And all of you cooperated with my investigation. Perhaps not always in ways I wanted, but you gave me information to work with, and I structured and collated them all.

Nine stories … Nine lives … I am not sure what to call it. I did not find my way to Mudritha, but I did to you. Enough to know why you chose to go on this trip. You had lost yourselves, each one of you, and there was no one to come looking for you. Like Mudritha herself. The journey helped you recover yourselves. Like summer weeds drenched in a sudden rain, you were refreshed.

I won't go into the details of all the journeys I myself went on in the course of looking for Mudritha. To be fair, there weren't that many paths I could take. I found a doctor who was a distant relative of hers, and he told me that it is possible Mudritha was a fantasy made up by the man who was your tour operator. I would have believed it too, except, it occurred to me, why would he take you to Odisha? Why would he, pretending to be Mudritha, entice you there with repeated descriptions of its rural beauty, its women-centred festivals? Why take you there of all places? He would not do that unless he had some strong motivation. I discovered that he had no previous connection, none at all, with Odisha. It was his first trip to that state. All of this led me to believe that Mudritha existed and that she had some connection with Odisha.

The doctor gave me another contact, another relative – he was a teacher – of the woman who we all thought to be Mudritha, who had lived in a large, decaying house all alone for over two years. She had lived there for longer than that, but with her brother's death she became truly isolated. A woman born with a physical disability that restricted mobility without the help of others. She was the one who had planned a trip involving trekking, boating and so on, with all of you.

The man, the teacher, used to help her. A relative, yes, but not someone close enough to wholly take on her care and responsibility. He visited her once a month, mostly out of sympathy, and helped her deal with necessary things. It was a large family with a lot of members but with no close, lasting relationship with one another. No one had much affection or concern for the two broken souls who lived in that falling-down house. Instead, they were secretly conspiring to evict them from the property. Can't blame them, to be fair, because she and her brother had no claim to the property although it was where she had lived ever since she was born. She, too, did not nurture relationships with her extended family, or call them or ask for help. The front door of Mullapparambil was open only for him.

She managed her own cooking, he said, albeit with a bit of difficulty. It was he who had, at her request, bought her a smartphone. She was already set up with a computer, internet connection, and so on. She was financially well off too. He had been, he said, amazed at how well she managed to take care of her needs with great inner strength. Around a year ago, he went off to the UK to be with his son. He told me that he had found her a part-time helper before leaving. He kept in touch for a while, called her every now and then, and then slowly lost touch.

This man, who claims to have known Mudritha from the time she was young, described her as someone who was a voracious reader and a bit of a dreamer. He suggested that she may have planned this whole thing as an antidote to her personal disappointment in not being able to travel.

It is easy enough to imagine the mental state of a woman living all alone in an old house. What if she also had a physical disability that restricted her independence? Desires and disappointments, repressed over a period of time, could overflow in fanciful ways, and it is possible that she became part of its currents. So did you, all of you, and you flowed with her, brimming, bountiful.

Why Odisha? The teacher gave me a plausible explanation for that, too, although I am not sure if it constitutes a definitive answer. I may have, in my desire to satisfy myself with an answer, made connections between the question and his explanations. We are all, for ever, looking for answers, rationale or plausibility notwithstanding.

In her youth, she had a friend who was from Odisha. Those were the days when newspapers advertised requests for pen pals. Perhaps that is how they became friends. How else would a young woman who barely left home meet someone from a different place? The teacher remembered his name – Madhukant. He was from a village in Odisha, somewhere near the border with West Bengal, and had come to Utkal University for higher studies. On several occasions, he had picked up her post which included envelopes with 'Madhukant' written in a beautiful script at the back. He recalled feeling somewhat jealous, and said, with what I think was not an inconsiderable sense of regret, that she would have made a good friend or lover.

He did not know what those letters contained, but he knew that this friendship that their seventeen-year-old daughter cultivated had made her parents suspicious. They were unlucky as parents, their only son had mental health issues and their daughter was born with a disability. Still, instead of encouraging her, they disliked the idea that their daughter learned about the outside world, branched out into that world. And they tried restricting her, confiscated her letters and scolded her. Especially her father, who was too sensitive when it came to his daughter. Perhaps it was only the natural concern that a father has for a vulnerable daughter. Let us choose to believe it was so.

And then, the letters from Madhukant stopped. He asked her about it once, and she showed him a news item in an old edition of the newspaper, *The Hindu*. It was a report, from a place called Bhadrak in Odisha, of an encounter between the police and some students from Utkal University that had resulted in several deaths. These students were engaged in revolutionary activities in poor, remote villages. The influence of Naxalbari, he assumed, the states of Bihar and West Bengal were so close after all. Fools who thought they could restructure the world from its natural order of things, with no understanding that the structure had taken centuries to be shaped and did not need dismantling and restructuring. That was his perspective, his political stance. To be expected from an old-time feudalist.

There was a reason he remembered this incident so vividly. After showing him the news item, she had broken down, and in the midst of her sobs, she had whispered in a frayed voice, 'I would have joined them.' A young woman, all of seventeen years old. Did she mean she would have joined them in the revolution, or that she would have killed herself in order to be with them in death? He did not know. And he did not know how to console her. He, too, was young then, after all. He had not seen her lose control like that before this incident or after that. She had always shown strength, was strong. The deaths of her parents and her brother, the loneliness that followed, none of it seemed to have touched her with such intensity, or, at least, she had never allowed her feelings to be known.

So, this is the summary of what I learned from the teacher. He also assured me that her name was not Mudritha. But we know she is Mudritha. It is impossible to find her now. She who had been forced to spend her life crawling within the constrictions life had dealt her and society had reinforced, where would she have gone? Were there vast, expansive spaces that were waiting for her all along? Nothing of her remains now, in any case – not her home, her room, or her books.

How am I to find her from nothing?

That is why, Ranjini, I am abandoning this search. You can tell the others all this, or don't tell them – the choice is yours. Maybe it is better not to tell them because the hope that Mudritha is around somewhere, that one day you will all meet her – that hope is a wonderful thing. Get together again, all of you, in her name, and go on other journeys. I, too, am hoping that, one day, I will join you on one of those journeys.

Bye,

Vanitha

LIGHT

Tomorrow, a message from Sarvaranjini will drop into the WhatsApp group named Silence.

It will be a tiny story.

A pandit sees a small child holding a lamp walking down a path in the middle of the afternoon.

'Where have you brought this light from?' he calls out.

The child blows out the light and asks, 'Where did the light go now?'

The pandit is unable to answer.

Sarvaranjini will say nothing more.

Tomorrow, through the course of the day, the members of the group will read this story and remember another light. They will never know where it had come from or where it had gone. But every time they think of that light, their eyes will fill with tears.

AUTHOR'S NOTE

Novels form a large part of my reading. Even as a child, I borrowed more novels than any other books from libraries, happy that their length meant I would not finish the books I checked out too quickly. Many of the books that I read are imprinted in my mind alongside memories of events and happenings in the days I read them. Anand's *Aalkkoottam* is a fever dream of days spent in bed. Ashapurna Devi's *Prothom Protishruti* brings up images of walking to the road and back through the trees, waiting impatiently for the newspaper-delivery man who also brought the weekly in which P. Madhava Pillah's Malayalam translation of the novel was serialized. Bibhutibhushan Bandyopadhyay's *Aranyak*, in P. Vasudeva Kuruppu's translation, and P. Madhava Pillah's translation of *Yayati* by V.S. Khandekar were read sitting on the cement bench in the Parali railway station platform. On days of heavy rain, pulling the shutters of the train carriage down did not stop the water from getting in. It was in these soggy and chilled window-seats that I read Dostoevsky's *The Insulted and Injured*, rendered into Malayalam by N.K. Damodaran. Vilasini's *Avakashikal* made the boredom of travel in the last passenger train, which was always late, bearable. So many such memories, experiences resurface when I reread these books. And this is why rereading the books we love is also a process of indulging in nostalgia.

I worshipped those who wrote these books; I was in awe of their talent for telling stories within massive frames without losing connections and continuities. Being not in possession of this talent, or the patience or the time required, I did not even daydream about writing a novel. Writing short stories, however, was a long-held dream, and, many years later, I wrote some and a few of those were published. Still, the thought of writing a novel remained outside my imagination, which is why when a few people who had read my short stories told me that my craft was better suited for the novel, I did not take their views seriously.

Across the road from the front gate of the college where I worked was an old, tile-roofed two-storey building with a row of rooms on both floors. The area lacked the vibrancy and attractiveness that surround colleges in cities. The ground floor housed a few chai shops, an old-fashioned 'cool bar', and a shop that sold stationery and fancy items. The risers of the stairs going up to the veranda on the upper floor had begun to crumble. Somewhere along the way, in the shadow of the veranda, I began to see Aniruddhan, a lonely, sorrowful man. With him, Mudritha also came into my mind; she, too, was lonely.

My first attempt was to write them into a short story. But, as I began to write, they left its confines and flowed out as though I had no control over them. I felt that I could not abandon them, so I let them flow and continued writing. When I had written three or four chapters, I began to wonder what I was writing, whether it would take the form of a novel, whether it contained the potential to be shaped into the structure of a novel, a story that would hold together. Mired in these doubts, the writing stopped. But there were some outside influences, loving encouragement, and above all, my own determination not to let Aniruddhan and Mudritha go.

I continued writing, still without clear ideas about the directions the story would take other than these two characters – Aniruddhan who dreams of travelling, who found joy in arranging journeys for other people, and Mudritha, who approaches him with the request to organize a women-only tour. I have often thought that my writing style is one that follows, once begun, the trajectories the story would take on its own. My stories are not written down after they have formed fully in my mind. Perhaps it was this uncertainty and ambivalence that had stopped me from pursuing my writing after the stories I wrote for literary competitions while I was a student, made me abandon my efforts whenever I was faced with a hitch in the storytelling. It took me many years to start writing again, and this time, when I was unsure about where a story or a character would lead, instead of abandoning it, I waited. I think I was also aware that perhaps I may not have another opportunity. And as I waited patiently, the characters in the stories I was writing began to reveal themselves, often finding their own trajectories and endings in ways that I would not imagine.

Mudritha was no different. When I began writing, I had not imagined that all the other women in the book would appear wanting to accompany Mudritha or that it would be to Odisha they would travel. Something I had read at some point about Chitrotpala, which had lain unremembered in my mind, might have triggered the idea that they would travel to Odisha. I remember being taken with the name of the river, and I imagined her, a tributary of the ever-raging Mahanadi, to be calm and gentle.

As I read more about Odisha, I was convinced that this would be the state most suited for my characters to explore. A land of women-centred festivals such as Karthika Purnima and Magha Panchami, a land that still retains markers of the culture and art of its indigenous communities. I was certain that the journey Mudritha plans should not be to its well-known and well-trodden paths, to its tourist attractions. Instead, she would take the women to its rural villages, to its joys, celebrations, curiosities. She has clear reasons to avoid the famous sun temple in Konark. Chandrabhagas who are victims of male power and lust are everywhere. The story of Chandrabhaga in the novel is not only about a river, or simply a retelling of the myth, but a reminder that the lives of women – and rivers – are wounds that still bleed. So, I decided to ignore Konark and send my characters to an old yogini temple instead. The group has one woman named after a yogini at this temple – Umanarayani. Uma and Narayani might be one person or two, but what I am hoping to convey are the parallels between women's lives, even within the diversity, in their bitter life experiences.

Placing a diverse group of women, who also have certain similarities, at the centre of the narrative helped me creatively. Each woman in the novel is made up of parts of the women I have met in my life. Like them, I, too, had hoped that we would get to meet Mudritha in the end. But somewhere along the way, as the story developed within me, Vanitha came to me and took over the narrative. Mudritha, in the end, never showed herself.

As I journeyed with Mudritha and her fellow travellers, other stories and poems came along to keep us company. I have always been fascinated by Sappho, her life as well as her poems. Like most people, I too believe the story that, after a life of writing poems that blaze like fire, of loving with as much intensity, of rejections, of retreats, she had flung herself into the sea. It seemed to me that her words were the most apt to reflect Mudritha's thoughts and dreams, the journeys she had never begun, the sights she wanted to see that remained unseen.

The other women in this novel are all adults with myriad life experiences, from different cultural backgrounds. Stories from the Bible and the puranas, other stories and poems I had read, known, which had settled quietly and deeply into my consciousness, surfaced as I wrote about their experiences, politics, convictions and standpoints. And so came Sylvia Plath and Virginia Woolf and others, and their words mingled with mine as I tried to draw out my characters and their lives. Each of us women carry within us a stranger, one who is fickle-minded, excitable, troubled by uncertainties and dilemmas. Ordinary language becomes inadequate to express her revelations, her confessions. It requires a language that is spiritual as well as material, into which flow poems and stories. As I wrote, the world that revealed itself was this other one, the secret one that this woman lived – desired to live – within the everyday life that she lived outwardly satisfying male-defined values and norms of social and public acceptability. What keeps her company in this existence is the deeply meaningful and intriguing writing and speech of other like-minded women, always, through all times.

This is my first novel. I wrote this feeling some anxiety: Does this work? Is there another novel already like this? Would readers find it interesting or boring? And so on. At the same time, I loved writing the lives contained in this novel, enjoyed being a voyeur in their worlds, thoughts, their homes. Perhaps because I was writing without preconceptions, I found the process relaxed and pleasurable, as though I was walking along with the story as it rambled down a peaceable path in the evening. The sights seen on such a walk have their own limitations, of course, and I acknowledge them too.

I know women who want to travel, to make friends, to sit together, who feel this need so strongly in them, and yet have no opportunities to do so. *Mudritha* was written for them, for those women who, having been forced to sit in one place collecting moss, then find the joy of discovering themselves. It reflects my own hope that we are creating our own spaces. Many are the messages I have received on WhatsApp and Messenger from women who, after reading *Mudritha*, found like-minded women and organized trips, made travelling in groups a regular part of their lives. Women like the ones in Mudritha's travel group, whose minds shake awake from slumber with thoughts of tastes, smells, touches they have not experienced before.

I have watched, my heart swelling with pride, Malayalam literature being translated into English and being read by ever-widening circles of readers. When I first met Jayasree Kalathil, writing a novel was not even part of my daydreams. Jayasree had translated the novellas of N. Prabhakaran (*Diary of a Malayali Madman*), and after the book received the Crossword Book Award for Translation, had come to Brennen College in Thalasseri where I taught. She spoke at the Malayalam department, discussing with us and the students the academic, literary and practical aspects of translation. A year later, she contacted me on WhatsApp to tell me that she had read *Mudritha* and that she was interested in translating it into English. It came as quite a surprise to me, and I wondered: Was *Mudritha* worthy enough to be translated into English by someone who read widely in English and Malayalam and had a deep understanding of both literatures?

Still, here we are now, with the English translation of *Mudritha*. When I read the translation, I felt that this is exactly how it would read if I had written it in English. I see my writing reflected in it so fully and deeply, except that this time my characters are thinking and speaking in English. The novel contains many references to poems, the Bible, Hindu puranas, and I had used Malayalam translations of these while writing. Available Malayalam translations of Sappho's poetry are free renderings far removed from their original, making the task of finding those originals rather difficult. But Jayasree took on those tasks with dedication. I thank her for translating this debut novel of mine with such care and passion.

My gratitude also to Rahul Soni and Rinita Banerjee who edited the book, and to HarperCollins India for publishing it.

Jissa Jose
Kozhikode, Kerala

I am often asked how I choose the books I translate. The answer is simple. I don't translate any book that I haven't read closely first, and I only translate books that stimulate me intellectually and emotionally. As a reader, I do not exist in a vacuum, nor are my intellectual and emotional faculties removed from the political realities of my time and place. Still, sometimes it is an image that grabs hold first. My love affair with *Mudritha* started that way. Aniruddhan walks into a police station to report that Mudritha, a woman he knew but had never met, has disappeared. And as he reveals this story, he describes a travel agent's office in a dilapidated building in a market. These buildings, mostly two-storeyed, housing a row of peedikamuri or shop-rooms, are a common sight in many towns in Kerala. Dusty, fronted with fading signs, they lie abandoned, their past lives still pulsating within their broody confines. The image took hold, and I could not put down the book until I had found out what had happened to this man, this woman, and all the others who are part of their story.

The second thing that captivated me was that *Mudritha* is the story of Kerala's women. It unfolds through the interconnected stories of eleven women and one man. Part detective story, part closely observed portrayals of intimate lives, it explores the intricacies and unwritten rules that govern women's lives and the ways we find to cope, to survive, to thrive, even, despite the often debilitating weight of these rules. It was impossible not to find myself reflected in some of the stories – experiences of strong and empowering friendships, family ties that are at once enabling and exhausting, growing up and trying to live in an atmosphere of constant moral surveillance, the deeply felt need for breaking out of boundaries. I shared Umanarayani's obsession with the Skylab, Madhumalathi's fascination with the world of stories (the Indrani teacher who nurtured the love of reading in my life was my own mother), Sarvaranjini's dream of another land where another life seemed possible, Hannah's memories of giving naughty names to nuns, just as my friends and I had done at my boarding school. I have heard it said that identifying with the characters in the book one is translating is inadvisable. Maybe so, but when the translator as reader shares similar social, cultural, political, generational milieus as the characters, it is sometimes unavoidable.

Written by a woman, with eleven major and a handful of minor women characters, it is easy to categorize *Mudritha* as 'women's writing'. 'Pennezhuthu' – variedly translated as women's writing, women-writing, and feminist writing – is indeed a historically significant literary movement in Malayalam literature, with women writing their worlds, their words, into the public space as well as about the world from their perspectives. In the male dominated space of Malayalam literature, pennezhuthu has often been relegated to women writing about 'women's issues' – defined as the realm of the family, home, relationships – as though these are not part of the public and political imaginary, as though these are somehow lesser than the spheres of male participation in society and community. And yet, women writers in Kerala have defied categorization and written about the world, from diverse perspectives, offering different analyses, revelling in storytelling, experimenting with form, language, voice and style. Jissa Jose is a contemporary writer who belongs to this strong tradition. As exemplified in *Mudritha*, her debut novel, her characters are fully realized social beings, even when constrained within societal boundaries, who interact intellectually, emotionally, politically and culturally with the life around them.

In telling this story, Jissa draws together aspects of the feminine and its eternal negotiation with the violence in the world. However, her primary purpose is to tell a story that centres women's lives and how they make meaning out of the choices – or the lack of choice – in front of them. Interspersing this story with interpretations of the stories of women from the puranas and legends, Jissa presents before us a history of women told through their desires and ambitions, love and anger, and their attempts to resist and rise above the encroachment over their bodies and souls, 'unleash[ing] the songs and stories suppressed within ... lips singing sweetly, bodies dancing, stepping and swaying in their own individual rhythms'.

Translating this novel was an unadulterated pleasure. Compared to some other books I have translated, it was also more straightforward. However, I had to pay special attention to the nuances of Jissa's language, layered and complex in places and simple and uncomplicated in others. My primary task as the translator was to follow these nuances as closely as possible, bringing out the individuality of each of the eleven women while also highlighting the collective nature of their experiences.

Equally important to the storytelling and the narrative voices is the engagement with the poetry of Sappho, Sylvia Plath and Zeynep Hatun. The lives of Sappho, Plath and Virginia Woolf – three creative, accomplished women who took their own lives – also run through the story as a mudra, a sign, a signifier, of loss, of disappearance and suicide – key themes that recur in the novel, of an act of 'going under' that is an annihilation of self. Jissa had used excerpts from Malayalam translations of these poets' work in the original text. Finding corresponding lines in the English poetry of Sylvia Plath and in an English translation of Hatun's poem (which I found in *Women in Sufism: A Hidden Treasure* by Camille Adams Helminski) was straightforward enough. But the lines from Sappho presented a challenge. Much of what remains of Sappho's poetry are remnants, translated and retranslated several times. Jissa had used a Malayalam translation (*Sappho: Nee Thottu Njan Theenampai* by N.P. Chandrashekharan), which turned out to be a version so 'free' based on English translations available online that identifying the source text began to feel like an impossible task. I referred to several English translations, including *Sappho: A New Translation of the Complete Works* by Diane Rayor and André Lardinois, *Sappho: A New Translation* by Mary Barnard, *If Not, Winter: Fragments of Sappho* by Anne Carson, and *The Complete Poems of Sappho* by Willis Barnstone. Identifying the exact remnants still remained elusive. In the end, the lines included in this text are created from these various translations as well as my own translation back into English of the Malayalam versions in Jissa's original novel. In some sense, then, translating Sappho for this novel has in itself become an invocation of her spirit, as woman, poet, lover, rebel, as, in essence, metaphor, just as she is for the women in this novel.

Interpretations of stories from Hindu legends and the Bible add another layer to the storytelling. Jissa told me that she had referred to a Malayalam prose translation of the Mahabharata as her source text. I have depended on corresponding English translations (mainly, Ramesh Menon's two-volume translation, *The Mahabharata: A Modern Rendering*). For quotations and verses from the Bible, I depended on the *New Revised Standard Version Catholic Edition* (Division of Christian Education of the

National Council of the Churches of Christ in the United States of America), the English translation that is closest to the Bible used by the communities represented in this novel.

Mudritha is a story about quest in its many forms. On the surface, it is about a journey to Odisha in which ten women are variously involved, and an inquiry conducted by one woman into the disappearance of another. The eleven women form a diverse group from different places and locations, with different jobs and interests. But they are also united by the desire to reach out and touch the world, to experience it, 'to slip away, anxious that their lives don't end in its everyday confines'. In the telling of this story, each of the women involved reveal stories of unique lives lived in complex and specific terms and yet sharing elements that bind them together. In that sense, it is also about the eternal quest for finding one's place in the world, journeying inward as well as out into the world.

I am grateful to Jissa Jose for trusting me with the translation of this story, and for the many calls and messages in which she answered my queries patiently and with grace. Rahul Soni at HarperCollins India saw the potential in this debut novel and commissioned it for publication. Rinita Banerjee's attention to detail while editing the book has been exemplary. Malayalam travel writer, Vatsala Mohan, was generous with her knowledge whenever I posed questions about puranic characters. Shefali Jha and Adley Siddiqi, faithful first-readers, read the draft manuscript and gave me comments, caught bloopers and saved me from embarrassment. Amit Malhotra designed the cover that beautifully evokes the many signifiers in the novel. My gratitude to all of them.

Jayasree Kalathil
Hampshire, UK

ABOUT THE AUTHOR

Jissa Jose's debut novel, *Mudritha* (2021), was twice shortlisted for the Kerala Sahitya Akademi Award (in 2022 and 2024) and honoured with the Samadarshana Puraskaram in 2024. The book is in its sixth edition. She is the author of four other novels, *Dark Fantasy* (2021), *Anandabharam* (The Weight of Happiness, 2022), *Mukthibahini* (2023) and *Blueberries* (2024), and three short-story collections, *Sarvamanushyarudeyum Rakshakku Vendiyulla Kripa* (Grace for the Protection of All People, 2020), *Irupathaam Nilayil Oru Puzha* (On the Twentieth Floor, A River, 2020) and *Pushpaka Vimanam* (2022). *Anandabharam* was awarded the 2024 Ankanam Shamsuddin Smrithi Puraskaram. She has also authored *Sthreevada Saundarya Shasthram* (2020), a book on feminist aesthetics, its praxis and representation.

Jissa is the principal of Government Arts and Science College, Kunnamangalam, Kozhikode. She has a PhD from the University of Calicut and received a post-doctoral award from the UGC.

Originally from Kottayam, she currently lives in Kozhikode district, Kerala.

ABOUT THE TRANSLATOR

Jayasree Kalathil is the author of *The Sackclothman*, a children's book that has been translated into Malayalam, Telugu and Hindi. Her translations from Malayalam have won the JCB Prize for Literature, the Crossword Book Award for Translation, the V. Abdulla Memorial Translation Award, Jury Commendation from Muse India-GSP Rao Translation Award, and been shortlisted for the American Literary Translators Association National Translation Award. In 2024, her translation of Sandhya Mary's *Maria, Just Maria* brought her the Crossword Book Award for the second time and a third appearance in the shortlist for the JCB Prize for Literature. As part of the global effort #readpalestine, she has translated Palestinian poetry into Malayalam, including works by Mosab Abu Toha, Mahmoud Darwish, Refaat Alareer, Hiba Abu Nada and Samih al-Qasim.

Originally from Kottakkal in Malappuram district, Kerala, Jayasree currently lives in the New Forest in Hampshire, UK.

Harper
Collins

4th

HARPER
FICTION

HARPER
NON-FICTION

HARPER
BUSINESS

HCCB
HARPERCOLLINS
CHILDREN'S BOOKS

HARPER
DESIGN

Harper
Sport

HARPER
PERENNIAL

HARPER
VANTAGE

हार्पर
हिन्दी